Praise for the airport thrillers featuring Alexandra Shanahan

"An insider [who] exposes how a major airline really works . . . dead on. . . . Alexandra Shanahan is credibly tough and genuinely sensitive at all the right times."
—Jeremiah Healy, author of *Spiral* and *The Only Good Lawyer*

Hard Landing

"Intriguing. . . . *Hard Landing* goes down easy, and will keep you flipping pages till three a.m."—John J. Nance, *New York Times* bestselling author of *Blackout* and *Headwind*

"This is a debut novel, but I like it because it is also a good novel."—*The Boston Globe*

"What really goes on behind the scenes at an airport . . . Lynne Heitman is a new name to the crime and mystery scene and this, her first book, is a good, tighly plotted page-turner."—*Publishing News* (UK)

"Terrific . . . [Heitman] clearly knows the world of airline management. She also has created a very likeable heroine. . . . On top of that, *Hard Landing* twists and turns and keeps you on the edge of your seat. Fasten your seatbelt."—*Kate's Mystery Book Newsletter*

Also by Lynne Heitman

HARD LANDING

Published by Onyx

TARMAC

LYNNE HEITMAN

AN ONYX BOOK

ONYX
Published by New American Library, a division of
Penguin Putnam Inc., 375 Hudson Street,
New York, New York 10014, U.S.A.
Penguin Books Ltd, 80 Strand,
London WC2R 0RL, England
Penguin Books Australia Ltd, Ringwood,
Victoria, Australia
Penguin Books Canada Ltd, 10 Alcorn Avenue,
Toronto, Ontario, Canada M4V 3B2
Penguin Books (N.Z.) Ltd, 182–190 Wairau Road,
Auckland 10, New Zealand

Penguin Books Ltd, Registered Offices:
Harmondsworth, Middlesex, England

First published by Onyx, an imprint of New American Library,
a division of Penguin Putnam Inc.

First Printing, February 2002
10 9 8 7 6 5 4 3 2 1

PUBLISHER'S NOTE
This is a work of fiction. Names, characters, places, and incidents either are
the product of the author's imagination or are used fictitiously, and any
resemblance to actual persons, living or dead, business establishments, events,
or locales is entirely coincidental.

For my mother

Prologue

The sky might have looked like this in prehistoric times. Before cities, before streetlights, before electricity, there was only the pale moon and distant stars to illuminate the night. On a moonless night, there was nothing. Only darkness so thick you could reach out and lay the back of your hand against it.

But in prehistoric times there would have been nothing like the mammoth airliner that lies shattered across the side of the mountain. From a very great distance, the gleaming wreckage would look like a constellation of stars clustered around the ancient peak. Closer in, it would look more like a bright carpet spread across the rolling ridges and spilling down the steep incline to where the last piece of the aircraft, torn and gutted, had lurched to a stop.

After a while, the mountain regains its equilibrium, enfolding the wrecked airplane in a deep, gentle silence that is interrupted only by the crackling of the burning parts and the small, intermittent explosions muffled within the twisted remains. Every now and then a tree catches fire and ignites like a blowtorch.

A large section of fuselage teeters on a ridge. With the agonized shriek of metal on metal, it rolls and settles on its side. No one hears. All two hundred and three souls on board are gone, their corpses strewn across the rough terrain with the struts and panels, books and tray tables, wires, seats, and insulation.

Investigators will find the captain's watch still on his

wrist, a Piaget given to him by his wife and four children to honor his twenty-five years as a pilot. It stopped at 2047, thirty-four seconds after the aircraft had dropped from the radar, fifteen seconds after one air traffic controller had turned to the other and said, "We lost them . . ."

At 2209, a distant sound from the valley below begins as a soft swishing, grows clearer, more clipped, then thunderous as helicopters explode from behind the ridge, bursting through the black smoke like two projectiles spit from a volcano. They swoop toward the wreckage with engines roaring, blades hacking—all identifying markings concealed. Anyone looking would not be able to see, behind the powerful floodlights, the heavy equipment, the special extraction tools, the masks that the men wear to work around the dead.

One helicopter passes quickly over the holocaust, flying as low as the heat and the flames allow. The second pilot steers his ship in search of level ground. The sooner he lands, the sooner he can get men and equipment to the scene.

Every second is critical. They have to be gone before the rescuers arrive.

Chapter One

The padded mailer was nine by twelve inches, barely adequate to hold its chunky contents. ALEX SHANAHAN was written across the front in blue ink, but the rest of my address was in black, as if the sender had filled it in at a later date. I stared at the handwriting for a long time because I knew I'd seen it before. I couldn't place it.

According to the postmark, the envelope had been mailed two weeks earlier from East Boston, Massachusetts. For a good portion of that time it had been sitting at the post office with postage due, which explained why it had taken almost two weeks to get from one end of town to the other. The idea of calling the police crossed my mind. Logan Airport was in East Boston, and anything mailed to me from Logan Airport should have been checked by the bomb squad. I decided against it. I hadn't worked there in a long time, and besides, whatever was in the package had the stiff outline and solid feel of a heavy book, not an incendiary device.

I went looking for a kitchen knife to use as a letter opener, forgetting that everything from my kitchen, indeed my entire apartment, was wrapped, packed, and stacked neatly against the wall in cardboard boxes. I found my keys and used one to slit open the end of the mystery package.

Whatever was in there was wedged in tightly, and I couldn't get a firm grip anyway because the contents came complete with a greasy film that rubbed off on my fingers. I picked up the envelope and studied the problem. The only way I was getting it out was by performing surgery. Using the key again, I made rough incisions along two of the three remaining edges and created a flap, which, when I folded it back, provided a clear view of what was inside.

It was a stack of pages, torn and smudged, attached to a single thick cover that was smeared with the black grease and soot that had come off on my fingers. From the orientation of the pages, it appeared to be the back cover. That meant I had to flip it over if I had any hope of figuring out what I had.

There was no point in risking my security deposit two days before I moved out, so I found a section of the day's newspaper to spread across the countertop. I used the Money & Investing section of the *Wall Street Journal*—superfluous to someone who is completely broke. Using the envelope like a hot pad, I lifted the damaged book and nudged it over until it flipped onto the newspaper. I was right. The front cover was a victim of whatever trauma had befallen this book. The pages had drip-dried into stiff waves of pulp, some sticking together, and whatever had soaked them had bled the ink. Most of the pages were gone forever, but then there were some that displayed entries that were remarkably legible. The first one I could read was a captain's report of a seat in coach that wouldn't recline. Beside it was the mechanic's entry—the date he'd fixed the seat and his signature.

I knew what this was.

The second was a write-up on a fuel indicator light that refused to go off, and the one after that on a landing gear problem, each duly noted by the cockpit crew, and each duly repaired by the maintenance team on the ground.

Someone had sent me an aircraft logbook, or the remains of one, the kind I used to see routinely in the cockpits of Majestic airplanes when I worked at Logan. No front cover meant no logo or aircraft number, so I couldn't tell which airline it belonged to, but I knew what all airline people knew—logbooks are never supposed to be separated from their ships. The information they carry on their pages is irreplaceable. It's the entire history of an aircraft, recorded event by event by the pilots who have flown it and the mechanics who have fixed it.

Logbooks are as unique to an aircraft as fingerprints, as much a part of the plane as the flaps or the wings or the seats. Standing alone in an empty apartment staring at this one, I had to admit to feeling a chilly whisper of airline superstition. A logbook without an aircraft is like a wallet without a person. You just know the separation is not intentional. To know that an airplane was flying around without its logbook, to see the book in this condition, felt like bad luck.

When I picked up the envelope and turned it over, a wad of tissue paper dislodged from one corner and dropped to the counter. It was stained black on one side where it had been flattened under the weight of the logbook. But it wasn't completely flat, and something had to be inside to make tissue paper thud. After I'd unpeeled a few of the layers, I began to feel it, a nodule in the center that had some weight to it. I pulled back the last of the tissue to reveal a sight that was at least as stunning as it was bewildering.

It was a diamond ring, but in the same way the ceiling of the Sistine Chapel is a painting. It was thick and heavy—a complex latticework of gold studded with what must have been fifteen small diamonds. In the middle of the setting was a massive oval diamond that rested like a dazzling egg atop an intricate diamond-encrusted bird's nest.

I spread one of the tissue paper sheets flat on the counter. BURDINES was printed in light brown ink and repeated over and over in diagonal rows across the sheet. I knew Burdines. I remembered it from a trip my family had made to Miami when I was a kid. We'd arrived in the middle of a cold snap dressed for the beach. My mother had marched us all over to the nearest department store—Burdines—for sweat suits and heavy socks.

The ring felt heavy in my hand. There was no way this piece came from Burdines, or any other department store. It felt old and unique, as if it had been custom designed for the hand of a woman who was much loved and treasured, and I had the sense that it was real, even though it made no sense that it would be real. No one sends something that valuable via U.S. mail in a wad of tissue paper.

I checked inside the band for an inscription. The absence of one felt like karmic permission to do what I had been dying to do since I'd unwrapped it. I slipped it on my own finger. There was no wedding band to remove first, and no pesky engagement ring to get in the way. Jewelry wasn't something I bought for myself, so the coast was clear for it to slide right on. It was too baroque for my taste, and *so* big. I didn't know how anyone could wear it without feeling a constant, unsettling imbalance, or without consistently smacking it into things. Wearing it gave me the same queasy sense of dislocation I had felt about the book—it belonged somewhere else.

I slipped the ring off and went back to the logbook. Toward the back was a place where the pages were less clumped together, almost as if there was a bookmark. I turned to the place. There was a bookmark, a single piece of white paper folded in half and stuck in between two soiled, damaged pages. My fingers were still black, so I went to the sink and washed my hands. Then I pulled up a dish pack to sit on and opened the note. When I read it, I felt myself growing cold from the inside out, starting with the marrow in my bones. A single line was written across the pristine page. This time I recognized the handwriting, but even if I hadn't, the note was signed.

I'll call you.
John

The logbook and the diamond ring had been sent to me by a dead man.

Chapter Two

The house was silent. Most houses are in the middle of the day. But the stillness in the McTavish home went beyond the quiet respite between the morning hours when a family disperses, and the evening hours when they drift back together again. There was a towering void in this house, a desperate emptiness made more achingly obvious by the raft of family photos that filled the walls and the shelves. I had felt it the week before when I'd been there for the wake, and I felt it now as I watched Mae stare at the diamond ring her husband . . . her late husband had sent me, holding it close to her face with a hand that trembled in short, subtle bursts.

"It can't be real," she said. "This isn't real." Her voice was solid, but her rhythms seemed speeded up and her speech pattern on fast-forward. She was talking about the ring, but she could just as easily have been talking about the sudden and horrible turn her life had just taken. "Is it real?"

"I took it to a jewelry store this morning," I said. "It's worth almost twenty-five thousand dollars."

"No. No, there's no way. This wasn't his. Where would John get something like this?"

"I was hoping you could tell me. You've never seen it before?"

She shook her head and handed the ring back. I set it back in the tissue paper nest on the low coffee table at our knees. Next to it was the lump of a logbook that had proved at least as baffling to her. She started picking at the nubby upholstery of her durable plaid couch, as if there were something encrusted there she had to remove. "The police are saying it was drug related."

"Drug related?"

With an abruptness that startled me, she stood up and, as if I wasn't even there, resumed the task I had obviously interrupted by knocking on her door. With brittle efficiency, she moved about the small den gathering her children's toys from the floor. A plastic dump truck, odd-shaped wooden puzzle pieces, two Barbie dolls—one without any Barbie clothes. She scooped them all up with a jerky, kinetic intensity that made my own springs tighten.

"I thought it was a mugging, Mae."

"Nothing was stolen from him."

"Okay, but where do they get drugs?"

"They said he was in Florida trying to pull off some kind of a drug buy. Can you believe that? My John, Saint John the Pure, in on a dope deal. If they knew him, they could never think that."

I had to agree. If anyone had asked me—which they hadn't—to list all possible motives for John's murder, no matter how long that list, drugs would have been at the bottom. His contempt for drug dealers and drug abusers was well known. He had actually turned in one of his union brothers at the airport for smuggling dope, an act of conscience that had not endeared him to the other union brothers. Even the ones that had no use for drugs had less tolerance for rats.

"Is that it? It's not a mugging so it must be drugs?"

"I think they have more they're not telling us. And he also called here early Tuesday morning and told Terry to lock all the doors and not to let us out of his sight until he got home on Tuesday."

"John did?" I didn't know if I was having trouble following her because she was moving and talking so fast, or because it was such astonishing information. As far as I had known, John's death had been a tragic and random murder in a city known for that sort of thing. "Did he tell him why he was so worried?"

"He said he would explain when he got back. The

police say that's all part of the drug thing. That the people he was supposedly involved with have been known
to threaten families."

She stood in the middle of the room. With all the toys
put away, she looked anxious and panicky, desperate for
something to do with her hands. Then a bright thought
seemed to break through. "I'll make coffee." She took
off, straightening the rug and scooping the remote control from the floor as she left the room.

Before I left the den, I took one last look at the gallery
of photos—the living, loving chronicle of what had been
this family's life in progress—and searched out John's
face. In a few of the pictures, mostly the posed shots, he
wore the serious expression I had known. Thick-necked
and determined, he had always looked to me like an
Irish laborer from the early nineteen hundreds who could
have just as easily raised the steel towers for the Wil-
liamsburg Bridge as loaded cargo for Majestic Airlines.

But in most of the pictures, especially in the candid
shots with his children, John was a different man. The
weight of responsibility that had so often hardened his
face was gone. The guarded expression he wore on the
ramp was nowhere to be seen, and I saw in those photos,
maybe for the first time, a man who was open and confident and comfortable in his role as husband, father,
teacher, and protector. I saw the man he'd wanted his
children to see.

I walked into the kitchen and the first thing I saw
grabbed hold of my heart and squeezed. The kitchen
table was set with three Scooby-Doo placemats. They
still had toast crumbs and jelly stuck on them.

Mae was moving purposefully from cabinet to counter
and back to the cabinet again, where she stopped long
enough to take down two cups. "How do you take
your coffee?"

"I'll take tea, if you have it. How are your kids
doing?"

"Kids are strong. I look at them and I wish I could be
that strong. I'm jealous sometimes because there are
three of them. They have each other."

"What about Terry? Is he helping you?"

"Terry is not doing well. He was just getting over the accident. This I don't think he'll ever get over. He needs to get help, and he won't. He worries me."

Just what she needed. Three small children to worry about and John's kid brother, too.

I dropped my backpack on one of the kitchen chairs. The non-Scooby end of the table was stacked high with papers and folders and files. One of the piles had slipped over, and the top few pages were in imminent danger of jelly stains. My intention had not been to riffle through Mae's private papers, but the one on top caught my attention. It was a photocopy of a Majestic nonrevenue pass coupon, the kind employees use when they travel. This one had the date and the destination filled in— March 5, flight 888, BOS to MIA. And it had John's signature. It was a copy of the coupon John had used to go on his doomed trip to Florida. The return trip information was blank.

Poking out beneath that was a receipt from a hotel in Miami called Harmony House Suites. It was also dated March 5. Then a pad of lined paper with a quarter of the pages wrapped over the top. The page left on top was filled with a task list. Some items were crossed out. Most weren't. The tasks still left to do included *Thank you notes for funeral, copies of death certificate to insurance co.s, change beneficiaries.* Everything related to the funeral was crossed off. There was a separate category titled MR. AND MRS.—REMOVE JOHN'S NAME. Underneath was listed *bank accounts, parish directory, safety deposit box, retirement accounts.* All the details and loose ends left over when one life that is inextricably entwined with so many others is abruptly ripped out by the roots. Toward the bottom was a shorter list. *Rental car. Cell phone. Harmony House Suites,* which was the name of the Florida hotel on the receipt.

I started to put the pad back on the pile when a couple of loose papers fell out.

One was a flight manifest for flight 887 from Miami to Boston for March 6, what I assumed would have been

John's return flight home. It showed the names of all passengers on board, along with standbys and crew. John's name was there, but there was no seat assigned, which meant he had called reservations to put his name in the standby queue, but hadn't made the flight.

I looked for Mae. She was at the sink washing the cups we hadn't used yet. "Mae, John was listed on a flight to come home?"

"Flight 887 on Tuesday morning," she said. "He called Monday night and said he'd be home on Tuesday, but we didn't hear from him. At first I wasn't worried because those flights out of Miami are so full you can get stranded for days waiting for a seat and I was sure he was going to walk through the door any minute and when he didn't I thought . . . I was sure he'd driven over to see if he could get one out of Fort Lauderdale. But he never called. Tuesday afternoon I was getting antsy. Tuesday night came and went and no John and I was really freaking out on Wednesday morning when still we hadn't heard and then Wednesday afternoon they called and told me he was dead."

The sound, sharp and sudden, cracked the quiet in the kitchen. Crockery against porcelain. It was loud and unexpected and made my heart shudder. I looked up to find Mae staring at me, and for a second I thought it was because I'd been prying, digging through her papers. But then I realized she was waiting for me to offer some adjustment, some correction to her recounting of events that would have changed the way it had all come out. When I couldn't, she turned back to the sink.

The cups hadn't broken. They rolled around and knocked against each other under the stream of running water. "He believed it was always on him to put things right," she said. "He shouldn't have even been down there. Some people just aren't worth the effort."

"Is that why he went down there? To put something right?"

"I am so angry with him." The muscles across her back tensed. "I hate him for going down there. I hate that he left me here to raise these three babies all by myself."

She dropped her head and reached up to touch her forehead with damp, shaking fingers. Her tears began to drop into the sink. "I hate him." I could barely hear her the last time she said it. She sounded as though she was afraid I would.

The steam began to billow up from the hot water that was still running. I turned it off, then reached down for the cups in the sink. For a moment we both held them. Her skin was red and warm from the hot water and I thought she might have actually burned herself. If she had, she showed no signs of feeling it.

Then she let go. "I don't really want any coffee," she said. "Do you?"

"No."

She walked to the table but could not bring herself to sit without stacking the placemats—crumbs and all—and taking them to the sink. When she returned, she started straightening the papers.

"This information about John's trip," I said, pulling out a chair, "is it for the police?"

"The cops don't want to know any more than they already know. No, it's for me." She sat, finally, with her hands in her lap and one leg pulled up underneath her in the chair. "I get these ideas. Just questions I want answered."

"Like what?"

"Like what was so important that he had to go see Bobby Avidor."

"Who's he?"

"He's an old . . . I won't call him a friend because he's not. He's an acquaintance from the neighborhood. We all knew him. He's a maintenance supervisor at the airport in Miami. That's who John went to see."

"A maintenance supervisor for Majestic?"

She nodded as she reached for one of the stacks of papers. "I've got his phone number here somewhere. Not that it's doing me any good. He won't return my calls. Not Terry's either."

I watched her flip back through the used pages of the

lined pad, searching for the number. "Do the police know about him?"

"They said they already talked to him. He wasn't any help."

"Why won't he call you back?"

"I don't know. Because he's one of those people who is just not worth it that John wouldn't give up on." After she'd flipped all the way back to the front of the pad with no luck, she pitched it onto the middle of the stack where it sat with its top pages curling from the bottom. She stared after it. "I'm not any good at this. I never have any time. I think I just want to know—"

We both heard the commotion at the same time. The back door opened and Terry McTavish was there, leaning on his cane, and trying to squeeze through without letting the family's big yellow Lab into the house.

"Turner, get back," he snapped. "You can't come in here."

Turner whined and pushed his big nose into the tight opening, maneuvering for leverage. He kept trying until Terry's cane fell through the door and onto the kitchen floor with a loud *thwack*. It startled the pooch for an instant, long enough for Terry to box him out with his good knee and slip through. He slammed the door shut from the inside, then stood unsteadily, catching his breath, braced by one hand still on the doorknob.

The sight of him, of what he had become, still shocked and disturbed me. Before the motorcycle accident, Terry McTavish had been a smaller, more compact version of his older brother—sturdy, solid, and one of the few men who could match John's torrid pace on the ramp. Now, with one leg shortened and twisted like a dead branch, the most he could do was count stock at a local hardware store. It had been a stunning physical transformation. And when he turned toward me and I saw his face, I knew what Mae had said was also true. What the Harley hadn't crushed in him, his brother's murder had. His eyes looked dead.

The cane had fallen at my feet. I picked it up and offered it to him. "It's good to see you again, Terry."

He barely acknowledged me. Mae reached out for his hand as he wobbled into her radius. "I thought you were working."

"They didn't have enough gimp work today."

She reached her other hand up and held his in both of hers. "Stay here and talk to us. Miss Shanahan has something to show you."

He pulled away. "I'm going upstairs."

"It has to do with John," she said. "I think you'll want to see it."

"I don't want to see anything having to do with Johnny, Mae. I told you that." His tone seemed flat and lifeless, like the expression in his eyes. But there was something else. Hard to grasp, but there. A hard, thin thread of warning.

Mae either didn't hear it or chose to ignore it. "Sit down and talk with us for a few minutes."

He turned slowly around his cane. "Why can't you let him rest in peace?"

She blinked up at him. "Because I don't think John was in Florida doing a drug deal, Terry. And I know he won't rest in peace as long as anyone thinks he was. Especially his children."

Her purpose may not have been to provoke him, but that last thought acted on him like an electric cattle prod. His face flushed and the words spewed out as if shot from a fire hose. "It doesn't matter what we think. When are you going to figure that out? If the cops say he was selling dope, then that's what it's going to be because *they* are the ones in charge and *they* can say and do whatever they want and there's nothing we can do about it because I'm a gimp who can't even drive a car, and you've got three kids to take care of, and we don't have any *goddamned money*." He paused to take a couple of rasping breaths and his gaze landed on me. "That's what it means to be in charge, doesn't it, Miss Shanahan?"

It wasn't a question. It was an accusation—one that caught me totally off guard. I wouldn't have called Terry a company man when he'd worked for me, but he had

valued his job, he had respected the work, and he had
never been anything but polite and cordial to me.

"I don't know what you mean, Terry."

"Everything bad that's happened to this family started
when Johnny decided to help you. Once he took your
side, everything went to shit."

"Terry"—Mae's tone was sharp—"stop this."

"We're working people, Mae. All we've got is the union.
All we ever had was the union. She cost us their support,
and after they turned on us, we never had a chance."

Mae let out a long impatient sigh, and I knew they
were touching on a subject that was not new. "John was
his own man and he made his own decisions. If you don't
like what he did, blame him. And stop blaming me for
not giving up."

"What does that mean?"

"It means you could be helping me, Terry. You could
be making phone calls, talking to the detectives. There
might be people up here in Boston you could talk to.
You could be doing something besides sitting upstairs in
the dark with the curtains closed."

"You are never going to figure out what happened in
Florida from the kitchen table in Chelsea."

"I don't accept that." She swallowed hard. "And John
never would have given up on you."

Terry paled. His face showed such a naked display of
rage and betrayal and disappointment and grief that I
felt like an intruder just looking at him. They were slashing deeper and deeper, and I knew these were two people who cared for each other and who had both cared
for John. There was so much pain there, in both of them,
but it was the fear that I felt more. The room was so
full of it, it was hard to breathe. It made me scared.
Scared that life could turn out like this for anyone. I
wanted to do something. I wanted to fix it.

Terry's arm came up and the cane came up and I
thought toward me so I scrambled out of the chair, almost knocking it backward. With one vicious slash, he
swept everything that was on the table onto the floor.

Mae looked as if he'd just shattered her best wine-glasses. On purpose. And then I thought she might take his cane from him and beat him over the head. But in the end, she slumped back in her chair and just looked tired.

"We will never know what happened to Johnny, Mae. We will *never* know. And all your little phone calls and notes and questions are not going to change it. We're fucked. Johnny's fucked. That's just the way it is."

Then he went upstairs, presumably to sit in the dark with the curtains closed. We heard every awkward step as he climbed the stairs. It took him a long time.

The papers were scattered all around me. I got down on my knees and started to gather them.

"Don't do that," she said, with a voice like lead. "I'll get them later."

I ignored her because that was what she was supposed to say, and kneeled down to gather the pages because that's what I wanted to do. Eventually, she crawled down next to me and started to help.

"I'm sorry," she said. "He's not himself."

"I know that." Not even close. People had always commented on how much alike the brothers had been. But what I had always enjoyed most about Terry were the differences. Terry had always had a sweeter disposition than John, a lighter hold on life, and a more spontaneous core. It was a contrast I had attributed to the difference between being the protector and the protected. And now Terry's protector was gone.

"He says he wouldn't have been laid off if the union had been looking out for him."

"Layoffs go by seniority. There's nothing the union could have done for him."

"He knows that. He's just looking for someone to blame for how he feels right now. In his mind, if he had never been laid off, he never would have lost his benefits, which means we wouldn't have had to pay all his medical bills, which means we would have the money to hire an investigator to go to Florida. And since he can't have what he wants, he doesn't want to do anything."

It may not have made sense, but it was a bitter, sulky

kind of logic I understood. "Do you have any friends down there who could help you?"

She had reached far under the table to retrieve a scrap of paper and was now staring at the three discrete piles I'd been constructing.

"I'm organizing your notes," I said. "Force of habit. The first pile is all related to his trip. The second one is a list of contacts you've made. The third one is for everything else."

She dropped the scrap on the miscellaneous pile, then sat back against one of the low kitchen cabinets. "I don't know why I'm doing this. I say it's for John or for the kids, but I'm not so sure. The whole thing was so . . . too fast. He was here. He was gone. I think I need to know what was in between. Is that strange?"

"Not to me." If I understood anything about what she was going through it was the obsession, the compulsive need to fill in every blank and answer every question in the hopes that understanding how and why it had happened might help in accepting that it had happened. I wasn't sure it would, but I was sure I would be doing the same thing. In fact . . .

The phone rang. She stood up, excused herself, and left me alone in the kitchen. I put the piles back on the table. And straightened them. I went over to the sink and looked out the back window at Turner the dog chasing squirrels. He was never going to catch them, but he had to chase them. Even though I knew it was a really bad idea, I tried to imagine a conversation where I told my new boss I needed time off before I ever arrived at a job it had taken me a year to find. It was inconceivable. I tried to work through the details of rescheduling a move that had been planned for a month. Impossible. I ran budget numbers through my head to figure how long I could really keep going without a paycheck. Not much longer. It was lunacy to even think about changing plans at this late date, and I could not afford to mess with this last best hope for salvaging my career.

That's what I had on the one hand.

On the other hand, if I took a week and tried to find

out what happened to John, I risked losing a job. It was
not a stretch to say John had once risked his life for me.

Mae was back. "I can't get used to my children calling
me on their cell phones."

"Problem?"

"Erin doesn't feel like going to her dance class and
wants me to pick her up. I have to go soon."

"Mae, I'd like to help you with your investigation."

"Really?"

"I'd like to take some time and go to Florida. I could
take this logbook to the police and at least find out
why—"

"You would do that?" She sounded calm, even skeptical, but she couldn't completely hide the tiny filament of
hope that had lit up in her eyes.

"Well, yes."

"Don't take this the wrong way or anything, but
why . . . I mean I would never ask you to do something
like that. How could you—"

"I owe John."

"He never looked at it that way."

"I can't look at it any other way." Her eyes were now
burning bright, not just with hope but with so much anticipation and gratitude it scared me, and I found myself
backing off almost before I'd even fully committed. "I
can't stay very long and I wouldn't want you to expect
too much. I'm an airline manager, not an investigator
and—"

She came over and hugged me, which felt awkward
because I didn't know her very well and because I felt
as if someone had opened the starting gate before I was
ready. "There are some things I'll need, Mae."

She sprang back into hyper mode, digging around the
kitchen counter until she found a stubby pencil. She retrieved her pad from the table and flipped to a clean
page.

"What do you need?"

"I need to know everything you know about John's
trip. You've got some of it here—where he stayed, if he
rented a car, restaurant bills, charge card receipts—"

"There won't be any." She had her head down, writing furiously. "John hated credit cards. He only carried one because I made him, and he never used it. He didn't even like carrying a mortgage. It killed him when we had to take out a second."

"The card could have been stolen. It's worth checking."

"I didn't think of that."

"I need a list of anyone you've already talked to down there, including the cops. And I need you to call John's cell phone provider. I want to know who he called while he was in Florida." I hesitated on the next request, thinking about Mae's family room and the kind of photos that were there. "I'll need a picture of John to take with me."

After she left the room, I spotted one more stray piece of paper that had landed on the stove. At first I thought it didn't belong in our piles. It was a soccer schedule. But on the back was the name and phone number that explained clearly why it did.

When she came back, I held it up and showed it to her. "I need one more thing," I said. "I need to know who Bobby Avidor is and why he wasn't worth it."

Chapter Three

"**B**obby Avidor is a worthless piece of crap. He's a prick. He's scum. He's a rat bastard, a two-faced, lying sack of shit—"

"Take a breath, Dan." His voice was the loudest in a small diner full of big voices.

He stopped, blinked, grabbed a couple of home fries from my plate, and slid back in his side of the booth. But he didn't relax. He never relaxed. In the year I had known him, I wasn't sure Dan Fallacaro had ever taken a breath. He seemed to run on adrenaline instead of oxygen.

"If you'd arrived on time," I said, "you could have had your very own breakfast."

"I don't have time to eat, Shanahan." He shot forward in his seat and began drumming the tabletop with his fingers, thumping out the chaotic beat that was his own personal rhythm. "I had two airplanes crap out on me before the sun came up this morning, both of them over-booked. I had a ramper who got thrown in jail last night for drunk driving and resisting arrest. I had my best lead agent at the ticket counter not show up for work because her twelve-year-old kid stole her car. To top it off, air traffic control had a radar tower blow over, which means we've been having ATC problems for three days."

"Welcome," I said, "to life as a general manager." Dan was thirty-six, two years older than I was, but I felt so much like his big sister I always had to resist reaching over and tousling his hair. And I knew for all his constant complaining he relished every moment of his life at the airport, which not too long ago had been my life.

"Life as a general manager sucks, Shanahan. Honest to God, I don't know how you did it all those years."

"Most of those years, I did it somewhere besides Logan Airport."

"Maybe so, but I've got a whole new respect for you, boss."

I hadn't been Dan's or anyone else's boss in over a year, and it felt good to hear him call me that. More than I wanted to think.

The waitress appeared, a solid block of a woman with a face sculpted from stone. She slipped a cup of steaming black coffee onto the table in front of Dan. "What can I get you, Danny?"

He smiled at her. "Just seeing your face is enough for me."

She beamed. Dan had lots of big sisters. "You gonna eat anything but her leftovers?"

"Nope." He reached over and took another deep-fried potato slug from my plate. I'd asked the waitress not to bring them with my egg white omelet, but here they were, a half-eaten testament to my crumbling willpower. Being unemployed had disrupted my routine, to say the least, and routine had always been the key to my discipline. I took one last forkful, wishing I'd never taken the first, and pushed the plate toward Dan. He applied a blanket of catsup and set upon the greasy pile.

"Bobby Avidor, Dan."

"Avidor used to work out at Logan throwing bags years ago. He was before your time. He's a maintenance supervisor now down in Miami."

"Mae told me he saved Terry McTavish from drowning. She said—"

"And it's the best thing that ever happened to Avidor, that rat-fuck. He used to fill in on the McTavish fishing boat when they needed an extra hand. So one day, old man McTavish is home drunk off his ass, Johnny's trying to get the boat home in the middle of this big storm, and Terry's out on the deck doing whatever it is they do on fishing boats. All of a sudden, *boom,* this big fucking wave comes along and washes him over. Avidor happens to be standing right there. He looks down. He sees Terry dangling from this line. He does what any moron would do, which is reach down and haul him back in." He'd gone through the fries like a buzz saw and shoved the plate aside, leaving one uneaten cantaloupe ball to roll around in the greasy dish. "And by the way, I'm not convinced he didn't push him overboard to begin with just so he could save his butt."

"Don't you think Terry would have said something if he'd been pushed?"

"All I'm saying to you is Avidor's an operator and he knows a good thing when he sees it. Mae's right. He climbed aboard the Johnny McTavish gravy train that day, and he's been riding it ever since."

"How?"

"When Johnny started working for Majestic, he brought Terry in first, and right behind him comes Avidor. Avidor loaded bags for about two minutes before he got tired of freezing his ass off out on the ramp every winter. He decided he wanted to become an aircraft mechanic. Work inside the hangar where it was warm. So Johnny loaned him the money to go to school. From what I hear, he never paid him back."

"Mae said he didn't."

"He's a piece of shit." Dan mumbled to himself as he dug around in the wad of suit jacket on the seat next to him. Somehow he found a toothpick. He started to stick it in his mouth, but something else occurred to him and he pointed it at me instead. "Avidor got caught stealing, too."

"Stealing what?"

"The union caught him stealing tools from some of his fellow mechanics down at the hangar. They went to Johnny and told him to take care of it, so he gave Avidor a choice—leave the station, or get turned in to management and get fired. Avidor did the smart thing and transferred out to the West Coast." He put the toothpick in his mouth. "Johnny should have cut him loose right then and there when he had the chance."

"Mae says John went to Florida to meet Bobby. She says she doesn't know why."

"She probably doesn't, but Terry does."

"He says he doesn't."

"He may not know the specifics, but he knows what everyone else around here knows."

"Which is what?"

He assumed his top secret, cone-of-silence pose, one I'd become familiar with during our time together. He leaned across the table and lowered his voice. "Ever since he got to Florida, Bobby Avidor has been sending wads of cash up here to his dear old mother. She still lives in one of those little towns up the north shore somewhere. It's been one of life's great mysteries for the boys on the ramp, at least the ones who used to know him. First of all, why does anybody give up mechanic's pay to become a supervisor? Avidor was probably making more in overtime than his whole salary now. And second, making the salary he makes, how does he manage to buy his mother a nice SUV?"

"And what have they concluded?"

"Drugs. What else could it be?"

There were lots of things it could have been, but there was no point in arguing with Dan. He lived by the drumbeat of ramp rumors and, at least so far, it had served him well.

"He's running drugs on Majestic?"

"Not into Boston. No way. I've had the dogs in, the FBI, corporate security. No fucking way that shit's coming into my station. I can't speak for any other station. Listen, Shanahan"—he checked his watch. He'd been getting more and more twitchy by the second—"I'd love to sit here and shoot the shit with you, but I've got to talk to the asswipes in schedules. They're trying to cram in another six flights a day, and I don't have the gates. So if we're done here—"

"This drug thing and Avidor, is this a new rumor?"

"Hell, no."

"Why would John wake up one day and decide to get on an airplane and go confront a problem that's been hanging out there for a while?"

"How would I know that, Shanahan? Maybe he got fed up."

"Are you thinking Bobby killed John? Is that the rumor?"

"Ahhh, Bobby Avidor is a pussy. Whoever got over on Johnny had to have been bigger, tougher, and stronger than he was." He shrugged. "Or else it was five guys."

I wanted to probe further, but I was about to lose my audience. Dan's patience was dwindling fast.

"Dan, I need you to help me with something."

"I thought you already found a job."

"Not that kind of help."

I pulled the logbook from my backpack, but checked around the diner before slipping it onto the table. Maybe because of its condition, maybe because the man who had sent it was dead—for whatever reason, I couldn't shake the feeling I had something I wasn't supposed to have.

Dan had no such compunction. He grabbed the book, freed it from its careful wrapping, and turned it over in his hands. "Jesus Christ. What happened to this?"

"Be careful. You'll get that black stuff—"

Too late.

"What is this black shit, anyway?" Since he had no napkin of his own, he reached for mine and wiped his hands, and then used it to open the book and flip the damaged pages. He looked up at me. "What the hell are you doing with a logbook, Shanahan?"

I told him.

"Johnny McTavish sent this to you?"

"Before he left for Florida. This, too." I showed him the ring. When I told him how much it was worth he thrust it back at me, stiff-armed. "Take it back. It's making me nervous."

I wrapped it up and stuck it back into the pocket of

my khakis, which may not have been the best place for
it, but I wasn't really set up to transport high-value cargo.

"Dan, do you think you can find out what airline this
belongs to?"

"Probably. What for?"

"Because I have two places to start, the ring and the
book, and I'm taking care of the ring."

"Whoa. Slow down. What are you starting on?"

"I'm going to Miami. I'm going to try to find out
what happened."

"I thought you were supposed to be in Detroit on
Monday. Hello? New job?"

"Temporary change in plans."

He stared at me. "Not for nothing," he said, "but
you're the one who was talking about how your severance was expiring and how bad you had to get back to
work and what a great opportunity this was—"

"They'll be there when I get back." I didn't want to
talk about it. "I made you copies of all the pages I could
read. There are several captains' signatures in there.
Some entries have part numbers and mechanics' license
numbers. I figured we could trace one of them back to
the airline."

"We?" He reached over and snatched the file almost
before I could get it out of my backpack. "Shanahan,
how come I feel like I still work for you?" He was trying
to sound annoyed, but had the file open and was paging
through the copies.

"Be discreet. Whatever's going on, I don't want anything to get broadcast on the ramp before I get a chance
to talk to Mae first."

He closed the file and looked down at the bag next to
my booth. "What time is your flight?"

"I'm listed on the two o'clock. But if you give me a ride
to the airport, I could probably make the ten-thirty."

He scanned the restaurant and caught the waitress's eye.
"Are you going to see Ryczbicki while you're down there?"

"It would be hard to avoid him. He is the station
manager."

He reached for the check when it came and pulled out his wallet to pay, which was the least he could do, given that he'd kept me waiting for almost an hour, then eaten all of my home fries.

"You tell him for me the next time he sends a damaged aircraft my way and blames it on Boston, I'm going to come down to his ramp with a fucking baseball bat and conduct my own investigation."

"Sure, Dan. That will be the first thing I bring up."

He glanced again at the check and threw down a twenty, which by my calculation represented more than a one hundred percent tip. Our stone-faced waitress would have another reason to smile today.

Chapter Four

The automatic sliding glass doors parted with a swish as I stepped from the warm, humid jetbridge into the terminal. The Miami International Airport was as I remembered it—an homage to marble, glass, and pink neon. Everything in it was canned, conditioned, and proudly artificial, especially the climate. Even the real potted plants looked plastic.

I hadn't spent much time in Miami, but what I always remembered was the slickness, the smooth and shiny surfaces that made me less surefooted, more aware that if I slipped and fell down here, I could get hurt.

I checked around and located the agent who had met the flight. "I'm Alex Shanahan. You paged me on board?"

She checked her clipboard. "Mr. Ryczbicki asked that you meet him in the lounge at the Miami Airport Hotel."

I almost asked her, but then it occurred to me she probably wouldn't know how Bic had known I was coming. "Can you point me in the right direction?"

"It's on the concourse between E and F just on the other side of the security checkpoint. Look for the sushi bar in front. You can't miss it."

I went to the concourse between E and F, located the sushi bar, and there it was—a hotel inside the airport. It struck me as almost too convenient. At most airports, you had to step out to the curb to catch the shuttle to the hotel, which afforded at least a few seconds of fresh air and natural light. Not here. Here the lobby doubled

as part of the concourse. I worked my way through and
landed at the cocktail lounge.

It was roaring, not exactly what you'd expect at a bar
at 2:20 in the afternoon, but then this was Miami International where people flew in and out from time zones all
over the world. One man's dawn was another man's
dusk. Phil Ryczbicki was perched on a tall stool at the
bar, chatting with the bartender. He looked like a puffy
frog on a tree stump. A frog sipping a martini. I set my
backpack on the floor next to him.

"Are you keeping office hours here, Bic?"

The bartender looked at me as if I were the school
principal and drifted away. "Heard you were flying in.
Decided I could use a few belts." Bic turned and peeked
at me over one of his soft, sloping shoulders. "What's it
been . . . two years?"

"More like three. Dare I ask how you knew I was
coming?"

"You don't want to know, and I've got enough problems of my own without you dropping in."

"It's nice to see you, too, Bic."

A few years and a few pounds hadn't made Bic any
more congenial. He was still five foot four, and no doubt
still bitter about it, which was one of the things that
made him so darned affable. Round as an onion and
balding on top, his distinguishing feature was a giant
blonde mustache that made him look like a whisk broom
with eyes. He was a kick-the-tires kind of guy who had
never come to terms with the concept of women running
airport operations, and never would come to terms with
the idea that some of them did it better than he did.
Dealing with him was not always pleasant, but he was
consistent and I'd figured out the key to him a long time
ago—give him a way to take all the credit and cover his
ass, and you were welcome to whatever was left over.

"Dan Fallacaro sends his love," I said. "He claims you
dropped a damaged aircraft on him. What's that all
about?"

He snorted. "He thinks my boys creased a B757 with

a Cochran loader, closed it up, and sent it damaged to Logan."

"Did they?"

"All I know is we both made our arguments and he got charged with the ding."

"You're a master, Bic."

"I don't make the rules, Alex. I learned to make them work for me. It's all in how you present it."

The couple to his left settled up their tab and left. Bic patted the newly vacated cushioned stool next to his. "We have to talk," he said.

I scanned the room. The Florida sun shone brilliantly outside, but only a sickly version of it made it through the wall of heavy Art Deco blocks, just enough to make visible the blue haze of dust and cigarette smoke that lingered over the cushy black leather seating pits and low cocktail tables.

"I'll catch up with you later." I reached down for my backpack and began to hoist it onto my shoulder. "I'm going down to claim my bag."

"Don't bother."

"Why not?"

"Because your bag is on its way to Honolulu."

"*What?*" My backpack hit the floor and I worried, belatedly, about my laptop.

"One of your pals in the Boston bag room misrouted it."

"That can't be. I personally handed my bag to Dan, and he personally loaded it into the belly. It never even went through the bag room."

"Then someone went to a lot of trouble to fish it out and retag it."

I sagged against the bar and started to feel that hopeless, helpless feeling I hated so much. The most deeply frustrating part of being harassed by a group, especially one as tight and organized as the International Brotherhood of Groundworkers, was that the act was always anonymous. There was never any way to find the one who had scrawled the filthy graffiti on the door to your office. Or the one who had made seventeen hang-up calls to your home in the middle of the night. The person who had slashed your tires in the employee lot was never going to be identified. It was hit and run. It was guerrilla tactics. It was none of them and it was all of them and there was never anyone to stand in and engage the fight. The only real choice was to endure it. And after a time your skin thickened until you almost couldn't feel anything, and your resolve hardened into a clenched fist, and it changed you. And then you had that to be angry about, too.

A hint of a smile twitched the broom on Bic's upper lip. "Are you enjoying this, Bic?"

"I never enjoy a misrouted bag, not even yours. It means more work for me. I just can't believe you checked a bag out of Boston. What were you thinking?"

"Dan asked me to check it. It was a full flight and he wanted some overhead space for his paying customers. And I was thinking sooner or later the boys in the Boston bag room were going to have to get tired of screwing me over."

"Now you see, there's your problem. They will never forget what you did. Not in Boston, not anywhere. You're on the shit list, and once you're on, there's no way off. My advice—never check another bag out of Logan. Maybe never check another bag on Majestic, period."

"How did you find out?"

"One of my rampers downstairs gave me a heads up. He's got a buddy up there who called to let the south-eastern local in on the joke. I've already put out a tracer. If you're lucky we'll catch it before it leaves the mainland."

I immediately began trying to inventory what had been in my bag. All the unique, irreplaceable things—my oldest, softest pair of jeans that weren't ripped, my Walkman and all my best running music, that cool little toothbrush holder I'd found at Target one day when I'd been shopping for shampoo. And there were all the things that seem so mundane until they're gone—hair

conditioner that I could find only at the shop in Boston
where I got my hair cut. Face scrub. Underwear.

"In the meantime"—Bic sat back and rested his little
hands on his thighs—"we have to talk."

"All right, let's talk. But not here. I make it a point
never to breathe air I can see."

"Where do you want to go?"

"Have you considered your office as a place to conduct business?"

"That's the last place I want to be seen with you. Why
do you think I met you in the bar? Where are you
staying?"

"Right here."

"How do you afford a place like this?"

"None of your business."

"Fallacaro got you a discount, didn't he?"

He was right, but no need to confirm that. He turned
to find his buddy the bartender. "Raymond . . . Ray,
we're going upstairs."

Glass in one hand, power spigot in the other, Raymond
nodded in our direction. "You want a roadie, man? How
about your friend?"

Bic shook his head. He threw back the last of his martini, set the glass on the bar, and hopped off his stool.
"Put it on my tab."

The Top of the Port was a combination snack bar,
lounge, and health club on the roof of the hotel. A turquoise swimming pool refracted the sunlight, and a green
running track wound around the perimeter of the deck.
It was a quarter mile at most, but it had a nice surface—
easy on the knees.

I followed the track, walking around until I found the
ramp-side view of the airport. We were high enough to
see the entire ground operation, and the barely choreo-
graphed convergence of people, vehicles, and aircraft
that made the whole thing go. That it worked as
smoothly as it did never failed to amaze and enthrall me.
A vast array of ground vehicles was on display—tugs,
carts, push tractors, fuel pump trucks, catering and lav

trucks, Bobcats, loaders, and buses. They flowed around the airplanes like tributaries around great, winged boulders. At that moment, the lineup for takeoff included an Aeroflot B767 probably destined for Moscow, an airbus from Turkish Airlines that had to be headed for Istanbul, and an El Al B747 that was most certainly bound for Tel Aviv. Behind them, I could see the colors of Lan Peru, Iberia, Qantas, Sabena, and Surinam Airways.

Bic stood and watched with me. We had our differences, but we shared one thing in common. I knew he could stand there as long as I could—which was a long time—and never lose interest.

"Have you missed it?" he asked.

I used my hand as a visor to watch the British Airways B747 lumber down the long runway. Just when it looked as if it might run out of concrete, it lifted off with impossible grace and climbed until it faded into the late afternoon sky. You could have carved the heart out of my chest and I wouldn't have missed it more.

"Not really."

He surveyed the deck. "Let's go sit over there. Maybe if we sit out in plain sight someone will come up and serve us a drink."

We settled into a couple of molded plastic chairs beside a patio table. The breeze whispered across the deck. It ruffled the leaves of the potted plants and brought with it an odor so strong I could almost taste it. "What is that smell?"

"Smoke," he said. "Feels like the wind is starting to shift."

"Smoke from where?"

"Wildfires."

I sat up straight and checked out the view of downtown Miami on the opposite side of the hotel. Hanging over the city was a yellowish gray haze that dulled the outlines of the buildings.

"We came through that stuff on the way down, but I thought it was air pollution."

"We had to shut down the operation yesterday for over an hour," he said. "Diverted almost fifty flights."

"Because of smoke?"

"Our visibility was about two hundred yards."

"Where's the fire?"

"All around us," he said. "Up north fifty thousand acres of the Okefenokee Swamp is on fire. This smoke comes from a big fire in the Everglades." He sniffed the air. "This is not bad. Wait until the wind picks up."

There was something eerie about the acrid smell, the way it clung to your hair and made your skin feel grainy. There was something unsettling about the way the smoke flattened and diffused the light from the sun, making everything that had been bright dull and dirty. It made my eyes burn—not much of an improvement over the bar.

"What do you want, Bic?" I knew he would be blunt with me, so I figured I'd jump in first.

"I want you to turn around and go back to Boston. I'll forward your bag when it turns up." His tone was even, his expression hidden behind that mustache and a pair of trendy narrow sunglasses he'd produced from his suit jacket. Mine were on their way to Oahu—without me.

I settled back into my lounge chair and put my feet up. This was going to be one of those unpleasant conversations. "Do you even know why I'm here?"

"Don't know and don't care." That didn't sound right. Bic had a reason for every ounce of energy he expended. He wouldn't have bothered with even seeing me if he hadn't had good reason. "People around you tend to have bad luck," he said. "I don't want to be one of them."

"Does Bobby Avidor work for you?"

"Why?"

"You know, that wouldn't be hard to verify, Bic. You could save us both a lot of energy by answering the easy ones, and fighting only on the hard ones."

"Yes, he works for me."

"And is he running drugs out of your station?"

"That would be a hard one, right?" He dropped his head back to let the sun fall on his face. "Who told you that?"

"Unidentified sources."

"Ramp rats in Boston."

"*Reliable* sources who relayed to me what appears to be common knowledge on the ramp in Boston."

"Let's say he was. Why would that be any business of yours?"

"Because a friend of mine came down here to meet him and went home in a box. I'd like to find out what Bobby knows about that."

"John McTavish was a friend of yours?"

"He was."

"I didn't think you had any friends on the ramp up there," he said.

"And you know more than you're saying."

"We shipped his body home last week. My station productivity has gone into the crapper ever since. No one around here can talk about anything else."

"Gee, what bad form for John to get himself murdered in your city. So what about Avidor?"

"He's not running coke out of here. Bob Avidor comes in, he does his job, and he never causes me any problems. And as far as any involvement with McTavish, the police have checked him out on that, and they've cleared him. So you've got nothing, except to say he's an asshole. As far as I know, there's no law against that."

"How can you be so sure about him?"

"You're not listening to me. If he was a bad guy, I would know, and I would take care of him myself. But I don't need you here, and I sure don't want you here."

The breeze came up again, stronger this time, and I thought I could feel the temperature dropping.

"You know, Bic, all this strenuous protesting is giving me the idea that you don't want me to look because you know there is something to be found."

He sat up as abruptly as his portly shape would allow and planted both feet on the cement. "Look, I've got nothing against you personally. From what I hear, that guy you killed up there was a piece of shit and he deserved to be dead."

"I didn't kill him. He got killed all by himself." I felt my voice flatten until it was all sharp edges. "And he was a murderer hell-bent on killing me, too."

"Whatever. He was a dues-paying member of the International Brotherhood of Groundworkers. He's dead, they blame you, and not just in Boston. They all hate you and they always will. There are assholes that aren't even been born yet who are going to join this union and hate you for what they think you did. That's how strongly they feel."

"What are you suggesting, that I crawl under a rock and hide?"

"I don't care what you do. I just want you to do it someplace besides Miami. I have a good relationship with my local. I'm on track for a promotion to VP, and I don't want you screwing it up. They've already been in to tell me if I do anything to help you, they're going to call a wildcat strike."

That was the motivation right there. Even the slightest hint of labor unrest would be enough to get Bic up off his ass and into my face. "Well"—I reached up and rubbed my temples. This was sounding all too familiar— "I hope you told them to go pound sand."

"What I told them was to get their butts back to work and never threaten me again. What I'm telling you is if you've got something on Bob besides ramp rat rumors, I'll nail his balls to the wall. But if you don't, keep your mouth shut because there's no way in hell I can defend myself against gossip and innuendo. You should know that better than anyone."

He stood up and shook out his pant legs so they weren't bunched up around his thighs. "You want to talk to Avidor, go ahead. Knock yourself out. He can take care of himself. But just Avidor. You want to talk to anyone else who works for me, you tell me first. And stay out of my operation. I'm not going to let you do to me what you did to yourself in Boston."

I watched him walk around the swimming pool and disappear into the hotel. After he'd been gone for a few minutes, I got up and watched a few more planes take off. This time they disappeared much faster after lifting off, swallowed up by the haze that had blown in, thickened the sky, and turned a beautiful sunny day to shit.

Chapter Five

C'mon, don't pick up. Keep ringing, phone, and roll me into voice mail.

Paul Gladstone's line was ringing at the other end and I was moving as best I could around my hotel room, which was basically a bed with four walls around it. The room did not benefit from the huge print on the bedspread—big, tropical flowers with blooms drawn in broad, looping strokes of pink and purple, yellow and lime green. At least it was a queen-sized bed. I chose to feel good about that.

By the third ring, I was thinking I was home free, mentally scripting the message I would leave for my future boss. "I tried to reach you," I'd say. "I hate leaving this message in voice mail, but since we're having so much trouble connecting—"

"Paul Gladstone."

Damn. I cleared the disappointment out of my throat. "Hello, Paul. This is Alex."

"Alex!" He sounded truly delighted to hear from me. "How are you?"

"You're working late tonight." I glanced at my watch, even though I didn't have to. I'd purposely waited until after nine o'clock in Detroit, hoping I would miss him. Again.

"I'm trying to keep my head above water. Where are you?"

"I'm in Miami."

"One last fling before the grind? Good for you."

"Not exactly. Listen, Paul—"

"Before I forget, we've got a couple of meetings on your calendar for next week. I should let you know . . . let me just find . . ." I heard the sound of keys clicking. "I thought . . ." More keys clacking. I stood up and started to pace. "I guess they're not on my calendar since you're going in my place." He chuckled. "That would make sense. How about this? I'll have my secretary give you a call when she gets in tomorrow morning."

"Paul, I'm not going to be able to make it in by Monday."

There was the tiniest pause, long enough for me to think about how long I had been without a paycheck. "That might not be a problem," he said. "I don't think the first meeting is until Wednesday afternoon. If you can get here by then—"

"I won't make it by Wednesday."

I could feel him going still at the other end of the line. He was listening more carefully now. The pause was longer and heavier. "How much time do you need?"

"I think a week will do it."

"Is everything all right?"

"Everything is fine. But I'm not in Miami on a vacation. Something has come up that's of . . . of a personal nature, and I have to take care of it before I start work." The words I had scripted for this conversation felt stilted. I felt evasive, and I felt him reacting to it.

"Is it something I can help you with? Because I'll be honest, if I can get you here on Monday, or even Wednesday, I would sure like to do it."

"I know. And I'm sorry to be dumping this on you at the last minute. I know you're busy. If there was any other way—"

"Okay, okay. Let me think about this." I pictured him sitting at his desk with one hand around the phone and the other flat atop his head, the way he'd done a few times during the interviews. "I'll have to cancel my trip this week, but I'll . . . we'll be all right. Are you sure there's nothing I can do? I mean on a personal level."

I fell back on the flower print bedspread and draped my arm over my eyes. I felt guilty enough without his genuine personal concern. "No, really, everything's fine, Paul, but thank you for asking."

"Then I'll see you a week from Monday."

"Right. I'll stay in touch and let you know if it's going beyond that."

"If it does, Alex, then this becomes a more complicated problem." Now his voice was taking on more gravity, and I felt the weight of his concern like a stone hanging from my neck. "I have to ask you, Alex, are you having . . . you're not having second thoughts, are you?"

"No. I'm still fully committed to being there, Paul."

"Good. That's all I needed to hear." He sounded relieved, and I felt queasy and I wasn't sure why.

We chatted for a few more minutes. He told me about the freak snowstorm that had moved in the night before. I told him about how it was 78 degrees in Miami.

After I hung up, I stared at the phone for a long time. Eventually, I reached over and wiped my perspiration off the receiver.

An hour later I was still emptying out shopping bags. I'd picked up the basic replacement gear—running shorts, T-shirts, khakis, a couple of polo shirts. I'd spent more time and money on my new pair of running shoes than I had on the marginally nice-for-the-price lightweight business suit. But then I knew I'd be spending more time in the shoes.

When the phone rang, I hoped it wasn't Paul Gladstone calling to be nice again.

"Hello?"

"I hear you're looking for me."

"Who is this?"

"Avidor. I have what you're looking for."

At first the whole scene struck me as surreal. When I stepped off the elevator and walked onto the concourse, I saw a woman in the beauty salon next to the hotel getting a manicure. A party of four was raising a toast in one of the restaurants, and next door to them, passengers shopped for that last minute bottle of duty-free Armagnac.

It was two-fifteen in the morning.

I blinked at colors that seemed too vibrant and lights that were too bright. Everyone moved as if they'd been dosed with caffeine. Then I realized I was the one out of sync. I was at Miami International Airport, where time had no meaning. It may have been the middle of the night for me, but the people who moved through this global way station came and went from time zones all over the world.

Bobby worked the night shift, mostly at the maintenance hangar, but he had agreed to take his dinner in the food court at Concourse F so we could rendezvous at the terminal. He was very clear he would be there no earlier than two-thirty and would stay no more than thirty minutes. But something told me not to be surprised when I rounded the corner and found him already settled in and halfway through his dinner when I arrived at two-twenty. He was at the Café Bacardi, a teeny restaurant with a massive bar long enough to warrant two television sets. They were both on and tuned to the same station, so we were treated in stereo to the hypnotic drone of a stock car race. Unless NASCAR ran at Darlington in the middle of the night, the few people scattered around the food court who were interested were watching a tape-delayed version of an earlier race.

"Are you Bobby?"

"The only people who still call me Bobby are from Boston."

"What do you want me to call you?"

"I don't care."

Bobby may have grown up with John and Terry McTavish, but he looked older. His hairline was receding and he had a thick, bottom-heavy shape that fit nicely into his plastic chair. He had buckled his belt one notch too far, bisecting a soft middle into two spare tires. His jittery eyes fixed on me briefly. It was long enough to see that his body may have been flaccid, but his eyes were diamond hard.

"May I sit?" I asked.

"Suit yourself."

I did. "What's up, Bobby?"

"I gotta set the record straight," he said, "on Johnny McTavish. I know that's why you're here."

"How did you know I was here at all?"

"We heard from Boston you were coming down. We heard about the bag. And Bic called and told me I should get this thing cleared up."

"Bic told you where I was staying?"

"Is it a secret or something?"

"No." *In fact, I'm thinking of posting my schedule on the web.*

"Terry sent you," he said. "Am I right?"

I didn't know this man except by his lousy reputation among some good people. But even if I knew nothing about him, I didn't want to give him any information he didn't already have. "Who said anyone sent me?"

"It was Terry. I know it was Terry." He shook his head. "God bless him. He thinks I'm the devil himself. You'd never know I'd saved his life. You probably already heard that story, right?" He gave me another one of those quick-flick glances, and I knew he wouldn't need much encouragement to tell me his version of events on that fateful day.

"Someone may have mentioned it."

"I hear Terry's whacked out. Gone off the deep end. Is that true?"

I gave him a "beats me" shrug.

"How's Mae holding up?"

"Mae is fine."

"I hope you'll give her my regards. No matter what's happened between us over the years, I still got a soft spot in my heart for the McTavishes. All of them."

His grin was so greasy, and not from the sub he was eating, it almost had me reaching for a napkin to wipe down his face. "If you're so fond of them, why aren't you taking Mae's calls?"

He laid his sandwich down. All the planes of his face flattened into somber concern. "Because I got nothing to say to her that will make her feel better."

"How about 'My condolences. I'm sorry you lost your husband'?"

"Believe me, anything I got to say about Johnny, she don't want to hear. Terry, neither."

"Tell me. I'd like to hear it."

He pondered that request as he looked left, then made a big show of looking right. No one was within ten feet. Still, he dropped his voice and spoke without moving his jaw much, which made it tough to hear him. "The truth is Terry McTavish knows what went down with his brother. He just don't want no one else to know. And if you're a friend of Johnny's, you won't neither."

"I'm listening."

"Johnny McTavish was down here because of a drug buy."

"A *drug* buy? John McTavish?" I almost laughed out loud. "That's an outrageous accusation, and you know it." And now I knew how the police came up with their theory.

"Listen to me. I didn't say he was down here to make a buy. I said he was here *because* of one."

"Could you elaborate on that distinction?"

"I said you wouldn't like it, and neither do I, but here it is. Last Monday, I'm down at the hangar working the end of my shift, when I get a call. It's Johnny."

"What time does your shift end?"

"0700 hours, but I worked over that morning, so it must have been around 0900 when he called."

"What did he say?"

"That he was getting on a flight and coming down to see me. I say what for? He says he'll tell me when he gets here, to just be at the gate to meet his flight. So that's what I did."

"You waited around at the airport for him? Until after two o'clock?"

"I didn't put in for no overtime, if that's what you're thinking. I don't even get paid overtime. I did some paperwork and other things I'd been needing to do. I haven't talked to the guy in years, right? I get a call out of the clear blue. I'm curious."

"How many years?"

"Since I went to LA, which was four and a half, maybe five years ago. Besides that he's done me a few good turns in my time. So he gets here and we go and have a cup of coffee. We're talking about this and about that and so on and so forth and then he starts saying why he's here. I'm listening to him and I can't believe what he's telling me, which is all about how his brother's surgeries and all the litigation had put him in a financial bind, him and Mae. They even tried to sell that business of theirs—you know about that business Johnny and Terry got going on the side?"

"The landscaping business."

"Only it turns out they owe more on it than it's worth. So Terry, who figures he caused the whole thing anyway, he decides he's gonna take matters into his own hands. He sets up a coke buy from a guy down here. Some connected guy. According to Johnny, it was a big shipment, a one-shot deal Terry was trying to do to get right, and get his family out of the hole he'd put them in. It's not like he can really work anymore."

I looked more closely at Bobby Avidor. Those light blue eyes, at least what I could see of them, did not seem at all connected to the things that came out of his mouth. His gaze kept jumping around, which made it hard to tell if he was lying. Dan had said it best—John would sooner cut off his arm than deal drugs, and anyone who knew him knew that. But I wasn't so sure about Terry. I thought about that display of anger back in Mae's kitchen, and I felt a little less comfortable because what I did know was if Terry had been in trouble, John would have done anything to get him out. Anything.

"If Terry doesn't have any money, how was he going to pay for a shipment of coke?"

"By providing the transportation. He was going to arrange to bring it up on one of our airplanes."

"How? He doesn't even work for Majestic anymore."

"He has friends that do."

If Bobby had concocted this story, he'd been shrewd enough to take into account both character and circumstances. "Let's say that was true," I said. "Why would John have flown down here and told you all of this?"

"Miami is a tough place if you don't know your way around. And Johnny was not a person who was plugged into the underbelly, if you know what I'm saying."

"And you are?"

He shrugged. "Being in Florida and working at the airport, he thought I might have heard some names I could pass along."

"Did you?"

"I don't know those kinds of people, and even if I did, I wouldn't have put Johnny in touch with them. He'd be a babe in the woods in that crowd."

"What did you tell him?"

"To go home and talk to Terry. And to tell Terry to talk to his priest."

I sat back, listened to the whining NASCAR engines, and tried to figure out what was wrong with this story, other than the fact that I didn't like its teller. "Let me make sure I understand this. You say John flew to Miami on Monday. The two of you spoke here at the terminal. He told you Terry was involved in a deal to smuggle cocaine on a Majestic aircraft, and he wanted you to help him stop it."

"Which I didn't do, because I didn't know how to."

"Did you see him after that meeting?"

"That was it. We shook hands, I went home, and I didn't hear from him again. I assumed he went back to Boston. I didn't even know he checked into a hotel."

He had an answer for everything, which meant either he was well rehearsed, or his story was true. "The police say you have an alibi for the night he disappeared."

"I was out with one of my buddies."

"I'm sure your buddy can verify your story."

"The cops already have, but you can talk to him if you want. I'll give you his number." He smoothed out a section of the butcher paper that had been wrapped around his sandwich. He took a pen out of the pocket of his short-sleeved shirt and wrote something on one corner. He ripped the corner off, folded it, and folded it again. Then he crumpled the rest of the paper into a tight ball that fit nicely into his fist. "By the way," he said, still fingering the note, "I hear your bag turned up."

From anyone else but him, that would have been good news. "Where?"

"Frisco." He squeezed the ball of paper and released it. "Don't quote me on this, but rumor has it it's coming in sometime later today. If it comes in before I leave, you want me to hold it for you? Maybe keep care of it for you?"

"I'm sure baggage service will take care of it."

"Okay. But I wouldn't want you being down here in Miami without the things you need." He put the note flat on the table in front of him and pushed it toward me. That same well-lubricated smile slithered across his face. Before it had been equal parts chummy and patronizing. This time I saw hints of a third element—menace—and I saw it in his eyes, too. They were dull and mean when he finally settled his gaze on me. Whether he was lying about Terry or not, we were on different sides of some very tall fences. He knew it, too. I just wondered how far he would go to keep me on my side.

"All's I'm saying is if you don't have everything you need to stay down here, it might be best for you to go back home."

"I appreciate your concern, but I can be very resourceful."

"That's your call."

He pulled back his finger, leaving the note in front of me. I picked it up and started to unfold it, but was jolted by a screech of metal on gritty linoleum that cut right through the sound of the speeding race cars and touched off a shiver down my spine. It was Bobby pushing his chair back from the table in the most ear-cringing manner possible. "I don't think," he said, rising slowly, "we have anything else to talk about."

"We might." I unfolded the scrap of paper and read the name he'd written.

When I looked up to find him, he was already gone, walking away with one hand in his pocket and the other wrapped around the balled-up butcher paper. From the way he was sauntering, it looked as if he might be whistling.

I almost went after him, but he wasn't the person I needed to be talking to. That would be the person who had been with Bobby the night John died, the person he said would vouch for his innocence. That would be Phil Ryczbicki.

Chapter Six

"**W**hat I'm asking you, Dan, is whether you believe Terry would do such a thing."

I had Dan on the phone and the early news on the TV, and neither one of them seemed to have good news for me. On the screen—huge clouds of black smoke boiling out of the flames and into the tropical jet stream as more and more of the drought-cracked Everglades turned into fuel for the raging monster. On the phone—a connection that was as balky as Dan as he did everything but answer my question.

"Where did you hear that?"

"Your friend Avidor," I said. "I saw him last night." I checked the clock radio next to my bed. "Actually, it was more like three hours ago. He said John was down here to undo a drug deal Terry had set up."

"That *cock*sucker. That shit-eating, crap-spewing son of a bitch. It's not enough he gets Johnny killed. Now he's smearing the whole family. Jesus Christ, Shanahan. Jesus *Christ*."

"Then you don't think it's true. Thank God." I sank down on the edge of the bed and, for the first time since I'd left Bobby, let myself feel tired. When I'd gotten back to my room, I'd pulled back the covers and tried to sleep. But the air conditioner had been too loud and the bed too soft. The pillows had been too flat—still were—and my brain would not stop working. What if it was true? What if John had been murdered trying to protect Terry from committing a felony? What if Terry went to jail? What would Mae do then? If it was true, what would I do?

I realized we had lapsed into silence, unusual in a conversation with Mr. Fallacaro, especially after he'd had his first cup of coffee of the day. "Dan?"

"I didn't say that."

"Didn't say what?"

"That Terry would never do something like that."

I was back on my feet. "What are you talking about? You just said—"

"Whether it's true or it's not, I don't like fucking Bobby Avidor talking about Terry that way. The McTavishes are good people. The kid's been through a lot. Tell me exactly what he said."

I found the remote control, which wasn't hard because it was bolted to the nightstand, and turned off the TV. I could only deal with one crisis at a time. I told Dan what Avidor had told me. "Just tell me objectively, if Terry felt desperate enough and guilty enough, do you think it's something he would do? I need to know what you really think. It's important."

"I've got to be honest with you, boss. Terry's different than he was before he cracked up on that motorcycle. I knew him pretty well when he worked out here, but since he got hurt, he's been hanging around with some of the hard-asses in the union and all they talk about is how the company owes him, how we screwed him out of his benefits. If he ever gets up in the morning one day and forgets to hate Majestic Airlines, they'll be right there to remind him. And the truth of the matter is Terry got screwed."

"Terry got a bad break, Dan. The worst, but—"

"Just stop right there if you're going to try to be rational, Shanahan, because Terry's not exactly in a rational mood right now."

I pictured Terry trying to maneuver around Mae's small kitchen with one good leg, one bad, and a cane. I remembered the look of bleak disappointment in his eyes, and the rage that had come off of him like a fever.

"So what's your answer, Dan? Do you think he'd set up a coke deal?"

"The old Terry wouldn't have gotten involved in anything like that, but now . . ."

He let out a long sigh and for once I wanted Dan to talk faster. "But now you don't know?"

"What do you want me to say, Shanahan? Do I think Terry McTavish would decide to take from the company what he thought he was owed to begin with? No. Would it surprise me to hear that he did? Not that much."

After I hung up, I sat down on the bed again and tried to figure out what to do next. I had a full day scheduled, meetings with people who saw or might have seen John while he was in Miami. But I should call Terry, I thought, and quiz him. I should give Mae an update. What would I tell her?

My muscles twitched and ached from too little sleep. I was mighty annoyed at the turn events had taken, and deeply pissed off that I never saw it coming. The sun was beginning to show through the slats of the plantation shutters. I lay all the way back and closed my eyes against the bright intrusion. The next time I moved, it was to get up and answer the door. The maid wanted to know if she could clean my room before her shift ended. It was after eleven o'clock in the morning. I was already late for my first appointment. Probably not a good way to start off with the Miami-Dade Police Department.

Chapter Seven

Betty Boop stared down at the squad room from a high shelf. Her round button eyes and Kewpie doll lips gave her an expression of extreme surprise, not inappropriate given that she was staring down at a man handcuffed to a chair.

Detective Patricia Spain leaned against the desk where I was sitting. Her white silk blouse gleamed against her dark skin, and her peach-colored linen suit hung on a frame that was all corners and angles—long legs, plank-straight shoulders, and flat stomach. With her ultrashort hair and unlined face, she could have been anywhere from thirty to fifty years old.

"Spell your name, please."

She wrote down my name in her pad as I spelled it. She was a lefty, the kind that wrapped her arm around and pulled the pencil from the top—a difficult maneuver since she was leaning against a desk, trying to use her knee as a writing surface. Homicide detectives worked out of Miami-Dade Police Department headquarters. As such, she was a visitor herself to the Airport Station squad room. She had borrowed a desk, one of ten packed into a space as big as a small master bedroom, and given me the chair.

"Tell me again about your relationship with the victim."

I didn't like the word victim. I shifted in my chair and accidentally bumped a stack of manila file folders on the floor at my feet.

"Don't worry about those," she said before I had a chance to lean over and straighten them. "They go up in that chair you're sitting in. I'll put them back when we're done."

"John and I used to work together for Majestic Airlines in Boston. We became friends."

"Ummm-huh. And tell me again why you're here."

It seemed like a simple question. And I had lots of answers. I could have told her how when I had needed help at Logan, John McTavish had been there. How he had helped me uncover a deep, dark secret that just about everyone had wanted to stay buried. How he had chosen to stand with me against his union brothers—men he had grown up with and worked with side by side—when doing so probably meant risking his life. I could have told her that John was a good man who had worked for everything he'd had in life and did not deserve to be labeled a drug runner.

I looked at the detective. "Mae . . . John's wife wanted someone down here who could be closer to the investigation. I'm between jobs right now, so I told her I'd come."

"Are you an investigator of some kind? Do you have a license?"

"No."

Her eyes as she looked down at me were as dark as a couple of pitted black olives. It was hard to read them, but I felt as she stared down at me that she had decided something right then. "I've already told the family everything we know." She had decided not to talk to me. "I don't know what else we can do for you."

"With all due respect, Detective, they don't feel that you've told them anything. Is that because you don't know, or because you don't want them to know what you know?"

She closed her notebook, crossed her arms, and leaned back against the desk. "When we have something to tell them, we will."

"Does that mean you won't tell me either?"

"There isn't much I could tell you that I haven't told them. Maybe a few unpleasant details."

"I'll take anything you've got."

She didn't sigh. She didn't roll her eyes. She just held eye contact for a moment longer than if she hadn't wanted me to go away. Then she reopened the notebook, flipped back a few pages, and began to read. Rapidly. "Mr. McTavish was stabbed in the throat with a serrated blade, probably a knife, long enough to go in one side and out the other. He was killed somewhere other than where he was found, we don't know where yet, but it wasn't his hotel room. We haven't found the murder weapon. He didn't die right away. From the position of the body, it appeared he was trying to climb out. The ME says he bled to death."

"Climb out?"

"The body was found early Wednesday morning in a Dumpster by a homeless man looking for breakfast."

"Oh." That was a detail no one had shared with me, and I wasn't sure I was better off for having learned it. Bleeding to death on a pile of garbage was a graceless exit for an honorable man. I thought about Mae wanting the details, wanting to know everything John had done from the moment he'd left her to the moment he'd died, and I wondered if that was something she would want to know. I was glad I had just given her an update. I had a day or two to figure out how to tell her.

"When was he killed?"

"Sometime early Tuesday morning. We know he called home around one a.m., so it was after that. There's only one person down here we know for sure he made contact with, and he's got an alibi."

"Bobby Avidor?"

"Ummm-huh. Do you know him?"

"I met him for the first time last night. I've heard rumors that he's running dope out of the airport here."

The information did not bowl her over. She didn't even blink. "Where did you hear that?"

"His former colleagues on the ramp in Boston. They're usually right."

"Well"—she flipped her notebook closed for a second time—"I've talked to the detectives who work here at

the airport and they've got nothing like that on him.
They're usually right."

Touché, Detective. "Do you have a motive?"

"Nothing we're ready to talk about."

"John's wife told me you suspect he was involved in
a drug deal gone bad."

"This is Miami. We assume everything is drug related
until we can prove otherwise."

"John McTavish would not be involved in any transaction related to drugs."

Detective Spain looked skeptical, and I didn't blame
her. She probably heard the same thing about everyone's
murdered friends and relatives. She responded with her
own question. "Why do you think Mr. McTavish was
in Miami?"

"It's possible he heard the rumors about Avidor and
he came down here to tell him to stop doing what he
was doing."

"Why wouldn't he have called us? Or the FBI?"

"John didn't trust authority, and he was comfortable
handling these kinds of problems on his own. He probably felt he had created it by bringing Bobby into the
company. It would have been like him to try to solve
it himself."

She'd asked the question, but seemed only half interested in the answer, and not at all interested in continuing the discussion. She tapped the end of her pencil on
her pad. I sat in my allotted space and felt the weight of
the logbook in my lap. It was inside my backpack, and
the time had come for me to do what I'd come to do,
what I'd told Mae I would do, which was turn over the
book and the ring to the authorities.

Detective Spain was now sliding the pencil in and out
of the little spiral at the top of her pad. When she got it
stuck there, I stood up, which wasn't a good idea because
wherever you stood in that squad room, you were standing in someone's way. Another detective almost tripped
over me.

"Thank you for your time, Detective." I pulled one of
the personal business cards I'd had printed out of my

backpack, wrote the number for the hotel on it, and offered it to her. "I hope you won't mind if I stay in touch with you while I'm down here." She took the card and slipped it into her notebook.

I waited. She stared at me. "Detective, could I have one of yours?"

She offered a card and I took it, thankful that I had gotten at least one thing I'd asked for from the good detective. I threw the backpack over my shoulder and walked out.

Chapter Eight

The Harmony House Suites was different from the place I had pictured when Mae had shown me the receipt. The lobby looked more like a sparsely visited shopping mall from the 1970s than the serene atrium it aspired to be. The indoor-outdoor carpet was too orange, the decorative goldfish pond in the middle of the lobby was too blue, and there was far too much glass, brass, and faux wood trim in evidence.

"Miss Shanahan?"

"Yes?"

"I'm Felix Melendez Jr. You asked to speak to me?"

He wore a beige and brown broad-striped tie and a tan polyester jacket with too wide sleeves. His Adam's apple was pointy, his spiky black hair had dyed-white tips that reminded me of cake frosting, and if he was a day over sixteen, I would have been shocked. "You're the manager?"

"I'm the acting general manager."

"What are you when you're not acting?"

"I'm one of the assistant managers. How can I help you?" His dark eyes conveyed a calm intelligence that was in high contrast to his eager, loose-hinged posture.

"I'd like to talk to you about one of your guests . . . a former guest. He stayed here a couple of weeks ago. His name is—"

"John McTavish."

"How do you know that?"

"Because the police have already been here. He's the dead guy, right?"

He stood with his hands behind him, head tilted attentively, waiting for confirmation or correction. He wasn't being a smart-ass. He wasn't even betraying a callous streak. He was just being young. "That's right," I said. "He's the dead guy. And I'm trying to find out what happened to him."

"Are you police?"

"I'm a friend of his." He continued to blink at me as if that explanation wasn't enough. "You don't have to talk to me," I said, "but if you can help me, I hope you will."

"That's no problem. I'll give you whatever you need. I was just wondering, is it true he worked for an airline?"

"Yes. In Boston."

"Cool."

"Is it?"

"Let's go back to my office."

The back offices of The Harmony House Suites were like back offices everywhere—drab and textureless, scuffed and cluttered with the accumulated detritus of an ongoing business. But Felix's office was a striking contrast. He slipped behind his desk, a veritable oasis of working space interrupted by only a monitor, a keyboard, and a mouse on a pad that said Limp Bizkit. He made up for the absence of windows with lots of framed posters—travel posters, including my all-time favorite from Majestic, Sacré Cœur at night—and his question about John's occupation made more sense. He must have noticed me looking.

"I'm trying to get into the travel business. An airport hotel is as close as I've come so far, but I'm thinking of going to school to become a travel agent."

"Why don't you apply to the airlines?"

"I have. Every one. They either rejected me or put my application on file."

He didn't seem dejected. He seemed cheerful about the whole thing, which made me think he was the kind of person who would not waste time worrying about the obstacles thrown up in his path. He'd find another way.

"I used to work for Majestic, too," I said.

He smiled and shook his head. "That is too cool. What do you need, Miss Shanahan?"

"When did you talk to the police?"

"I didn't. The other assistant manager talked to a detective the week it happened. But she told me about it."

"Did the detective leave a name?"

"She left a business card." In what seemed like a conditioned response, Felix's hand moved to the mouse and his index finger went to work. When he found the screen he was looking for, he turned the monitor and showed it to me. "I scanned it in. I had to put it in our activity report for the home office. Do you need a copy?"

I looked at the information on the screen. Detective Patricia Spain.

"I already have one of—"

Too late. He'd pointed and clicked and somewhere a page began to print. In keeping with the austere look of Felix's office, the printer was hidden from sight.

"Did you ever see John?"

"I never saw him. I worked nights that week, and he checked in during the afternoon before I got here. But one of our room service waiters took dinner up to him. The detective showed him a picture of Mr. McTavish, and Emilio said that was him."

"Can I have Emilio's full name?" I started to go for a pen in my backpack.

"Sure. It's Emilio Serra. He'll be back in at"—Felix turned in his chair and with his eyes fixed on the monitor, clicked the mouse—"five this afternoon."

"And when is his shift over?"

"One o'clock in the morning. After the kitchen shuts down. You don't have to write any of this down. I can print it all out for you."

I found the pen anyway, and a piece of scratch paper, and put them on the desk in front of me on the off chance there was a bit of information floating about in the world he couldn't access with his mouse.

"When did John check out?"

"He checked in Monday night and checked out on Tuesday." He was reading again from the monitor.

"And he left nothing in the room?"

"No. The police checked, but there have been four different guests in there since he was. If he'd left anything, we would have known by now. Or else it would be gone."

"How about phone records, a copy of his credit card receipt, or anything he may have signed at check-in?"

"The police took all of the originals. But I can print copies for you. I can tell you right now he had one phone call from his room, which the detective said was to his house in Boston."

"What time was that?"

"One in the morning on Tuesday." It was the call he'd made to Terry, the one warning him to watch the family. Had to be. I reached for the pen.

"I can print all of this out for you."

"Somehow it sticks in my head better if I write it down myself." I recorded the time of the phone call, which had been, as far as I knew, the last communication from John to anyone.

"Incoming calls?"

"We don't track those."

"Does the hotel have a voice mail system?"

"Yeah. It's called the front desk. No one there remembered taking any calls for him. If you want . . ." He paused, tapping his finger on the side of the keyboard. Right there on his face, I could see Felix's internal struggle playing out. His lips pursed and unpursed and his thick, dark eyebrows danced up and down as his expression teetered between cautious and excited. Excited won out. "I can give you his whole schedule while he was on our property."

"How can you do that?"

"When you check in, you get a unique card key, and every time you use it, the activity gets recorded. All that information goes into the system as a stream of data. I can tell you everything he did that required a card key. And what time he did it, too."

"Like coming and going from his room?"

He gave his head a quick shake. "Only coming. He wouldn't use it to go out. Do you want it?"

"Absolutely."

I took my scratch paper, walked around, and stood behind Felix's chair to watch him work. He was already clicking on a desktop icon that looked suspiciously like Felix the Cat. A menu came up, one that seemed navigable and well designed. He typed John's name into one of the blanks, hit enter, and leaned back. "We'll have to wait. The hotel system sucks. It takes forever to compile the data. Oh, and you can't, like, tell anyone where you got it."

"Why not?"

"The data belongs to the hotel. I wrote my own program to access it."

"You hacked into your own company's system?"

"I had to. We have a lot of repeat business, and I like to know if a guest likes to use the health club, or always orders the same thing from room service. I tried to get our systems people to do it. My request has been sitting in some programmer's in-box for eighteen months. I'm like, 'Dude, it will take you an hour to write the code,' and he's like, 'Write it yourself. Just don't tell anyone.' So I did." He shrugged his narrow shoulders. "Why collect the data if you're not going to use it?"

The boy manager looked up at me as if I could explain why big corporations can be bureaucratic, territorial, insular, and at times downright prehistoric when it comes to embracing available technology. I couldn't.

"Felix . . . do you mind if I call you Felix?" "Mr. Melendez" didn't seem to fit and he didn't object. "You'd be perfect in the airline business."

That drew a big grin, a loopy, high school marching band grin. I liked this kid. I liked how he was smart without being cynical or ironic. And I liked that he had a mass of perforations in his right ear, though sans earrings for the moment. He was, after all, at work.

"Here it is. Mr. McTavish checked in at four o'clock in the afternoon on Monday." He glanced over as I wrote down that time. "He booked for one night, and . . . that's weird." His fingers flew over the keys. "He specifically stated when he checked in that he wanted to pay cash, but he ended up charging the stay to his card."

"MasterCard," I said.

"How did you know that?"

"His wife told me he hated credit cards. She had to remind him to carry one." I leaned in toward the screen to see what Felix was looking at. "Does that give you the name of the agent that checked him out at the front desk? I'd like to talk to that person."

"No one checked him out. He walked."

"What do you mean 'walked'? He didn't check out?"

He pointed to one of the fields on the screen. "His checkout time shows as noon on Tuesday. Noon is the default time the system uses for automatic checkout. That means he left without stopping at the desk. We must have used the credit card imprint he left when he checked in. That's what we do when people walk. See? It's not signed."

I wrote down "Tuesday, 3/6, noon—checkout."

"It wouldn't have been like John to walk out without paying," I said, "and he wouldn't have left the charge on his credit card."

"Then someone must have snatched him."

"What?"

"You know, abducted him. He wasn't killed in his room and you say he wouldn't have walked the bill, so either he left and never came back or someone came and took him. They gathered up all his stuff and let the system check him out. That way no one knew he was missing for a few days. In the meantime I've had two guests in there and the room has been cleaned up, wiped down, and vacuumed."

It made sense—I had no activity for John after the phone call to Terry—but I couldn't get my head around the idea that anyone could have taken him someplace he didn't want to go.

"Here—" Felix started the printer and turned the monitor so I could see it. "I made this for you."

It was a timeline, his version of the one I had been

trying to construct. "Felix, this is great. Is this what your
program comes up with?"

"Basically, but I added a few things."

"Felix, I love this."

"Piece of cake, Miss Shanahan."

I looked over the list of activities, trying to picture
John going through each one.

Day	Date	Time	Activity	Comments
Monday	March 5	3:47 P.M.	Check-in	
		3:55 P.M.	Arrived room	
		5:32 P.M.	Health club	
		6:45 P.M.	Gift shop	*Purchase*: 32 oz. Clear-Water—bottled water
		6:53 P.M.	Returned room	
		8:27 P.M.	Room service order	*Purchase*: Cuban sandwich (extra sauce); mashed potatoes; 2 Bud Lights
		10:11 P.M.	Room service order	*Purchase*: Pint Häagen-Dazs Vanilla
Tuesday	March 6	12:45 A.M.	Return room	
		12:49 A.M.	Phone call to Boston	
		Noon	Checkout	

"Did your room service waiter see John to give him
the ice cream?"

"Emilio saw him both times—to take him dinner and the ice cream."

"So John went out after ten o'clock, came back before one, walked in, picked up the phone immediately, and made the call. Where did he go?"

"He had a rental car, too. Did you know that?" Felix was on to another screen. "Red Ford Taurus, Florida license plate DK614V."

"I did. In fact . . ." I reached for my backpack again and fished out the receipt I'd taken from Mae's kitchen table. For its compact size, it had lots of information. "The car was dropped off at six o'clock Tuesday morning," I added the time to the list. "That narrows the window considerably. Now we're talking about a five hour time frame. If he was abducted, he probably didn't return his own car, which means . . ." I scanned the receipt. "Yep. The charge went to his MasterCard. I'll bet they hit his credit card the same way you did."

Felix had been paging through screens, and found one that warranted his close attention. "Hold on." His eyes scanned and his lips moved silently until he had his thoughts straight. "If someone took him from his room, it was probably closer to one a.m. than six."

I looked over his shoulder at the screen. Whatever he was seeing was not obvious to me. "How do you know that?"

"See this entry?" He pointed to a small "NS" in a field next to John's name. "That means no service. Housekeeping puts it in the record when they don't have to make up the room, in case someone complains. That was my idea. They didn't change the sheets at all, which means he never slept in his bed."

"Felix, your talents would be wasted as a travel agent." He beamed.

"Can you print this stuff out for me?"

"No sweat." He clicked his mouse, and the printer began to clatter again. This time, he turned, opened a door in the credenza behind him, and revealed the printer's nesting place.

"Is there anything else you can think of, Felix?" I

almost hated to leave. This kid was a treasure trove of information.

He sat back in his chair and blinked up at the ceiling. "I might be able to get you a list of cars that were in the lot that night that weren't supposed to be there."

"Surveillance cameras?"

"Way more low-tech. We use a security company to make sure no one uses our lot for long-term airport parking. What they do is drive around the lot once an hour and write down the license plate numbers for any car that doesn't have one of our parking permits, which you get when you check in, so then if the car is there for more than two hours we can tell and we get it towed, only it usually takes forever to get a tow truck out here—"

"Felix, I would love to have that information."

"Okay. I'll have to make a few phone calls."

"Can I see the room John stayed in?"

"Oh, yeah. Sure. Absolutely. Let me just check . . ." He pulled up another screen. "Yeah, there's no one in there right now. I'll take you up."

He gathered the printouts and handed them to me. I followed him out to the front desk, where he made a room key. We stepped into the elevator and swooshed up to the sixth floor of a seven-story building.

This hotel had a totally different feel than mine. It was in Miami, but it could have been in Omaha for all the accommodations to the locale. I suppose if you're on the road for two hundred days a year, it's comforting to always see the same orange carpet and wide wooden doors with brass kickplates and doorknobs.

After a sharp knock, he slipped the flat key into its slot, opened the door, and flicked on the lights. He started to give me the grand tour when his radio crackled. He was urgently needed at the front desk. Something about a room mix-up. He clearly didn't want to go.

"Can I call you if I come up with anything?"

I gave him my card. "Please do. Use my cell phone number. It's the only number on the card that's still good."

"Cool." And he was gone, sprinting for the elevators, off to solve another problem.

That left me alone in the guest room, the last place anyone had seen John besides the Dumpster. As promised by the name on the bath soap, the room was a suite. The front room was made up as a sitting area with a couch, a console television, and a wide window that opened out onto a large center atrium. Heavy curtains covered the window in the bedroom. The room was spacious with two queen-size beds and a dresser. The air conditioner was going full blast, which I assumed signaled the expected arrival of another guest later in the day.

I didn't know what to look for—mainly I tried to get a feel for the place—but what I saw made me sad. Durable carpet, cheap phones with plastic overlays on the keypads, assembly line paintings on the walls. The place was spotless, antiseptic, and sterile—so different from John's house back in Chelsea where well-used toys littered the floor, and the most important use of walls and shelves was to display the family photos. What were you doing here, John, so far away from home?

Chapter Nine

It was dark by the time I made my way back to the airport. I'd stopped for dinner on the way, not because I was particularly hungry, but because it further delayed the assignment I'd given myself for the evening, which was to call Terry McTavish in Boston and ask him if he was doing a dope deal that got his brother killed. I made another pass around level six of the Dolphin Garage, which, with its light green signs, was not to be confused with the Flamingo Garage and its orangey pink signs. The sodium lamps that lit the vast concrete space made it seem even darker outside than the hour would suggest. It was a heavy traffic day. I ended up in a far corner of one of the higher levels and felt good about snagging that space. I felt even better when a kidney red sedan showed up just behind me and began circling. Good luck, buddy. Try the next level.

I dragged myself toward the elevator, slithering between the Mercedes coupes and Dodge Rams and Ford Explorers that were packed together well within door-dinging range. The sound of the airport hummed in the background, but in the top levels of the parking garage, it was quiet enough to hear the pings and ticks of recently extinguished car engines. I also heard the kidney car cruising around. If he was waiting for someone to pull out and vacate a space for him, he was in the wrong place. There was zero foot traffic on this level besides me.

As he turned onto my row and approached from behind, I stepped to the left to let him pass. As he puttered slowly by, I caught a glimpse of his face in the rearview mirror. He was staring straight back at me. When our eyes met, his cut away and he immediately sped up. My heartbeat turned to an anxious flutter as he passed right by the turnoff that would have taken him up or down to another level. The flutter advanced to pounding as I watched him and realized he was not searching for a space. He was moving too fast.

I looked around to make sure there really was no one else within earshot. This was a public garage, for God's sake, at one of the busiest airports on earth. Where was the traveling public when I needed them?

He made the turn to my row and came around again. This time he didn't pass. He hung back, matching my pace, which felt far too slow. I slipped between a Jeep and a pickup truck, putting a row of parked cars between us.

Get the license number, I thought. Get a description, dammit. Do something besides acting like a scared rabbit. But when I tried to see inside the car, to put a face on the faceless pursuer, the overhead lights were too bright. All I could see was a black glare. And all I could hear was the quiet thrum of his engine. More like a vibration than a sound, it crawled up my back, up my neck, and laid its hand on the back of my skull. I was shaking.

What if he had a gun? What if he wasn't alone? I hadn't seen anyone else in the car, but that didn't mean they weren't there. That's what did it. The thought of being pulled into a strange man's car and driven somewhere. Somewhere dark and isolated. I turned and ran. His motor roared. His tires squealed on the slick cement. The acrid odor of burned rubber filled the air. He was in reverse, backing out of the row as fast as he could.

I made it to the elevator bank in seconds and without looking back shoved through a heavy metal door to the stairs. The echo of my footsteps bounced around the tall, narrow well of unfinished concrete and iron. My knees, stiffened by adrenaline, made each of the stairs feel awkward and narrow.

Halfway down. Stop. Listen for following footsteps. Hold my breath so I can hear. None. Take off again. Move fast.

At the crossover level, I stood behind the half-closed door, peeking through the crack. Other cars were circling, but no sign of the kidney car. And there were lots of people making their way on foot to the terminal. I took a deep breath, stepped out, and jogged the full length of the garage. I didn't stop until I arrived at the other end. I turned to scan behind me. If the red car was there, I couldn't see it.

Inside the terminal the moving sidewalk didn't move fast enough, so I motored along beside. I didn't slow down until I was standing in the blessedly crowded lobby of my hotel, with the elevator on the way. I bent over to catch my breath and ease the pain in my side. Perspiration ran down my nose and dropped onto the marble floor. When I felt a hand brush my shoulder, I bolted upright and almost took off again. If I had, I would have bowled over the man standing in front of me.

He took a look at my face. "Miss Shanahan, are you all right?"

"I'm fine."

It was the front desk agent who had checked me in. "I do apologize, but I called to you from the desk and I don't think you heard."

"No, I didn't. I'm sorry." The doors to the elevator I'd been waiting for were closing by the time I noticed. I reached for the call button, hoping to catch it. Too late. My heartbeat was coming into normal range, oxygen was flowing through my bloodstream, and the dizziness was fading when I looked at him again.

"I just wanted to make sure you got your message." He handed me a slip of paper. "The caller said it was important."

The message was from Mae, and it was information I'd been waiting for.

"Thank you," I said.

The elevator had come again. I stepped in and studied the list of phone numbers she'd left, calls John had made from his cell phone while he was in Florida. Two went to his house, one to what she described as a bar in Salem, Massachusetts. The last one was the most interesting. With a 305 area code, it was a local Miami number. When I got back to my room, I picked up the phone and dialed it. The call was answered in less than one ring by a woman with a crisp, authoritative voice.

"Good evening," she said. "Federal Bureau of Investigation."

Chapter Ten

There's a good reason not to go running in South Florida after the sun has been up for a while. The air outside turns sticky and thick and all the oxygen leaches out. If there's a fire raging nearby it also turns smudged and dirty, conjuring images of ash and soot darkening the tender, pink linings of your lungs. Your face throbs, your body loses copious amounts of fluids, and no matter what you wear on your head, you can still feel the sun baking your scalp.

But I had new shoes. New running shoes made everything right with the world. They made me faster and lighter because they came out of the box with Mercury's own wings. So despite Bobby Avidor and his dismal accusation, despite being chased around by an unknown pursuer, it had been a fast, hard run, and as I stood cooling down in the lobby of the hotel, I dared to feel good. It was the shoes.

"You just missed Mr. Ryczbicki," I was told when I stopped at the desk for messages. "He was here looking for you not two minutes ago."

"Did he leave a message?"

"He said to tell you your bag was here."

I didn't like the scene as I came down the escalator and approached the Majestic Airlines baggage claim office. The ramp-side door was open, held that way by five or six baggage service agents clustered in the doorway. They stared out into the bag room, hands over their mouths as if they were telling secrets.

Baggage service agents are the most cynical of a cynical breed. By definition of their jobs, the only customers they ever see are the ones ready to unload with both barrels because their bags are missing, damaged, or pilfered. Eventually, even the best ones come to see the world through the warped prism of customer discontent. The unabashed curiosity of such a group on its own would have been cause for concern. But it was the smell from the bag room that really had me worried. As I got closer, I realized the agents weren't covering their mouths to whisper; they were blocking out the overpowering stench that hung like a putrid mist in the dense tropical heat.

My stomach started to churn.

I approached a petite agent with smooth olive skin and long black hair pulled into a thick ponytail. "I'm looking for Phil Ryczbicki. I'm supposed to meet him down here."

She asked for my name, and when I gave it, heads snapped around. The other agents stared at me with ominous recognition. Bic's voice boomed from inside the bag room. "All you people get back to work. Joe, go down to the freight house and get a forklift for this thing."

Forklift? My anxiety deepened. It was never a good sign when a forklift was summoned to the bag room.

The agents shuffled around so I could get through. They gave me a wide berth, careful not to get accidentally soiled by my sweaty running clothes. The gap closed behind me . . . and no one went back to work.

The odor inside the bag room was so rank the first whiff withered all my sinus membranes and forced tears from my eyes. Bic was there, standing over what was without question the source of the odor—my bag. "Close that door," he barked at the employees in the doorway. His voice ricocheted off the concrete walls like a bullet fired from a high-powered rifle. "Get back to work. *Now!*"

My bag was unzipped, splayed on the floor like a pig

with its belly sliced open, and I wondered who had ventured close enough to unzip it. Everything that was pushing out was mine—except for all those dead fish. There was a big pile of them folded in among the underwear and T-shirts, the toothpaste and the blow-dryer, complete with heads, tails, scales, and rheumy dead eyes.

Bic had me fixed in a coldly furious blue-eyed stare. He didn't seem affected by the stench. Must have been the anger clogging up his sense of smell. "I told you I didn't want any of this crap starting here." He snapped the words off, leaving the sharp, ragged points. "This kind of garbage might be acceptable at Logan," he said, "but not here. Not in my station."

I was angry, too, and not just because all my stuff was marinating in fish guts. I was mad at myself for checking the bag in the first place and leaving myself open for a sucker punch. And that's what it felt like. A hard punch in the gut that had ripped a few internal organs loose.

"The boys in Boston may have misrouted my bag," I said, "but they're not the ones who added the fish of the day. That had to be your guys. This is an organized racket."

"I don't care."

"You don't care?"

"If you're not here, this—" He pointed to the bag. "This fucking *bull*shit doesn't happen. My operation is not in an uproar, and I'm not standing here getting stink all over my suit. That's on you and I am not taking the hit for it."

"Thank you for your concern."

"I don't deserve this shit you're bringing down on me."

"No one deserves this kind of shit." I wanted to kick the bag for emphasis but was afraid to get fish juice all over my new running shoes. "Including me, Bic. And if you had any balls you would find whoever did this and put the blame where it belongs."

"Where would I even begin to look? They hate you, Alex. They all hate you. That's what happens when you off one of the brothers."

That was it. I moved so close, I smelled his aftershave instead of the fish. "This is the last time I'm going to say this to you. The man got himself killed. All I did was get out of the way before he killed me, too. You were not there, Bic. You can't possibly know what happened, and I'm tired of your flip comments. I never want to hear another word about Boston from you. Do you understand?"

He didn't seem to know how to react. At heart, Bic was just another insecure, resentful, self-loathing short guy with an overcompensating ego who took out his miserable life on anyone who was smaller, weaker, and willing to put up with his crap. It was no coincidence three wives had dumped him.

We stared at each other for a long time. He didn't move and he didn't say anything, but in his eyes he backed down.

And not one second too soon. I held it together long enough to get out of his face and his bag room, far enough out on the broiling open ramp that if I broke down in tears, which is what I felt like doing, he wouldn't see me and no one would hear me.

He was right. A man was dead because of me, and lots of people hated me for it. I was right. I had been perfectly justified in what I'd done and the people who hated me for it were morons. And I could still see his bloody, mutilated body lying in a heap in the falling snow every time I closed my eyes. I felt responsible. I felt justified. I felt angry.

I felt responsible.

The pressure of the hot air felt good. It felt right, and as I stood in a sweat feeling sorry for myself, I took a moment to hate everyone back. I hated the weasel who had misdirected my bag. I hated whoever had put the fish in it. I hated Bobby Avidor for the things he had said about John and Terry. I hated him for lying, and if he wasn't lying, I hated him even more for telling me a truth I didn't want to hear. I hated Bic for not taking my side, for blaming me, the victim. I *hated* being the victim. And at the bottom of it all, I hated myself for being so confused and befuddled about what I had done in Boston, for constantly teetering on the fence between guilt and anger, anger and guilt. Pick a side and jump down, for God's sake. Handle it. But I couldn't. I couldn't jump down and stay down on one side or the other, and jumping back and forth was wearing me down.

And the sun was wearing me down. If I stood there long enough, I'd simply melt like a candle into a puddle of wax on the concrete. The forklift would roll over me on the way to dispose of my bag, leaving me imprinted with its tire treads.

"You're right." I wasn't sure if the voice had come from inside my head or from the real world. It was Bic. He had followed me out and was standing next to me, looking out of place on the ramp with his loafers and tie. "I'm going to launch an investigation to find out who did this."

"Good luck." I tried to sound more sardonic than hopeless and bitter. We had never caught a single soul in Boston for similar fun and games.

"Even if we don't catch him, it'll send a message."

He stared across the field. I looked where he was looking, which was probably at the forklift motoring our way. I looked down at the top of his head. "You know, Bic, you and I have had our differences over the years, but I never would have figured you for being the drinking buddy of someone like Bobby Avidor."

He whipped around and faced me. "Who told you that I was his buddy? Did he tell you that? Bob Avidor is a piece of crap. I would like nothing better than to kick his ass out of here. But he does his job, and if he's doing something wrong, I don't know what it is, and I can't catch him at it."

"And you don't want me to catch him, either?"

He turned and disappeared into the bag room behind the forklift, which had finally rumbled up. I took one last deep breath and followed him in. In the closed space, the diesel fumes mitigated the foul stench, but I still needed my hand as a filter. And I had to lean toward Bic to make sure he could hear me over the grinding of the engine. "Why didn't you tell me you were Bobby's alibi?"

"I told the police."

"Why would you keep that from me?"

"Why should I tell you anything?"

"Because," I said, "if he's running drugs out of here, I would think you'd want to know."

"He's not."

"Why are you so sure?"

"You're not the only one with sources on the ramp. And I am not his drinking buddy. I'd never been out with him before or since."

"But you do think he's up to something. I can tell."

His lips had tightened. He didn't look as soft as he usually did, and . . . Wait a second. "You've never been out with him before or since?"

"That's what I said, isn't it?"

For the first time I started thinking perhaps I wasn't the sole reason for his perpetually bad mood. Imagine that. It wasn't all about me. "It was Bobby who asked you to go out drinking with him that night, wasn't it?"

Bic's eyes narrowed to a squint even though we were in the deep, cool shade of the bag room, and I knew I was on the right track. He signaled to the driver to drop the fork assembly to the floor and scoop the bag from underneath. The bag was too light and the flat arms too far apart to gain purchase. The driver began a back and forth stuttering dance as he tried to hook some part of the bag on one of the tongs.

"Bobby set you up, didn't he? He needed an alibi for that night and what better alibi than his boss? He used you." Bic tried to peel away, but I followed him. The bag room wasn't that big. "And you don't want anyone to know. How's it going to look? The station manager out drinking with the potential suspect."

"He's not a suspect. If he was with me all night, then he's not your guy."

"No, but if he knew he needed an alibi, it was because he knew something was going to happen to John that night. He set John up and he made you his alibi."

He took a few steps away, as if he needed to watch the bag lift operation from a different angle. I tried to think about the situation the way Bic would—maximum credit for the least amount of personal risk.

"You've got a short list of bad options, Bic."

"How do you figure?"

"If I come out of here with something on Avidor, it looks as if you're not doing your job. And if I don't, I've managed to stir up enough shit for people to wonder. There's no way to defend yourself against rumors. Isn't that what you said? You should be working with me. That's the only way you're coming out of this whole." Another alternative occurred to me. "Unless you're involved in what's going on."

"I'm not involved."

"And I'm not going away. You help me, and I promise you I'll do everything I can to make you look like a star."

The driver had managed to work the tip of one of the tongs inside the bag and raise it. A large, greasy smudge was all that was left on the ground where it had been. A few of my shirts dropped out of the bag as it dangled, along with a couple of fish heads that thudded to the concrete and glared up at me through dead eyes.

The driver leaned out and yelled at Bic. "What do you want me to do with it, chief?"

"Burn it. And get Facilities up here to hose down the floor."

The sound of the airport, as always, hovered in the background, but when the forklift motored out, a relative peace descended over the bag room, and the air seemed to clear immediately. I could breathe again.

Bic turned and looked at me without a trace of emotion. "Why should I trust you?"

"There's nothing in it for me to cut you out, Bic."

I could almost hear the gears grinding in his head. "You keep me informed of everything you're doing."

"I will."

"But nothing that will get me into shit. I'll leave it to you to know the difference."

"Plausible deniability. I understand the concept."

He didn't offer to shake on the deal. He didn't even change expression. "What do you want?"

I told him I wanted to know everything he knew about Bobby, and everything he'd done to try to catch him. I wanted to know all about the night John died, and I wanted access to the ramp so Bobby couldn't hide from me on the field. I had more questions, particularly about anyone he knew who drove a kidney red sedan, but he was late for a meeting. We made plans to meet in a few hours, but I caught him with one more question before he turned to go.

"If you hate him so much, why did you go drinking with him?"

"It was the end of another shitty day with divorce attorneys, I wanted a drink, and he told me he might have information on some gambling that has been going on downstairs on the ramp."

"Did he?"

"Nope." He walked into the terminal and let the door slam behind him.

The last time I saw my bag, the forklift driver was scraping it off into the cart that would take it to the furnace to be incinerated.

Chapter Eleven

I couldn't get the smell off.

I'd showered. I'd showered again. I'd scrubbed my skin raw and rinsed all the essential oils out of my hair. I'd gone to the hotel laundry and washed my running clothes, but they seemed, like me, to be permanently tainted. Almost twelve hours after I'd inhaled the first whiff of dead-fish bouillabaisse, the stink was still with me, sitting like an unwanted guest in the passenger seat of my car.

Bic had come through with some interesting details about Bobby, but the only one that seemed actionable was the rumor that he liked to disappear from the field in the middle of his shift. Guys had disappeared from the midnight shift all the time in Boston, but Bic claimed it was unusual in his city, and I didn't have much else to go on. So there I sat in the middle of the night in my Lumina outside the maintenance hangar, with my adrenaline-hard stomach and my twitchy muscles, swinging between hoping for Bobby to come out to relieve the unrelenting boredom, and praying he wouldn't because I wasn't sure I could tail him without being spotted. I'd never followed anyone before.

He came out at a quarter to two. He wasn't hard to spot, driving out of the employee lot in the muscle car Bic had described, the black Trans Am with the big bird painted on the hood. I scrunched down in my seat, even though I was across the road parked in a lot with twenty other cars—a good place to hide, but not a good place to be when he took off like a rocket. By the time I'd turned onto the road, his taillights had turned into red pinpricks.

I caught him at a traffic light. Even then it wasn't easy keeping up. He turned onto LeJeune, a wide, chaotic, congested artery that was as bright as the Las Vegas strip, but sold burgers and gas instead of sex and gambling. Bobby was one of those people whose driving personality matched his car. He liked following closely, darting between lanes, and flashing his brights at anyone who displeased him. But I didn't have to worry that he would see me. He didn't seem to have much use for a rear view.

After a few hair-raising blocks on Chaos Street, he cut a woman off, sailed in front of her, and turned sharply. I checked my blind spot and found someone in it. Bobby had caught a green light and was moving away. I had to do a squeeze-in maneuver to stay with him, something I'd learned in Boston, which instantly set horns yowling. I risked the tail end of the yellow light, then had to floor it to keep him in range. Just as I did, a jet flew overhead on approach to the airport, gear down, roaring loudly enough to shake the plaque from my teeth. A few more screamers flew over before even that ear-splitting ruckus began to fade. The road signs began to stretch farther apart and the streetlights became more infrequent. We were on a highway that felt like the only lighted passage through an ocean of darkness.

We went a long way on that road. The bright half-moon and the stars became more prominent as we distanced ourselves from the city lights, and it occurred to me to pay closer attention when road signs did appear so I could find my way back. I didn't want to be lost out there. Ft. Lauderdale. Orlando. Florida City. I couldn't feel the direction we were going. Key West. Tamiami Park.

After another fifteen minutes, we were in a deep, swampy darkness going deeper. The shoulders next to the roads had disappeared. Lit only by the beams of my headlights, the snarled vegetation that had replaced them looked as if it would reclaim the right of way completely if not beaten back with a machete on a regular schedule. The hairs on my arms stiffened, and I felt more and more relieved to be in the company of other cars when they appeared.

Then we were the last two out there, and I wasn't sure what to do. The only thing I could think of was to keep adjusting my intervals, letting him slide ahead until I could barely pick out his taillights. I would wait until I thought I was about to lose him, then reel him back, usually on the rare occasion when another car showed up and I could tuck in behind it.

Thirty-five minutes out. The thought of turning around came up more and more, but I kept pushing it away, kept thinking we had to be closing in on wherever he was going. But my body was having none of it. The back of my damp T-shirt stuck to the car seat because the instinctive part of me, the part that knew when to flee from danger, understood that I was taking a real risk, that Bobby could be fully aware of my presence and leading me to a place where no one would ever find me. The farther I went, the deeper we drove into the swamp and the less opportunity I had to change my mind.

Then he disappeared. One second he was there, then he was gone. I blinked in the darkness, hoping to see the taillights farther down the road. He wasn't on the road. I took my foot off the gas and coasted. Had he gone left? Had I seen it or imagined it? I took in a deep breath. I rolled the car forward slowly and scanned the brush and the trees for the place where he must have vanished.

It was there. A narrow gap to my left. Another road, this one the least roadlike of all. From the only light available, my headlights, it looked like a dirt path cut out of dense brush. It was the only place he could have gone. But no taillights. No sound of gravel under tires. Something was there, though, maybe a mile away. Lights in the trees.

I parked the car and got out. I climbed onto the hood, and when that wasn't high enough, onto the roof of the Lumina. From the higher perch, I could see a dim arc

over the trees, a muddy center of light in an endless pool
of darkness. Bobby was there. I didn't know what else
was, but I knew that's where Bobby had gone. I felt it.
Nothing else was stirring, at least not human, for as far
as I could see.

I climbed down and stood staring at that dark road. I
wanted to go down there, but my knees were shaking so
much, just staying upright was draining all my energy.
The rational me, the parental me was mortified by the
idea, stunned by its recklessness, fighting for control and
losing because I wanted to go down that road. Yes, I
could come back in daylight when the whole situation
would be, or at least would *feel,* less menacing. I didn't
want to wait. I wanted . . . I didn't want to be scared.
And if I went down that road, it would prove that I
wasn't scared.

I got back in the car, started the engine, turned off
the air conditioner, and opened the windows so I could
listen as I went. The windshield instantly steamed up. I
cleared it with the palm of my hand, put the car in gear,
and nosed it into the narrow opening. Room enough for
one car only. I thought of going in with the lights off.
Impossible. It had looked like a dirt road but now
seemed to be composed of nothing but gravel. I felt each
ping as if it were bouncing off my rib cage instead of the
undercarriage of the car. Then there were the ruts and
bone-jarring potholes that snuck up in the dark. And the
music. It sounded like . . . It was mostly the thrum of a
bass, but as I kept going I started to hear the grinding
of the electric guitars over the beat.

A violent bounce into a crater nearly ripped the steering wheel from my hands and left the car pointed at an
odd slant. As I straightened the wheel my headlights fell
across a silver mailbox marked JZ SALVAGE. Beneath was
a big reflective arrow that pointed to a break in the tree
line to my right. Beyond the break, I could see the
lighted area I'd spotted from the road.

I killed the headlights and nudged the car forward,
close enough to see that the arrow pointed to a long
driveway blocked by a wide swinging gate—closed—the

kind you'd expect to see on a large corral to keep the horses in. Attached to it was a handmade sign with bold, slashing letters that spelled PRIVATE PROPERTY. UNLESS YOU HAVE BUSINESS HERE KEEP OUT. Beyond the welcome sign, the drive ran across a swath of open field and down to what looked like a residence. It was a stucco cube with a crown of awnings and a perfectly flat roof. That's how they built them down here. No need for pitched roofs so the snow would slide off. It was also the source of the music, which was clearly audible now. Behind was a large warehouse, marked with a bigger JZ SALVAGE sign. Reclaiming the entire complex from the darkness was a couple of tall stadium lights with about half the bulbs lit. I couldn't see clearly what was behind the warehouse. It looked like a field of heavy equipment or even a used car lot. But I could see what was parked out front—a speedboat on a trailer, a couple of SUVs, a motorcycle, what looked like an airboat, a pickup truck, and toward the back Bobby's black Trans Am, which pleased me to no end because it meant he wasn't lurking behind me.

I sat in the car with the lights off and the windows open, fighting off the urge to be sensible and bail out. There was no way I was going down the front path and through the front door, but if I could get across the entrance without being spotted, I could drive for a ways shielded by the brushy perimeter that seemed to surround the property. I tried to stop breathing so shallowly, wiped the sweat off the steering wheel with my shirttail, and pressed slowly on the gas pedal. I drifted out into the open as quietly as I could. It seemed to take forever to glide past that fifteen-foot opening. When I was safely across, I paused behind a cluster of trees and listened. Nothing but me, the night crawlers, and the sound of heavy metal thumping through the fern and fauna. I rolled on.

My fuzzy intention had been to follow the road around to the back, but the road looped and lapsed and didn't follow the property line. When I realized the light was behind me, I pulled to the side and killed the engine.

I had to get out. I knew I had to get out of the car and go on foot. I spent a minute gripping the steering wheel and releasing. Gripping and releasing. Gripping. Gripping. My muscles didn't want to release. I counted to ten. I opened the door. I got out.

The air smelled loamy and damp. It was thick and alive with sounds I hadn't noticed before. Clicking and twittering and rustling down in the bushes and overhead in the branches. I still heard the music, but from the new angle also heard loud banging—the sound of metal on metal, heavy objects coming together with force. Power tools, too, like drills.

It took four steps to cross the road, but I had to hike a long way through a dark, close thicket. I made my way by moonlight that came and went, wished I had thought to bring a flashlight, and kept an eye on the stadium lights ahead. I hiked as fast as I could, trying not to trip over the roots and vines and brittle, cracked branches that grabbed at my feet and slapped at my bare arms. My jeans protected my legs, but my shirt had no sleeves. I knew I had reached the property line when I found a chain link fence that cut straight through the thick collar of trees. I tried to see beyond it, but the growth was too heavy and extended too far.

Time to redefine my goals. More information would be instructive—like who was in that warehouse with Bobby and what they were doing. The banging or sawing or drilling or sanding was still going on. The sound of men's voices was now part of the soundtrack, drifting toward me on the night air whenever there was a pause.

What I really needed was to find a perch and it needed to be high enough to see over the fence and the trees. I began to move laterally. Every now and then the moon would appear as I came to a place where the brush thinned enough that I could see something of what was on the property. It looked like machines, and lots of them. Some kind of mechanical equipment. It was too far away to see what kind, and they were down in a depression. They didn't look like cars, but they were lined up that way, dim shapes in rows among the weeds, and I wondered what it was exactly that JZ Salvage salvaged.

As I moved, the mosquitoes and gnats that orbited my head came with me. I was breathing hard, but tried to remember to do so with my mouth closed. Eventually, I found my spot. It was a tree, a good one for climbing, with a thick and gnarly trunk, and tall enough that I could see what I needed to see. It had one serious drawback. It was inside the fence line about a hundred feet onto the property. I did another quick rationalization and decided it was far enough outside the range of the stadium lights that I would still be in the dark.

Scrambling under the chain link was an option—the fencing job was not that enthusiastic—but I didn't want to crawl through whatever felt slick and vegetal on the ground. I went over the top, came down on the other side, and waited at the bottom to see that all was still quiet. This time when I began to move, it was into the field and away from the fence and the only thing to hide in was the darkness. My skin tingled under my damp clothes.

I stayed low, moved fast, and when I got to the tree, dried my palms on my pants, and started climbing. The coarse and peeling bark scored my palms and made them burn, especially with the profuse sweating I was doing. My foot slipped once and I dangled until I could latch back on. Running shoes are not ideal for tree climbing. I was already winded from the dash through the jungle, so I hoped the first branch that I came to that could hold my weight would be high enough for me to see what I wanted to see. I climbed up, threw my leg over, turned around, braced myself with my back against the trunk. I sat for a moment, looking out across the field, listening to myself breathe, and trying to comprehend the sight in front of me.

It looked like a giant garden of airplanes, a rich bounty of Cessnas, Bonanzas, Piper Cubs, Learjets, and Beeches. Most were small aircraft and most bone white, or at least looked that way under the glow of the moon. Every now and then a painted fuselage stood out. But the dusty light turned what probably had been bright reds and yellows and greens into dim shades of brown and beige and gray. On some that were closest to me, I could make out the corporate logos still on the tails.

JZ Salvage salvaged airplanes, which meant they had been pulled from trees, dredged from the bottoms of lakes, and scraped from gouges in the earth. Their wings had been detached, either from the force of the collision or after, and were stacked, mismatched and upright, in large racks at the ends of each long row. With missing or mangled landing gear, most rested on their bellies in the weeds. The rows and rows of upright tails looked like tombstones, which was fitting since all these airplanes were dead.

The men's voices continued to drift up from the warehouse and out over the field. It was easy to imagine them as the voices of ghosts that might linger in these hollowed-out echo chambers. It was easy to imagine the harsh, strident strains of the electric guitars as the cries of the people who had spent their last moments on earth hurtling toward it.

The first sign of movement from the warehouse caught me by surprise. I pulled my legs up under me and crouched on the branch, holding steady with my hands on the trunk behind me. The back doors were open, allowing brighter light to spill out from the interior work space. A man walked into the light. He was too far away for me to make out anything but a lanky build. I crouched lower in the tree as if that would help me see better. What I wouldn't have given for a pair of binoculars.

And then I saw something that made my stomach try to squeeze up through my throat. There was a dog. A big, guard-dog kind of dog with a dark, shorthaired coat, a thick square head, and a wide chest. He may not have been one, but he was certainly built like a rottweiler. The sign on the front gate had said nothing about a dog. BEWARE OF DOG would have given me pause. BEWARE OF ATTACK DOG would have turned me around for sure. And now I was thinking that this was not fair. And I was thinking it was too late.

The dog had shot out of the hangar behind the lanky one, and now pranced and spun as the man walked with him through the airplane graveyard . . . toward *me*. He hadn't . . . surely he hadn't seen me. I was much too far away. And besides, they weren't moving very fast. If that dog had sensed me, he would have shown it. So what were they doing?

They kept walking until they were a ways beyond the graveyard, but still on the other side of the field separating the airplanes from my tree and me. The dog danced and crooned until the man reared back and heaved something. It went high into the air, and into the field. The dog took off, kicking up grass and dirt and dust as he launched himself toward the object that fell just at the edge of the light. It was a tennis ball. I could tell by how far it went and the height of its bounce. The dog ran it down like a fuzz-seeking missile, snatched it out of the air, squeezed it in his pincer jaws of death—and did not run right back. He stopped. He dropped the ball. When he raised his great head to sniff the air, I pressed against the trunk of the tree so hard, the bark was going to leave an imprint on my back. I prayed the strong odor of rotten fish was in my head and not out in the air around me. The ball tosser yelled. After one last skeptical snuffle, the dog picked up his ball and hauled ass back to the hangar. I blew out a long breath and peeled my back off the tree trunk.

Jump down? Hang in? Wait for the game to be over? I bit off the sliver of thumbnail I'd been chewing. Go. *Now.*

I twisted down out of the tree, dropping at least six feet to the ground, and started to move, slowly at first. The ball was in the air again. With one eye on the charging animal, I moved faster, hoping my new running shoes still had Mercury's wings.

When I got to the fence, I stopped, leaned down to look through a couple of low branches at the progress of the game, and panicked. I couldn't see the dog. The man must have thrown the ball farther this time. I scanned the field, trying to will my eyes to see in the dark. Couldn't. *Jesus,* he could have been steaming for me right then. The man yelled. "Bull" was what he was calling out. I went down lower until my ear was almost flush against the moist ground, and strained to hear any sound at all that wasn't guitar strains or insects. Nothing.

I waited, so tense that if he had leapt upon me at that moment, I might have shattered into pieces. When Bull finally reappeared, ball in his mouth, I felt so much tension release I was afraid I wouldn't have enough energy left to stand up.

No problem. With Bull dashing in the opposite direction, I crawled up the fence, swung over, jumped down, and landed in a hole. My foot collapsed, my left ankle took all of my weight, and should have snapped in two. I had one numb moment to anticipate how much it was going to hurt. A charge of pain ripped up my leg, jumped to my spine, and would have come out of my mouth if I hadn't clamped my jaw. Instead it emerged through my eyes, which immediately sprouted tears. A wave of nausea rolled through.

I sank to the ground, sat in a heap among the dead palm fronds, and waited for my heart rate to stabilize. When it did—at about two hundred beats a minute—I got up and started moving again. The ankle was swollen and angry, but mechanically it worked. Every time I stepped on the foot, I got the sharp needles. Bad enough, but what if it gave out? Get back to the road and into the car. I hobbled along the fence, looking for the place to turn, the opening, the way I had come in, but . . . I didn't know where I'd come in. I couldn't figure out where I had come over the fence. Stupid, stupid, *stupid* to have wandered so far away. Insane not to have identified a landmark.

The cold blanket of panic started to descend. Which way? Couldn't decide. Searching for a familiar branch or leaf. A footprint. And then the air exploded. A metallic roar ripped through the humid night and sent me to the ground. I looked up in time to see Bull as he launched himself against the fence, a barrier that hadn't seemed substantial to begin with. It swayed out on impact and strained against the posts that were supposed to keep it upright.

He stopped and I saw him spot me. The sound that came out of his throat was like nothing I'd ever heard, vicious and guttural and wild.

I jerked to my feet, pushed off with the bad foot, fell down, scrambled up, and thrashed along the fence line. He was right there, step for step, on the other side. I could smell his frenzy.

The man was on the move now, his yelling getting closer. I veered into what looked like a solid wall of prickly, thorny trees and brush, and crashed a new trail. *Boom*. The fence rattled and shook behind me. And then it was quiet. The sound of my own gasping filled my ears. Get to the road, was all I could think. Get to the road and into the car. Wrap that steel and glass around me.

And then he was coming again. I heard him. He'd crawled under or crashed through or chewed through the steel mesh, but he was on my side now and coming fast, choking on his own drool, announcing himself with a low, rumbling, murderous fury. I pushed ahead, tripped into plants and brush, scraped off of trees, ripped through leaves and hanging vines.

And then a surge of energy. I'd found the road. But which way? Which direction was the car? *Dam*mit. I started right and heard Bull charging toward me. I turned and ran the other way. I could feel him on my ass. I could feel him closing the gap. And then I saw the car and I felt a stab of hope and I pushed toward it, arms pumping, heart thumping, feet barely touching the gravel. Almost there when . . . when . . .

A bright, cold light shot through my eyes and into my brain. I froze, caught in the high beams of my own car. Someone was in my car. I raised a hand to shield my eyes. Bobby? There was yelling. The dog was closing. I could hear his nails on the gravel road. There was more yelling from behind me, and now ahead of me.

"Keep moving. Hurry up." A voice from the car. "Get *in. Get in!*"

Jesus *Christ.* A split second to decide. Dog will shred me without a doubt. I sprinted toward the car.

"Other side, dammit. Other *side.*"

Too late. I was headed toward the driver's side. The dog was coming fast. The backseat window was coming down. Just as I pitched through, I heard a door open and a heavy thud, almost at once, and yelping. The driver's door had swung open and the dog . . . the dog must have . . . the driver had opened the door and the dog had run into it, and somewhere in the back of my brain I wondered how I was going to pay for the damage. I hadn't taken the optional insurance.

The car rocketed forward and slammed me against the backseat. Dust billowed. Stones flew. There was bumping and fishtailing. The dog's hysterical frustration.

I lay facedown with my eyes closed and my nose buried in the upholstery. My ankle screamed, every painful throb a rebuke for having abused it so completely.

"Are you all right?"

It was a man's voice. I turned over on my back. I wanted to sit up, but I couldn't will myself to do it. I had to lie flat and breathe. From there I could see only his hands on the wheel, hands in black gloves. He wore a dark ball cap. He seemed tall in the seat.

"Hey!" He turned and I could see his profile. Roman nose. Strong chin. I couldn't see his eyes. Understandably, he kept them on the road. "What's going on back there?"

"I'm all right."

"Get up and see if there's anyone behind us." There was urgency, but no panic.

The blood drained from my head when I sat up, but I steadied myself long enough to squint through the back window, trying to see through the cloud of dust. "It's too dark to see very far, but no one is there right now."

He let out a long sigh that seemed to tighten the tension, not relieve it. "That doesn't mean they won't be coming."

Chapter Twelve

He looked like a commando. The black gloves had only been the beginning. His jeans were black, as were his socks and running shoes. Despite the heat, he wore a long-sleeved black pullover. Any skin that showed, including his face, was smeared with black camouflage paint. When he glanced over, what stood out most in a dark car on a dark road were the strands of silver laced through brown hair. His hair was long enough to poke out from under the black ball cap he wore pulled down low over his eyes.

And there was the gun. A pistol. It looked like an automatic, and it had been resting on the seat next to him until I'd crawled over to join him in the front, at which point he picked it up and tucked it back into a hip holster.

"Put your seat belt on," was the first thing he said.

I did, and then I looked at him again, but all I saw was that big gun. "Who are you?"

"I'm the one asking the questions," he said. His voice sounded like a well traveled back road—dusty, littered with rocks and stones, and pitted with potholes. "Who the hell are you?"

I hadn't totally calmed down and I wasn't thinking completely straight, but I was clear enough on a few facts. I had a sprained ankle, scratched and bloodied arms, sore ribs and pelvic bone where I'd slammed around going through the window, and a complete stranger behind the wheel of my car, which he had apparently hot-wired because the keys were still tucked in the pocket of my jeans. He was armed and I wasn't. He was bigger than I was, and if I'd had to guess, I would have said it wasn't the first time he'd been in a scrape like that.

The dynamics of the situation didn't favor me.

"I'm . . . my name is Alex Shanahan."

"That doesn't tell me what I need to know, Alex Shanahan. What were you doing back there?"

"I was following someone."

"Who?"

"Someone who went into that warehouse." I was stalling, trying to figure out what to reveal.

He was having none of it. "What is the guy's name?"

"Bobby Avidor."

He checked the rearview mirror, which he had done every thirty seconds since we'd turned back onto a real road. "What kind of car?"

"A black Trans Am."

"Yeah, I saw him." He nodded. "Why did you follow him?"

He looked at me sternly, and I suddenly felt that no answer I gave would be good enough. I wasn't sure there was a reason good enough to do what I had just done. No need to share that with him. "I'm not telling you any more," I said, "unless you tell me who you are."

He reacted as if I'd reached over and tapped him on the nose. His neck stiffened, which had the effect of pulling his chin toward his backbone.

"I'm the one who just saved your ass. Remember?" Obviously the dynamics of the situation weren't lost on him, either.

"You did, and I'm grateful. But I don't think it's a lot to ask for you to tell me who you are. I told you who I am."

"You told me your name. My name is Jack Dolan. What does that tell you?"

"Not much."

"How about this?" he asked. "Me first, and then you."

"Deal."

"The guy your buddy went in to see, the guy who owns the salvage yard, I'm watching him. And you walked right into the middle of my modest little stakeout."

"Oh." I felt mildly guilty, but mostly inept. "Are you a cop?"

"Private."

He must have finally felt that we were clear of the dog and whoever else was back there. He slowed down and took time to adjust the seat. He pushed it all the way back.

"Why are you watching him?" I asked.

"Someone paid me to do it. And the target is not someone you'd want to be introduced to under any circumstances, but especially not sneaking around his property. That was his dog, Bull."

The target. Annoying that he'd gotten me to reveal Bobby's name, yet was clever enough not to come across with the name of his guy. "Is 'the target' a drug runner?"

"That's not his business." He glanced over as he took a right turn. I was so glad to see that he knew where he was going. "Why?"

"Bobby Avidor is rumored to be running drugs out of Miami. He works for Majestic Airlines, and people who know him there—"

"This one works for an airline? This Avidor?"

"He's a maintenance supervisor."

He nodded as if that made perfect sense.

"What? Does that mean something to you?"

"Maybe." He took in a long breath, checked the mirror, took off his gloves, and relaxed a little more. He seemed to be coming down from high alert in stages. "Your turn. Why are you following Avidor?"

"He may be responsible for the murder of a friend of mine."

"And you were going to do what? Make a citizen's arrest?"

"I had no plan to approach him. All I wanted to do was follow him and see where he went."

"What were you going to do once you found out?"

"I was going to take that information and add it to what I already know and . . . process it."

From the side I thought I saw the beginning of a be-mused smile. Apparently he found me more amusing than threatening. I didn't know if that was bad or good. He looked over and another part of him emerged from the black mask. He had a nice smile.

"You have no idea what you're doing, do you."

It pained me to agree, but it would have been difficult, absurd, even, to ignore the facts. "I'm new at this."

"Are you armed?"

"No."

"I can guarantee you the boys in that yard were armed tonight. Heavily. You have no idea how much danger you were in back there."

"I'm beginning to appreciate how much. But once you get to a certain level of danger . . . I would say to the point where your life is threatened as it probably was tonight—"

"Not probably."

"Then incrementally speaking, increasing amounts of danger on top of that don't make the situation worse. In other words, the risk does not increase proportionately with the recklessness of the act, once you pass the point where it's your life that is at risk, because that's the ultimate risk."

He gave me a sideways glance.

"You can only die once, is all I'm saying, no matter how stupid you are."

"Maybe so," he said. We drove for a few more miles before he spoke again. "Is that how you respond to being scared? Intellectualize? Analyze the thing that scares you?"

"No." I shifted in my seat. "That's how I respond to everything."

He chuckled. "Here's more input for your calculation. Bull was very close to chasing you down back there. If he had caught you, he would have pulled you to the ground so he could get to your throat, because that's how animals kill. They attack the most vulnerable spot. You would have tried to fight him off, and his teeth would have shredded your arms down to the bone, and you wouldn't have been able to push him off anyway because he's too heavy. He would have wrapped his jaws around that soft tissue"—he made his right hand into a vise and placed it on either side of his throat and for a second reminded me of how John had died—"sunk his teeth in, and ripped everything out. There would have been blood everywhere—your blood—because he would have torn the major arteries, and then—"

"What is your point?"

He left a long pause before he answered and when he looked at me, he wasn't smiling. "There are ways to die, and there are ways to die. Being mauled by a vicious animal is not one of the better ones."

I stared out my window at a drainage canal that paralleled our road. It was bone dry. I ran my fingers over the cuts and scratches on my arms. Superficial wounds from the bushes and branches. Mr. Jack Dolan had done what I had failed to do for myself. He had scared me.

"Avidor is not running drugs," he said, changing the subject at just the right moment. "So if your murder victim—what was his name?"

"John McTavish."

"If John McTavish was killed over drugs, you've got the wrong man."

"No." I turned my attention back inside the car. "It's not the drug piece we're sure of; it's the other way around. We know John came down to Florida to see Bobby Avidor, and I'm reasonably sure Bobby set him up to be murdered. That it was about drugs is the speculation."

"By whom?"

"John's family. His friends. Coworkers."

"Which one are you?"

"Friend," I said. "John and I worked together at Majestic in Boston."

"Is Boston where you live?"

"For another week. If it's not drugs, then—"

"Here's why I'm asking. Wherever your home is, you should go there. You don't belong in places like we just came from."

Of course he was right. I just didn't like being told. "How do you know I'm not FBI or DEA or ATF? I could be a private investigator. I never told you I wasn't."

He looked at me with raised eyebrows and half a grin that said he didn't take the comment any more seriously than I did.

"Just tell me what it is they do," I said. "What is Bobby into if it's not drugs?"

"Parts."

"Parts?"

"Aircraft parts," he said.

"Stealing aircraft parts?"

"At a minimum. My bad guy does the whole buffet—stolen parts, recycled, counterfeit, back door, strip-and-dip. You name it. If Avidor is hooked up with him, he's into parts. Bad parts."

"You won't tell me the name of this bad guy? This J.Z.?"

"Who said it was J.Z.? Where can I drop you?"

I hadn't even noticed that we had made our way back to civilization. The lights were on. Traffic was flowing. We were back in Miami. "You can drop me at the airport."

"Now you're talking. What airline?"

"No airline. I'm staying at a hotel there."

He checked his blind spot and changed lanes. "You're not going home?"

"Not right now. And you can't take my car. I need it."

"I wasn't planning on taking your car. Where do you want it parked?"

"The Dolphin Garage. Where is yours?"

"My truck is back at the salvage yard where I left it. But it's parked far enough away that I can get to it without anyone seeing me." He enunciated clearly, just in case I didn't catch the instructive tone.

"I can drive you home," I said. "Where do you live?"

"No thanks. Plenty of cabs at the airport."

"How do you think a cabbie is going to respond to your camouflage?"

"This is Miami," he said. "The cabbies have seen worse."

We were at the airport now, approaching the parking garages. "Let me take you to get your car tomorrow. It's the least I can do."

"Did you say the Dolphin Garage?"

"We can talk more on the way out there. I have more stuff to tell you."

"No."

"Why not?"

"Because you don't know what you're doing."

"Which is exactly why I need help."

"I generally get paid for providing that kind of help."

"Okay, that's fair." He pulled the ticket at the garage and the gate went up. I had to think fast. "I could hire you. And I could pay you. Eventually."

"I already have a job. I just told you that."

"You could do both jobs at once. Obviously we're after the same players. Earn two fees for one job. It's synergistic. Economies of scale and all that."

"Economies of scale?" He was circling the garage looking for a space. "I'm going to try to get close to the elevator," he said. "So you don't have to walk far. These damn places are dangerous for women."

"I have something—" Something to show you, I thought, if I trusted him. I'd been burned before. I took another look at him in the better light offered in the garage. Strong jaw. Hands resting easy on the steering wheel. Eyes that were always moving, but with the purpose of seeing, as opposed to Bobby's jittery eyes, which seemed to rove incessantly for the express purpose of not being seen. I decided to trust Jack Dolan.

"I have something that might be useful to you. My friend, John, before he died, he sent me an aircraft log-book and a diamond ring."

"Why?"

"I don't know. Maybe for safekeeping. I think his intention was to talk to me about it when he got back from Florida. But he never came back."

"Are you sure it's a logbook?"

"I used to work for an airline. I know what one looks like. And it's trashed. It's muddy and sooty and ripped up. I'm trying to track down which airline."

"You need to work through the homicide detectives," he said. "Whatever you have, give it to them."

"The police think it was a drug killing."

"Then it probably was." He pulled the car into a spot and killed the engine. "They're generally right about those things, which is because they do investigations for a living." There was that instructive tone again.

"They're not right about this," I said. "At least not completely."

"What does that mean?"

"They think John was setting up a drug deal. He wasn't. He might have been doing something for his brother, but—"

"His brother?"

"It's complicated. That's part of what I have to tell you."

The first thing he did when he got out of the car was check the damage to the door from Bull's head. I walked around to see for myself. My ankle had settled down during the long ride in, but now that the blood was flowing, it was really thick and sore.

Bull must have had a rock for a head. There was no way I was getting away with a dent like that on a rental car, which meant I was going to have to pay for it because I hadn't paid for the insurance, which reminded me of my financial crisis, which reminded me of my call to Paul Gladstone and the ticking clock. I had already used up two of the extra seven days he'd given me to get to Detroit. The thought made my head throb as much as my ankle.

"Just let me run you out tomorrow to pick up your car," I said. "Please?"

"You're trying to rope me in. You think if you have

another couple of hours to work on me tomorrow, you'll talk me into it."

"Pretty much."

He smiled. "At least you're up front about it."

I followed him to the elevator, which wasn't far. It arrived with a clear *ding* that felt loud in the deserted space. He held the door so I could limp in.

"Do you know South Beach?" he asked.

"Not at all."

"I'll be at Big Pinks in South Beach tomorrow for breakfast. Meet me there. You can give it your best shot."

And then we walked, he in his black face and me with my limp, all the way across the garage, through the terminal, and to the elevator at the hotel.

Chapter Thirteen

The phone had probably been ringing for a while. The sound seeped into my awareness gradually, like a tune I was humming without knowing what it was. It took a long time for me to realize it was a phone ringing, and an equally long interval to remember what I was supposed to do about it.

"Hello?"

"What, you don't answer your phone down there anymore? What the hell's going on?"

I was lying on my stomach with my head on one of the flat pillows, which was like no pillow at all. I adjusted slightly so I could see the clock radio. "Dan, how can you call me at six o'clock in the morning?"

"Were you asleep?"

"I was in a coma." Every nerve ending in my body objected when I rolled onto my back, reminding me of what had happened last night. Actually, a few short hours ago. Parts of my body that weren't twitching, aching, or stiff were hard to identify. The makeshift ice pack I'd rigged around my ankle was now a soggy, gooshy, cold towel under the sheets at the foot of my bed.

"What do you want?"

"Your logbook belongs to Air Sentinel."

I sat up. Fast. "What?"

"I said your logbook—"

"No. I heard you." My head was swimming and it was hard to get my thoughts together. To top off everything else, I hadn't gotten enough sleep. And there was something bothering me. Something floating out there in the ether that I thought I was supposed to be paying attention to. "How did you figure it out?"

"I traced a couple of the mechanics' signatures by their license numbers. Turns out they worked at Sentinel. Then I took one of the part numbers that was in the book and called their maintenance manager here at Logan. He's an old buddy of mine. So I call him and I ask him to look up the part for me as a personal favor. I figured he could tell me what aircraft it belonged to and we'd know where the book came from. Ten minutes later he's standing in my office."

"It's at least a twenty-five-minute walk from Sentinel to your office."

"This is what I'm saying. The guy's sixty pounds overweight and he's sucking wind when he gets here, all red in the face, asking me where I got that part number."

"What did you tell him?"

"Something about how Sentinel borrowed it from our inventory at O'Hare and I was trying to track it because we thought it had been stolen and . . . I don't even remember. It was a complete load of crap."

"What did he say?"

"Nothing. That's the weird part, Shanahan."

"Why is that weird, Dan?"

"This guy, my buddy, he's usually got diarrhea of the mouth; I can never get him to shut up. But this thing, he wouldn't say another word. I ask him, 'How come you blew a gasket hauling your ass over here? Is there something special about this particular part?' All he said was that I could stop looking for it, that he would make sure Majestic got paid for it. And we should do lunch sometime."

"What do you think that means?"

"Beats the shit out of me. I thought you would have had it all figured out by now."

"I've got some pieces coming together. It's just that they're from an entirely different puzzle than the one we've been looking at." I told him what had happened the night before, about chasing Avidor out to the salvage yard and meeting Jack Dolan. I left out the parts that made me sound like a complete bonehead, which left only the marginally boneheaded moments. "Jack says this guy that Avidor went to meet is a known player in the bogus parts trade, which means Bobby is probably involved, too."

"No shit. Involved how?"

"Probably stealing them." I knew I sounded like more of an expert than I was. "And reselling them on the black market. Maybe worse."

"Stealing from Majestic?"

"Maybe."

"No wonder Johnny was so pissed at him."

"Yeah." I peeled the covers back to sneak a peek at my ankle. Ugly, as expected. As I stared down at it, an awareness started to emerge from my subconscious. I was supposed to be doing something. I had left something undone somewhere. I had no idea what. I swung my feet around to the floor, intending to get up and start the blood flowing. That was until the blood made it to my ankle and the throbbing commenced. I tossed a couple of pillows down to the foot of the bed, leaned back against the headboard, and propped up my injured limb. There would be no running today. Walking was going to be a challenge.

"Doesn't it seem to you," I said, "that a logbook would have more to do with parts than drugs?"

"Like what?"

"I don't know. Maybe Avidor is stealing from Sentinel. Or selling to them. Maybe he sold them a bad part. Or he sold it to a broker who sold it to them. Dan, Sentinel had a crash not too long ago."

He was quiet for a microsecond. "Oh, shit yeah. A bad one down in Ecuador or Salvador or some fucking place. Took them forever just to get to the site."

A thought had popped into my head and tumbled into another couple of thoughts rattling around in there and pretty soon they were starting to stick together and form a critical mass and, damaged ankle or not, the momentum lifted me off the bed and pulled me across the room to dig around on the dresser where I'd dumped my keys and my money from the night before. "I have to find . . ."

"Find what?"

"Find my messages from last night." That's what it was. That's what was bothering me. "I had a message from the jeweler."

"What jeweler?"

"The one who appraised the ring, and I think the message was that he figured out who it belonged to, but it was this long, confusing message that went over to the back of the page and I was so out of it when I came in . . ."

The messages weren't on the dresser with my keys. I looked around for my jeans, which turned out to be on the floor in the bathroom.

"How in the hell could he figure that out? There were no marks on that ring anywhere. I looked all over it."

"This Gemprint thing they do. They have this laser process where they can read the way a diamond is cut, which is never the same way twice, apparently. So it's like—"

"Snowflakes?"

"Yes, but more to the point, it's like fingerprints. People can have their diamonds identified and the information banked so that if the stone gets lost or stolen and turns up, it can find its way back. Only most people don't know about this process, so the jeweler said it was a real long shot but he took the reading anyway and I think . . ."

I'd tried three pockets of the jeans. The messages were in the fourth, folded neatly, right where I'd stuffed them. One from Dan. One from Paul Gladstone in Detroit. One from the jeweler. And I was right. His message was that the diamond ring matched one in the Gemprint database belonging to a Belinda Culligan Fraley. Something else was written there that was trying to pull together all the other things I'd been thinking, but not comprehending. I was already moving toward my laptop.

"Hey!" Dan was still there, and he wasn't pleased to be left out. "What's up?"

"The woman who owned this ring is dead. I'll call you back, Dan."

"*Shan—*"

The image that filled my laptop screen was dim and blurry. The figures that moved through it looked like ghosts in hazard suits, stepping through a dark landscape, picking their way over dangerous terrain in the herky-jerky motion of an Internet video feed.

The first time I'd watched the short clip, my face had burned hot, almost as if the waves of searing heat from the fire had transcended time, distance, and the limits of technology and come through the screen. With my heightened sense of smell, I even thought I could detect the faint odor of jet fuel as it leached into the soil on a mountainside six thousand miles away.

The plane had crashed two months before—close enough in time that images of the catastrophe could still be easily retrieved from the memory bank, but distant enough that they had receded just out of reach of every-day consciousness. The stories and articles from the Internet had reminded me of the details.

An Air Sentinel B777, almost brand new and operating as flight 634, had completed most of its journey from Miami to Quito, Ecuador, when it had dropped from the radar screen at 2046 local time. The next time it had been seen was several days later when rescuers finally made it to the crash site on the side of a mountain north of the city.

When the clip stopped, I restarted it and this time looked for the neon orange flags used to mark locations of human remains. They were hard to see, but they were there. I ran my finger over the rough diamond surface of the ring John had sent, and wondered which flag marked the spot where Belinda Culligan Fraley's remains had been found.

Chapter Fourteen

I almost hadn't recognized him without the combat gear, but Jack Dolan had been the only patron at Big Pinks who was not crowded under a big striped awning in a hubbub of eating, drinking, chatting, and smoking. Relaxing in the sun in a billowy, short-sleeved cotton shirt and baggy shorts, he had seemed younger than I had perceived him the night before, when his weathered voice, the glints of silver in his hair, and perhaps the whiff of paternal concern had put him in his late fifties. Maybe it was the huarache sandals, or the fact that he still had all his hair, which wasn't as long as I'd suspected, but neither was it meticulously tended, private investigation being one of those professions where tonsorial maintenance was optional.

He sat forward in his chair, took off his sunglasses, and studied the diamond ring. "How do you know," he asked, "that it came from the crash site?"

"I told you about the Gemprint thing where—"

"Gemprint I understand, and I believe you when you say the ring belongs . . . or belonged to this Fraley woman. What I don't understand is how you knew she was on the airplane."

"That part was easy. I went online and pulled up a list of the deceased. She and her husband, Frank, were both on Air Sentinel 634 when it went down. They died along with everyone else on board."

"Why would you think to do that?"

"Because the logbook is from Air Sentinel. Air Sentinel had a terrible crash a few months ago. The logbook is damaged in a way that is consistent with a crash. Bobby Avidor is involved in selling bad parts. This Fraley woman had died recently. It was a theory that seemed to make it all fit together."

"How do you know she was wearing this ring when she died?"

"I don't have *proof* that she was wearing the ring. I don't have *proof* of anything. But I believe the logbook came from the crash site, and if the logbook came from the crash site, wouldn't you have to think the ring did, too?"

It all came out too fast and with a higher acid content than I had intended, and I was immediately remorseful. Not smart to piss off the one guy I thought could help me, especially since he'd done nothing to deserve it. But my left ankle was bigger by half than my right, I was on the downside of a three-hour-old adrenaline rush, and I had really expected him to be more enthusiastic . . . okay, impressed by my discovery. I wasn't sure what to make of my own reaction. Maybe I was trying to compensate for screwing up the night before. Trying too hard.

He stared at me, and I couldn't read anything in his eyes except that they were brown. And intelligent. "I think you're right," he said.

"You do?"

"I'm testing your theory. Is that all right with you?"

"Ummm . . ."

"That's a technique we investigators use. Asking questions for understanding. An alternative approach would be for me to simply assume that you're right. Maybe you're always right, which means we don't have to investigate at all. I'll just wait for you to tell me the answer. That would be easier, of course. And quicker."

A grin was tugging at the corners of his mouth, but a gentle one, making it all right for me to smile at myself. When I did, he started to laugh. He was making his point without making me feel stupid, a technique that I thought

I might need to brush up on. He held the ring out for me, and I took it.

"Okay," I said. "All right. I don't know that Mrs. Fraley was wearing this ring, but I made that leap, perhaps an incautious one, but one that I think is logical given all the other circumstances. I suppose I could call the family and try to find out."

"There you go," he said. "Now tell me about the car that followed you."

I told him about the kidney red car that had chased me around the parking garage, and, from the tone of his inquiry, flunked the investigator lesson on being tailed. No license plate. No description.

"Kidney car," he said, putting the glasses back on.

"Not much to go on," I admitted.

"We're going to have to work on that. But in the meantime, what do you think all this means?"

"I think the crash might have been caused by a bad part, that Avidor was involved, maybe with the guy you're chasing, and that the logbook is some kind of proof."

"Of what?"

"Of the cause of the crash."

He sat back, stuck his legs straight out, crossed them at the huaraches, and clasped his hands together on his belly. It looked like his thinking pose. "That could be one explanation," he said. "If your friend McTavish found out about it, that would be a motive for murder. Do they know the cause of the accident yet?"

"Officially, they're still investigating," I said. "It's only been a few months. But I'm wondering if they already suspect something, because of the way that Sentinel maintenance manager reacted in Boston."

"Is it an NTSB investigation? Or the Ecuadorans?"

"Ecuador called in the NTSB."

"Good," he nodded. "That's good. Now I've got a question for you. You said you talked to Pat Spain over at Miami-Dade."

"I did."

"Why didn't you give her the logbook? For all you know, it's evidence. Why didn't you hand it over to the detective working the case? That's what most civilians would do."

"I almost did. I took it over there to give it to her. But then I got this feeling that it wouldn't have . . . not that she wouldn't have done the right thing, but that it wouldn't have helped John, or John's family, for her to have it. I feel responsible to them, and it seemed at the time that it was better for me to have it than for her to have it."

"You thought you could do more with it than she could?"

There was a delicate but unmistakable emphasis on 'you.' "I'm saying even if she *could* do more with it, I *would*."

"Subtle distinction."

"It didn't seem subtle at the time. Detective Spain had a theory and she seemed to be happy with it. She didn't seem interested in discussing alternative scenarios."

"Because something is obvious," he said, "doesn't mean it's not true."

"I know that. But I also knew John, and her theory doesn't make any sense."

"You said something about his brother last night. What's that all about?"

I told him.

"You know," he said, starting slowly, "one reason cops can do what they do is because they bring an objective point of view to proceedings. Sometimes people crack. Sometimes it's the people who've worked the hardest and the longest. I've seen it over and over. Sometimes you don't know people as well as you think you do."

"If you're saying I have a personal stake in this matter, you're right. And if you're saying you think the good detective should have the logbook, I'll take it to her. But I don't believe John was involved in a drug deal. Not for his brother. Not for any reason. He was a good man and he worked hard for everything he ever got."

He looked up into the awning, studying the undercar-

riage as if he wanted to see how it worked, what held it
up. I couldn't see behind the shades but I felt a crack in
his resistance. I saw it in the tilt of his head, in the way
he pressed his fingers together. A bubble of anticipation
started way down deep, but I kept it in check.

"Let me talk to Patty on my own," he said. "I know
her from when I worked at the Bureau. She might tell
me things she wouldn't tell you."

The bubble turned to a rush. "You worked for the
FBI? Where?"

"Mostly down here, but I spent time in the New York
office. Why?"

"Because John made a call to the FBI from his cell
phone while he was down here."

His interest level was rising steadily. "Was it the
main number?"

"Yes. Is there a way to trace his call to a specific agent,
or are we stuck with a call to the generic Feds?"

"Not traceable. The only way we could—" He stopped,
smiled to himself, and shook his head.

"The only way we could find out who he called," I
offered helpfully, "is for you to ask around at the FBI
and see what you can come up with."

He let his sunglasses drop down his nose and peered
at me over the rims. "I didn't say I'd do that." He paid
the check and stood up. "Let's walk."

Walking slowly and at a distinct list to the left, I followed him down a small side street, past a pile of rebar
that would turn a quaint old hotel into a featureless new
condo development. We crossed another street and went
through a park the size of a postage stamp where dogs
inspected the grass, looking for their spot, and people
with sand on their feet stood in line at public restrooms
and changing booths. We went over a grassy swale, onto
a wooden boardwalk, and there it was. I took in a deep
breath and enjoyed my first real look at the ocean since
I'd been there.

"Nice," I said, leaning against one of the plank rail-
ings.

It was more than nice. It was as if someone had lifted

the lid off of the world, had opened it up to air it out, to make space for the uncoiling of the neighborhood, of the city, of the continent into the wide-open, endless repository known as the Atlantic Ocean.

He leaned next to me, and we stood side by side, looking out to sea. "It's nicer without the smoke."

It was true. The light from the sun was dulled by the haze of smoke, but the heat was full force, and it felt good on my arms and my face after the long winter in New England and the long night in a Florida swamp. I felt my own uncoiling inside. Jack must have felt it, too.

"The man your buddy went to meet," he said, "is named Jimmy Zacharias."

Jimmy Zacharias. J.Z. I squinted into the sun and smiled. "What is the case you're on?"

"Jimmy killed two men."

"He killed two men and he's still walking around in the world?"

"He's responsible for the helicopter accident that killed them."

"Oh."

The muscles in his forearms tensed. "Just because he killed them with shoddy maintenance instead of a hollow point bullet doesn't mean he's any less responsible. And it doesn't make it any less criminal."

"I agree with you. I just had a different image in my mind is all. Who's your client?"

"The insurance company for the manufacturer of the helicopter. Both widows are suing, but the manufacturer had nothing to do with this. This accident was caused by bad parts or bad maintenance or both."

"I assume Jimmy worked on the helicopter."

"One of his shops refurbished it and did some follow-up work. He has a financial interest in a handful of repair stations in the area. That's how he launders his dirty parts."

"Are you talking about FAA-certified repair stations?"

"No one would do business with one that wasn't certified. That's the whole point. He finds a business that seems perfectly legitimate, usually one that's in trouble and needs cash. Then he slowly starts to mix the bad parts in with the good. He dummies up the paperwork, and that shit flows right on through and into airline operations and inventories all over the world."

"Don't these stations get inspected on a regular basis?"

"Some of these repair shop guys know a lot more than their inspectors ever will. A lot of them were mechanics for Eastern and Pan Am. And when he does get into trouble, Jimmy just changes the name of the place and gets recertified. He ran one station under four different names that I counted."

"Where does he get the bad parts?"

"Wherever he can. From people like Avidor who steal for him. Jimmy was in the military, so he has access to a lot of military surplus. He has his own aircraft recovery and salvage business. That's what you saw last night. He also keeps an eye on the junkyards. He's not above doing a little strip-and-dip."

"Strip-and-dip? Do I even want to know?"

"He gets scrapped parts from the junkyard, cleans them up, paints over the corrosion, dummies up the paperwork, and sells them."

"Painting over the corrosion," I said, "that must be the dip part."

"You'd be amazed at how good they look with a new coat of paint."

"Jimmy sounds like a real peach."

"You don't know the half of it," he said.

"Why isn't he in jail?"

"He's smarter than your average swamp rat, and what he does, it's hard to prove."

"Do you think you'll be able to prove what Jimmy did on this helicopter accident?"

"I don't know. We've just identified the part that caused the crash. It's pretty badly damaged, but we've got metallurgists and mechanics and engineers looking at it. If we can demonstrate that it's bogus and tie it back to Jimmy, then we've got him."

"Tie it back how?"

"Maintenance records, purchase orders. The logbook. In this business there is always a paper trail. It's required. It's just that the paperwork is sometimes forged. But I have a feeling about this. I think we're going to get him this time."

"This time?"

"If there's no legitimate paper trail, I'll find someone to flip on Jimmy. That's why I've been watching him. I wanted to see who he's working with these days. The parts business tends to be a closed community. Jimmy and I, we know lots of the same people."

"And now you know Avidor. Maybe he'll turn out to be a talker."

"Maybe so."

We drifted into an easy silence. I watched a group of noisy volleyball players and realized for the first time I hadn't seen many children around. I looked as far as I could see from one end of the beach to the other. There was not one small person in sight.

"Look, Jack, I really would like to work on this with you. I can scrape together ten thousand dollars from my retirement accounts. That's all I have to spend on the whole deal, including my expenses. So here's my pitch: You take my case and I'll give you all of the money that's left when we find John's murderer."

"We?"

"You and me."

"Together? That would be highly unusual."

"Do you really think I'm going to sit around the pool reading *Vanity Fair* and drinking Cuba Libres while you're out doing all the scut work?"

"Cuba Libres?"

"Isn't that what you people drink down here?"

"Not since 1954. Don't you have a job? Some place you have to be?"

"That's a long story, but what it comes down to is this is where I have to be, and that is my deal."

"Why are you so adamant about this?"

"Will knowing that make a difference in your decision?"

He gazed out over the turquoise waves and seemed to give the question serious thought, which I liked. "It might."

"John and I got involved in something together at Logan. The truth is I got involved and he decided to help me."

"What was it?"

"My predecessor there, the woman who was the general manager before me, had died. That's why the job was available for me. The police thought she'd committed suicide and that was the company line. The people who knew her couldn't accept that she had killed herself, and it turned out she didn't."

"Murdered?"

"By a ramper. One of her own employees."

He smiled lightly. "And you got involved?"

"He was my employee, too. I inherited him."

"Ah."

"I could have left it alone. Things in Boston had been left alone for a long time by a lot of different people. But there was something . . . I felt that I knew this woman—Ellen was her name—even though I'd never met her. We had a lot in common, and I couldn't let it go until I had figured out why she had died."

"Did you figure it out?"

"Yes."

"And John helped you?"

"He provided me with information from the ramp that I never could have gotten without him. Things I had to know to understand what had happened to Ellen and why. He warned me a few times. Even though I was a member of management, he took my side against his union brothers. These were people he'd worked with side by side for years. Some of them he'd known since they were kids. And they weren't happy about it. No one's ever stood up for me like that."

"That's important to you, is it? Having someone stand up for you?"

"Yes."

"What happened to the murderer?"

A cold wave passed through me, the same one I always felt at this point in the story. "The man who murdered Ellen died."

"How?"

"He was chasing after me on the ramp. There was an accident and he died. Horribly."

He turned slightly, enough to see my face when he asked, "And you feel bad about this?"

It was my turn to stare at the shimmering ocean. "Sometimes."

He held out his hand. "Let me see that ring again." I gave it to him and he studied it, turning it slowly. "I'd like to see this piece get back to the family it belongs to. It looks as if it might be important to someone."

"And I'd like to find out who killed my friend. If it was Jimmy and we can prove it, maybe we both get something good out of the deal."

"Ten thousand dollars?"

"Whatever's left."

"I'll do it." I felt a quick flush of excitement, which he moved quickly to squash. "And I have a few conditions of my own. You have to do what I say when I say it."

"I will."

"You have to be available whenever I need you, day or night."

"I've given up sleeping, anyway."

"And you take the notes."

"Excuse me?"

"And drive."

"What?"

"All investigators take notes," he said, clearly seeing more and more merit in the idea. "And you said it. I'm the professional. I know you don't want me slowed down by administrative duties. It wouldn't be cost effective."

"Are you making fun of me?"

"Yes." He laughed, but again in that comfortable way.

"It's been pointed out to me," I said, "that I can be a little structured at times."

"That's all right," he said. "I can use a little more

structure in my life. Let's go get my truck. But first we have to stop at the office supply store around the corner."

"What for?"

"A notepad and pencil for you."

The route Bobby had taken me on the night before, as I had suspected, felt more benign by daylight. The masses of tangled trees and thatched brush lining the roadways were lush and full under blue sky and bright sun, not forbidding. The quiet that enveloped us as we moved farther and farther from the city was calming, not frightening. But then I wasn't alone this time. Jack was in the passenger seat.

I'd spent most of the drive out talking, filling him in on the details of what I knew so far. I'd given him the timeline Felix and I had made.

"What did you find out about the rental car?" he asked.

"Not much. Whoever turned it in left it in the rental car lot way off in a corner by a fence. This agent I spoke to found it and checked it in. It was the same deal as the hotel. John had wanted to pay cash—it was in their records—but they charged it to his credit card when he didn't show up in person to pay. Like the hotel room, the car has been rented a half dozen times since the murder."

He set my timeline on the seat, leaned forward, and searched the trees. "Go up half a mile . . . right here, where it looks like there's no road, and make that corner up there. My truck should be back in the bush."

I pulled around the corner and stopped. We both got out. I didn't see any truck, but that was, I imagined, the whole point. Jack struck out on a nontrail into the undergrowth, and I wobbled after him as best I could, careful not to step in any more holes. I found him standing next to a gray low-slung truck that looked as if it had been in all the rough places Jack had been.

"An El Camino," I said. "I don't remember the last time I saw one of these."

His stance was odd—back rigid, arms straight at his sides, eyes turned skyward.

"It was two cops," he said.

"What was two cops?"

"The helicopter crash I told you about, the one I'm investigating. The two men who were killed were county cops up in the Florida panhandle. The county had purchased a helicopter for search and rescue. It was just this small county sheriff's department that was trying to do a better job. And what they bought was old, but it had been refurbished. They'd never even had it up before. A little girl went missing. Six years old. They weren't in the air fifteen minutes when it fell out of the sky—and crushed them both. They never had a chance." He started to go on, and didn't. The bundle of bone and muscle that hinged his jaw to his skull was working hard, clenching and unclenching. I'd known him for less than twenty-four hours, but I could feel the agitation churning beneath the calm exterior, and his struggle not to let it show.

"Did they find the girl?"

"They found her body."

I leaned back against the truck. It was dusty, but I felt the need to sag against something. "I'm sorry. Did you know any of these people?"

"I know Jimmy. I know he cut some corner or shaved a little something off here or there to put in his own pocket. And then he went home, went to bed, and slept like a baby."

He was very still as he stared up into the high afternoon sky.

The tight line of his shoulders under his lightweight shirt, the way he seemed to be searching the treetops, and especially the tilt of his head all reminded me of something I had seen the night before. The dog Bull had sniffed the air that way as he'd picked up my scent and had stood all aquiver with anticipation of the chase, and I suddenly felt as if I'd walked into a movie after it had started.

"Jack, is there something between you and Jimmy Zacharias?"

"Jimmy is just another scumbag in a long line of scumbags."

A little too much indifference, a slight turn away, and I wished all the way back to Miami that I had asked the question when I could have seen his face as he answered.

"Holy Christ, Shanahan. Are you sure about that?"

Dan and I were experiencing the usual techno-interruptus that comes along with mobile communications. But this time he was on a landline in his office and the problem was at my end. I was trying to get back to my hotel, but had to keep driving in a circle to keep my cell phone far enough away from the airport's electronic interference.

"Think about it, Dan. The impact and fire explains the damage to the logbook. The fact that the airplane crashed explains why no one's been looking for it. Everyone thought it was destroyed."

"And you're saying you think it was caused by a bad part?"

"Bad part or faulty maintenance. I think that's why your buddy over at Air Sentinel was in such a twist. He knew the part you asked him about came from the accident airplane."

"If that aircraft came down because of a bad part and the word gets out, Sentinel has got a big fucking problem."

"They're probably trying to figure out right now how to deal with the backlash."

A tollbooth loomed ahead. I had somehow gotten twisted around myself in my meandering route. I had to stop talking and pay attention to the road. That didn't mean Dan had to stop talking.

"This makes Avidor more of a scumbag than I gave him credit for. If Johnny knew about any of this—"

"John knew about it, Dan. He had the logbook. I don't know how he got it, but he must have known it had something to do with that crash. Proof of what caused it . . . maybe a record of a bad part that was used. I think that's what got him killed."

"That logbook is a mess, Shanahan. I don't see how it could prove anything."

"It's possible the killer didn't know that." I took the last exit before the tollbooth, turned back toward the airport, then found a quiet strip mall where I could park and finish my conversation. "I don't have it all figured out, Dan. All I know is it never made sense to me that John would wake up one day and decide to fly to Florida to confront Bobby on being a drug runner if he'd known about it all along. John would have roared into Miami if he'd heard Bobby was trading in bad parts."

Dan was silent, an event unusual enough for me to take note. "What's the matter?"

"I was just thinking . . . How many people went down on that ship?"

"Two hundred and three. No survivors."

"Jesus God."

He was thinking what I was. An airplane accident is bad enough when it's just that—an accident. A crash caused by a sleazy, back alley transaction between a couple of low-rent, self-dealing criminal entrepreneurs that may have netted each a couple of hundred dollars was so monstrous, so malevolent that trying to comprehend it just made your circuits melt down. It was mass murder.

"Listen, Dan, I don't think we should be talking about this to anyone. It's pretty volatile stuff."

"I don't even like talking to you about it."

"Good. And I need more help."

"That's a big fucking surprise."

"I have a theory on how John got the book. According to his phone records, he called a bar in Salem from down here."

"So?"

"So Salem isn't far from Gloucester, and Gloucester is where Avidor and the McTavishes all grew up. Maybe Avidor still has friends back there, or he and John had a mutual acquaintance. So here's what I need you to do. I need you to drive up there—"

"Shanahan, do you know what kind of a week I'm having here? It's spring break. My loads are off the wall. Not to mention my own kid's out of school and she's up here with me . . ."

"A nice drive up the north shore will get you out of the airport and give you a little father-daughter bonding time with Michele. You can take her to lunch, have some chow-dah, and while you're there snoop around this bar and find the connection to Bobby."

He was quiet. I hated horning in on his time with Michele, limited as it was. But I couldn't fly up and do it. Given her circumstances, I wouldn't ask Mae to take time away from her children, and Terry couldn't even drive. "Dan, if it's true Bobby is selling bad parts to commercial airlines, or to anyone for that matter, wouldn't you do anything to make him stop?"

I heard a light thud and knew he had put the receiver down on the desk. I'd seen him do it when we'd worked together. It's what he did when he wanted a moment to think. I watched the rush hour traffic ebb and flow and waited. Dan had long ago surrendered himself—body, soul, and marriage—to the business of flying people from here to there. Like all good airline people, he preferred that the passengers who put their lives in his hands got *all* the way to where they were going safely. With their bags. Besides, he hated Bobby Avidor's guts. There was only one conclusion he could come to.

He picked up the phone and I heard him breathing. "Give me the name of this dive."

Chapter Fifteen

Jack's bungalow on South Beach was one in a long row of low-slung boxy structures that were painted peach and topped with terra-cotta tile roofs. The complex reminded me of pictures I'd seen of officers' quarters in the Pacific theater during World War II. I wouldn't have been surprised to see Douglas MacArthur, or at least Gregory Peck come striding out with a pipe in his mouth and an aide in tow. But the only one who came out was Jack carrying a cup with a lid. When he got in, the aroma of his coffee filled the car.

"Where to?" I asked him.

"Go back out the way you came and get on I-95."

"North or south?"

"North. We've got a very busy day ahead."

The landscape on I-95 north wasn't much to see. Thunderboat factory outlets, truncated strip malls, and tire dealerships hunkered off to the sides. What there was could only be glimpsed intermittently through a solid wall of eighteen-wheelers, tour buses, and hulking SUVs with trailer hitches, all moving over twelve lanes of concrete at speeds that left no margin for error.

After he finished his coffee he settled back and got comfortable. "I thought," he said, "you spent fourteen years in the airline business. Why don't you know more about bogus parts?"

"I did. And what I knew about the maintenance function was all I needed to know—'How soon can you fix my airplane so I can get this angry throng out of my terminal?' What exit am I looking for?"

"I'll tell you when we're getting close."

Jack's navigation was making me rethink my commitment to being the designated driver. He was dribbling out the directions as we went, which I despised. I wanted to know in advance where we were going. I wanted to know how far it was and how long it would take to get there. I wanted to have in my mind a route of travel. But I'd quit arguing about it when I finally realized his brain didn't work that way. He went strictly by feel, and he liked the flexibility of keeping all his options open.

"I do know this—" I said, checking my blind spot for a lane change. "Majestic Airlines never had a problem with bogus parts."

"Dream on, kid. Majestic has a problem. All commercial carriers have the problem. They don't want you to know about it, and the FAA is helping them cover it up."

"That sounds vaguely paranoid, Jack. Slightly conspiracy theory-ish."

"The FAA won't even acknowledge the term 'bogus parts.' Their accepted term is 'Suspected Unapproved Parts.'" He laughed. "That doesn't sound as menacing as counterfeits. Or scrapped and sold as new. Or old and damaged military parts buffed up and sold 'like new.' Or new parts sold for unapproved purposes because they're cheaper than the right parts. Or hot stamped parts."

"What are those?"

"Parts with paperwork that says they were inspected when they weren't. The FAA has literally gone through their databases and reclassified accidents that the NTSB attributed to bad parts."

"There have been accidents attributed to bogus parts?"

"What do you think happens when an airplane is flying around with a car part in it?"

"Car parts? Could we be just a little less hyperbolic?" I adjusted my position in the seat. I'd been there for a long while, and my ankle was stiffening up.

"Lancer Cargo about five years ago," he said. "They got a couple of starters in that their mechanics didn't think looked right. They opened them up and found scrap and car parts inside. These were ten-thousand-dollar parts. But that's better than having a counterfeit or back door part slipped in on you because at least you have a chance of spotting a car part that's not supposed to be there."

"What's a back door part?"

"Say a foreman at a legitimately approved machine shop keeps the assembly line running after he's supposed to have shut it down. He makes an extra ten combustion liners that his boss doesn't know about, sells them out the back door to some dirty broker, and pockets whatever he gets. This is your exit."

I hit the brakes, sailed into the outside lane, and made the exit, barely. The black Mercedes following too closely on my tail honked his displeasure. If Jack noticed I couldn't tell. He was on a roll.

"A back door part doesn't get tested, which is bad enough, but at least it's been properly designed and is made out of the approved materials. You can't say that about counterfeit parts. These dinky little machine shop guys look at parts selling for ten or fifteen thousand bucks a pop and they say, 'Sheeeeeet, I can make me one of them.' And they do. Maybe they reverse engineer it and make it out of whatever material happens to be lying around. As for accidents, there was a Norwegian charter flight a few years back, I think it was a Convair, that fell into the North Sea. Do you know why?"

"I'm sensing a problem with bogus parts."

"The fasteners—the bolts used to hold the tail on—were made from a lower grade of steel than the standard demands, and they hadn't been tested. When the airplane flew into turbulence, metal fatigue caused the bolts to snap. The tail fell off, and everyone died."

"If it wasn't reported, then how does anyone know?"

He reached over to adjust the air vent. I couldn't tell if he was too warm or too cold. I was feeling chilled myself. "Because the Norwegian version of the FAA wasn't afraid to say what happened. In this country, between the FAA and the airlines, they don't have the

manpower, the resources, or the balls to solve this problem. Since they can't solve it, they have to hide it because
if they didn't, no one would ever fly again."

Even with the windows closed, I could still feel the air
taking on that familiar humid, swampy quality as we
drove farther and farther from the interstate. We kept
passing signs on the side of the road that promised tours
of the Everglades, alligator shows, and airboat rides. I
saw an official National Park visitors' station with a tall
totem pole in the front yard.

Jack seemed to be searching for a specific street, staring at the infrequent signs until they were past.

"Jack, do you know the actual names of any of these
streets?"

"No. What do you think would happen if John Q.
Traveler found out the fan blades in the jet engine on
his airplane came from Rudy's Chop Shop?"

"*Came* from, or *might* have come from?"

"You would be amazed, Alex. You *will* be amazed."

"If it's such a big problem, how come we don't see
more commercial airliners plunging from the sky?"

"It's more insidious than that and it's not at that stage
yet. It's like termites that get into your house and start
chomping away. You have no idea what's going on because the damage is underneath, and the truth is you're
not looking all that carefully. What's even worse is when
the guy you hire to inspect your house looks it over and
tells you everything is copacetic."

"That would be the FAA?"

"Right. You think your house is stable and strong.
You think it's going to last forever right up until the
day it collapses around your ears. That's what's going to
happen to the U.S. airline industry and its vaunted safety
record one day."

"How do you know all this stuff?"

"Because it's one of the things I used to do at the
Bureau."

"I think you're exaggerating."

"That's what you're supposed to think. It's the FAA's
job to shill for the airline business—your business—and

it's the job of the airlines to sell tickets. My job was to chase the termites, no matter where they went. I saw a lot of nasty bugs. Take your next right, go down and park in front of the first trailer in the third row."

"Am I about to meet one of your nasty bugs?"

"No. Ira was a good mechanic who never should have tried to run a business. Unfortunately, those are the only ones who ever seem to get caught."

Ira Leemer looked like Rod Stewart without the benefit of your glasses. He had the elfin face, the sharp nose, and the tapering chin. He even had blonde highlights in his gray hair. But whereas Rod's features were still crisp and distinct, Ira's were puffy, droopy, and soft. And when he opened his mouth to speak, he sounded like what he was—a half-Cajun South Florida ex-con salvage dealer who lived in a trailer on the edge of a swampy marsh.

He was talking to me and he was on a roll, perched on the top step of his porch. The door was open and I could hear the sound of an oscillating fan inside. Ira was explaining himself and the unfortunate decisions that had sent him to prison.

"Well—" He twisted around to face me more fully. "Ever'body knows there's bad parts, and then there's bad parts. You take a B747. There's over six million parts on that sucker, and most of them don't make that airplane fly. If you know what's what"— when Ira said "what," it came out like "whuuut"—"which I do, you know never to muck around with nothing that's flight critical." He wet his lips with a sip of Fresca from a sweaty can. "The worst thing I did was fudge a little bit when I had to. I'd take parts from one unit that just come in to be fixed and use them in another one I had to get out the door. You weren't supposed to do that, swap parts around, but there ain't no real reason you can't do it other than they told you not to. And besides that anyways, these parts they call bogus, a lot of the times they're just as good as the real ones. They don't have the paperwork behind 'em is all that is."

"Ira," Jack said, "you weren't working on crop dusters

in the backyard." He was sitting across from Ira in a
folding beach chair, the kind with the aluminum frame
and the woven nylon strips. "You were an FAA-certified
repair station doing work for major commercial airlines.
You weren't allowed to run by the seat of your pants."

"I know that. All I'm saying is I paid attention to the
things that mattered. Maybe I wasn't so good with the
paperwork, all the manuals you got to keep on hand and
updated and so on. I just never had the money to do it
right. These fellows coming up in the business now, they
just don't care if the engine runs or the airplane gets off
the ground or even if it stays bolted together while it's
up there."

Between declarations, Ira puffed the life out of a hand-
rolled cigarette that was shaped like a knotty twig. Every
time he exhaled, I felt my own lungs withering. I moved
a few more inches upwind. "How did you get into the
business?"

He shaded his eyes with one hand and pointed up at
me with one of his yellowed fingers. "See now, that there
was one of my main problems. You think of it as a business. To me it was just fixing airplanes like I'd always
done. I was a mechanic for Eastern before that asshole
Lorenzo showed up. Other buddies of mine, they'd
started their own repair shops, so when I finally got laid
off I figured what the hell, I'll give it a whirl. And so I
did. Ended up doing twenty-one months. It don't sound
like that much, but I'll tell you what, I could'na done
one more day. But I never went into it to be no crook.
I really didn't. All I was trying to do was feed my
children."

I reached up to rub the back of my neck. I'd worn my
hair up because it had been so hot. It wasn't even nine
in the morning and I could already feel the sunburn
starting.

Ira nodded at Jack. "What about you, Bobo? I hear
you retired from the FBI a few months back."

Bobo? Jack was busy ignoring me. Was this a nick-
name with meaning specific to Jack? Or was it Ira's catchall
name for everyone? He hadn't yet called me Bobo.

"I left three years ago," Jack said.

"Whooo*eeee!* You sure do lose track of time when you're in the joint."

Jack stood up and stretched, pushing the arch in his back with both hands. "Ira, did you get anything on Avidor?" The catching-up-with-each-other phase of the interview was now apparently over.

"Well, I did. After you called I did me some checking around." Ira took a long drag of nicotine and checked back and forth with his eyes, as if he might catch someone sneaking around the side of his trailer to eavesdrop.

Jack glanced over at me. And he kept looking at me, eyebrows raised. I'd figured my role in this interview was to listen closely, learn what I could, and not disturb the flow. But after he stared for a while longer, it hit me that my role was to listen closely, learn what I could, not disturb the flow—and take notes. I reached into my pocket, pulled out my nifty notebook, and christened it with Ira's name and the date.

"What I hear—and I don't know nothing for sure 'cause I ain't never worked with this boy myself—is he's a good steady source. He works out there at the airport and he's in management, so he can get you what he says he'll get you, and he delivers on time. He'll get you papers, too, if you pay extra."

"What's he pushing?"

"Anything he can lay hands on, but mainly new parts. He's getting hisself a reputation, too. They're all still talking about a deal where he had this ol' boy stealing from out of his own airline's inventory and then selling them back to the same outfit. They was paying for the same gizmo twice and didn't even know it."

"Was it Majestic?" I asked the question, then braced for the answer. In spite of all that had happened, I still felt protective of Majestic Airlines. I'd left fourteen years of my life there.

"No. He don't shit in his own bed, apparently, which is the smart thing to do. I hear he uses these rent-a-mechanics a lot." He looked at Jack. "You know the ones I mean?"

Jack nodded. "Temps with mechanic's licenses."

"Thing is, they don't make much money, and they got access to everywhere because they go wherever they're needed." Something in the water caught his eye. He went over to a splintered deck that hung out over the mud and the water. "Look over there, Missy, in the sawgrass. See that? See 'em moving out there?"

I joined him and scanned the brown water where he pointed. And near as I could tell everything was moving. Everything was alive. Bugs crawled on the carpet of lily pads or swarmed across the surface in huge undulating clouds. Mysterious creatures pinched at the surface from underneath, leaving no trace except dissipating concentric circles. The drought had pulled the waterline down, exposing large expanses of black mud, tree roots and rocks that were slimy and encrusted, covered in black and green mold and algae. And then I did see what he was showing me and it gave me a shiver. It was a nest of small alligators—at least eight of them—knifing through the shallow water with only their snouts and bubble eyes visible.

"They're babies," he said. "The mother must be around here somewhere."

"What's Avidor doing for Jimmy, Ira?" Jack obviously wanted to get back on course. We went back to join him. He was still at the trailer, having shown no interest in checking out the indigenous wildlife.

"He's recruiting mechanics," Ira said, settling back in. "Dirty boys. You know the kind I mean. They got the feelers out. Somebody even asked me if I was interested."

"Recruiting them for what?"

"Don't know, Bobo." Ira's tone had turned cagey. "I try not to know stuff like that no more. And I told them no. I ain't going back to prison no way no how." He reached down and knocked on his wooden steps.

"Speculate," Jack said. "What is Jimmy up to these days?"

Ira took a last long drag and dropped the cigarette into the soda can at his side. The still burning butt hissed when it hit bottom. "I really can't, Bobo."

"Yes, you can."

Jack didn't move and Ira didn't move. All they did was look at each other. But something had shifted between the two men. Jack's approach still felt casual and relaxed, perfectly in tune with the hot and still weather that slowed the world to an underwater pace. But there was an underlying firmness of tone that had crept in, a directness in his speech, a no-bullshit attitude that seemed perfectly pitched to Ira's frequency. And he responded.

"Far as I know, Jimmy's doing the same old shit. Pulling in parts from wherever he can get them cheap, and selling them for what the market will bear."

"Is he still pushing them out through the usual outlets?"

"Yeah, I guess. I don't know who specifically he's using these days, but it's got to be three or four of them little repair shops around town that got their FAA certificates and not much else. Probably the ones couldn't stay in business if it weren't for him propping them up." He reached into the slush-filled cooler by his side for another can of soda, and smiled as he popped it open. Then he reached into a deep pocket of his baggy pants for his tobacco pouch. "You after Jimmy, are you?"

"Maybe."

"What for?"

Jack looked as though he were considering how much to tell Ira. "The helicopter thing. The one that went down up in the panhandle."

"Those deputies, huh? I heard about that. You ain't never gonna get him on that, Bobo. Take my word. He's got hisself covered six ways from Sunday."

Jack paused before answering. "We'll see."

Ira sat shaking his head and staring down into his lap, absorbed by the intricate process of rolling another tobacco twig. "Nobody ever used to get kilt in this business. But it's what it comes to when you get these drug people coming in."

Jack looked at him closely. "Drug people?"

"The business has changed since you and me were part of the landscape. It ain't the friendly, neighborly sort of confab it used to be. It's growing. New people are coming in, and some of them are crossing over from the dope trade. Not a good class of people, neither, if you want my opinion."

"Drugs and aircraft parts," I said. "That doesn't sound like a natural crossover to me."

"Why not? You can make almost as much money, the FAA is a hell of a lot easier to hide from than the DEA, and even if you do get caught like I did you don't do much time. I mean twenty-one months ain't nothing compared to a life sentence. Or the needle in the arm."

"Do you have the names of any of these drug people?" Jack asked him.

"No. You never know who these people are. They're used to keeping themselves hidden. They don't know nothing about fixing airplanes. That's the whole problem. The government grabs up the ones like me that don't mean no harm, really, and leaves the ones who are a menace to society out on the street. At least I always made sure anything I fixed would work."

"Ira"—Jack was still in that firm tone—"I need to know why Jimmy is putting together a crew of mechanics."

"Why don't you ask the Avidor fellow?"

"I plan to." Jack moved a step closer to Ira. The toes of his shoes were almost touching the bottom step. "But I also need to know what you can find out. You said they contacted you. Call them back."

"All righty. I'll do that for you, Bobo."

"I want to know something else, Ira. Air Sentinel 634."

Ira was busy firing up his cigarette. His eyes narrowed as he looked up at Jack. "What about it?"

"Do you know what I'm talking about?"

He studied the burning end of his cigarette. "I know about that airplane that flew into a mountain in Ecuador, if that's what you're asking me."

"What do you know about it?"

"Not a damn thing."

The answer came too fast. Ira knew it too—and didn't care. My inclination was to lean in because this was getting really interesting. But Jack stepped back and tilted his head to the sky. "You ever remember a fire season like this one, Ira?"

"No sir. Not in all my days. It's the drought is what it is." He nodded out to the swampy morass just beyond the deck. "Water levels are four or five feet low. It's so dry out here, you can see bottom in places. Yes sir. See things we ain't never meant to see."

Jack put one foot up on the step and moved his face closer to Ira's. "Tell me about the crash."

"I don't know nothing about that." Ira kept passing his free hand over his chest as if he were trying to wipe something off the palm of his hand. Then he started to rise, but Jack reached over and put one hand on the smaller man's shoulder, keeping him in his seat.

"Do you know something you're not sharing? Because it feels to me as though you know something you're not sharing."

"No sir."

"I need you to get me something. A name. A place to start."

Ira's body began to list slightly in favor of his right shoulder where Jack's hand seemed to have gotten heavier. "That might be dangerous, Bobo. Might there be a little something in it for me if I get you what you want?"

"Get me something and we'll see."

Jack let go. Ira popped instantly back to center as if nothing had happened. "I'll scratch around a little for you," he said. "But I'll tell you right now, I ain't going too deep. I don't want no ex-drug runners on my ass."

We sat in the car with both doors swung open, waiting for the cabin to cool down. Jack was on the phone checking with his service for messages. He was having a hard time getting a signal. I was taking in the surroundings, things I had felt or heard but not seen when I'd been out Jimmy's way. Everything was green or brown, like plants and the water, or gray like the trunks of the ancient trees. Most of the flowers were purple. Purple seemed to be a big swamp color. There was an amazing variation of plant types, thousands of different textures and shapes and shades of green. Ferns that were six feet tall, bamboo stalks, twisted tree branches sprouting leaves as big as both my hands together.

"What do you think of Ira?" Jack had finished his call and was staring at the trailer. Ira had taken his cooler of Fresca and pouch of tobacco and trundled inside.

"If he turned down the work," I said, "he didn't do it without finding out what it was. But if he didn't take the work, what other reason would he have to lie or withhold?"

"He's a snitch. He sells information. He could be playing both sides. The trick with someone like Ira is to get as much information as you can while revealing as little as you can. We'll wait and see what he comes up with." He closed his door and strapped in. "What do you think about this drug connection he mentioned?" He asked the question as though he knew I wouldn't like it.

I adjusted the vent on my side so the struggling air conditioner wouldn't blow hot air in my face, and tried to choose just the right word. "Interesting."

"Interesting?" He didn't seem satisfied with the one I'd chosen. "Did you tell Terry McTavish what Avidor said about his drug deal?"

"His alleged drug deal."

"What did he say?"

"He said it was more of Avidor's bullshit and he threatened to fly down here and beat the crap out of him with his cane. John's wife thinks it's a preposterous story. My friend Dan says no one on the ramp in Boston has heard anything about it. Terry hasn't been out of Boston since his accident and he's offered his phone records to demonstrate that he hasn't called any drug connections. No calls to Florida or South America."

"All right."

"I think it's a dead end, Jack."

"Okay."

"Aren't you going to argue with me?"

"I don't think it would be productive," he said.

The temperature of the air blasting out of the vents was approaching tolerable so I closed the door, put the car in gear, and pulled out of the trailer park. Dust flew and I was glad we had the windows up. Jack seemed content to stare out his window.

"What are we going to talk about all the way back to the city if you won't argue with me?"

"You can guess who we're going to talk with next."

"That doesn't sound productive."

"First clue—it's someone you already met."

Chapter Sixteen

Detective Patricia Spain had not offered her hand to me when we'd met at the police station. When she arrived at the restaurant and saw me sitting with Jack, she thrust it right out there and told me to call her Pat. It was a confident handshake. None of that stuff where you reach out and grab a dead jellyfish. I always admired that in another woman. I liked her better already.

As she settled in at our table, she reached over and touched Jack's arm, then did a double take on his face. "Baby, you look like hell."

He leaned over and kissed her cheek. "Thanks, Patty. You look great as always. I ordered for you. A large stack of banana pancakes with extra butter and extra syrup, a side of scrambled eggs and bacon—crisp—and a tall glass of orange juice. Is that going to be enough?"

She studied him critically, as if he were an oil painting at the museum. "You eat it, lover. You look like you could use the protein. And next time you want to meet with me, you make it someplace besides the airport. Could you have *picked* a more inconvenient place?"

"We're seeing someone here later. Besides, I thought you'd like a chance to get out of the office."

"Tell me what you need so I can get up out of here and go do some real work."

He sat back in his chair, looking marginally insulted. "Why do you always think—"

"I know you wouldn't be calling if you didn't need

something." She nailed him with her black eyes, but I could tell she was teasing him. Half teasing, maybe.

Jack's protest was interrupted when he had to push forward and let a family of six squeeze by our table, one at a time, each with their own large, clumsy rolling bag. Pat looked at me. "Why didn't you tell me you were running with this fool? I wouldn't have had my game face on."

"We hadn't even met at the time. I thought you weren't interested."

"That's not true. And I am sorry about your friend. I called the family after you left to see how they were getting along."

"Patty," Jack said, "you gave her the brush-off?"

"I wasn't even supposed to be talking to her. I've been instructed to refer all inquiries to the FBI. If I could save her from the experience of dealing with Agent Hollander, it's the least I could do." She spit out the agent's name as if it were a bug that had flown up her nose.

That was a name I hadn't heard. I dug out my notebook and wrote it down.

Jack pressed for details. "The Bureau took your case?"

"They did. And don't even ask me why. Ask Agent Damon Hollander. Maybe he'll tell you more than he told me, since all you Feebs come from the same DNA."

Jack shrugged. "Am I supposed to know him? I've never heard of him."

"He's too young for you, baby. He brought his tight little ass over to my office and snatched Mr. John McTavish right out from under me. Didn't say this. Didn't say that. Didn't say boo."

"You let him do that? That doesn't sound like you, Patty."

"It's not like I don't have enough murders to fill up my idle hours. Besides that, the boss came in and told me in his quiet voice, which he only uses when he's serious, to let it drop. So I did. I let it go."

I looked at Jack. "Maybe that's who John called at the FBI."

"It would be a good place to start. When did he swipe your case, Patty?"

"Two days ago." She turned to me. "I'm surprised you didn't see steam shooting out of my ears when you came to see me because I was still hot about it."

"I thought you just didn't want to talk to me."

"But—" She sat back, straightened her shoulders, and let an exaggerated aura of calm and serenity come over her. "I've let it go now."

The waitress brought our breakfast. Pat pushed her pancakes toward Jack, ordered a side of toast, asked for extra cheese for her eggs, and proceeded to crumble the bacon strips into the scramble. This was a woman who liked to eat. My egg white omelet with fruit and dry English muffin seemed anemic by comparison. I picked at it while I turned the pages back and reviewed my notes from our first meeting.

"Pat, you said you thought John's murder was a drug killing."

She nodded, but waited until after she'd swallowed to respond. "The MO, sugar. The whole thing with the knife, the serrated blade, the through and through in the throat, lots of blood—that's Ottavio's signature."

"Ottavio?" Jack knew enough to be surprised.

"Who is this person?" I asked him.

"Ottavio Quevedo. The DEA boys call him Ottavio. Or just O."

"Spell it."

"Octavio, only with a double *t* and no *c*." I wrote it in my book. "Colombian drug lord. One of the more vicious strains of the disease."

"He's been a busy boy, too." The waitress had brought Pat's extra cheese and she was busy sprinkling it on her eggs. "He's duking it out with a bunch of Mexicans who have been trying to move in on his East Coast market. Stiffs have been piling up in Dumpsters all over town, all linked in some way to O and his gang."

"I didn't even know there were Mexicans in the market," I said.

"Oh, sugar, two of the most powerful drug cartels in

the world today are run out of Juarez and Tijuana. The Colombians are just not what they used to be. Medellín and Cali are shadows of their former selves."

"Correct me if I'm wrong on this, Patty, but the guerrilla armies run the drug trade in Columbia now—"

"They do."

"And Ottavio is lined up with them."

"That's right. He's got a whole damn drug army behind him, and they've got more firepower, more sophisticated equipment, and all around better toys than the official military." Pat had finished her eggs and was trying to get the top off a tiny container of grape jelly. It was a struggle. Her fingernails were too short. "So that's one big vote for a drug killing. The MO. And then there's the story Mr. Bob Avidor gave us."

"He's lying. He's lying about everything." I hadn't meant to be quite so curt, but I was annoyed by this drug accusation, by the *persistence* of an accusation I knew in the deepest part of my heart to be false. "I can't explain the MO, but I can tell you that John McTavish's life couldn't have been any further away from some international drug lord smackdown."

Pat had managed to peel back the foil top and was digging out the deep purple spread with a knife. "I didn't say I believed him. We haven't found anything linking the vic—John McTavish or his brother to drug activity. At least we hadn't by the time I had to give up the case. But Avidor is not your man. His alibi is good."

Jack had eaten half the pancakes before putting his utensils down and concentrating on his coffee. "What's the alibi, Patty?"

"He was over at the Broken Arrow playing pool until almost two a.m. with his boss, Phil Ryczbicki. The bartender identified them both. Called them Mutt and Mutt. He remembered them because Avidor asked him to find him a hooker."

I didn't even look up, just wrote down *Avidor. Hooker. After two a.m.* The more I learned about Bobby Avidor, the less I understood John's loyalty to him, notwithstanding the rescue of his brother.

Jack took it in stride. "Did he find him a hooker?"

"Officially, no. Off the record, he gave me her name."

"So," Jack said, "Avidor stayed with Ryczbicki until the boss went home, then bought himself an alibi."

"Correct. Avidor was seen by quite a few people after he left the bar getting a blow job in his car in the parking lot. Then he took the young lady home. She was with him the rest of the night."

I amended my notes. *Avidor. Hooker. Blow job.*

"He couldn't have been much more conspicuous," Jack said. "Did you show McTavish's picture around the bar? He left his hotel room to meet someone between ten on Monday night and one the next morning. That's one place he could have gone."

Pat gave him an exasperated glance. "Baby, with you gone from law enforcement, I don't know how we manage to stay out of our own way."

"I'm just asking—"

"I may not be the FBI, but I did manage to establish that neither one of those boys saw McTavish that night, and neither one killed him. Avidor was doing his thing and Ryczbicki went back to the airport and slept on the couch in his office. He was seen by several members of his staff."

I stared down at Ottavio's name in my notebook as if it were a code or anagram that might rearrange itself and give me some answers. It didn't, but it gave me a question.

"Here's a thought. It makes no sense to me that John was moving into drugs, but does it make sense that Ottavio could be moving into parts?"

"Parts?" Pat looked across the table at Jack and seemed gently amused. "Are you still chasing aircraft parts?"

"Old habits die hard. We heard there's been some crossover between the drug and bogus parts industries."

"Where did you get that?"

"I tapped Ira Leemer on the back of the head and that's what rolled out."

"Good lordy, I hope that's all that rolled out." She looked at me with eyes wide. "You might want to consider getting a tetanus shot."

"Patty, let me float a theory here and see what you think. Air Sentinel 634."

"What's that?"

"It's a triple seven that crashed down in Ecuador not long ago. We have reason to believe the crash might have been caused by a bad part or bad maintenance. If that's true, the Bureau would be all over it."

"So?"

"If Avidor had something to do with the crash and McTavish found out about it and was murdered for it, it makes his death crash related, which could explain why Hollander showed up to take your case."

"I just told you Avidor was otherwise occupied."

"He could have set him up. I saw him out at Jimmy Zacharias's place the other night. Jimmy might not have an alibi, and he's perfectly capable of jamming a blade through a man's throat."

Pat crossed her arms over her chest. It made her seem broader and more formidable. "What were you doing out there?"

"It's another case I'm working on. Avidor walked into it."

Pat stared at Jack with what looked like concern. "You need to stay away from Jimmy Zacharias, sweetie."

"He's the target of my investigation."

With her arms still crossed she looked like a fortress. "Because he's a legitimate suspect, or because you can't stand his skinny ass?"

"I hate his skinny ass, and he's a legitimate suspect."

There was a moment where something was supposed to be said and wasn't, and all that was left was a silence that felt particularly awkward between two people who obviously liked each other. Jack was inscrutable. Pat was giving away nothing in her expression, but she seemed to want to say something. It was no doubt something I would have loved to hear, because there was clearly a history between Jack and Jimmy Zacharias, one that was beginning to feel more and more significant to what we were doing. I wanted to know what it was. But I wasn't going to hear it from Pat Spain.

"Your theory about the plane crash is nice, baby, except for one thing. Damon Hollander is a drug man. Came down from New York not too long ago. Brought with him some high-level sources in the drug trade from what I hear. And he's working on a case right now that's got everyone's attention."

"What is it?"

"It's not a what, baby. It's a who."

"All right. Who?"

"Ottavio Quevedo. That's why he took my case. Not because of parts or some crash." She looked at me. "I wouldn't have told you this was a drug murder unless I thought it was. Personally, I think it's Avidor that's involved and your friend ended up being in the wrong place at the wrong time. I'm sorry, baby."

The three of us sat quietly. I closed my notebook. I couldn't think of anything else to say. Jack broke the silence. 'Patty, do me a favor and ask around a little. See if you can come up with anything about this crash or what Jimmy's up to these days."

"Ask around yourself. You've got a cell phone just like I do."

"The difference being you are still on the inside, and I am now on the outside."

"A distinction you'd best keep in mind, lover. I've been told in the quiet voice to stay away from this case. Why should I risk my job for you?"

"Because I bought you breakfast."

"These eggs weren't that good. And you ate my pancakes."

"Then do it because I never once treated you like Damon Hollander did."

"Let's take a walk," I said when we were out on the concourse. "I have some questions about what she said. Let's go check out Bic's operation."

We headed over to the Majestic concourse and cleared security. We found a spot near one of the gates where we could stand by the window and talk privately.

"I like your friend Pat," I said. "How did you get to know her?"

"We worked together on a task force once. She's good and she doesn't get the respect she deserves."

"She likes you."

"She's been a good friend."

"She seems worried about you."

He turned toward the window and ended up gazing into bright sunshine. Instead of turning back, he slipped on his sunglasses. "It's so clear today," he said. "You'd never know half the state was on fire."

"Jack, what is it between you and Jimmy Zacharias? And don't tell me he's just another scumbag."

He didn't even seem to have heard the question, but I decided to wait him out. "There are people in this world," he said finally, "who have no conscience, and he's one. He can do anything; he can do the worst things, and still get up in the morning and look himself in the mirror. That bothers me."

"I would venture to say that during your long career in law enforcement, you ran into more than one unrepentant criminal. What is it about *this* man?"

He left another long pause in the conversation. I figured he was trying to decide how much to tell me, and I was busy reacting to the idea that he would exclude me at all. I didn't want to be excluded. I liked him too much.

"What do you see," he asked, "when you look out there?"

"You mean on the ramp?"

"Yeah."

From where we stood we could see four, maybe five gates clearly, and there was an airplane being worked on each one. I scanned as I used to do in Boston, looking for any big problems. Saw none. I picked out one crew and watched as they loaded bags, boxes, parcels, and kennels from the cart to the belt loader to the belly.

"It's a tidy operation. The guidelines are all freshly painted. Everyone's in uniform, but that's easy. All they wear down here are short-sleeved shirts and pressed cotton shorts. It's hard to screw that up." I watched the crew working the flight. "They treat the oversized items with appropriate respect. Looks as if they have lots of

golf clubs and surfboards down here. In Boston we had
skis. Tractors, tugs, and carts are all painted, and parked
where they should be. I don't see any rust or broken
windshields. No debris lying around that could get
sucked into engines. Everyone's wearing their ear protec-
tors and their safety vests, and things seem to be moving
smoothly. Bic runs a good operation. I have to give
him that."

"You see things I would never see."

"That's my training. I've looked at a lot of ramps."

"And I've worked a lot of cases over a lot of years."
He took his glasses off and turned to face me and I
realized where he was going. He'd been a few steps
ahead of me. "What's between Jimmy and me has nothing to do with you. It has nothing to do with this case."
His voice caught. He cleared his throat and looked down
at the glasses in his hand. "I'm asking you to trust me
on that."

With his back to the sun, I had to squint to see what
I wanted to see. "When you talk about Jimmy, Jack, your
face changes. Your whole body reacts to the mention of
his name. Something that powerful has to affect what
you do and how you think, so I don't believe you when
you say it won't affect this case." His forehead bunched
and his chest rose and I could see the defensive response
forming around his eyes, so I hurried to finish the
thought. "But I trust you, Jack."

He shifted his weight to his other foot and looked
harder at me. He seemed to be searching for signs of
trickery. There were none. I wanted to know what was
going on. I wanted to stand there and wheedle, coerce,
or otherwise try to pry the story out of him, but it
wouldn't have worked. He was a locked safe on this subject and I didn't have the combination. Not yet.

"Good," he said. "Let's go see Mr. Avidor."

Chapter Seventeen

We found Bobby Avidor at the maintenance hangar. He stood with one balled fist on his soft hip as he stared up at the stabilizer of an MD-11, where two mechanics were working on a lift. When he saw us coming, he ignored me and spoke to Jack.

"Who are you?"

"Jack Dolan. I need to talk to you."

"What about?"

"John McTavish."

"Are you a cop?"

"Private." Jack had left his sunglasses on. He looked very cool when he said that.

Bobby looked at me. "Ryczbicki put me on the day shift."

"So I heard."

"What did you say to him?"

"Only that it was easier for us to find you on days. And he should keep an eye on you."

He didn't bother to conceal his contempt as he used his collar mike to radio the mechanics on the lift. He told them to let him know as soon as they'd found the problem.

We followed him into the hangar and up an exposed set of iron stairs to the admin areas on a second-floor landing. His office seemed like a palace compared to places I'd seen and worked in up on the line, but then hangar space wasn't quite as dear as airport terminal space.

His desk was tan metal with a laminated top. On top

was a carved wooden slat that read R. A. AVIDOR that could have come from a souvenir shop at Niagara Falls. A couple of guest chairs faced the desk. The only other major piece of furniture was a bookcase crammed with all sorts of binders and manuals. Proudly displayed on his cork bulletin board, among other things, was a postcard photo of three exotic women posed elbow to elbow on a sunny, sandy beach. The caption below their bare breasts read: "Wet and Wild in Hawaii."

Avidor unclipped the radio from his belt, took off the collar mike, and rested his thick hips against the arm of one of his guest chairs. "What can I do for you?"

"You can't do anything for me except listen to what I have to say to you." Jack still had the shades on. "You claim that John McTavish was here to bust up his brother's drug deal, but you made that story up to cover your own ass."

Avidor's laugh was like the nervous twitter of a teenager. He crossed his arms, which made his stomach pooch out even more over his chronically too-tight belt. "I don't know what you're talking about."

"You're in the business of dirty parts. We know that. And you're in business with Jimmy Zacharias. We know that, too."

"I don't know any Jim—"

"I saw you with him, so shut the fuck up and listen." Bobby fell silent.

"You know something about the crash of Air Sentinel 634. Maybe you even caused it. We know this because John McTavish had in his possession the logbook from that airplane, and a piece of jewelry that belonged to one of the victims."

"Where would Johnny get something like that?"

Jack sighed. Bobby didn't seem to be much of a challenge for him. "From you."

Bobby's normally active eyes looked like pinballs. "That's crap."

"You're the only connection that makes any sense," I said. "John found out what you did and came down to confront you. He probably threatened to turn you in."

Jack took a step closer to Bobby. "In my old line of work, we called that a motive."

"A motive for what?"

"For murder."

Bobby jerked up, walked around to his own side of the desk, and stood with his hands in his pockets. His big, high forehead was starting to flush. "I have an alibi."

"All that means is you weren't on the scene when it happened, but you did set him up. You called someone— my money's on Jimmy—and reported the situation. Then you got yourself an alibi, a good one, and proceeded to make up this ridiculous drug story. That's something I've always hated. Tarnishing the good name of a victim, a solid citizen who can't defend himself, just to save your own ass."

"That's not what I did."

Jack followed Bobby around to the other side of his desk and leaned against the inside edge. "There was no drug deal. There was a plane crash, and I think you had something to do with bringing it down. Sold a bad part . . . installed a bad part . . . the proof is in the logbook, isn't it?"

I watched Bobby closely. I figured Jack was throwing stuff at him to see what stuck. Bobby was lapsing into serious fidgeting—rubbing the ball of his thumb across his forehead, turning back and forth in the limited area behind his desk, trying not to trip over Jack's feet. "Last I saw Johnny McTavish, he was sitting up at the terminal drinking a cup of coffee. And I don't know anything about that plane crash, and I don't know anybody named Jimmy."

"Here's what I came to tell you, Bobby. You are way, way out of your league. You're a small-time dirty parts pusher who got mixed up with the big boys. Now you're in for a plane crash, a murder, and, if you're not careful, for the same thing that happened to McTavish. And I'll tell you why. John was only a threat to them because he knew you. And now that you have participated in his murder, you're an even bigger threat. In fact, I don't know why they didn't kill you instead of him. Maybe I'll ask Jimmy when I see him."

Bobby's expression froze. He wasn't even blinking.

"That's right." Jack said, "I know Jimmy better than you do. We go way back. I hate him and he hates me, and before this thing is over, you're going to find yourself squeezed between the two of us, and that's a bad place to be. You know what you should do, Bobby?"

If Bobby knew, he didn't say.

"Cut a deal while you still have the leverage, because depending on how much you know and when you knew it, you could be in line for the death penalty. We have that here in Florida, and we're not one of those pussy states that's afraid to use it."

Again, Bobby rubbed his thumb across his forehead. He adjusted his tie. He rocked back on his heels. And then he shook his head. "Any leverage I have I'll use where it counts and that's with the Feds, not you. You've got nothing to offer me."

Jack stood up and smiled down at him. "Call the cops. Call the Bureau. Call whoever you want. Just make your deal and don't take too long. And if you get stuck and you need help in trying to decide what to do, picture yourself bleeding to death in a Dumpster with a blade in your throat. See if that doesn't get you motivated to do the right thing."

Bic had provided a ride for us down to the maintenance hangar, but Bobby hadn't been so gracious as to provide return transportation. We were outside on foot, navigating the circuitous pedestrian route, since we weren't allowed to cut across the active ramp. We'd been walking a few minutes before Jack spoke again. "What did you get from that interview?"

"Besides the fact that Bobby Avidor is a loathsome pig?"

"Try to work around that."

"That would be tough."

"When you're talking to someone who may have done

a murder, or committed any crime, you're going to get a lot of subterfuge. You have to make yourself look past it for what's important. And you can't let it be personal. When I look at Bobby Avidor, I don't see the worthless piece of crap I know him to be."

"What do you see?"

"I see a man on the other side of a business transaction. He's got a piece of this puzzle I have to solve. He's the connection between John and Jimmy, and if Jimmy did kill John, that's a key piece. We'd be doing well to get him to talk to us."

"Won't Jimmy know that, too?"

"Jimmy knows," he said. "If he did kill John and Bobby knows it, I don't understand why Bobby is still walking around. Jimmy doesn't leave loose ends."

"Maybe Jimmy still needs him for something."

He reached up and took his glasses off. "Maybe," he said, wiping the sweat from his eyes, "he just hasn't gotten around to this particular loose end."

Watching him sweat made me realize how hot I was. I lifted my hair off the back of my neck and held it up, waiting for a cool breeze. "So our job is to first help Bobby define his options, and then to help him see that we're the best one."

He smiled. "Exactly. And hope he's smart enough to make his choice before it's too late."

"How does Bobby know the FBI has this case? He didn't even mention the local police."

"Another good point," he said. "I plan to ask Patty if she told him. If she didn't, he might have been contacted by this Agent Hollander."

My cell phone rang. I flipped it open to answer, saw that the call was from Detroit. "What day is this?"

"Friday."

"Uh-oh." I flipped it closed without answering. My heart pounded out the classic I-overslept-for-the-exam panic.

"What's the matter?"

"I'm supposed to start my new job on Monday."

"Your new job?"

"Yeah. I sort of forgot about it, but I'm due in Detroit on Monday." I'd quickened the pace so much that even Jack, with his long legs, was having a hard time keeping up.

"Alex, you forgot you were supposed to start a new job?"

"I've been distracted. Can I catch up with you later, Jack? I have to go and take care of this thing."

When he didn't answer, I turned to find that he had stopped and was several paces behind me. Then I realized it was because I'd broken into a full-fledged trot. The good news was my ankle was feeling much better. I jogged back to him.

"How are you going to take care of it?"

"I'm not sure. I have to go make some calls. But you can use my car if you need it. You know where it is."

I started to reach for the keys, but he waved me off. "Call me later when you've got your life worked out. I can't wait to hear this story."

Chapter Eighteen

"**W**ow." I appraised the crowd. It spilled out the door and snaked halfway down the block. "I would like to eat sometime tonight."

"Don't worry." Jack put his hand on my back and led me past the line. The guy at the door—I wouldn't exactly call him a maitre d'. More like a bouncer—stuck out his hand the minute he saw Jack. "Hey, man," he yelled, "good to see you back."

Jack returned the gesture and leaned in so he could be heard. "Can you help me out tonight, Al?"

Al glanced at me. "Two?"

Jack nodded and we were in. I'm sure I felt more than one laser stare into the back of my head from the poor schmoes at the door who had to wait their turn.

Al took us through the small dining room, a bright, noisy place. Waiters and cooks were yelling over the serving bar. There was a lot of clanging—silverware on plates, plates going into the dishwasher, dishes shoved onto the counter. Several patrons in bibs worked on crab claws and lobsters. And there was lots of skin showing. This was the kind of place people came to in boats. Indeed, when we emerged onto the deck, I spotted a whole line of boats tied up in the boat parking lot, or whatever you call it.

"You sit over here." Jack held a chair for me, the one that faced the water. "That way you don't have to sit and stare at me all night."

The waiter came right over as we took our seats. He

greeted Jack as if they were a couple of old pals and left two large plastic menus. When the waiter left, Jack was grinning.

"What are you smiling at?"

He shrugged as he unfolded his napkin. "I like this place."

"I guess so. I've never seen a red carpet rolled out so fast. How come they know you so well here?"

"I did one of the owners a favor once when I was on the job."

"Is Al the owner?"

"Al's his nephew. Ike and his brother Bernie own the place. It's been in their family for fifty years." He kicked at the splintering deck. "It hasn't changed much in all that time, either."

"What did you do for them?"

"Bernie likes to gamble. Ponies, dogs, football, basketball, jai alai—you name it. He got into some trouble once on some money he owed. He was about to have his liquor license yanked. I helped him work out a deal where he got to keep it if he paid off all his debts and entered a twelve-step program, which he did. It all worked out."

"That was a nice thing you did."

"Hey, I didn't want them going belly-up. They have the best stone crabs in town."

"It was still a nice thing you did."

He stared down at his plate, then rolled back in his chair and gazed out across the deck. Jack never seemed to know what to do with a compliment. "I hate these wildfires," he said. "But the smoke sure makes for some beautiful sunsets."

I opened the menu and checked out Bernie and Ike's offerings. A few items cooked simply. I liked it. "What is a stone crab anyway?"

He leaned forward and settled into a lecture pose. This was a subject he could obviously warm to. "It's a special kind of crab with huge claws. That's the only part you can eat. If you see one it looks like a couple of huge claws with this tiny crab body attached."

"What makes them so special?"

"Wait until you taste one."

"What makes them so expensive?" According to the menu, an eight-crab-leg dinner was almost twenty dollars.

"They're protected. It used to be you could walk out the back door and pick them up off the beach around here. Development pushed them south, so now you only find them in the Keys and along the Gulf Coast."

The waiter returned and we ordered. With a build up like that, I had no choice but to order the specialty of the house, the stone crab plate. I also ordered a beer, a compulsive move since I rarely drank beer. But it seemed like the only drink possible on a balmy early spring evening in Florida with stone crabs on the way.

Jack ordered club soda. When our drinks came, he took the straw out and settled back in his chair with it. "So, tell me about this job you forgot you had."

"I didn't forget I had a job. I lost track of what day it was."

"Airline job?"

"I'll be the Vice President of Operations for a start-up in Detroit."

"That's impressive."

"We have two airplanes," I said. "Everyone but the president is a vice president."

"Will you be doing something you like?"

"I'll be working like a dog. My already limited social life will shrivel up and die. I'll be running the field operation, which is the part of the business I love, but I have to do it from headquarters, which is the part of the business I hate. I'll live in Detroit and I'm not sure how to feel about that." My entire body blanched at the very thought of one of those wicked winds skidding across the Great Lakes. "I've never been to the city, only the airport. It is a good sports town."

"Sounds like a great job," he said in a complete deadpan.

"But . . . ?"

"But nothing."

"This is the perfect job for me. I'll love it. Why are

you saying I won't? Are you saying I shouldn't take this job?" I twisted in my chair and fortified with a sip of beer. It was cold and quenching and had definitely been the right call. "I've already accepted. They've turned off all their other candidates. I can't do that to them. Sure, they gave me another week, but only because I begged and pleaded and they didn't have any better alternative. I've probably already damaged their confidence in me, and I don't know when I'll be able to reschedule my move. I'm going to have to put everything in storage."

He set his drink on the table and crossed his hands in his lap.

"All right. The truth is, I've had a hard time being unemployed. It's been scary. I've always worked. I don't know what to do with myself when I don't work."

"You're doing something now."

"I'm not earning money. I need money. My severance is gone. I'm using the last of my savings to be down here. What if I get sick? I need health insurance and disability coverage and a retirement plan. I have to work. There's no one to take care of me."

"There's no one to take care of anyone. In the end we all take care of ourselves. Some do it better than others. Don't say you're taking this job because you need an income or benefits. There are lots of ways to earn money. You don't have to do what you've always done."

"I need structure." I used my finger to draw a line in the condensation on my beer glass. A straight line. "I like structure."

"I noticed. What I'm saying is to build your own structure. You're smart enough. You don't have to take the easy way out."

He smiled. I brooded, because he was on to something. I'd never been excited by the Detroit opportunity, and accepting the offer had felt like agreeing to move back home with my parents. There had to be something to the fact that I had forgotten about it. Completely.

"Look at it this way," he said. "If you really wanted that job in Detroit, why would you be sitting on a deck in Florida?"

I was left to ponder that question as the waiter served up our dinner. There was barely enough room on the table for the two big plates. The claws, as advertised, were huge. They were served cold with coleslaw on the side, a big basket of assorted rolls that smelled homemade, lots of drawn butter, and a metal pail for the refuse.

I waited until the waiter left to lean over and ask Jack, "Are they always served already cracked like this?"

He had already plowed in and was sucking a piece of meat from a tiny crevice in one of the big claws. "Unless you travel around with your own ball-peen hammer, I don't know how you'd get them open. Feel how hard the shell is."

The shell was indeed as hard as any I'd ever encountered, but not being a crustacean connoisseur, that didn't mean much to me. And it didn't matter anyway once I started to eat because he was right. Stone crabs were well worth the trouble. The meat was tender and sweet and firm—a rare and delightful experience, especially with all that drawn butter, and most especially when eaten on an open-air deck in good company and the presence of a violet sunset.

Jack tossed a shard of crab shell into the bucket. "Let's review the case," he said. "Start from the beginning."

"Me?"

"I want to see what you're writing down, what you're paying attention to."

A test. A challenge. That was all I needed to hear. I wiped off my fingers—eating stone crabs was a messy business; you had to peel off the shell with your fingers and dig out the meat. I pulled out my little notebook and flipped to the first page. "Okay. John flew down to Miami on Monday March fifth from Boston and arrived in the early afternoon. He met Bobby Avidor for a cup of coffee. Bobby says they talked about Terry's drug deal. I say John was here to confront him on parts. Whatever they talked about, John left for The Harmony House Suites and Bobby made sure he had a good alibi for the night. He asked Phil Ryczbicki out for a drink. They stayed out until after two. After that, Mr. Avidor was observed in the parking lot enjoying a blow job in the front seat of his car.

"John checked in at The Harmony House Suites, did normal hotel things. Sometime after ten he left his room. He came back just before one in the morning. Wherever he went and whomever he saw, he heard something that worried him enough to call his brother in the middle of the night and assign him to look after his family. And he told them he was coming home. Sometime after that call and before six, he disappeared. Someone packed his things and returned his rental car so he wouldn't be reported missing." I flipped back to my notes from the first discussion with Pat Spain. "John's body was found on Wednesday in a Dumpster. He was killed someplace else and left there. None of his valuables were missing, and the murder weapon has not been recovered. Since then, we've established that Avidor is in the bogus parts business, probably with your pal Jimmy Zacharias, and that John was in possession of the logbook from an airplane that crashed in Ecuador. He had a diamond ring from the same crash. I think those are the high points . . ." I thumbed through the notes. "Oh, and the FBI has an interest in this case for reasons unknown."

"I think their interest has to do with the crash," he said.

"Why?"

Jack put down the claw he'd been working on to go for some bread. "I tried to reach Damon Hollander today. I was told he would be 'unavailable for several months and could someone else help me?' "

"That's no way to do business. What's that all about?"

"I suspect he doesn't want to talk to us, but the really strange thing was no matter who I spoke to over there, whenever I brought up the Sentinel crash, the conversation stopped dead. There is definitely something going on that no one wanted to tell me about."

"Can someone else help us? Don't you have any buddies over there like Pat who will give you the inside scoop?"

"No. Listen to this. Patty called me back. There's a group of detectives that work out of the airport station that specialize in crimes against the airlines. She asked around and found out they also had a case that was recently yanked out from under them by the Bureau. It's a repair station that they suspect is moving dirty parts. They think it's one of Jimmy's places. Guess who took the case?"

"Damon Hollander? He's supposed to be a drug guy. Why would he be interested in them? Unless it has something to do with John's murder."

"Exactly." He picked up the claw he'd been working on and resumed peeling.

"This is good," I said. "It feels like progress." I picked up my pencil. "What's the name of this repair station?"

"Speath Aviation."

"Speath?" I grabbed my notepad and felt that tingling thrill that meant something was about to fall together in a way that would make me warm all over. "I know that name."

"How?"

"Because Felix . . ." I couldn't find the page I needed.

"Who's Felix?"

"He's the kid I told you about who works at The Harmony House Suites. He's been trying to identify the cars in the hotel parking lot the night of the murder." I explained the low-tech security system and Felix's idea about finding cars that weren't supposed to be there.

"He found some?"

"Yeah, he called me back. I talked to him just before I came over here. Here it is." I'd written the notes on the back of a page. "He got two hits. A black Volvo registered to The Cray Fund, which is an investment firm here in town. And the second one was a green Subaru Forester. It belongs to a George Speath."

I looked over at Jack. He was leaning in, listening intently, holding his buttered fingers in the air like a surgeon. "That's him," he said. "He runs Speath Aviation. He was at the hotel the night of the murder?"

"He was there and not checked in or he would have had a placard in his windshield." I scanned my notes. I'd been writing so fast to keep up with Felix, they were almost illegible. I'd had to make him stop and take several deep breaths. But now I was starting to feel the same way. "Heavy aircraft maintenance facility. Been in business twenty-eight years. Started by a guy named Howard Speath and now operated by his son George—"

"Who was at the scene of the murder," Jack said, "and is being investigated by the FBI." He seemed more satisfied than excited, as if he knew we were running a marathon and I was trying to sprint. But I had a deadline.

"We have to talk to him," I said. "Tomorrow. This Speath sounds like the key to everything."

"Hold on. Slow down. Drink your beer and let's talk about this."

I sipped my beer, but hardly tasted it. My mind was going too fast and my sense of urgency had been heightened considerably by my discussion with Paul Gladstone. I had one week and one week only. There would be no more extensions on the Detroit job after that.

"From what Patty told me, it sounds as if George Speath is part of the business community and has never had any trouble with the FAA or the law. He's not the usual kind of partner who hooks up with Jimmy."

"So?"

"If he's not a pro, and the detectives don't think he is, then we might be able to turn him easier than we could Avidor. I want to find out a few things about him before we go blowing into his business."

"Like what?"

"This is the investigation part, Alex. We'll talk to some of the employees. Check out his inspection records. Talk to the FAA, vendors—"

"I don't have an unlimited amount of time down here, Jack. Or cash. The clock is ticking."

"It takes as long as it takes."

The motor on a boat kicked in behind me. I stared up into the palm trees. "Do you know if Speath does work for any of the major airlines?"

"Probably. Why?"

"I have a better idea." I pulled out my cell phone. "I have a guaranteed way to gain total access to his business."

"Without him knowing?"

"With his enthusiastic assistance. All I need is a little help from Bic."

The restaurant was even more crowded when we left. Jack put his hand on my shoulder to guide me through the ever-burgeoning group thronged around the door. It was one big party out on the sidewalk. Blonde women and tan men with big plastic cups of beer swirled around each other. It was later in the evening, so this was the crowd that had already drunk their way through happy hour and was out in search of something to eat. They were raucous. They were ribald. They were all having a good time.

After we'd made it through the gauntlet, Jack moved his hand to the small of my back, and kept it there as we crossed the street to my car. He'd touched me before, but this felt different. Purposeful. I liked the way it felt, and it started me thinking about how his hands would feel in other places.

He took my keys and opened the door for me. I turned and we stood for a moment and I looked at his face as if I had never seen it. I saw the curve of his mouth. How warm his brown eyes could be. And there was something else in his eyes. A connection. An attraction. That he was thinking what I was thinking, too. It was thrilling and unexpected and stimulating on so many levels and I wanted—

"I'm going to take a cab home," he said, stepping away.

"I'll . . ." I had to stop myself from stepping with him. "I'll drive you home."

"It's a long way out of your way. You should go home and take care of that ankle."

My ankle? I hadn't been thinking about my ankle. Is that what he'd been thinking? I looked into his face again. There was something there. There was a lot there. I was getting so I could read him, but there was too much for me to work out without a few clues from him. He didn't seem willing to offer them.

"I'll talk to you tomorrow, then?"

"Yeah." He turned and went back toward the restaurant, presumably to get Al to call him a cab. I looked for him as I drove by, but the crowd had swallowed him up.

Chapter Nineteen

Speath Aviation was expecting me. I could tell, not because anyone was there in the small reception space to greet me—there wasn't—but because of the letter board sign standing just inside the door. It had WELCOME and my name spelled out in magnetic white letters, only they must have been short on *n*s because the last one in SHANAHAN was a sideways *z*. But that was the only thing that appeared to be improvised in the neat, carefully ordered offices. The rubber tile floors were scrubbed. The bulletin boards on the pale yellow walls were hung with directives and reminders and alerts that were carefully spaced and clearly visible. Lining one wall was a row of twelve five-drawer file cabinets. All sixty drawers had typed labels.

That's what businesses look like when they're expecting an audit. It had taken one more day than I would have liked, but due in large part to Bic's assistance, Speath Aviation was expecting an auditor dispatched by Majestic Airlines to check them out for possible overhaul work. They had been encouraged to provide full access. To everything. I was about to embark on my first undercover assignment.

Something caught my eye at the end of a short hallway. There was a door there that seemed to lead out to the hangar. The door had a window about chin high, the kind with safety glass. I wasn't sure, but I could have sworn I'd seen a man looking through it at me. A man wearing a cap. A baseball cap. It was one of those deals where the second I saw him—or thought I saw him—he vanished.

"Miss Shanahan?" I turned to find a large block of a man lunging toward me with his big, outstretched hand. His face was as wide as a stop sign, his features emphatically blunt, and shaking his hand was like trying to grip the wrong end of a Ping-Pong paddle. "I'm George Speath. I'm sorry to have kept you waiting."

"I just got here."

"Good. Did Margie take care of you?"

"Margie?"

I gazed about the empty office. A cup of hot coffee on a desk steamed in silent testimony to the fact that someone had been there recently, but not since I'd arrived. George looked around when I did and seemed to notice for the first time that we were alone.

"Shoot." He gave himself a verbal smack in the forehead. "Sorry. Margie must be in the back. Can I get you anything? Coffee? Tea? Cookies? We usually have these really good butter cookies. They don't look like much, but I can't stop eating them. I wish she wouldn't buy them, but she does."

"No, thank you. I'm fine for now."

"Okay. Well, then . . ." He started to lead the way out of the reception area to a long hallway, but then in a gesture that seemed both courtly and awkward, stepped aside and let me go first. As I passed, I felt again the presence of someone watching me. I took a quick look at that door with the window. Nothing.

George's office had the low-ceilinged feel of someone's basement family room. A Foosball table wouldn't have been out of place in the corner. Hung on the walls in inexpensive and mismatched frames were pictures of George and various people, and George and various airplanes. He looked happiest with the airplanes.

"Now," he said, standing in the middle of the durable, rust-colored carpet and rubbing those big hands together, "where would you like to begin?"

"First let me apologize for the extremely short notice, and I'm sorry to get you in here on a Sunday."

"That's no problem at all. We work seven days a week here."

"I assume you've talked to Mr. Ryczbicki," I said.

"He called me yesterday. He's a nice fellow, isn't he?"

"Yes, he is." Bic must have really laid it on thick. "Maybe you could tell me what he's told you so we don't have to cover the same ground." When telling a lie, always best to see what has already been communicated by your coconspirator.

"Sure, sure. Whatever you want." He gestured for me to sit, then eschewed his big desk chair to settle across from me. The couch he sat on was too low for his frame, putting his knees almost up around his ears.

"Mr. Ryczbicki said he was interested in asking us to bid on overhaul work for Majestic Airlines, mainly overflow situations. He's having trouble handling the volume, and he's hired you to do a pre-audit to make sure we're in compliance with FAA and Majestic standards."

"Just so there's no confusion," I said, "I'm not an employee of Majestic Airlines. I'm an independent auditor, and I'm not affiliated with the FAA, so you don't have to worry. Whatever I find here is between you and Mr. Ryczbicki and me."

George put his hands up, palms out, and shook his head. "You're not going to find anything out of order. Needless to say, Miss Shanahan, this is very exciting news for us. We'd be so pleased to work with Majestic. We'd do a good job. I think I can convince you of that while you're here."

"Good." I pulled a pad and pen from my backpack. I was trying to look like an auditor, but I felt like an imposter, and the nicer he was to me, the more false my false persona felt. "I'd like to start by asking you a few questions."

He sat forward on the couch, ready to rumble. "Fire away."

"I understand your father started this business. Is that right?"

He smiled, revealing a crooked lower front tooth. "How did you know that?"

"I did my homework." Actually, Felix had done all the work. "When did you join him?"

"Seventeen months ago. After he'd already left. I was working at Honeywell when he began thinking about selling, so I talked him into letting me run it. He started five different businesses over the course of his career, and do you know he made successes out of every one? Five different industries, too." His expression was quizzical, as if he'd been studying this phenomenon for years and still hadn't cracked the code.

"Is he still involved here?"

"Oh, no. He's busy with a group of college kids that are starting up one of those dot-com companies. I'm not even sure what it is they do." He nudged his silver aviators farther up the bridge of his nose. "I always was more comfortable with a product I could touch and feel." He held up his big hands as if he were cradling a crankshaft between them. "I like standards. I like things I can measure."

"Is your father still involved in your business?"

"No." A rueful smile flashed and disappeared. "He doesn't have much time for aviation parts and repairs anymore."

Nor for his plodding son, I imagined. So far, it was hard not to like George.

I asked him questions from the list Bic and I had made up, things he and I had agreed we'd want to know about any business doing repair work on our airplanes. It was a long list. George answered every question thoroughly, but not succinctly, and a full hour had passed before I'd realized it.

"I'd like to see your operation now, George. Can we do that?"

"Sure. What do you need?"

"I'll need to take a look at all your certifications, all of your procedures for ordering, tracking, and receiving parts. I want to see your file of FAA directives. I'd like to take a look at your accounting system, your inventory system, and I want to talk to the person who receives your parts. I also need a list of customers."

"That's very thorough."

"Majestic has requested a full audit. They're selective about who works on their airplanes. And they only work from a list of approved vendors."

"I sure hope we can get on that list."

"Oh." I'd been scanning my list again. "How about a business plan. Do you have something like that? Something recent?"

He was up and to his desk across the room in two long strides. "I've got exactly what you need. I made up a business plan for the bank. For a loan I needed." He rummaged around, looking first through a thick stack on top of the desk. Then he turned and thumbed through a pile at eye level on one of his built-in shelves. Finally, he punched a button on the phone.

"Margie, do you have my copy . . . *any* copy of the business plan?"

A voice came right back. "You have them all in there with you, George."

"Where? I can't find them." George was now down on his knees behind his desk. "Margie?" His voice grew muffled as he dipped down and his head disappeared behind the desk. "They're not in the drawer."

There was no response until the office door flew open and a woman—Margie, I presumed—stepped in. She stood for a moment with her hands on her hips, sizing up the situation. I could tell right away that she was a gold woman, although a younger version of this new species that I'd discovered in Florida.

Gold women usually had blonde hair, and however they chose to wear it, it always looked as if it had been painted over with clear fingernail polish. Their lipstick was lighter than their tanned faces, which were usually on the way to leathery, and they could never wear enough gold jewelry. The most evolved of the gold woman species, usually women in their late fifties or early sixties, had additional coordinating accessories such as gold handbags and shoes.

Margie had all the basics, including a pair of hose that

made her long, tan legs a shade darker, but not too dark to dull her pedicure, which was shown to good advantage by the open toes of her high-heeled shoes. She walked on those very high heels across the office and straight for the credenza. "Move your feet, George."

He did as he was told. She opened a cabinet, pulled out a thick spiral-bound document, and handed it to him with a look that said, "Honestly, George." On her way back around the desk, she punched a button on his phone and hung up on herself.

George got to his feet—being a big man, none too gracefully—and started thumbing through his business plan. "Margie, did you meet Miss Shanahan?"

She looked at me with hazel eyes that shone brightly against nutmeg brown skin. "I must have been out in the hangar when you came in. You're the auditor?"

"Yes."

"I keep all the books, and I'm the only one around here who understands the filing system, so just ask me for anything you need. I'm usually out front, but if you can't find me, I'm back in the hangar with the boys. Just yell out there for me."

"Okay. Thanks."

She was as crisp, almost to the point of being brusque, and as direct as George was meandering. They probably made a good pair. She left me with George, who handed me the business plan. Then he stood, looking as if he were waiting for direction.

"Shall we go through your operation, George?"

"By all means."

He walked me through his operation. He had a reasonably large facility, with seventy-five employees working three shifts. I did a quick scan for the baseball cap. Everyone I saw had one on. They appeared to be standard issue at Speath, so I assumed whoever had been staring at me from outside the door had been a curious employee.

The main part of his space was a huge hangar where he did engine, airframe, and structural work. George made an effort to introduce me to as many employees as he could as we walked around. Everyone seemed happy to see him, and the ones that were too far away made a point of waving or shouting a greeting.

"Is this your only facility?" I asked him.

"This is it. This is all I need. Watch out." His arm shot toward me in a move so quick I reacted without thinking. I jerked away from him, but not far enough. I felt his big hand on my back, nudging me forward a few steps.

"What?" I pulled farther away. "What are you doing?"

He pointed to a still wet, white grainy splat on the ground, perilously close to where I'd been standing. "Pigeons. That was a close one." He tilted his head back to search the rafters for the perpetrator of the poop bombing.

I looked up to where he'd been looking, intending to gaze sternly at the feathered offender, but what I saw was an entire squad perched overhead on the exposed steel struts. I had to settle for a blanket squinty-eyed condemnation.

George sighed. "We can't get rid of them."

I thought back to my own experience with hangars and pigeons. "Have you tried owls?"

"Look over there."

He put his hand on my back again and, as if he were turning a telescope, redirected my line of sight until I saw what he was pointing at. It was a fat, dark gray, in-your-face pigeon that had chosen the head of one of George's plastic owls as a perch.

"Tough birds," I said.

"It's a problem. Most of my guys make sure to keep their hats on when they're out on the floor. Would you like one? I recommend it if you're going to be out here."

"Sure."

George snapped the radio off his belt and raised Margie. She appeared almost immediately to deliver one of the heavy-duty black baseball caps with the Speath logo on the front and SPEATH AVIATION stitched in red across the back.

"What are you doing?" George stared at my hands as

I rolled and shaped the bill of the cap, something I did without even thinking.

"I'm—" I started to say "making it less geeky-looking." Instead, I said, "I'm making it more comfortable. It's a great hat." I put it on and smiled at him. "Thank you, George."

He stepped back and regarded me with a bashful grin. The nicer he was to me, the worse I felt for lying. If George Speath was a bogus parts dealer, he had to be the kindest, most gentlemanly one ever. "It suits you," he said. "Come outside. I want to show you something."

I was glad for the hat as I followed him out onto the ramp. It kept the direct sunlight off my face, although it didn't help much with the sneaky rays that bounced off the concrete and ricocheted back up. But I forgot all about them when I got a glimpse of what he was so excited about.

It was an old twin-engine prop, with a polished aluminum skin that looked as fresh as if it had rolled out of the factory that morning. It had no logo or other markings, only an elegant maroon stripe that followed the classic lines of the fuselage, down both sides, and all the way to the tail. Powerful propellers fronted the engines, one each on elegant wings spread beneath the sun.

"Pretty impressive, isn't it?" George couldn't have been more excited if he had just given me my first glimpse of the Grand Canyon. And to be honest, for me it was almost as dazzling a sight.

"It sure is. Is it an Electra?"

He turned and looked at me with a new appreciation. "You know your airplanes. It's a Lockheed L. 12 Electra. They used one just like it in *Casablanca*. Or so the legend goes. I think they just used a cardboard version."

I made a complete circle, walking around the aircraft and taking in the grand sight. The aircraft sat on the tarmac with all the poise and presence of a movie star from the 1930s. Sleek and glamorous, it was definitely out of its time and place, but there was nothing about it that was faded. "This is . . . this is great, George. What are you doing with it?"

"I'm restoring it for an aviation museum out in Kansas City. I'd take you into the cabin, but it's a little dicey in there. We haven't even started the interior."

"What does it seat?"

"Six passengers and two crew. The engines are Pratt & Whitney 985 Wasps. She was built in 1936, and do you know there are some still being used today? This one will fly when I'm through with it. I'm going to take her up myself."

"You're a pilot?"

"I've got my own plane," he said. "But it doesn't come close to this baby." He walked over and put his hand flat against the throat of the aircraft and held it there as if he were calming a wild horse. "Can you picture one of these Electras," he said, "propellers spinning, flying around the world in a trip that might take weeks and make a dozen stops? Those were the days, huh? They must have been, anyway." He gazed up at the airplane, squinting into the bright sun, and his smile was bittersweet. "Sometimes," he said, "I think I was born in the wrong time."

"How did it go?" Jack was at the other end of the line. I was in my car. We were cell phone to cell phone.

"George Speath is a very nice man," I said. "He gave me a nifty hat." I checked it out again in the rearview mirror. It really was a nice hat.

"Are you telling me," Jack said, "you've already been compromised as an undercover operative?"

"As far as I can tell, George Speath runs a good shop. His documentation is all in order. His inventory and his stockroom are well organized and properly secured. He deals with the same vendors over and over, only the ones he knows. His receiving procedures are layers thick with checks and double checks to make sure the part he's getting is the one he ordered. I talked to his FAA inspector, who loves him. Every employee I talked to loves him. His customers love him. Either he's too nice to be a crook, or he's too crafty for me to catch him."

"And he was at the murder scene and he's being

looked at by the Bureau. There has to be something there."

"I wish we could find Agent Hollander and ask him what it is."

I searched the side of LeJeune Road for the Miami Sub Shop I'd designated for dinner.

"I've left several more messages for him," he said. "Patty has tried to reach him for me."

"Why don't we just go over to the FBI offices?"

"I told you he's not working out of the offices. He's set up off-site somewhere. If he doesn't want to be found, we're not going to find him. I know that better than anyone."

"You do? Did you used to hide when you were an agent?"

"I'm trying to tell you we shouldn't count on getting anything from Hollander, and I don't think we should give up on George. He's the best lead we've got so far."

"I'm not giving up. I'm on my way over to see Felix now." I found the sub shop. It was, of course, on the other side of the street and nowhere near a left turn lane. I was going to have to go down, turn around, and come back, which made me reevaluate whether it was worth it. There was always sushi at the hotel. Or the California Pizza Kitchen in the food court on Concourse F. I decided to skip it and went on to The Harmony House Suites, which was starting to feel like my home away from home away from home.

"Felix," he said. "Is that the hotel kid?"

"He's a hacker who happens to work at the hotel. I think he can help me with a little research I want to do. Where are you? Do you want to meet me here?"

"I've been out looking for Ira. He's gone AWOL. No one's seen him."

"That sounds bad." I pulled into a space and turned off the engine, which made it much easier to make out what he was saying.

"Maybe not. Ira can make himself scarce when he wants to. It could be he just doesn't want to talk to me."

"Are you going to keep looking?"

"No, I'm beat. I'm going home."

I felt a sinking disappointment that I was going to spend a whole day without seeing Jack. "Don't forget our appointment tomorrow," I said. "I'll come by and pick you up."

"What's tomorrow?"

"We have a ten o'clock appointment at The Cray Fund offices downtown."

"The financial people."

"Right. Their car was in the lot that night as well."

"Waste of time," he said. "Waste of time."

"You're the one who said we should keep all the possibilities open."

Chapter Twenty

It was dinnertime at The Harmony House Suites and the lobby was crowded with conference goers turned loose from their white tablecloths, cold Danish, and flip charts. Felix was easy to spot and not just because of his bleach-tipped hair. It was the way he moved, shambling through the crowd all floppy and loose-limbed like a young bird dog.

I fell in step behind him. "Felix Melendez Jr."

He spun around, ready to be of service to whoever needed him. "Yes, can I help—Miss *Shan*ahan." He took a step back and broke into that loopy grin. "What are you doing here?"

"I came to see you. Are you on your way somewhere?"

"It can wait." He stuffed his hands in his pockets and kept grinning, his head bobbing like a cork in mild seas.

"Felix, could we go somewhere where we can talk?"

"Oh. Oh, sure. Sorry." A hint of subversive curiosity stole into his eyes. "Somewhere private?"

"That would be good."

"There's someone using my office right now." He stood on his toes, craned his long neck, and searched every corner of the lobby. "Um, how about the health club? I can see it from here and it's empty."

"Lead the way."

The health club at The Harmony House Suites was like most hotel health clubs—a sorry collection of mismatched workout equipment picked out of catalogues by people who've never seen a sweat towel. The centerpiece was the obligatory Universal gym, the kind with myriad hooks and ropes and attachments that combined to give you four hundred different exercises. There was one old treadmill with a fraying belt, a couple of dumbbells in the corner, a slant bench, and two stair climbers.

Felix went straight to the thermostat—someone had left the air conditioner on full blast—mumbling about conservation and the destruction of the environment. I found the remote for the TV and muted the soap opera rerun. We came together at the Universal gym, where he draped his arms over a dangling straight bar.

"Would you like to do some work for me, Felix?"

His eyes widened and it's possible his spiky hair actually stood up a little straighter on his head. "Are you *ser*ious?"

"I can pay you a little, not much—"

"Wow!" He let go of the bar, causing it to swing perilously toward my head as he darted around. "I'd do it for free. *Wait!*" He stopped and patted himself down, searching his shirt pocket, suit jacket, and pants pockets, front and back. "I don't have anything to write with. We should go—"

I pulled out my pad, jotted down what he needed, ripped out the page, and handed it to him.

He read what I had written. "Speath Aviation." He nodded. "The dude whose car was in the lot the night Mr. McTavish was killed." I could feel Felix's enthusiasm rising as his voice dropped inversely. "Is he a suspect in the murder of your friend?"

"Don't know yet. I want to take a close look at his business from the inside out. You've also got the password there, which George says should provide full access to all of his systems."

"Cool. What are we looking for?"

"We think it's possible he's been laundering bogus parts through his business."

"*Way* cool." He stuck his thumbnail between his teeth, and I could see the wheels spinning. Fast. "Okay, okay." He started moving around the room, taking large steps in the small space, changing course every time he was about to smack into something. He rubbed his forehead. He took long, deep breaths. He talked to himself. "Parts, parts, parts."

Then he stopped. "What's a bogus part?"

I explained to Felix about how there were people in the world who made a living making, stealing, and selling used, damaged, counterfeit, and otherwise substandard parts to people and businesses—including commercial airlines—that unwittingly purchased them and installed them on their aircraft. He listened in rapt attention until I was finished, at which point he blinked and said, "That is harsh."

"Way harsh," I said. "I thought you could do that thing you do with your computer and see what you can come up with."

"That means inventory," he said. "And vendors. You're probably looking for who they buy from, who they sell to, background checks on the employees. I can roll through their inventories and figure out what they've purchased and sold in the past few months. Maybe get you copies of corporate ledgers, check registers, purchase orders, invoices, lists of accounts payable and accounts receivable, customer files. Is this a public company? No, private. I saw that when I looked him up. Okay, but someone does their books. I can find out who and possibly get in that way." He looked at me, face open and eager as if to ask, how am I doing?

Pretty darn well if you compared his list of specific ideas to my sketchy list of questions. Of course, I was limited by the fact that I didn't think like a hacker.

"Cut the data however you think it makes sense and see what you can come up with."

I looked up to see a man in track shorts, ratty shirt, and running shoes walking through the lobby and coming our way, clearly intending to work out. I remembered that John had worked out in this room. I looked around again at the equipment and wondered when I'd stopped thinking about him as a person, as a friend, and had started thinking about him as everyone else in Florida did—as

McTavish, murder victim and case number. The thought of him, the feeling of his strong presence left in the room like sweat on the machines, caught me by surprise and pulled me into a sad place. I decided I needed to call Mae. I hadn't been talking enough to Mae.

"Miss Shanahan?" Felix was looking at me as if he had noticed something, but was too shy to comment. Or wouldn't know what to say. How old was this kid, anyway? Twenty? Twenty-two? I almost didn't want to know, didn't want to think how tender was the age at which I was introducing him to one of the more corrupt and sordid elements of a business he was trying to be excited about, and I was still trying to love.

"You still have my card with my phone number, don't you, Felix?"

"I scanned it in." Of course he had.

"Look specifically for any indication that Speath ever did work for Air Sentinel," I said. "He claims no, but I still want to check."

"Why?"

"There's a possibility, and I have nothing to prove this, that his shop could have installed a bad part or in some other way caused a plane crash."

"Oh." He thought about that, and seemed to come to terms with it rather quickly. "Okay. When do you need this stuff?"

"The sooner the better, but don't ignore your job."

That cracked him up. "My job mostly ignores me."

I started for the door. "Miss Shanahan?" He was standing still, feet together which seemed weird. "This is really cool. Thanks for asking me."

That may have been the first time I'd ever been thanked for asking someone to do me a favor.

The California Pizza Kitchen was sounding like a much better choice for dinner than sushi when I arrived back at the airport. On the other hand, I hadn't been running lately because of my ankle. Sushi would be less satisfying, but also less of a carbo load.

At some point, as I was resolving the dinner dilemma,

I became aware that he was back there. Behind me. Moving as I moved. I stopped once abruptly to browse in the window of a bookstore. Out of the corner of my eye, I caught him trying to match my movements, but his reaction was a beat behind, enough that I could see him do it. He was definitely following me. Damn.

He wore a cap pulled low enough over his eyes that his face was impossible to see, which meant I couldn't see when he was looking at me. He might have had a beard. He wore a black mesh T-shirt with the sleeves ripped out over jeans that bagged around his light-skinned, pointy-toed cowboy boots. A big, angry looking tattoo covered one upper arm. I was too far away to see what it was.

I stood at the window of the bookstore with one eye on him, trying to figure out what to do. Drift over to the Flamingo Garage and the airport police station. That's what made the most sense, but it was a long way away. A good ten-minute walk. He'd follow me until he figured out where I was going, peel off, and come back to haunt me another day. Frankly, I was tired of being followed around.

The airport was busy, and I kept getting buffeted and brushed aside by great moving tourist flows, clumps of people wearing loose, sunny smiles and big name tags. First it hit me that it was cruise ship day and I was in Miami, which meant the big air-to-water transfer and vice versa were underway. Then it hit me that I was in one of the greatest places in the world to get lost—a crowded airport—and I came up with a better idea.

I glanced over at my pursuer, who didn't seem to have moved a muscle the whole time he'd been standing there. Then I picked out a particularly animated tourist clump, steadied myself, and dove in. I had to really clamp down on the adrenaline to match their pace, which felt excruciatingly slow. I had to if I wanted to stay nestled in their midst. I went a short way with them before I saw another group coming from the opposite direction, and moving more swiftly. I wanted to go the way they were going and needed to shift over, but couldn't find Mr. Mesh

Man. They were approaching fast when I picked him out. His back was to me. I waited as he turned, turned in my direction . . . waited . . . waited . . . there. He saw me. Go . . . *now*.

I crossed over, began flowing in the reverse current, hopefully pulling him behind me, and, if I'd done it right, without his knowing.

Always keeping him in sight, and letting him keep me in sight, I made a couple more shifty moves. He wasn't very big, and had to stop frequently to stand on his toes and scan. Every time he didn't spot me, he grew more agitated. I could see it in the set of his shoulders and the way his head swiveled. At one point he turned completely around and I wasn't sure he'd pick me up again. It was so crowded it was actually hard to keep him in sight.

By the time I landed in the snaky check-in queue for LOT Polish Airlines, my heart was hammering, but I was weirdly exhilarated by this game of cat and mouse. Perhaps it would have been better to be the cat . . . but still, I was exactly where I wanted to be—around the corner from the security checkpoint.

I did a radar sweep for Mesh Man and found him—staring straight at me. And approaching. Fast. I pushed through the line, past a skycap and his overloaded rolling cart. I went around a herd of flight attendants with rolling bags. I was moving fast, but when I looked back, Mesh Man was closing. When I looked ahead, I saw what I didn't want to see. A line at the security checkpoint.

If I hadn't been carrying my backpack, I could have gone directly to the front of the line and sailed through the metal detector. If Mesh Man was armed, there was no way he was coming through behind me, and if he wasn't and followed me in, I'd simply turn around and ask him to state his business, right in front of all these people. But I had to get through, and fast. My Majestic ID had always been good for cutting the line. I wished I still had it. What I did have was the temporary one Bic had provided. I was almost running now and my hands were shaking. When I slung the pack forward, I almost dropped it. I had to try two zippered pockets before I found it. I was already standing at the front of the line, having cut in front of at least twelve people, when I finally extracted it. I flashed my ID. They made me throw my bag on the belt for x-ray, but let me pass through the metal detector. As I stood waiting for my backpack to come through, I tried to spot Mr. Mesh Man. Couldn't. I was tingling all over and breathing hard. My ankle was sore and my legs were stiff when I finally saw him . . . the back of him, hauling ass away from the checkpoint. I stood there for a long time, cooling off and calming down, watching people come through, and wondering if he had just given up, or if I had been playing cat and mouse with an armed man. I didn't feel quite so exhilarated any more.

Chapter Twenty-one

The receptionist at The Cray Fund was a slim Latino man with long graceful fingers. His short dark hair and soulful brown eyes stood out against the overtly white walls, his white reception counter, and a white-and-gray marble floor that practically glowed in the bright light from the floor-to-ceiling windows. Once again I sorely missed my sunglasses, which had been incinerated along with everything else in my bag. Jack had his on.

"Cray Financial Services, how may I direct your call?" I thought he was talking to himself until I spotted the translucent earpiece and microphone sprouting from the side of his head. His fingers moved expertly across a console as he went back to a call on hold. "She's off the line now, I'll transfer you."

"May I help you?" he asked, glancing up crisply between calls.

"Alex Shanahan and Jack Dolan. We have a ten o'clock appointment."

"With whom?" He was exasperated with us.

"We're not sure," I said, courting even more derision. "I called yesterday afternoon and spoke to a gentleman, maybe you, who told us to come in this morning. We have questions about one of the firm's cars."

"Have a seat." His constantly moving fingers punched up another call.

Jack had already found a spot on the edge of the white leather couch. He picked up a copy of the *Miami Herald*.

I sank down next to him and picked up one of the company's prospectuses.

"Ten to one," he murmured, "the car in the lot in the middle of the night was this Cray out porking his secretary."

I gazed about at our well-appointed surroundings. The place reeked of money, in a tropical sort of way. "I doubt if he'd choose The Harmony House Suites for his romantic interlude, you're the one who says we have to be open to all possibilities, and *porking* his *secretary?*"

"I'm just going off years of experience running people and their dirty little secrets to ground." He set down his paper and took in the surroundings. "What do they do here, anyway?"

"They're investors. They run a hedge fund."

"Is that like a mutual fund?"

"Sort of, except a hedge fund is an investment pool for rich people. It's not regulated like a mutual fund is, so it allows much riskier investing, which can mean much higher returns. According to this"—I pointed at a summary page in one of the company's brochures—"their return last year was over seventy percent. Of course the converse is also true. The downside can be as big as the upside."

"You understand all that stuff?"

"I've had a few finance courses in my day."

A set of handsome double doors off the reception area opened and a man and a woman emerged. The man was large, muscled, and dressed like one of the Bee Gees. His polyester white slacks were tight across his thick thighs and flared below the knee. The rest of his outfit was all black—silk T-shirt, leather belt, and woven leather loafers. No socks. On his left wrist were a large gold watch *and* a thin gold bracelet, and on his right pinky, a thick gold ring in the shape of a cross. He was Hispanic, so the chest hairs that curled out above the rounded collar of his shirt were also dark. He walked past us without so much as a sideways glance.

Jack leaned over to whisper. "He wasn't the one following you last night, was he?"

I shook my head. Too big. Way too big.

The woman lingered in the double doorway, pausing—
or posing—momentarily as she gave the two of us a good
once-over. She was angular and elegant enough to have
just stepped from a Richard Avedon photo—the long
graceful neck and those high-fashion bones. What she
didn't have was the proudly vacuous stare. In keeping
with the blinding color scheme of the office, her silk suit
was ivory and her hair shimmering blonde. I didn't think
high heels were stylish at the moment, given all the
chunky shoes that had been stepping on my toes lately.
But she had that kind of style that made everything she
wore look as fresh as if it had been designed for her the
day before and whipped up that morning.

"I'm sorry to keep you waiting," she said, slinking my
way first. "I'm Vanessa Cray."

And you're a girl, I thought, as I pushed myself up
from the couch to greet her. "Alex Shanahan," I said.
"This is Jack Dolan." I glanced at Jack, anxious to see
how this unexpected development fit with his porking
theory. Vanessa had turned her attention to him as well.
She was tall enough in her heels to gaze directly into
Jack's eyes when she turned to greet him, which was
enough for him to finally remove the sunglasses.

"Mr. Dolan," she said, "it's a pleasure to meet you."

She had smiled at me with polite obligation. The way
she smiled at him, the way she demanded eye contact
and touched his arm with her left hand as she took his
hand with her right made me think of how I'd had different résumés when I went looking for work, based on
who the audience would be. Vanessa Cray was one of
those women who had one personality for her own gender, and a very different one for the other.

Jack seemed very pleased to have caused such a response and was suddenly much more interested in taking
the meeting. "The pleasure is mine."

"Won't you come in?" She detached from Jack and
swept us through the double doors.

Two things hit me right off about Vanessa Cray's office. It was vast and it was cold. Really cold. This was in

spite of her floor-to-ceiling windows that opened out to a gleaming South Florida day that was only slightly tarnished by today's serving of smoke and ash. The glass in her windows must have been heavily insulated because I couldn't feel any warmth from the sun. Seeing the brightness outside and feeling the cold inside made for a strange, disorienting sensory experience.

Another thing that was hard not to miss was the proliferation of flowers. One would think an office filled with flowers would have had a homey charm. But these flowers looked more like exotic specimens growing in petri dishes. The plant on her desk had neon orange blooms that were shaped like lobster claws and looked to be made out of rubber tubing. They were all like that, graceful little sculptures that practically shouted "hands off."

"May I get you a hot drink?" She addressed me from behind her desk, which was not much more than a piece of glass stretched across two fancy chrome sawhorses. She glanced up—but only for a second—from whatever had drawn her to her flat screen monitor. "You seem uncomfortable."

"Not really." It's just that my eyeballs were beginning to frost.

She continued to keep us waiting for what was turning into an uncomfortably long period as she tapped her keys and perused the screen. "Please excuse my obsessive-compulsive behavior," she said lightly, making it clear we had no choice. "I'm trying to keep my eye on things. We made some big trades today."

"How did you do?" I asked.

She smiled. "As it happens, extremely well."

Jack leaned over the dish of lobster claws on her desk. "You like orchids?" he asked.

Vanessa shifted her intense concentration instantly from the screen to Jack. It was like a heat-seeking missile acquiring a target. "Do you know orchids?"

"Not really, but my mother loved flowers. She had them all over the house when I was growing up. I couldn't help but pick up a few things from her, although I don't remember any that looked like this."

She swooped around her desk to stand next to him, and they both leaned over the dish while I stood to the side, feeling as if I hadn't been picked for the kickball team.

"It's unlikely your mother would have had these." She ran a finger gently, lovingly along the outside of one of the blooms. "They're *Masdevallia velifera*. Their shape is quite unusual for an orchid. This one is called a Solar Flare because of the shape and the bright neon color. They grow mostly on trees in Andean cloud forests, where it's cool and shady and always bathed in mist. Their ideal temperature is fifty-five degrees."

That explained why she worked in a refrigerator. It was probably the least of the concessions she made to her passion. She was probably good at passion.

"They must be a challenge to grow in Florida," Jack said.

"That's why I grow them. And because they are so magnificent." She gazed down at the orchid in the same way a parent gazes upon her child—with endless wonder, as if it filled her with both pride and bewilderment to behold what she had made.

"Perhaps we could get started," I said. They both looked at me. "So we don't take up too much of your time."

"Certainly." She directed us to a cluster of chairs, small couches, and tables at the other end of the sparse office. I pulled my notebook from my backpack, opened it up, and noted the date and time and attendees.

"My assistant tells me you have a question about one of our cars. Of course I'll provide any information I can, but may I ask why you're interested?"

She was glancing over at my notebook, but addressing her questions to Jack, who sat forward on his chair with his elbows on his knees, and his hands clasped together in a posture that made him look both relaxed and alert. I listened carefully to hear how much he would tell her, and how he would couch the information.

"The license number came up in a case we're working on."

"What kind of case?"

"We're looking into the murder of a man at The Harmony House Suites. A black Volvo 580 registered to your company was in the hotel parking lot that night."

"How," she asked, "do you know this?"

"Surveillance."

She tipped her head and gave him a teasing smile. "I'm sure my car wasn't the only one in the lot that night."

He countered with his own crooked grin. "We're eliminating possibilities."

"Then the car does belong to you," I said, climbing into the conversation.

"It belongs to my company. But you already knew that. That's why you're here." She glanced again at the notebook on my lap. "Are you Jack's assistant?"

If I had been a dog, all the hair on my neck would have stood up right then, although it was certainly her right to find out who she was talking to and why. And I *was* in a way acting as Jack's assistant, although I didn't understand why she felt the need to point that out, unless it was to make me feel as if I didn't belong there, as if I didn't know what I was doing, as if she and Jack were the real thing and I was an imposter, an interloper, a party crasher—

"Ms. Cray," Jack said, "I—"

"Call me Vanessa."

"Ms. Shanahan is my client. I work for her."

"I see." She had barely glanced in my direction and was now addressing Jack again. "I have a fleet of six Volvos registered to my company. All the same model. All the same year. All black."

"The license number is unique," I said, trying not to behave as if she'd just blown me off completely. It was tough.

"I'm afraid that won't tell you who was driving."

"The cars are not assigned?"

"Anyone who works here is welcome to use any car. I had intended them for business use only, but I must admit we've never kept careful track." She shrugged delicately, making it clear that keeping track of six forty-

thousand-dollar vehicles just didn't make it onto her
radar screen.

"How many em—"

"I have thirty-five employees."

"And no procedure for signing the cars in and out?"

"None."

"Does that mean your employees could hand the keys
over to friends or family?"

"I don't see the need for stringent controls. I trust
my employees."

Which meant we had to consider not only all thirty-
five employees, but their friends, their families, and anyone else they may have felt like handing the keys off to.
She couldn't have made the situation more complicated
if she'd tried.

Jack picked up the ball. "Ms. Cray—"

"I asked you to call me Vanessa." She gazed upon
Jack as if he'd disappointed her. If he felt disappointing,
he wasn't letting it show.

"Can you provide us a list of employees and contact
numbers?"

"Of course." She reached over, picked up her phone,
and asked whoever answered to bring a copy of the company's employee roster. A young woman wearing a serious suit and an expression to match appeared almost
immediately with the file, and took the opportunity to
say gently but firmly that Vanessa was late for her conference call with London. They'd started on time, she
explained, and had gone as far as they could without her.
I checked my watch. We had been with her less than
twenty minutes and spent at least half that time watching
her stare at her monitor.

"Tell them I'll be right with them." The assistant de-
parted. Vanessa paged through the file quickly and
handed it to me. "I think you'll find what you need in
here." She took two business cards from a holder on the
table next to her and gave us each one as well. "And if
you'd care to look at the cars, I'll have my assistant call
downstairs. Now I really must—"

"Your name is not on this list." My tone was more

blunt than I'd intended, but then I wasn't trying too hard.
This time when we locked eyes, I felt as though she were
seeing me for the first time. I'd finally managed to get
her attention.

"You asked for an employee list. I'm not an employee."

"I assume you have access to the Volvos."

"Yes, but I don't use the cars. I have a driver."

"I understand," I said. "What I'm asking you is if there
is anyone else with access to the cars whose name is not
on the list."

"Oh, I see. No, there's no one that I can think of
right now, but if you'll leave your information with my
receptionist, I'll certainly call you if anything comes to
mind."

She had walked behind her desk and settled in again
to watch whatever it was she found so mesmerizing on
her computer screen. If that wasn't enough of a signal,
she punched up her assistant on the phone and requested
to be hooked up to the London call.

We were dismissed. Actually, I had been dismissed
even before we'd begun, but now she was apparently
through with Jack as well.

We took the express elevator down from the Andean
rain forest. The two of us stood, as people do in elevators, side by side facing forward. Jack stared up at the
floor counter while I studied our images in the polished
metal elevator doors.

I was studying Jack's image more than mine. He was
an attractive man, especially spiffed up the way he was
with his hair combed and a nice jacket on. I enjoyed that
about him. Also his intelligence, his complexity, his sense
of humor. His mysterious side. That sense that there
were many more layers to him than he was showing. I
didn't like that Vanessa Cray had just tried to crawl up
his pant leg.

He noticed me looking. "What?"

"Do you think she did that to keep you off balance?"

"Did what?"

"Flirted with you?"

He brushed something off his jacket lapel. "Are you saying you don't think she finds me attractive?"

"I think she finds you attractive in the way a lion finds zebra meat to be attractive."

He grinned. "I've been called a lot of things, but never zebra meat." He scraped the edge of her business card along his jaw, and I could hear the sound of stubble. "I've seen her somewhere before. I can't remember where, but I know I've seen her face."

"She's hiding something," I said.

"You just don't like her."

"I don't like her, and she's hiding something."

He turned his attention back to the floor counter overhead. "Did you ever consider that she was flirting with me to get to you?"

"Why would she do that?"

"She likes to play. And she recognizes you as the bigger threat."

"How am I a threat to her?"

"She's used to controlling men. That's obvious. But you're smart, and so is she. You like to be in control, and so does she. And you're a woman. You are more of a challenge for her."

We dropped a few more floors as I considered that. Better to be neutralized for being too much of a challenge, I supposed, than to be dismissed for not being enough of one. I decided to feel marginally better. Even so . . .

"I think she's hiding something."

"That's because you don't like her."

"Yeah."

We had to cross to another elevator to get to the garage, where we found the six black Volvos in reserved spots on the bottom level. They were all in, presumably because everyone was at work in the building. We identified the one we wanted by the license plate, and as promised, a parking attendant gave us the keys.

Jack piled into the driver's side and I slipped into the back seat. "What are we looking for?"

"Anything that might tell us who has driven the car lately."

I pulled an empty Snapple bottle off the floor and showed it to him. "All we're likely to prove is that someone drove the car at some point, not who drove the car to the hotel that night and for what reason."

He leaned over and opened the glove box. "Don't overanalyze. Keep looking."

"I'm not optimistic." I reached down into all the cracks between the leather cushions and felt around. All I came up with was a Tic Tac, a penny, some hairs, and a lot of really disgusting lint and grit that made me want to flee to the ladies' room and wash my hands.

"You know, Jack, they could have switched the plates."

"That's why we're going to search all six."

We did. It took two hours. The most interesting thing we found came from the first car we'd searched, the one with the license plate that had matched the surveillance. It was a credit card receipt for a gas purchase dated the Tuesday afternoon after John had been killed. The person who had signed was named Arturo. I held it up to the light and tried to read the last name. Impossible. It was nothing more than a long, illegible squiggle.

"I'm going to have to get someone to run that down," Jack said.

"I've got a better idea. There's someone I'd like you to meet."

Chapter Twenty-two

All the rooms on this side of The Harmony House Suites had interior windows that looked out to the hotel's wide center atrium. In answer to my knock, room 484's curtains twitched. The deadbolt clicked, and the door opened, but only a crack. I could have fit through just fine if I was Gumby.

"Felix?"

"It's me, Miss Shanahan." Felix's voice was quiet, but not subdued. It was hard for Felix to restrain his innate enthusiasm for just about everything. The crack expanded to reveal the white-tipped hair, the dark eyes. "Are you alone, Miss Shanahan?"

"No. I brought someone to meet you." Jack stepped out so Felix could see him. "We have another assignment for you."

"Cool."

I waited. And waited. "Can we come in, Felix?"

"Oh. Oh, sure. Absolutely. Sorry. Come in."

He opened the door and let us slip through. Apparently, he'd taken over room 484 at The Suites and turned it into his command center. It looked like the one John had stayed in, only the floor plan was reversed. It also had a few additions. There were multiple electronic products around the room—a couple of printers, one of which seemed to be in many pieces on the floor, a scanner, what looked like some sort of external high-density drive, a CD player, and lots of hardware I couldn't identify.

The center of all the gadgets was a laptop, which sat on the coffee table in front of the couch. With all the wires and cables running out of it, it looked like a post-op patient in the trauma ward.

"Felix, this is Jack Dolan. He's a private investigator."

"Hello, son." Jack extended his hand and Felix shook it. They were quite a contrast, these two. Jack with his calm, squinty-eyed, seen-it-all PI's stare, and Felix Melendez Jr. with eyes that couldn't have gotten any bigger, so clearly delighted to meet a real live private investigator. I loved this kid's transparency. He moved to the seat on the couch in front of his laptop. The maestro preparing to work.

"What is a Limp Bizkit?" Jack was staring down at the mouse pad on the coffee table.

"It's a band," Felix said, waiting for the next question.

"We need to know whose signature this is." I handed him the credit card receipt. "Can you work with that?"

He snapped it out of my hand and checked it over. His face began to glow. He was like a kid at a spelling bee who had been given an easy word. "Just give me a couple of minutes, okay?"

"Can I watch?" I asked.

He was already deeply immersed. Jack settled into the armchair next to the couch, stuck his legs out, and crossed them at the ankles. I sat on the couch next to Felix and watched what he was doing. I didn't understand a lot of it, but eventually he got to some program that seemed to be doing a high-speed comparison between the credit card number we'd provided and a large database of other numbers.

"This is going to take a few minutes." He relaxed, but only slightly.

"Anything on Speath yet, Felix? Anything suspicious in the financials?" I asked.

"Nothing so far, Miss Shanahan, but I haven't had much time to work on it. We had a fire alarm yesterday and then there was a problem with a parrot that got loose and my restaurant manager called in sick—"

"It's okay," I said. "I told you not to ignore your day job. In fact, are you sure you should be using the hotel to do this work for us?"

"I'm not working on the hotel's time. They're getting, like, totally more coverage from me since I'm around here so much. I'm using my own computer and equipment. And I plan to bill you for the room and the phone calls. But," he hastened to add, "I get an awesome discount."

"You know, Felix, we haven't talked about this, but I should be paying you. What's the going rate for someone like you?"

"To do this kind of work, maybe $100 . . . $150 an hour."

"Oh."

"Don't worry, Miss Shanahan. I figure if you can help me get a job at the airport, it will be worth it." I was definitely getting the better end of that deal. "I'll have something to you on Mr. Speath as soon as I crack the firewall. It shouldn't be much longer."

"Firewall?" Jack asked the question, but only because he beat me to it. "Speath has a firewall?"

"Oh, yeah. It's a good one, too. Most of his data is really accessible, but there's this one section he has walled off. I tried every way I know of to get past and I couldn't. But I will. I've been talking to some of my friends about it. We have ideas."

"It must be sophisticated," I said, "if *you* can't get in."

Felix's olive skin flushed, starting at his throat and rising all the way to his white tips. "Thank you, Miss Shanahan. And I will find a way in. I've just never seen one like this before. It's, like"—he stared up at the ceiling—"wicked tight, you know? It's a vault."

I looked at Jack. "Why would a little aviation repair company have a need for a data vault?"

"I don't know," he said, "but I'd like to know what's in there. I'd also like to know why he was here at the hotel that night."

"I have a theory on that," I said. "We're interested in Speath because the FBI is interested and because his car was in the lot the night of the murder."

"Yes," Jack said. "We hate coincidences."

"What if it's not a coincidence? What if the two things are not independent variables, but dependent?"

"What does that mean?"

"What if the FBI is interested in George *because* his car was in the lot, and his car was in the lot for totally innocent reasons?"

"Like what?"

"Why do people go to hotels in their own city? Maybe he got a room with Margie."

"Who's Margie?"

"She's his assistant, and she's an attractive blonde. A few too many ankle bracelets for my taste. But still, maybe we're looking at an appropriate application of your porking theory. Or maybe they were in the bar having a drink."

"I can check that." We both looked at Felix. "I mean I can try to see if they were here for other reasons, like . . . you know, like if they got a room together. We already know they didn't register their car with us, so they probably didn't, you know, use their real names. But they might be regulars. I can see who was registered that night and if they've been here before. I can check the registration cards for local addresses. After a while, you get so you can recognize certain things. I can also ask the bartender to go through credit card receipts. Sometimes people park out there who are just here for a drink."

"Do that," I said. "Maybe we can eliminate George from consideration altogether."

"Oh, hey. It's up." Felix checked his screen. "Here it is. Your data's up."

Jack came around to Felix's other side. "What are we looking at, son?"

Felix pointed out the highlights with his finger. "The credit card was issued against a Cray Fund corporate account, and here's the list of people who have cards." He ran his finger down the list. When he stopped, I leaned in to see who the winner was. "There's one Arturo," he said. "Arturo Polonia."

"I'll be damned." Jack shook his head. "This is supposed to be secure data. And you hacked in? Just like that?"

Felix puffed up his narrow chest. "One way or another, I can get in almost anywhere. And I'll crack Mr. Speath's vault, too. I'll figure it out."

"How about an address or social security number on this Arturo character? I can get someone to run it and see if he has a record."

"Piece of cake, Mr. Dolan."

While they looked for that, I found the file Vanessa had given me and searched the list of employees. I read over it twice.

"I think we just narrowed our search, Jack. There is no Arturo Polonia on the Cray employee list."

Chapter Twenty-three

Jack paused between bites of his *chile relleno*. "Maybe she forgot," he said.

"Does Vanessa Cray strike you as a scatterbrain, Jack?"

"No. But she did strike me as someone who could get absorbed in what she was doing to the exclusion of everything else. She checked out on us before we ever left her office."

We were at the Texas Taco Factory for an early dinner, a storefront fajita bar in Jack's South Beach neighborhood. It had a neon Corona beer logo in the window and a hand-lettered sign that announced a senior citizens discount, although the place didn't strike me as a seniors' kind of hangout. It was dark, with scarred heavy wooden tables and long benches to sit on. Next door was Pucci's Pizza and the Top Dog Gun Shop. Shorty and Fred's Ford Dealership was across the street.

"I still think having Felix do a background check on her is a good idea. He's dying to help us. All he would have to do is a quick search of the periodical databases at the library—magazines, newspapers, especially the business publications. I'd also like to know where she went to school, and if she worked anywhere before she started that fund of hers. That extremely successful fund of hers."

"You wouldn't be jealous, would you?"

"You mean because she turned out to be sexy and glamorous and beautiful and successful, probably rich, and undoubtedly more together in her life than I am in mine at the moment?" I threw back a mineral water chaser. "Heavens, no. I'm not jealous."

Jack crunched a few more taco chips. I took another bite of my fajita. I was trying to space them out, since I had to towel down after each bite. The salsa and other unidentified juices tended to leak out of the sides of the soft tortilla and run down my arm.

"What I want to know," I said, "is why you're dismissing her. Her car was at the hotel, she lied to us about this Arturo guy, and I still don't get why she would have screwed with us the way she did if she wasn't hiding something."

Jack was working on his main course—scrambled eggs, a choice for dinner I always found strange. But he said he'd had a taste for *huevos rancheros* all day. "She answered every question," he said. "She gave us what we asked for, and she volunteered her cars for inspection, so I don't see how she screwed with us. I'm not dismissing her. I'll get someone to run Arturo Polonia for me."

He took another long drink of ice water from a tall plastic glass. He was throwing down lots of water, no doubt to counteract the extra-hot salsa he'd ordered on the *huevos*.

"I'm just trying to get you to think about this critically," he said. "You don't see many women in the dirty parts trade, especially ones who wear silk. She's way, way out of Jimmy and Bobby's league, and if you're saying you think she killed John, I don't see how. He was stabbed, which means he was physically overwhelmed. And someone had to lift him into that Dumpster. You told me he was a big man."

"Maybe someone helped her. Maybe this Arturo person."

"Then let's talk about motive." More water. "You dismissed Ottavio because you couldn't conceive of a motive that made sense, and yet you think John might have come in contact with this woman? John was in no way involved in drugs, but he may have invested in a hedge fund. Is that your speculation?"

I had to smile. Jack's sarcasm was too gentle. Good

sarcasm was supposed to be sharp enough to make you bleed. Yet he always managed to make his point.

"All right, that's fair." It was time to make another fajita, a process at least as treacherous as eating them. I pulled out a tortilla and started piling—meat and peppers and guac and salsa. "How about this? I get to consider the idea that Vanessa is involved if I open up to the possibility that Ottavio could also be involved. Be open to all the possibilities. That's what you said." Sour cream, rice, some refried beans. "I can do that. I would never want to be accused of being less than rigorous in my analytical approach."

"Now you're talking."

"I just feel something from her, Jack. I can't explain it."

"I understand. I don't feel it about her, but I do feel it about Jimmy. I think he's a much more promising suspect. I think George Speath is going to wind up being the key. He's a nice guy, right?"

"He seemed very nice to me. More than nice. Sweet."

"Nice guys are always suspect."

"Where do you get that? The only thing we've determined about George is he likes to keep hackers out of his data. He's an engineer. Maybe he just knows enough to protect himself. It would be hard to hack Felix, too, but that doesn't make him a bad guy."

Jack looked at me. I had become a tad more forceful in my defense of George than even I would have expected. "Why," he asked, "do you like him so much?"

"He loves airplanes. He can't be all bad."

"So it's a perspective you've gained through careful and diligent data gathering and analysis."

"Exactly. Similar to the approach you've taken with Jimmy."

"Jimmy is a bad guy. There is no question about that. And I submit that the man following you through the terminal the other day was one of Jimmy's people."

"Jimmy doesn't know I exist."

"Avidor does."

"True. Why would he be following me?"

"To scare you. To scare me. I'm going to find out."
He scarfed down another handful of tortilla chips. Between the two of us, we were going through them pretty
compulsively. "If you feel that strongly about Vanessa,
you should pursue her."

"*I* should pursue her?"

"I'm going to track down Ira and see what news he
has for me."

"Tonight?"

"I do my best work at night. So does he. And I have
to follow up some leads on my helicopter case. I do have
another client, remember?"

"Oh, yeah. I'll call Felix and ask him to do the background check. Maybe we'll come up with something
that will help you remember where you know her
from."

"Tell him to look at the orchid societies."

"That's a great idea. And what about this employee
list?" I asked. "Am I going to have to interview thirty-
five people and all their friends and family by myself?"

"You said you wanted to be an investigator." He said
it with a twinkle in his eye.

"Actually, I think I said I wanted to watch you investigate."

"Give it to me." He took the list and folded it until it
fit into the front pocket of his shirt. "I'll see if Patty
would like to have something the Bureau doesn't have."

"Excellent." I finished off the last piece of skirt steak,
wiped down, leaned back against the wall, and stretched
my legs out on the long bench. My ankle was mostly
fine, but it still throbbed at the end of a long day.

"You're not going to see Jimmy tonight, are you, Jack?
By yourself?"

"Why do you ask?"

"I don't know. But it strikes me as not a good idea
for you to do that."

"Why?"

"Because you keep telling me not to get emotionally
involved. That it clouds my ability to get to the right

answer. You have something going on with Jimmy that you choose not to share with me . . ."

I glanced over for a reaction, thinking I could guilt him into sharing with me. There was none. Nothing. His face had gone blank. I picked up my knife and concentrated on rolling it across the wooden table. Flat implements don't roll well. "Anyway, whatever it is, it seems intensely emotional to me."

"I'm not emotional about Jimmy." Now his voice was blank, too. Flat.

"I can see it in you right now." I had cleared a space and was twirling the knife, spinning it like a top. Harder and harder. Faster and faster. "You're so cool about everything else, so in command. But when you talk about him—just me talking about him now—your reactions are different."

"Different how?"

I shifted on the bench. It felt narrow. I hadn't meant to go so deep with this line of discussion. I looked again into his eyes and couldn't find anything to hold on to. It was as if a shroud had come down.

"Vulnerable, Jack. You seem very vulnerable around the subject of Jimmy. That's the only way to describe it. It's like he's a flat spot for you. A place you can't see and since you can't see it, you can't defend it. I don't know him. I don't know anything about him, but you said he's pretty smart and—"

"Where did you get your psychological training?"

I stared at him, hoping for the mild curves and rounded corners that usually accompanied his ribbing. It wasn't there. His eyes were hard. Mean, even.

"On the ramp in Boston," I said. "Crash course."

"And who's going to protect me? You?"

His tone had moved beyond flat to sharp, sharp enough to make me bleed. He was getting the hang of this sarcasm thing, trying to hurt me, or at least push me away. I'd poked around in something that was none of my business. The restaurant had turned festive since we'd been in there. A large group had come in, gathered around the bar, and started doing shots. Loudly. They were just warming up while the temperature at our table had dropped below zero. For the first time, I felt uncomfortable with Jack Dolan.

"I'm sorry for digging around in your business and making assumptions I have no right to make. I do that, and I do it without permission." I swiveled around, put my feet on the floor, and sat up straight. "But don't ridicule my concern. I like you, and no, I can't protect you from Jimmy. From anything, probably. Surely you know someone who can. All I'm saying is I don't think . . . I would like for you not to go out and confront Jimmy on your own."

When I had faced forward, he had taken my pose, turning to lean his back against the wall and putting his feet up on the bench. He drank again from his big plastic cup of water, finishing off the slushy ice-water mix. He stared up at the ceiling fan, which was turning at a lethargic pace. "There's nothing you need to know about Jimmy and me," he said. "All you need to know about him is he killed your friend."

It was impossible not to feel the blunt finality of the statement. Nerves all through my body were twisting themselves into knots. It was as if the scenery I'd become familiar with had shifted and I was lost.

I took out a twenty and put it on the table. "Do you want me to drive you home?"

"I'm not going home." He made no move to get up.

I didn't want to leave, but I could feel everything in him pushing me out. I hated that he wanted me to leave. "You don't want me to go with you tonight?"

"I told you from the start I worked better on my own. I don't want you worrying about me." He turned his face away to look through the window to the street. The beer signs cast a neon glow across his face that made him look like an Andy Warhol portrait. "I don't want anyone worrying about me."

I waited, but all he would show me was the side of his face. His jaw was set and his muscles tense. I gathered my things and left him sitting on his bench. In the parking lot, I checked to see if he might come through the restaurant door and perhaps look my way. I only looked once, but I looked for a long time.

Going back over the causeway to the city, it wasn't quite dark enough to need headlights. Downtown Miami looked calm and beautiful with the lights just starting to emerge against the gray dusk. In the sky over the ocean, the sun was sinking behind the flat horizon. It looked as if it were being lowered on a crane into the water. The sky above it was streaked in that stunning array of colors that get left behind when the sun departs—mostly pinks and oranges. It was so beautiful it made me cry.

Chapter Twenty-four

I woke up all of a sudden, as if someone had reached out of the darkness and tapped me on the shoulder. I rolled over on my back, held still, and listened hard. All I heard was the laboring of the air conditioner. It was pumping fast, like my heart, but it was no match for the humidity that hovered over my bed like the sea of smoke that pressed down on the city outside. It was almost one in the morning.

It could have been the fajitas that had disturbed my deep sleep. More likely it was the specter of raging wildfires that had been planted in my consciousness by the evening news. Topping the headlines had been an eighteen-vehicle crash in central Florida, attributed to a nearby band of brushfires whose smoke had mingled with fog and drifted across the interstate. As I slept, a blaze was roaring north of I-75 near the Broward–Palm Beach county line, and had already consumed fifty thousand acres of tall saw grass. Yet another band of fires had threatened a warehouse in Miami-Dade County. The message seemed to be that we were surrounded by fires and they were moving closer.

I threw back the covers. I flipped my pillow, which was as soaked with perspiration as my hair. The sheets were also damp with the sweat that trickled down my face, under my arms, between my legs. It even seemed that the soles of my feet were sweating. I imagined an imprint of my body on the mattress that looked a lot like a chalk outline.

It was hard to breathe, harder when I thought about smoke and fumes and fog and fire, so I concentrated on inhaling and exhaling as deeply as I could, forcing air into my lungs and bad thoughts out of my head. But it was no use. When the phone rang, I was almost expecting it.

I sat in the Lumina, parked roughly where Jack had told me to park. I had followed his directions back to the swamp, driving almost forty-five minutes south and west from the city. It had been a nerve-wracking experience, driving dark and narrow roads, checking the rearview every few minutes along the way. If the kidney car, or any car, had been following me, I wanted to know before I'd gone too far from civilization. I had already worn myself out by the time I found Jack's rendezvous point.

According to him, if I was in the right place, I was half a mile from an old airfield and a large abandoned hangar. I was in the vicinity of the swamp I had visited while chasing Bobby, but supposedly a different section. It was hard to tell from the scenery. The roads had been just as black and forbidding with the same tunnel-of-horrors atmosphere that practically guaranteed something would leap out of the darkness at me when I least expected it. Jack had suggested killing my headlights at the final turn, but I had tempted fate, two eerie beams of light cutting through air that was as moist as a limp washrag and smelled like someone's basement after the flood.

When I'd reached the meeting place, exactly two miles in, I was supposed to have pulled to the side. There were no sides. I stopped the car and killed the engine. Now I was waiting, listening through closed windows to a darkness that throbbed with the same otherworldly sounds I'd heard the other night. They came from everywhere—from the trees overhead, from the ground underneath, from great distances, and from very close by.

Jack had been all business on the phone. Nothing about our conversation earlier in the evening, which was probably best given what we were about to do. He'd told me to wear black. I hadn't purchased any replacement clothes that were black, so I used what I had. New jeans that were as dark as indigo ink and stiff as Styrofoam, and a dark blue T-shirt I'd bought for running. I'd solved the problem of the big, silver Dallas Cowboys logo on the front by turning it inside out, but I couldn't do anything about the short sleeves. My pale, bare arms felt incandescent in the dark.

With the windows up and the air conditioner off, it hadn't taken long for the windows of the Lumina command capsule to steam up, so the sharp, fast knock seemed to come out of nowhere. It ruptured the clammy silence and nearly sent me through the roof. My hand went instinctively to the ignition. Another knock. I saw a flash of light, and heard Jack's voice. "It's me. Open up."

He slipped in. "Here—" He placed a small flashlight in my hand. "Hold this. And keep it low."

The flashlight was damp with what I assumed was his perspiration.

"You got here fast," he said.

It hadn't felt fast, especially the last ten miles. "Where's your truck?"

"Not far. It's in another clearing."

Another clearing? Was this car-sized space in the trees considered a clearing? "I take it you found Ira?"

"Yeah. He was over on the Gulf Coast fishing."

"He doesn't sound conscientious about his snitching duties. Are you sure we can trust him? What is this place we're going to?"

"It's an old airfield that was used mostly for crop dusters years ago. The people who owned it got sued. I don't even know who officially has title. It's been in receivership for years."

"What's so suspicious about it?"

"There's an old aircraft hangar on the property. Ira told me there's been a lot of activity in and out of it recently. Heavy equipment. Flatbed trucks. He said they even had a helicopter land in there. Whatever Jimmy is doing, Ira says this is ground zero."

"Is anyone there now?"

"I've been out here for hours. Nothing's happened except a car comes around every two hours for a drive-by."

"Jimmy's security?"

"Must be. But they're not all that serious if it is. All the better for us."

Jack must have noticed my glow-in-the-dark arms. He reached into the garment he was wearing—it looked like a fishing vest with numerous pockets and flaps and openings—and pulled out a round, flat can. With benefit of the flashlight, I figured out it was camouflage paint and not chewing tobacco. "Put this on your arms," he said, "and your face."

While I did that, he took the flashlight back and laid it on the seat so the beam caught his hands under the dashboard. And in his hands was a gun, the big automatic I'd seen before. A Glock, he'd told me. A 9 mm. With a few practiced strokes, he released the clip, checked it, and rammed it back in with a loud click. He slid the top back and pushed another small lever that I thought might be the safety. It all seemed terribly complex to me. I finished blackening my arms and started on my face.

He holstered the automatic, went back into the multifaceted vest, and came out with another gun, this one smaller. "Can you shoot?" he asked.

This question made my temples pulse as I tightened the lid on the camouflage paint. "And hit anything?"

"Okay." He held the gun low so the light would catch it. "This is only a .22. It's not going to do much, but it's better than nothing." He checked the safety, then turned it around and offered it to me.

I hesitated. "I hate guns."

"You'd hate worse being dead."

"Are those the only two choices?"

"It would make me feel better if you had a firearm. If something happened to me, or if someone got past me—"

"Then I'd be in deep shit. Jack, I'd be just as likely to shoot you as anything else."

"No, you wouldn't."

He was right. I didn't really think I'd shoot him. But

I didn't want the gun. It felt wrong. It felt as if I would be playing at something I wasn't. I was still an average citizen who in less than one week was going back to a life somewhere else. I needed to believe that.

"No," I said. "I don't want it."

He didn't respond, but I heard a protracted sigh, one with a hint of "You're more trouble to me than you're worth." It was a legitimate reaction. I felt bad about it, but I couldn't make myself carry a gun.

"Do you want me to stay back?"

"No." He put the gun back in his pocket. "Take the floor mats."

"What?"

He opened his door, leaned back in, and pulled out the front floor mat. Then he opened the back door and did the same. "We're going to need these. Roll them together so you can carry them."

I opened my door as wide as I could, given the close and steady presence of the surrounding brush. It felt good to unfold from the seat where I'd been crammed. As I labored in the small space to maneuver the floor mats into a manageable bundle, every sweat mechanism in my body proceeded to move into high gear.

"Let's go."

Jack was off down the road, which was more passable on foot, and I followed. He'd brought an extra flashlight, which I tried to keep pointed at my feet. I didn't want a replay of the twisted ankle fiasco. Even though the ground was dry, I couldn't shake the feeling that at any moment I would step into quicksand.

We ran for about five minutes. I didn't catch up with Jack until he stopped. It was hard to tell, but it felt as though we had emerged on the periphery of a flat, wide-open field. I could feel the openness, especially compared to the thick brush behind us. I crouched next to him.

"We're going across that field," he said, confirming the geography. "It goes right up to a fence that surrounds the hangar. Go as fast as you can, but watch the ground. There's a lot of junk lying around. Don't stop until you get to the fence. And don't lose the mats." He turned to look at me. All I could see were his eyes, but they were calm and steady enough to make me feel that way, too. "Ready?"

"Ready."

Without the thick cluster of trees around us, the bright moon cast enough light that I could see oilcans, car parts, parts of parts, and garbage bags with contents unknown. I moved quickly, trying to stay close as he ran ahead of me. I hadn't even noticed the large structure looming ahead until the fence appeared and we had to stop. Up close, the hangar was gigantic—tall enough to block out the moon and wide enough that I couldn't see either end of the building in the limited light.

The fence was chain link, topped with a generous twist of razor wire, and went around the outer perimeter of the hangar. We stayed low at the base for a full five minutes and listened. There were no city sounds to be heard, no cars or trains, factories or shopping centers. The sounds were from the swamp. There was no sign of any other humans.

I had assumed Jack would pull a set of wire cutters out of that hardware store of a vest he was wearing. Instead, he unfurled a car mat, stood back, and tossed it up and over the razor wire. Aha. He did the same with his second mat and with the two I was carrying. With all four spread out side by side, we were able to scramble up and over, although it wasn't easy. The Cyclone fence was tall and old and sagging. It was like climbing a thick, billowy curtain.

We dropped down on the other side and waited for the fence to stop shaking. I stared at the structure in front of us. From our location, I couldn't see any obvious points of entry. The hangar doors on this side were pad-locked shut. The walk-in door was most certainly locked. The foundation was solid concrete, so there would be no tunneling in.

"This way," Jack whispered.

"Where?"

"There's a window on the other side."

Indeed there was. It was around the corner and halfway down the length of the building. The bottom of it was high enough for me to reach, I figured, if Jack lifted me up and I stretched my arms out.

"Give me a boost," I said.

He stuck his flashlight in his belt and offered his two hands as a step. I climbed up and, with my fingers on the sill, crept up enough to see that the window was open a crack. I uncoiled a little more to shine the flashlight and look in. I saw a toilet reflected in a mirror over a sink. I could also see the door was closed. I tried to lift the window with one hand. No dice. I shoved the flashlight into my waistband and tried it with two. It was stuck so tight I had to bang it with the heels of my hands. I did it once. An avalanche of dust, rust, and dried paint flecks fell down and stuck to my damp face and hair. I rubbed my eyes and listened for an answering sound. Nothing. I banged it again, this time with my head down and my eyes closed. It came loose and opened all the way to the top. Without even looking down at Jack, I braced my arms on the sill and climbed through. I knew if I'd waited to think about it I would have stiffened up.

The whole enclosure wasn't much more than a toilet surrounded by sheets of plywood paneling. The toilet didn't have any water in it, so it smelled like a Port-O-Let at Woodstock. The door had a hook-and-eye latch and opened out. I pushed it open a crack, just enough to see and hear that it was quiet in the hangar. And dark. Jack dropped in behind me just as I pushed it open. The hinges squeaked.

"Let me go first," he said, plowing ahead. "I *am* the one with the gun." He didn't waste time or a single motion as he slipped out. I tried to move in the same economical fashion, staying low and following the beam of his flashlight, which was woefully inadequate in the vast building. What dim light there was inside the hangar came from moonlight through a high bank of windows and large, intermittent holes in the roof. It came down unobstructed in places, especially from overhead, and created deep shadows in others. It was too diffused to be of much use, but I did have the sense of being closed in and surrounded, much like the swamp outside. It was a creepy sensation in such a big space. There was also a smell—strong and heavy and mostly gasoline or some other fuel. But that wasn't all. Underneath it was the odor of something dead or decaying.

"I can't see a damn thing," Jack said. "I think . . ." He held up his flashlight. "Those look like worktables a little closer to the front. Maybe there are some lamps or lights on them."

He headed in that direction with me on his tail. I tried to take small, cautious steps. Every time I got overly confident, I ran into a pile of something unidentified on the ground. Whatever it was grabbed at my feet. Cables? Wires?

And then there was light. Jack had found a lamp. When he turned it on, it made a small pool on a short section of a long workbench. Using his flashlight, he found a second lamp not far away, and I found a third.

"Okay," he said, picking up small items around the space and studying them under the flashlight. "Fuses . . . O-rings . . . bolts . . . switches . . . valves." He raked the light over the back of the bench and a neat line of cans and bottles. "What have we here?" He picked up a large brown bottle and read the label. Then he leaned down and read the other labels.

"What is it?"

"Spray paint, chemicals, soldering materials. All the things you need to cover over half-assed repairs, change serial numbers."

"Strip-and-dip?" We were talking quietly, but our voices seemed to echo anyway.

"Yep. Among other things. I think we've found Jimmy's bogus parts factory." He ran the light farther down and touched on a neat hutch of drawers, the kind my dad used in his garage to organize his screws and nuts and bolts. Jack opened one of the drawers, pulled something out, checked it, and handed it to me. I held it under the light. It was a small metal plate with a series of numbers engraved in it.

"It's a data plate," he said. "Probably stolen."

He moved down the table and found another light. When I caught up, he was holding up a component. He turned it one way, then the other. "This is a rotor segment," he said. "Brakes." He rubbed over a rough section with his thumb. "This is where they've ground down the part number. They'll stamp a fake one on." He put it down and picked up another part. "This is the housing for a starter. If you look under the light"—he pointed to a thin, crooked line across the outer casing that looked like a healed scar—"you can see the solder marks. They'll clean it up, paint over it, throw on one of those data plates, and sell it as new. Or like new." He put the unit down. "I'll bet if we look around here, we'll find some fake packaging. And it will look as good as the real stuff. Also paperwork." He kept moving along the workbench until he found something and brought it back. "See these?" He showed me a stack of papers. "These are yellow tags."

They were single sheets of white paper—8½ by 11 inches. "They're not yellow. And they're not tags."

"They don't have yellow tags anymore. But they still use the term. This document, when attached to a part and signed by a licensed mechanic, means it's been repaired according to all the standards and specs and is ready to go back on the airplane or helicopter. That's what a yellow tag does. It's the mechanic's certification."

"So this is all that stands between me and an airplane flying with a car part?"

"This and the skill and integrity of the mechanic who hangs the part on the airplane."

I looked down at the stack. They were blank, and they were all signed. "This is like a stack of blank checks."

"Exactly. Jimmy fills them in for every part. He probably paid a hundred dollars each for the signatures."

I took a step back, tripped over something, and almost went down.

"Be careful." Jack directed the light down to my feet. It was a box I'd stumbled over. He moved the beam back to the workbench, so I used my own light to see what it was. I picked up an in-flight magazine out of the box and held it under one of the lamps.

"Jack, look at this."

He turned, caught sight of the cover, and stared at it.

"Look at the date," I said.

He didn't say anything, but in the silence I heard his breathing slow down. He swung around and tried to use his flashlight to sweep the hangar behind us. It was useless. The beam was feeble against the overpowering space.

"I'm going to find a light switch for the overheads."

"Are you sure that's smart?"

"I'm sure it's not, but I can't think of what else to do." He used the flashlight to check his watch. "We should still have over an hour before that car comes around. I'm not leaving until we know what's going on in here, and we're not going to figure it out one lamp at a time. I'll flip it right off again."

As he moved away, I followed his progress in the dark by the light in his hand and listened to him carefully picking his way forward.

It took a long time. While I waited, I tried to make out the dark shapes that were all around, towering above me, and crowded into the back of the hangar. Some were as tall as the high windows along the ceiling. The longer I waited, the more my skin prickled. I rubbed my arms and felt the goose bumps forming. I came away with black paint on both my sweaty palms. I tried to wipe it off on my stiff jeans.

"Found it," Jack said. And the lights went on—overhead lights blazing so brightly and so suddenly, my eyes squeezed themselves shut.

But not before I'd seen it. Not before I'd seen enough to make me afraid to open them again.

I did it in degrees, looking first at the small space around me just to get oriented. Then I broadened my scope, looking up and out.

The first thing that registered was the tail because it was the least damaged and most recognizable piece of the thousands, perhaps tens of thousands, of airplane parts that lay spread on the concrete all around me. Except for the odd angle at which it was tipped, and the fact that there was no fuselage attached to it, the tail appeared as it must have the day the airplane had rolled out of the factory for the last time. That would have been the day Air Sentinel had taken delivery, because that's whose logo was emblazoned across the stabilizer. And that's whose in-flight magazine we'd found in the box. It was from January, the month of the accident in Ecuador.

I did a complete 360, and what I saw literally sucked the air out of my lungs. It was what looked like the entire aircraft in pieces. Broken pieces. Ripped and cracked and scorched and shredded pieces. Enormous structures and assemblies ripped apart with the force . . . well, with the force of a jet flying into a mountain.

I looked across the hangar at Jack. He didn't say anything, but the lights stayed on. He was probably, like me, too stunned to move. I started moving toward him.

Close to the front of the hangar where the two of us were standing, the parts were more or less organized into groups. Seats all together along one of the walls. A group of boxes that all had cables poking out. Sheet metal stacked on end in racks. One of the massive engines was mounted on a base of some kind. Pieces of it were scattered around it in boxes, on more workbenches, and on the ground.

Then there were the cosmetic pieces, some of which, like the tail and the in-flight magazines, looked eerily undisturbed. Carpeted bulkheads, first-class leather seats, tray tables, laminated safety cards. I could see them here and there, interspersed with severed cables and frayed insulation, smashed fuses and electronic components, valves, cylinders, and huge slabs of bent and twisted aluminum skin. It was like seeing a jumble of body parts—a face next to a ruptured kidney, or a couple of manicured hands lying next to a shattered spine and a broken fibula.

Toward the back, the parts were less organized. They were thrown together in a large jumble as if some mas-

sive force had lifted them off that mountain in Ecuador
and flung them across the continents until they hit the
back wall of this hangar and came to rest, piled at odd
angles, almost to the ceiling.

There was also that strong smell. Aviation fuel and
grease and something decaying and rotten, and I started
thinking about the bodies and the blood and the tissue—
the people who had been in this accident, and what such
a catastrophic force had done to them. My mouth began
to water, and fill with the taste of something sour coming
up the back of my throat.

"This is the accident aircraft," I said, just to see what
it sounded like out loud. "This is the wreckage from
Ecuador."

"It's the Triple Seven that goes with your logbook,"
he said.

"What is it doing here?"

"I don't know how, but Jimmy must have stolen it."

I looked around, trying to process Jack's statement.
Some of the parts were gigantic. Besides the tail and the
engines, there was a large slab of wing, and what looked
like the landing gear. "How do you figure he did that,
Jack?" It seemed impossible to me.

"Maybe he stole it from the company that salvaged it.
Maybe he bought it from them out the back door." He
shrugged. "Maybe he took it off the side of the mountain himself."

"How does a private U.S. citizen get access to a crash
site in South America? How would he get up the mountainside ahead of the authorities, whoever they may be,
and cart off an entire airplane? Where does he get the
equipment? How does he even know there's a crash?"

"I don't know the how." Jack nodded toward the
worktable where we'd seen the soldering equipment.
"But I know the why."

And that's the moment when it all came together for
me. I took a step back, and then another, as if another
few feet of space and distance might make it easier to
comprehend the incomprehensible. What was even more
overwhelming than the sheer volume of parts and the

magnitude of whatever operation had to have been mounted to bring it all here was the notion that these parts, bent and broken and burned, were being readied to go back into the inventories of active commercial aircraft.

Jack stood shaking his head with an expression bordering on admiration. "Fucking Jimmy. He's got balls. I have to give him that."

The unmistakable sound of a slamming car door cut through the thick silence in the hangar. I looked at Jack just as the second slam sounded.

"Go. Go," he hissed. *"Go."*

He pushed me back in the direction we had come and followed right behind me. The lights were on this time, which made it easier, but it was still dangerous to maneuver through the obstacle course of dense coils, sharp edges, hanging cables, and cardboard boxes.

The walls began to rattle and a dull rumble filled the hangar as the big doors opened. If there had been a warning—the sound of an engine or the tires rolling over cracked pavement—we had been too insulated, too stunned, or too far away to hear. And now it was too late. I looked up at the plywood bathroom door where we had come through. So close. We weren't going to make it. If we were going to use the noise of the rumbling door as cover, we had to do it fast.

My instinct was to drop to the floor. From there I saw Jack lunge toward a piece of the wing leaning up against the wall. It offered good cover if he could narrow himself enough to wedge in. The door was open and I could hear voices. I went all the way down, flattening myself to the ground, flashlight in hand. My jeans protected my legs, but I could feel on my bare arms that the cement floor was stained with grease, and thick with the dust and grit and God knows what else that had settled in it. It was also cold, probably because my skin felt feverishly hot.

I didn't dare lift my head. I turned it as far as it would go, which meant one ear was pinned to the ground. I was glad I hadn't worn earrings. I spotted a large piece of scorched sheet metal that had enough of a bow shape that I thought I could crawl under. I started toward it, inching on my stomach, stopping every few seconds to remind myself to breathe and to listen. Whoever was out there was loitering toward the front of the hangar. There were two different voices.

The edges of the sheet metal were as sharp as German kitchen knives. Once in, I didn't know if I could get out unscathed, but I had no time to go anywhere else. I stuck my head in and tried to angle my shoulders through. It was a very tight fit, and the sharp ragged edges kept catching my shirt.

They were coming toward the back, toward us, rummaging along the way. The voices were getting louder. I wriggled out and flipped over on my back. I used my hands to keep the jagged edge away and was able to squirm quietly into the hiding place. It was dark inside, and the air was close. I stuck the flashlight into my waistband. It was uncomfortable, pressing against my pelvic bone, but I didn't want it rolling away at the wrong time, and I wanted both hands free. I could see through a ten-inch hooded gap where the sheet metal didn't quite touch the ground. Hopefully, I was back far enough that no one could see my blackened face there.

It took a long time for the two of them to cross the distance from the front of the warehouse because they were picking their way through the parts field, stopping every now and then to rummage around in the pieces of the aircraft.

I picked out the voices. One was deep and mellifluous. I pictured him as a big man with a barrel chest and a wide mouth. Like a bass. The second man's voice was thinner and grainier. He sounded like a tall, reedy smoker. They were getting close enough that I could begin to understand what they were saying.

". . . *shit*, man . . . *believe* this . . . what kind of . . ." That was Wide Mouth. His voice was louder and easier to hear. I couldn't understand everything he was saying, but from his excited and breathless delivery, my impression was he was seeing this stash for the first time.

I listened through every pore in my skin, trying to

make out the words and put them together. "Take whatever you want . . . ," said Reedy Man. ". . . you got it."

"I might . . . some of them seats over there"—Wide Mouth was getting closer—"because I can sell them on the Internet. Put them up on one of them auction sites. I read an article the other day that told how some fool bought some B727 seats for six hundred dollars on eBay, some that weren't even in no crash."

"Whatever you take . . ." Reedy Man sounded exasperated. ". . . can't tell anyone where it's . . . fucking Feds . . ."

"Well, shit, Jimmy. That's what makes them worth anything at all."

Jimmy? A drop of sweat trickled off my forehead and ran back into my hair. It felt like an ant crawling across my scalp. That was Wide Mouth talking which meant Reedy Man was Jimmy Zacharias. Knowing that changed the atmosphere, made the air more combustible. I wondered what Jack was thinking.

"Then pick something else, something you can sell straight up." Knowing it was Jimmy made him sound different, more menacing.

"You'll throw in all the paperwork?"

"Hurry up. They're going to be coming back soon. Fucking assholes left the lights on again."

One of them moved something that made my metal cover rattle. A jolt shimmered from the top of my head right on down my spine. They were that close? Of course they were close. If I could hear him that clearly, they were very close. There was more movement and someone's leather Timberland boot appeared next to my face. Close enough that I could smell the sweaty leather.

I stopped breathing and closed my eyes and concentrated every thought on being somewhere else. I pictured myself floating on a river in a tube on clear, cool water under a brazen blue sky. When someone started moving things around over my head, I tried to float along and relax my muscles and my brain and let the tension flow out.

Then it got worse.

The instant I heard the nails clicking across the concrete, I knew Bull was coming. He must have been out doing his business before, but he was there now. He didn't seem to be coming for us—his trot wasn't intent enough—but that didn't mean he wouldn't pick up the scent any second. I felt all the air go out of my hiding place. I imagined the grease on the ground as a pool of my blood, blood that would gush from my throat after Bull had ripped it out.

"I reckon I'd be better off with some of them smaller components up front." Wide Mouth was moving away. I heard him leaving, and then the boot—it must have been Jimmy's—started away as well. But the dog didn't. I heard him again. His gait was more purposeful. I imagined his nose to the greasy cement. I imagined him picking up the scent. I held my stomach muscles tight to keep from shaking.

"What's the matter with him?" Wide Mouth asked.

"He likes to scrape around in there for the rats. That pile is mostly cabin parts and it's crawling with them because of the dried blood and skin and shit. He's going to get hurt. Bull, get out of there."

No way. He came closer, his four paws dancing in primal anticipation. I couldn't see his head, but I heard his excited yelping.

"BULL!"

Bull was down on his stomach, his snout to the pavement, snuffling forward, trying to make himself flat enough to crawl under a piece of fuselage that was between him and me. It was me he smelled. It was my uninvited presence he sensed, and he looked as if he would chew through solid steel to get to me.

Jimmy jerked him back hard. The dog's squeal was pained and high pitched. "It's nothing but rats!" he yelled. "I told you that. You go in there you're going to get cut. Go on outside."

Bull was down on the floor heaving with all his strength against Jimmy's restraining hand. He did a frantic visual sweep, snout low to the ground. Just before Jimmy yanked him up by the neck, his eyes locked on mine. He went insane, and all I could think about was his powerful jaws closed around my throat.

Wide Mouth shouted. "Maybe there's something in there."

Bull bared his teeth and thrust his slobbering face toward mine. I could smell his breath. It took every ounce of concentration not to jerk away from him. Jimmy struggled for control, and I prayed he could find it. I could see Bull's hind legs as he leaped and yelped and tried to twist away. My arms were going to sleep at my side, the flashlight was pressed so far into my stomach I could feel it in my backbone, and I hadn't breathed in so long I was about to pass out. And if he found me, I didn't want to be lying there like a dead fish with arms that wouldn't work.

I used the cover of Bull's racket to bring one hand up from my side. That worked out okay. When I brought the other one up, my shoulder brushed my metal shelter, which caused something else to shift. Jimmy must have clamped his hand across Bull's snout and held his mouth shut. The dog held still and made the only noise he could, which was a sore, pinched whine. Jimmy kneeled down on one knee and started to lean over. But it took him a second because his big dog occupied both of his hands. I saw his knee come down. I wrapped my hand around the flashlight, the only weapon I had. I saw his hand touch the ground. I pictured him leaning down, but in that last second, something—a blur, a solid mass—skittered past my face. When it crossed my line of sight, a cold shot went straight through me.

It was a rat. A huge furry rat with tiny eyes, a long tail, and a pointy nose. It made a dash out from under my metal umbrella. It must have been mighty disoriented because that was also toward the crazed canine. It scampered right over Jimmy's hand. The thought of those rat claws crawling over bare skin made my shoulders shake and my jaw clamp and both my hands curl into fists without any conscious direction from my brain.

Jimmy wasn't taking it well, either. When he spotted the rodent coming straight toward his face, it startled him enough that he stumbled backwards and landed on his butt.

"Goddamn mother*fucker*," he yelled.

When Bull spotted the rat, he jerked away from Jimmy and took off, following the rodent to another part of the hangar.

I heard Wide Mouth rushing over. "Look at the size of that thing."

"What the fuck, Jimmy? What are you doing here?" That was . . . that wasn't the voice of either one of them. It was a new voice, a third voice coming through the door, and right behind it the sound of two more car doors slamming. "Get the fucking dog in the car, now."

Jimmy stood up. He and Wide Mouth moved away, talking the whole time. Jimmy was calling for Bull. I heard a lot of raised voices, but outside the hangar and too far away to hear what they were saying. Whoever had just arrived was very angry.

I heard all the sounds in reverse. The lights snapped off. The walls rattled again as someone pulled the big door shut and locked it. It sounded like a chain and a padlock. The voices faded out, and it was suddenly, blessedly quiet enough that I thought I could hear my own heart beating.

I wanted to cry from the release of the brain-boiling tension that had built up inside. A lot of good that would do. Instead, I took in many big breaths, unballed my fists, flexed my fingers, and kept my eyes peeled for more rats. It wouldn't be good to get startled again.

I don't know how much time passed before I heard Jack's voice somewhere close by. "Alex."

"Over here." I started to crawl out and snagged my shirt on the lip of the metal sheet. He reached down and carefully lifted my protective armor just enough that I could scramble out. The dimness felt comfortable, like an invisible force field.

"Are you all right?" he asked.

I didn't know, but I nodded yes. It was more for myself since he couldn't see it.

"Let's go," he said.

I followed him out the way we'd come, through the window and back over the fence, grabbing the floor mats as we went. This time as I crossed the field, I was less picky about where I put my feet as long as it was one in front of the other. I kept thinking about Bull, about the way he'd chased me before, and I kept looking back for him. As we moved into the trees, we had to slow down, but we still made enough of a disturbance to agitate the wildlife.

The return trip from the hangar seemed a lot faster than the trip in, but then we ran full speed all the way back. The car loomed ahead sooner than I expected. We were going to make it. We were going to crawl out of the swamp and back into civilization and take showers and wash the grease and the grit and the dog's slobber off and feel human again.

A cramp grabbed my side just as I reached the car and I had to stop and lean over to breathe. There didn't seem to be enough oxygen in the air. I set the mats down, stared at the car keys in my hand, and took a few more deep breaths. I straightened to put the key in the lock. A loud thump. The car shook. There was yelling and shouting. Men appeared from out of the brush and surrounded us. They all had guns. They were all shouting.

I looked for Jack. He was already pinned against his side of the car with his arms behind his head looking back at me. Someone pushed him toward the front and over the hood and pulled his arms behind him. I felt a hand on my shoulder and something cold and hard against my neck. My hands went straight over my head. I was so scared I didn't even realize until after I was handcuffed what they had been yelling.

Federal agents, they'd said. Step away from the car and put your hands behind your head.

Chapter Twenty-five

Jack and I had been put into separate cars for the drive into the city. We hadn't had a chance to speak at all, but I had searched out his eyes as they had snapped the cuffs on. He had shaken his head and I had taken that to mean I shouldn't talk to these people. And I didn't. I didn't say one word to the two agents who drove me in. They didn't attempt to talk to me, and barely spoke to each other, which just made the ride seem longer. After about twenty minutes, a cell phone rang. Mine. I recognized the ring. The agent who was carrying it opened it and turned it off without a word.

Inside the hangar I hadn't had time to feel afraid. But now I couldn't stop thinking about a time when I had gone out hiking late in the day in an unfamiliar place and gotten turned around. I kept remembering the moment, the sinking, gut-stabbing moment when I realized I had taken a wrong turn or chosen the wrong fork in the path and no matter which way I looked, nothing was familiar. Nothing. I was lost. It was getting dark. I knew I was in trouble.

Sitting in the back of a car in handcuffs, staring at the taciturn profiles of two agents, and thinking about the events of the evening was like an extended, slow motion version of that moment. At least in the woods, I had been able to act, to do something. All I could do here was sit and feel the panic growing.

The sun was coming up when we arrived at our destination, a nondescript office building in an area of town

I didn't recognize. We took an elevator to the fourth floor. The best and worst moment came when they removed the cuffs and let me stop in the bathroom in the hallway. I was so relieved to have a moment alone. But when I stepped in front of the sink to wash my hands, I glanced in the mirror and wanted to cry. I had forgotten my face was smeared with greasepaint. Twigs and leaves stuck out of my hair at odd angles, and black-stained sweat had dribbled crooked trails down my neck and throat and pooled in my ears.

I put one hand on either side of the sink, closed my eyes, and tried to let my head drop forward. But the muscles in my neck were so tight, trying to stretch them touched off a sharp pain that knifed across my shoulders and all the way down my back. When I looked in the mirror again, my eyes were full and beginning to run over because I knew I was in over my head—way over my head. What about my new job? What if they found out about this in Detroit? Would I ever get another job? How was I ever going to find my way out of this mess?

I tried to stretch the muscles anyway, breathing through the pain, reminding myself that I had made it out of the woods when I'd been lost, mostly by being calm, backtracking, and reasoning through a logical way out. Jack had said that I should build the kind of life I wanted. Looking in the mirror at my fright mask of a face, I didn't know if this was a life I wanted, but it certainly was a long way from any life I'd ever lived. Maybe that was the point. Maybe Jack was right. If I truly was interested in the job in Detroit, I wouldn't have been drinking beer last night on an open-air deck in Florida, and I wouldn't be standing here right now.

Hot water and paper towels took care of most of the paint and grime. Then I went through the door to start searching for the way out of the woods.

The agents led me into a mostly deserted, generic suite of offices complete with cubicles and identical computers on every desk. Without a word, they left me in a cold, windowless conference room with the door closed. There was no telephone. There was no clock, and I had no sense of how long I spent pacing around the small table, shivering in my damp, sweaty clothes, wondering what had happened to Jack and what was going to happen to me. I concentrated on staying calm. Eventually, the door opened and I was taken to a larger meeting room. This one had a big conference table, a woman, three men—and Jack.

I was so wound up and happy to see him I almost started right in with my compulsive questioning. What happened? Who are these people? What is going to happen? Am I going to jail? Am I screwed for the rest of my life?

But the room had a bad vibe, and Jack didn't even look at me. I assumed everyone there was a federal agent, although no one had bothered to identify which agency, and it hadn't been written on the door. They were all dressed casually except the one who was standing. He was about my age, mid- to late-thirties, blonde, blue-eyed, and proportioned like an athlete in a well-cut suit. Not the football player kind with a neck as thick as his waist, but more like an extremely fit golfer, or a world-class tennis player. He must not have gotten the memo about casual dress day.

"Please sit down." He spoke in my general direction, but not exactly to me.

I had just been nose to snout with a crazed dog who had wanted to rip the flesh from my bones, so a guy in a suit in a conference room didn't seem all that intimidating.

"Who are you?"

"Damon Hollander. I'm a special agent with the FBI."

So this was the famous Agent Hollander, the one who had treated Pat Spain with so much respect. I checked out the others around the table. They all looked so damn smug in their clean polo shirts and neatly combed hair. "Can I see some identification?"

Agent Hollander reached into his inside suit pocket, whipped out a thin black wallet, and flashed his badge

and ID. He did it with such cool, dramatic intensity I
knew right away it was his favorite part of the job. The
phrase Junior G-man sprang instantly to mind.

"Sit down, please."

I took the seat across from Jack, who finally glanced
up. He had also washed the black from his face, so it
was easy to read his expression, and it wasn't what I had
expected. He was supposed to be angry. I was entitled
to be scared and angry, but he was supposed to be bris-
tling with uncomplicated outrage at this high-handed
treatment we were receiving from his former employer.
He wasn't. He was subdued.

Damon joined us at the table, pulling his chair out far
enough that he could sit with his legs crossed. After he
was settled in, he unbuttoned his suit jacket and smoothed
it so that it dropped loosely at his sides and wouldn't
wrinkle.

"We have a little problem here," he announced. "You
people have stumbled into a federal investigation."

He was looking to Jack for a response. Everyone in
the room was, including me. After an uncomfortably long
silence, I spoke up. "What are you investigating?"

"I can't discuss that with you."

"Are you investigating the murder of John McTavish?"

"You'd be better off staying out of this discussion, Ms.
Shanahan. We're giving you the benefit of the doubt, so
the less you say, the better off you will be. The less you
know, the better off you'll be."

"It's good to hear you're so concerned for me,
Agent."

He offered yet another smug expression, from what
seemed like an endless assortment. He reminded me of
all those young, strapping corporate officers that used to
work at the airline. Young alpha males, every one, with
the blessed-by-the-gods attitude. They had all come from
the best schools, all dressed alike, all thought alike, and
because of it had been given more responsibility than
they had ever earned. Only this man carried a gun and
had behind him the full force and authority of the federal
government. Or did he?

I glanced around at the less-than-official-looking offices. "Agent Hollander, you followed me tonight. You stuck a gun in my ear, put me in handcuffs, and dragged me down here. You are now holding me against my will. By what authority have you done all of this?"

"He won't tell you." All eyes shifted to Jack. He was alive after all, and though his voice was thick and halting, it sounded wonderful to me. "And he won't answer your questions because he wasn't supposed to be out at that hangar tonight. Isn't that right, Damon?"

The young agent merely tipped his head in an attitude of patient benevolence. Jack sat forward in his chair and for the first time seemed to be present in the room. I started to review the events of the evening, trying to remember as much as I could, starting with the overheard conversation between Jimmy and Wide Mouth.

"You didn't follow her," Jack said, watching Damon for a reaction. "Or me. You were already out there." He nodded to the people sitting around the table. "You're the ones who are securing the hangar."

Damon had no reaction, but I remembered that Jimmy had referred more than once to the "fucking Feds." That didn't necessarily mean anything, but he had also said the assholes had left the lights on again. He'd said they had to get out before someone came back. If the two men in the car had been Jimmy's security, as we had assumed, why would Jimmy have been worried about them? On the other hand, why would the FBI be securing a hangar that housed a stolen aircraft?

"A secret hangar full of stolen aircraft parts," Jack said. "How does that fit into your investigation? And why doesn't anyone know about it?"

Damon's delicate hands stiffened just enough to convince me that Jack was right. I didn't know exactly what it meant that he was right, but he was. We weren't the only ones who had snuck into the hangar. Jimmy had, too, only he'd had a key.

"You're not with the Bureau anymore, Dolan. You don't get to ask the questions." Damon checked his watch and looked at me. "I'm requesting that you turn over the logbook that was stolen from the Air Sentinel crash site. And don't even bother asking how I know you have it. I won't tell you." He stared at me as if my complete predictability bored him.

"I'm not denying I have it." Who had told him that? Why wasn't he asking for the ring as well? I glanced over at Jack. A little help would have been nice.

Damon had followed my gaze. "Don't concern yourself with Mr. Dolan. You're the one who hired him. Without you, he has no reason to be involved."

That's when it occurred to me that Jack must have already had discussions with Damon Hollander. Jack hadn't . . . surely Jack hadn't told him about the logbook. I looked at the other agents, the two men and the woman. They seemed to be following the conversation closely and contributing nothing. I wondered why they had to be here. The whole thing was making less and less sense.

"Agent Hollander, do you or any of your colleagues here drive a nondescript sedan? One that's the color of a kidney bean?"

"Why do you ask?"

"No reason. Maybe I should give the book to Air Sentinel. Or Barbara Walters."

"Stealing evidence from a crash site is a federal offense," he said. "I can subpoena the evidence if you refuse to cooperate."

"I didn't steal it from the crash site and you know it. I think you know who did."

"You're withholding it."

"Does it have something to do with your investigation of John McTavish's murder?"

"Go home, Ms. Shanahan. Turn over the evidence and go home."

"Why?"

"Because I'm telling you to." Agent Hollander's pitch had changed ever so slightly. He was getting frustrated.

"Do you normally have good luck with this approach, Agent Hollander? 'Do as I say for reasons I won't tell you.' "

"Why are you protecting Jimmy Zacharias?" There was Jack again, dropping another bombshell out of nowhere. "Here's how I've got it figured, Damon. Jimmy stole the parts from the site in Ecuador with the intention of reselling them on the black market. He got them into Miami. I don't know how, but he did. The Bureau found out, because it's pretty damned difficult to hide an entire Triple Seven stolen from a high-profile crash, even from you. But instead of hauling Jimmy in, and Avidor, and everyone else who was involved in this thing, you're covering it up. You've got the lid on. You told Jimmy to stay away from the hangar, locked the door, and put two guys out front. Why would you do that?"

Jack was on to something. I could feel it. The other agents in the room had gone perfectly still.

"All I can figure is you want Jimmy out on the street, at least for a while longer, and maybe that's because he's one of these high-class confidential informants you're supposed to have. As if Jimmy could be a high-class anything. But that's neither here nor there. What's important is that it would be a pretty big coup for a kid like you at this point in your career."

"What would?"

"Nailing an international drug lord."

"Drug lord?" Damon seemed sad that anyone could be so misinformed, but he didn't deny it.

"Let's let our imaginations run wild. You're set up here off-site in some kind of ongoing operation. Let's say your target is a big fish from Colombia named Ottavio. It wouldn't hurt your career to be the one who reels him in, and you seem like the ambitious sort. Would it be fair to say you would do anything, or you would let your source do anything, to make that happen?"

All eyes shifted back to Damon. He was tightening up again, but in a controlled way. It was hard to see, but it was there in his voice and in the way he held his head. He seemed to communicate most directly through the angle of his head.

"I don't know what it was like in your day, Dolan, but even if that were true, we have specific policies and guidelines as to what sort of activities will be tolerated from a confidential informant. Even you can remember that."

"How about stealing an airplane? Would that be tolerated? What doesn't hang together for me, Damon, is that you're a drug guy. You're after Ottavio, and Jimmy is a parts man all the way. Parts and the occasional weapons deal. Even if Ottavio is in on this Sentinel parts scam, that wouldn't be enough for you. You want the big-time bust. Not some pissant, penny ante parts rap."

Damon crossed his soft hands over his knee. "That's a pretty complicated theory," he said, "coming from someone like you, Dolan. I'm amazed your brain can still handle complex thought." He turned to me. "I'm afraid Mr. Dolan has misled you and put you at risk. He's wrong about this, among other things. But I suspect he can get confused."

"Why would he get confused?"

I had asked the question without thinking and was immediately sorry because I knew I had done exactly what he wanted. And I had an idea what the answer was going to be. I saw it in Jack's face, which was tense enough to make mine hurt. I saw it in the deep furrow that creased the bridge of his nose, and the way he stared straight down at the table. And I saw it in Damon's keen interest in my reaction to what he was about to say.

"Dolan here spent most of his time with the Bureau in a bottle. That's why he's no longer with us. He's an alcoholic. They called it early retirement"—his eyes slid over to Jack—"but he was fired. You knew that, didn't you? That he's a slobbering, falling-down, blacking-out drunk?"

I didn't look at Jack, but at the other agents around the table, the two men and the woman, and I understood why Damon had wanted them there. Only one of them, one of the men, had the decency not to stare.

Damon had asked me a question and was waiting for my response. I gave him the only one I could, the only one that made sense, given the circumstances. "Yes, I knew."

"I don't think so. If I were you, I'd think carefully about whether or not you want to trust your future, maybe even your life to someone like him. I wouldn't."

It was best, I thought, not to prolong this conversation, so I sat quietly and stared, as Jack did, at the tabletop.

"Your cars," Damon said, smoothing his tie, "are in the back. Ms. Shanahan, I'll send an agent over to your hotel to pick up the logbook and give you a receipt."

When Damon stood up, so did the others. When Damon looked down at Jack as if he were a despicable waste of a human being, so did the others. Jack's hair was a mess and his eyes looked as if he'd been up all night, which he had. He still had a trace of camouflage paint on his chin and under one ear. He held himself perfectly still and endured the scrutiny, and I had the strong feeling it wasn't the first time he'd felt it. The fluorescents overhead threw light that was bright enough to catch the flecks of gray in the stubble on his chin, and harsh enough to show all the lines in his face. And I felt such a sense of loss from him. For him.

"You've been gone from the Bureau for three years," Damon said, "and you're still screwing up. Don't screw this up for me."

Chapter Twenty-six

I found Jack just where he'd said he would be. He was the only patron at the Miramar Coin Op Laundry, a laundromat situated in a quiet enclave in the shadow of downtown Miami under a canopy of tall, leafy trees. The space was narrow and deep—what the real estate agents in Boston refer to as a floor-through. He was unloading a machine all the way in the back, taking out a load of whites and pushing them into a dryer. It was quiet enough that when he slotted his quarters, I heard them fall.

When he turned, I knew he hadn't slept since I left him early that morning. His face was almost gray, as if he'd been sketched in charcoal, and his eyes were as sad as the shabby surroundings. "I see you found me," he said.

"Only because you let me. This would not have been the first place I looked."

"Let's sit outside," he said.

We settled in the *al fresco* seating arrangement on the sidewalk. It was a lot like sitting outside on the Champs-Elysées in Paris, except the metal tables and chairs were rusted, the sidewalk was cracked, and there was no one to serve us. There was a restaurant at the end of the street, but in place of quaint little tobacco shops and hotels, we had a beauty parlor—closed for the evening—and a boarded-up bar across the street.

"Did you get any sleep?" he asked, folding the newspaper he'd been reading.

"I slept all day," I said. "I really like sleeping. What about you? How did you spend your day?"

"Looking for Ira. Trying to find Patty. I didn't find either one. All in all," he sighed, "not a successful day." I was glad to see a hint of irony in his smile, but I wasn't sure how to respond. We had said nothing about the morning's events when we'd parted, preferring, at least in my case, to defer until I'd had a chance to sleep and let things seep in. So it was all still there, everything Damon had laid on us, hanging in the air, as pervasive and hard to ignore as the sweet and heavy scent of the dryer sheets that kept wafting out of the laundromat. I decided to defer a little longer.

"When do you suppose someone at Air Sentinel is going to find out where their airplane is?"

"They might know. But it's better all the way around if no one else does for now. At least not until Damon gets done whatever it is he's doing."

"And you think what he's doing is hunting down Ottavio?"

"Without a doubt. And I'm pretty well convinced at this point that Jimmy is his snitch. I just don't know what he could tell Damon that would be useful to him."

"Jack, you didn't tell Damon about the logbook, did you?"

"Name, rank, and serial number was all he got from me. Why?"

"I was just wondering how he would have known about it. He knew about the book but not the ring. I think that means something."

"Maybe." From the sound of it, he didn't much care to think about it. A quiet breeze riffled the corners of the newspaper, and we lapsed into a silence that went on for a while. The predominant sound was that of the dryer drum rumbling around.

"If you live in South Beach, Jack, why do you come all the way over here to do your laundry?"

"It's not that far. It's just over the bridge. Besides, I like this neighborhood." He nodded to the boarded-up storefront across the street. "When that bar was open, I could throw the laundry in and sip a cold beer while I waited. They used to know me over there a little too well. I think they went out of business when I stopped drinking." He laughed, but with more bitterness than humor.

"Those things Damon said to you . . . about you this morning, the way he did it . . . He's a piece of shit."

"He is that. He's also right." He looked up at me, maybe trying, as Damon had, to gauge my reaction, and the thought flashed that I was glad it mattered to him. "That's the problem. Everyone has always been right about me. My ex-wife. People at work. You noticed, didn't you, that I don't have many friends left there. Patty Spain is one of the few who still takes my calls, and she's not even with the Bureau."

"Did something happen?"

"Nothing happened. It was all the little things that accumulate over time when you're a drunk. It's the way they pile up, eventually, into this big stinking heap that people can't ignore anymore." He shook his head. "I let everyone down. My wife. My son. My bosses . . . many bosses who kept giving me chances. Sooner or later, I let them all down." He was holding his reading glasses in his hand, opening one temple, then the other, closing one, and then the other.

"You're sober now."

"Two years. I spent a lot longer than that drinking. I have many amends to make. Some I never can."

"Why not?"

He shrugged, and kept flipping those temples up and down. I thought if he did that enough, he was going to loosen the screws and the glasses would fall apart in his hands.

"Where is your wife?"

"She took my son a few years back and moved up to your neck of the woods. He's going to college at Dartmouth." He glanced over at me, I thought for a response or affirmation of some sort.

"That's a good school," I said, trying to give him what he needed.

He nodded, seemed satisfied, and dropped his glasses into the front pocket of his cotton shirt. Then he stretched his legs out under the wrought iron table, shooed a tiny winged visitor away from his face, and stared up with tired eyes into the trees overhead. He looked as if he might not ever get up. "Do you do that?" he asked, after a while.

"Do what?"

"Get used to certain places and keep going back to them?"

I'd tossed my keys on the table when I'd arrived. It was a mesh surface, and the longest key, the key from my rental car, had lodged itself in one of the openings. I set about dislodging it as I thought about that question. "The thing about the airline business is you're either unpacking from one move or packing for the next. There's enough time in between to find a dentist and dry cleaners. Then it's time to go again. There's no time to get attached to a place."

"Or to people, huh?"

"That, too." The key came loose with a minor tug.

"Sometimes I think I should leave Miami," he said. "But I never do. No matter where I go, I always end up back here."

"What keeps you here?"

He lowered his gaze until he was staring across the street at the bar that had gone bust. "I like living in a place where I know I can always find my way home. It's useful to know the geography when you're a drunk."

I thought about all the places my airline career had taken me—airports and offices, ticket counters and freight houses, cities large and small. I'd lived in apartments, hotels, studios, condos, duplexes, and houses all over the country, and never once had felt that I had found my home. "There's a lot to be said for feeling at home," I said, "no matter who you are. Or how you define yourself."

He took in a deep breath and let it out slowly. It sounded almost as if it hurt him to draw breath, hurt somewhere deep down in his lungs. I had to keep myself from reaching out and touching his face and trying to make him stop hurting.

"I'm sorry," he said.

"For what?"

"For letting you hear those things about me from that little prick. I should have told you."

He was again staring up into the leaves, which were becoming less and less distinct as the evening wore on. I looked where he was looking, and wondered if we were seeing the same thing. I was pretty sure that even if we were, we were seeing it from different angles. "That would have been easier on both of us," I said.

"He's right about the trust thing."

"No. I trusted you immediately, Jack, and not just because you saved me from Bull and my own stupidity. I believe you know what you're doing, and I don't believe you'll let me down."

"One of the things I thought about today, all day, was about what could have happened to you in that hangar. All the different things that could have happened."

"I don't recall you forcing me to go in there with you. And you offered me a gun. I should have taken it. I should have listened to you. I will next time."

"You should go home, Alex."

"Is that what you want?"

He stared down into his lap and I tried so hard to see into his eyes, but it was too dark.

"You should go home and get moved and start your life and your job."

"Right now, this minute, Jack, I couldn't care less about that job. I'm asking you if you want me to leave. If my being here makes it harder for you in any way, personally, professionally, or otherwise, I'll go. But if you're saying I should leave because you think that's what's best for me, then I respectfully ask that you mind your own business."

His head was resting on the back of his chair. He turned it so he could see me, but didn't speak.

"I will not let that asshole Hollander step over John McTavish's body to get a promotion." My voice felt clear and strong and I knew it was because I was speaking the truth—my truth—saying what I wanted to say. "I hate what he did to you this morning, and I'm not wild about the way he treated me. If leaving here makes Damon's life easier, that's reason enough for me to stay. Beyond that, I want to finish the job I came down here to do. So sit up and look at me and tell me if you are asking me to leave."

He sat up slowly, and turned in his chair. He rested his arms in front of him on the table and seemed to sit stiffly. When all he did was stare at me, I figured he was searching for the words to tell me that I was making his life a mess and I should go home. Now, if not sooner. He didn't seem to want to look at me, so I braced for rejection and started thinking about how to tell Mae that I'd had to give up. She would be nice and maybe take my hand and—

"Stay."

"What?"

He was looking at me now, and giving me that crooked, endearing grin he'd used on Vanessa. I liked it better when he aimed it at me. "If you want to stay, I like having you here."

"Good." And it was good. I felt good. I felt the way I do after I've run six miles. Worn out, but exhilarated. "Now, tell me what is going on between you and Jimmy. I want to know everything."

Chapter Twenty-seven

While Jack had moved his load of darks to the dryer, I had run down to the restaurant for a couple of sandwiches. It turned out the top floor of Perricones was a restaurant, but the bottom floor was a deli, and an excellent one. We both felt better for having a little protein in our systems—hot pastrami on rye with sauerkraut for him, and turkey on wheat with lettuce, tomato, and mustard for me. We were finished eating and I was still waiting to hear about Jimmy. By the time the streetlights came on, I wasn't sure I ever would.

A car rolled slowly by, the first in almost an hour. The driver found a place to park down the block on the street. A couple disembarked and headed into the restaurant. After they'd passed, Jack leaned over in his chair and kicked at a few stray pebbles on the sidewalk. "Did I tell you I served in Vietnam?"

I looked over at him. There seemed to be no end to the surprises he could come up with, and always in the most casual way. "No, Jack, you never mentioned that. What did you do in Vietnam?"

"I was a grunt. I got drafted and me and my low lottery number humped around the jungle like everyone else."

It never would have occurred to me that he had been a soldier, although it made perfect sense. He was the right age for it. But I was from a generation that didn't know war, at least not the low-tech version with ground troops, and without Scud missiles and CNN. I didn't know any soldiers. I never assumed anyone I ever met had been one.

"I thought . . . didn't you go to college?"

"I went after I came home. Uncle Sam paid for it, then I went to work for the Bureau. Everything I am I owe to the U.S. government." His laugh was bitter and I couldn't tell if the scorn was meant for his former employer or himself.

"How old were you?"

"I'd just turned twenty when I got there."

He sat back in his chair, turned his face to the dark sky, and went quiet again. I pulled my chair closer to the table. I sensed that everything he was about to say was something I wanted to hear.

"Thirty years ago." He shook his head. "Over thirty years. I can't believe it's been that long."

"Do you think about it much?"

"There are things that take me back there. The sound of a helicopter. Rotor blades always do it. Living down here, it can be the way the air feels when it has a certain weight to it. These fires out in the Everglades remind me a little of what it was like there."

"The smell?"

"Not the smell. The way the air presses against you. Vietnam had its own smell. I got it on me the first day I landed, and in some ways, it's never left. It's still so clear to me. You almost can't even describe it. Sweat. Jet fuel. Cordite. You always smelled cordite, no matter where you were."

"Cordite is—"

"It's gunpowder. Dust . . . fish . . . rain . . . chemicals. Bombs leave a chemical smell in the air. You mix it all up together with the blood and the corpses. And then it gets hot."

"I imagine that's a smell that would stay with you."

"You see things in a war . . . in battle . . . things you never expect to see and can't forget. I carried wounded and dying men out of the bush to helicopters to be evacuated and I still see their faces. It does something to you to know that the ones who died, yours was the last face they saw."

He was looking at the sky and he was talking to me, but he was remembering for himself. I could see in his face that there was a lot he was seeing he could not, maybe would not describe. If he had tried, I wouldn't have understood. I couldn't imagine what it must be like to carry around, like cards in your wallet, the images of men who had died in your arms.

"Jimmy and I served in Vietnam together."

He said it using that same dry, matter-of-fact tone and I wasn't sure I'd heard right. "You and Jimmy knew each other in Vietnam?"

"We met there. He was from Everglades City and I was from Miami. We were in the same unit and we hooked up. Almost from day one."

I sat up straight and leaned across the table. The mesh surface hurt my elbows. "The Jimmy Zacharias who runs the salvage yard, you've known him for thirty years?"

"Off and on."

I drifted back again in my seat. I wasn't sure what to make of this news. It changed the way I thought about Jimmy, even though I'd never met him. And it changed what I thought about Jack because it changed what I knew about him. I was getting used to that phenomenon. "What was he like back then?"

"He loved being a soldier. He grew up out in the Everglades so he was at home in the jungle. He used to say he could smell the NVA. He always knew when they were around. He never got surprised and he saved my ass more than once. It was like he had a sixth sense for it. Jimmy was a good soldier."

"This is the same man you suspect of killing John?"

He drew in a deep breath that seemed to take a long time to come out. "You learn things about the people you serve with," he said. "A lot about yourself, too. Some things you'd rather not know. What I learned about Jimmy in Vietnam was how much he liked to kill. What I learned from watching him was how cheap

human life can become under the right circumstances."
He thought about that. "The wrong circumstances."

He sat up straighter and shifted his weight. The chair
he'd been sitting in for hours seemed uncomfortable to
him now. "I watched Jimmy shoot an old man in a rice
paddy once from long range. This was someone's father
or someone's husband or grandfather who took three
bullets in the back of the head from a man he never saw
for reasons that had nothing to do with him. His head
exploded. He went"—he made a weak gesture with his
hand—"he went right over, face forward in the mud.
Jimmy killed that man and never looked back."

"Why?"

"He was lining up the sights on his rifle."

He'd been finding points in the distance to focus on
as he'd talked, but now he was looking at me, hard.
Waiting, I figured, for a reaction. I wasn't sure what to
say. What he had described struck me as the act of a
man who at best had lost his way, and at worst was a
psychopath. But I didn't feel I had the right to judge,
and I was very aware that whatever Jimmy had done,
Jack had been there, too. "This old man, I assume he
was a civilian?"

"Jimmy's philosophy was there were no civilians. You
couldn't tell NVA from friendlies. You couldn't tell the
children from the booby traps they sometimes carried.
He killed everything and everyone that got in his way."

A cricket started chirping and I became aware of the
deep silence we'd been sitting in. The dryer had stopped
spinning. Jack was still watching me.

"When you're in a war," he said, "when you're actually in it and not thinking about it or wondering about
it or training for it, you're in it up to your ass and you
have to stay in it, it's like you've gone to a different
planet. You're breathing different air than those people
back in the civilized world. The rules are different, but
you don't know that because everyone else around you
is acting the same way. All your reference points shift
and you can't get any perspective on it until you get back

to the world. You can't wait to get back to the world, but once you're back, you start to realize what's happened to you. You begin to understand how completely and profoundly you are not the same person you were. And you never will be."

The light from the street lamp high overhead showed every line in his face, tiny threads that held him together and kept him from blowing apart. He looked as if he was in pain, and had been for a long time. "I don't know if Jimmy went over there that way, or if his time there made him that way. All I know is when I met him, I liked him."

He put his hands on his knees and started to get up. He paused for a beat, and then he did stand. I reached for his hand and held it because I wanted to touch him, and because I didn't want him to walk away. But I didn't know what to say. I could feel the barrier that stood between us, the one made up of all those things he had seen, and all the things I never would. It was an insurmountable barrier for me. Impossible for me to ever get to the other side. But Jimmy was on the other side with him. Impossible for him not to be.

He pulled his hand away, leaned down, and kissed the top of my head. Then he did walk away.

I followed him and watched him from the doorway of the Coin Op as he pulled the clothes out of the dryer and piled them on a folding table. His back was to me as I approached him. I laid my hand between his shoulder blades and felt how warm his skin was through his shirt. And I felt him responding. I moved my hand up, following the line of his backbone, reached over the collar of his shirt and touched the skin on his neck. It was lined and leathery and the muscles underneath were stiff and tight. He straightened and closed his eyes, leaning into the rhythm of my hand as I wove my fingers into his hair, across the curves and contours of his head. When he turned around, I held his face in my hands and ran my thumbs gently along the deepest lines in his face, the ones that made him look the saddest. I wanted to kiss him. I wanted him to kiss me. He put his hands around

my waist and lifted me onto the table, onto the clothes
still warm from the dryer. I wrapped my legs around
him, pulled him to me close enough to feel the glasses
in his front pocket between us. Our lips brushed. He
opened his mouth and I tasted him. He tasted like Florida to me—sunny and tart, not sweet—and he smelled
like clean clothes. I wrapped my arms around him and
it felt so right to be holding him against my body, feeling
his breath on my neck.

My arms fell away as he stepped back—I thought to
kiss me again—but he kept moving back, out of my embrace. Out of my range. He caught my hands in his on
the way back and kissed them, once in each palm. "Let's
not . . . do this. This is not . . . it's not good . . ."

The expression in his eyes when he looked at me made
me feel that I'd done something very wrong. "I'm sorry,
Jack. I didn't mean—"

"It's not you. I'm not any good at this, especially now.
For me it would be for all the wrong reasons. I like you
and it's hard for me not to mess things up." He pushed
a strand of hair that had fallen into my face and wrapped
it behind my ear. "Do you understand?"

"Yeah. Okay." I let him go and we had this awkward
moment where he didn't know what to do and I didn't
know what to say and I was sitting in the middle of his
laundry. When I jumped down from the table, I felt the
pinch again in my ankle. It hurt.

I didn't stay long after that. Jack stood on the sidewalk
in front of the Coin Op and reminded me not to park
too far away from the elevator in the Dolphin Garage.
I walked up the street toward the restaurant and my car,
and knew that he was watching me all the way there.
That felt good. Having him in my arms had felt better.

Perricones looked like a tree house the way it nestled
under the leafy canopy. It was going full blast by then.
Some of the tables were on the open-air deck, and dinner
was being served to a lively New Orleans jazz accompaniment. The bawdy, brassy rhythm spilled out and rolled
down the streets of the quiet neighborhood like coins
tossed from the open doors and windows.

The smoke haze was not so bad, so I opened my windows to breathe unprocessed, non-air-conditioned air for a change. I could still hear the faint strains of the jazz band as I passed by the Miramar Coin Op and saw Jack, the only patron, sitting inside on one of the washing machines, hands on his knees, staring at the wall.

Chapter Twenty-eight

Ira Leemer turned and greeted me with a yellow-toothed grin that was surprisingly engaging. "Hello, missy. Want a bag of peanuts?" He offered me a small red-and-white-striped paper bag lumpy with what must have been peanuts in the shell. It was a surreal moment. Ira cocked his head. "Fresh off the roaster and on the house."

I hesitated. I always liked those peanuts. But so much fat content. What the hell. "Thank you, Ira." I accepted his offering, which seemed to make him happy. The bag still felt warm.

This time Jack and I had gone to find Ira at his sometime place of work—Ft. Lauderdale Stadium—where he was a peanut vendor and a spring training game was in progress. The Baltimore Orioles and the Mets. The three of us were in the cement-cooled shadows underneath the stands, but not too far from a ramp that led to the bleachers. I could see the bright square of sunshine at the top and hear the communal muttering of the crowd that always accompanies a game in progress.

"You work out here, Ira?"

"Since I been out. Yessirree. Only thing is they won't let me sell beer on account of I been in jail. That's where the real money is as far as the concession business goes. Anyhow"—he held up one of the bags—"these are the only parts I'm selling these days."

Jack was pacing, clearly not interested in peanuts.

"Why didn't you tell me what we were walking into out at that hangar, Ira?"

"Hold on a minute, Bobo. Just let's all calm down and let me get myself situated." He set his peanut tray on an unmanned snack bar counter, which freed his hands to dig out his cigarette paper and tobacco pouch. "I didn't know myself," he said as he started to roll one. "I just found out." He looked at me. "Saw them parts with your own eyes, did you?"

"Up close and personal."

"What was it like?"

Even if I could have described what I'd seen, what I'd felt, what I'd smelled and touched, I didn't get the chance. Jack was getting up close and personal with Ira, getting right into his face. "How did Jimmy get those parts? And don't give me any bullshit. I'm not in the mood."

Ira had to take a step back to look up into the taller man's face. "Went down and got 'em hisself, is what I heard."

"C'mon, Ira. How did he get them off the mountain? Where did he get the manpower and equipment? How did he get those huge units and assemblies into the country?" He articulated each question, as if his being clear might inspire from Ira a like response. "You know what I'm asking you."

"Hooked up with someone who was down there, I suspect, someone with some presence, who got in there, took what they wanted, and got out."

Jack looked as though he might take a swipe at Ira, so I gave it a try. "How did the bad guys get in there before the authorities? How did they even know there was a crash to go and scavenge?"

Something good happened on the field for the home team. A languid cheer drifted up from the crowd. It was, after all, spring training. By the time it petered out, Ira was rolled and ready. He fired up the cigarette and took a long pull. Then he spit out a piece of tobacco.

"I can't tell you what happened on account of I don't know, and that's the truth. I can tell you the story I've put together based on some of the things I've been hearing."

Jack took a step back and crossed his arms. It must have convinced Ira that he was in no eminent danger of being leveled, because he started to talk.

"As far as how they knew about it and the approximate location, they was monitoring radio frequencies. That was the easy part. Finding it and getting to it that fast, that was . . . that must have been the hard part. But once they got there . . . you know everybody's always talking about that airplane like it flew into the side of a mountain, but it didn't. It was a belly landing. Not much fire, so there was lots to take. But as far as getting there first, you are talking Ecuador here, missy."

"They have authorities in Ecuador."

"What they don't have is an NTSB Go-Team ready to show up on a remote mountaintop at the drop of a hat in the middle of the night. And who are the authorities down there anyway? You got your federales, your local authorities, your guerrilla armies—left and right wing. Who the hell is in charge? Probably whoever gets there first and whoever's got the biggest gun."

"Who got there first in this case?" Jack asked.

"Don't know, Bobo. That's what I keep on trying to tell you. But whoever it was had resources, because they took it all. You saw that. Every last thing that wasn't burning or bleeding, and some"—he narrowed his eyes and looked left and right, just as he had done at his trailer—"some that was bleeding, is what I hear."

I hesitated, but went ahead with it anyway. "What does that mean?"

"They was in such a hurry, them boys didn't even bother to dump out all the body parts. Just lifted the whole kit and caboodle the way it was. Lock, stock, and barrel. Whatever fell out, fell out. That's what I heard. Looted the bodies, too. Got it all before the peasants climbed up there and picked over what was left. By the time the airline got up there, you could gather up what was left and carry it down in baskets."

More casual cheering from the crowd above, and

though I was trying as hard as I could not to, all I could think of was climbing around in those parts, lying on the ground in the grease and other unknown matter. I remembered the smell—aviation fuel and something rotten. I thought I had imagined the something rotten. And the rats. Jimmy had said the place was crawling with rats. It all made me feel sick, and I wanted to give the peanuts back. Instead, I tried to focus on the task at hand.

"Ira, do you think it would be possible for someone to find a ring, a diamond ring, and the logbook in the wreckage that came up here?"

"Oh, sure, missy. You'd be surprised at the things that survive a plane crash. An aircraft goes nose down at full speed and turns into a burning hole in the ground. But around the crater, you might still find a pair of eyeglasses that ain't broke, or a fifty-dollar bill stuck in the mud. I didn't hear about the logbook, but sure, someone could have pulled it out of that mess. No telling what you might could have found tucked away in all the nooks and crannies."

"You wouldn't happen to have any firsthand knowledge of that?" Jack asked.

"Like what, Bobo? You mean was I down there in Ecuador? Hell, no. What do I keep trying to tell you? I'm telling you all that I know."

"I'm asking if you were one of the dirty mechanics working out at that hangar for Jimmy. Maybe doing a little strip-and-dip. You seem to know a lot about it."

"That's 'cause you told me to find out. No sir. I didn't want nothing to do with them parts. I ain't going back to jail. Besides, you know what they say. Even touching dead parts like that is bad luck. You remember that seven-two that went down around here back in the late seventies, don't you, Bobo? Went down in a bad storm."

"I remember. It went down in the Everglades."

"That's the one." He turned and directed his story at me. "The airline salvaged some of them parts and tried to reuse them, mostly galley parts. The company mechanics, of course, knew about all this and refused to even lay hands on equipment from a dead airplane, so they hired contractors. I tell you what"—there was that whuu-uut again—"one of them contractors was electrocuted on the job. Another one's wife delivered a stillborn baby, and once them parts were in the air, the stews started seeing ghosts in the galley."

"What happened?"

"The company hired one of them exorcists, but that didn't work. Finally they ripped the parts all out, took 'em to the smelter, and destroyed them once and for all. That's when the ghosts left and not before. They went belly-up anyway, but not because of no ghosts."

It was a good thing Jack had plenty of room to roam because he'd started moving and couldn't seem to stop. "What's the point of your ghost story, Ira?"

"I'm just telling why I didn't want nothing to do with them parts out in that hangar. It's bad luck. That's all there is to that. Bad luck. Whoever did disturb that crash is going to pay the price. It's like grave robbing is what it is. I don't want no part of it."

I reached back and lifted my ponytail off my neck. It was making my sunburn itch. I remembered how the big diamond ring had felt on my finger, and how the logbook had felt in my hands. Bad luck. That was the best way to describe the uneasy feeling. I had taken the ring off and Damon Hollander now had the logbook. But the feeling had never gone away.

"How much would you figure Jimmy could get for what's in that hangar?" Jack asked. "He had the landing gear, both engines, which looked to be in decent shape, probably avionics—"

"The tail," I said, "intact and in good shape."

Ira leaned back against the snack counter and ran that one through his computer while he smoked. "New Triple Seven. Depending on whether they go domestic or over-seas, piecemeal it, or find one buyer and move the whole load. Maybe three to four million."

"Plenty of motive for murder," Jack said.

"And a good way to tie Bobby to the whole opera-tion," I said, "if we can tie him to the book."

Ira was staring up the ramp. "It's probably getting

toward the seventh-inning stretch. That's when I do some good business, Bobo. Let me get out there. I'll keep nosing around for you."

Jack didn't even seem to hear him. "The Bureau has taken down Jimmy's operation out there. He's locked out of his own hangar, but he's still on the street. What do your sources tell you about that?"

"Is that what happened? 'Cause they were going great guns when all of a sudden everything just stopped. I'll be damned. How did he get hisself out of that one? You know Jimmy always said he'd never done one day in jail and never would. That's a puzzle, yes sir, that is."

"Tell me what you think of this idea." Jack had stopped moving and now leaned against the snack counter next to his snitch. The two of them looked as if they could have been discussing gardening tips, or the game outside. "Jimmy is a confidential informant working for the Bureau in an operation targeting Ottavio Quevedo. Do you know who that is?"

"Everybody knows him, Bobo."

"Jimmy's got something on Ottavio the Bureau wants and they're protecting him."

"I don't know what that could be."

"Let's think about this logically. What I saw in that hangar, to get it down off a mountain, you said it yourself, Jimmy would have had to have had access to cranes, probably crane helicopters, trucks, extraction equipment, earthmoving equipment. Plenty of manpower. Right?"

Ira cackled. "It weren't no donkeys carried them jet engines down off that hill."

"Who would have resources like that sitting around? Or access to them?"

"Bobo, I couldn't say. It would have to be the military, I guess. Maybe it was an inside job. Is that what you're getting at? Maybe them Ecuadors did it themselves, the army or what have you, 'cause they're the ones that would have all that stuff."

"I was looking at a map. That airplane went down not too far from the Colombian border." Jack was talking to me as much as to Ira now, maybe even to himself, and it was getting very interesting. "What you were saying about whoever gets there first, I think you're right. Who got there first in this case could have been one of the guerrilla armies from Colombia. Or the militias. They're better armed and better equipped than the real thing, and that's because they're funded with drug money."

"Drug money. Drug armies from Colombia. I think I see where you might be going with this, Bobo. That might explain the C130, too."

"A C130? A U.S. military aircraft?"

"Yes sir, an old one, but it can still carry plenty. They loaded it up and flew the whole mess up here. Don't ask me how they got hold of one or how they got into the States because I don't know."

A Colombian drug army. A Colombian drug lord. We were right back where we always ended up. I looked at Jack. "Does Ottavio have a C130?"

He shrugged. "He shouldn't, but that doesn't mean much."

"You're saying . . . I get what you're saying now, Bobo, without really saying. Maybe this Ottavio fella is the one Jimmy hooked up with down there. Maybe that's what Jimmy is snitching about." His eyes lit up and burned almost as bright as the tip of his cigarette. "Whooooeeee! Can you feature what would happen to old Jimbo if word got around that he's a stoolie for the Feds?"

Jack put his hand on Ira's shoulder, just the way he had on the porch of his trailer when he wanted to make a point. "That's exactly what I want to happen. I want to put Jimmy under pressure. Funny things happen to people when they're under pressure. All I want you to do is start floating the word that Jimmy is working for the government. Discreetly, Ira."

"That's all, huh?" Ira pooched his lips out and shook his head. He dropped his cigarette butt to the cement and stepped on it. "That's like saying you're gonna blow up his house, discreetly. That's like putting my head into the mouth of an alligator, discreetly. Are you sure you want to do that?"

"I'm sure."

I wasn't. "Why wouldn't we, Ira?"

"Because he's going to know right where it's coming from." He turned and looked at Jack. "He's going to know it's you, Bobo. He knows you're out here asking questions and making trouble for him. He's already put the word out for anyone who can to let you know to come ahead and come on. 'Get it over with' is what he says." He lifted his peanut cart off the counter, slung the strap around his neck, and shrugged. "Whatever's going to happen is going to happen I guess."

Ira the philosopher. He was obviously a determinist. I tended to come down more on the side of free will. I liked to think that we had input into how our lives turned out. That outcomes were shaped by the decisions we made rather than predetermined by the finger of fate. Jack was busy peeling twenties out of his wallet. I looked at him and wondered which philosophy he subscribed to. He handed Ira a few of the bills and nodded in the direction of the red-and-white-striped bag of peanuts that was still in my hand. "That's for the peanuts."

Ira took the money, leaned over, and stuffed it into his sock. The peanut tray bounced up and down as he adjusted it on his shoulders. "I'll see what I can do about putting the pressure on your old buddy Jimmy, if that's what you really want."

"That's what I want."

Ira made his way up the ramp and disappeared into the light. I couldn't be that close and not go up and take a look myself. Jack waited for me while I walked up the dim underground tunnel and into the sunshine. It was like walking out of a long dark winter devoid of box scores and *Baseball Tonight,* and into the bright spring of a brand new season. I loved baseball, and it hadn't occurred to me once since I'd been down here that spring training was in full swing.

The stadium was small—about eight thousand seats. It felt even smaller because of how close the seats crept to the field. The ballplayers seemed oversized at that distance, and even from several sections up I could hear sounds from the field I'd never heard before—the pop of the first baseman's bubble gum, and the scratching of the pitcher's spikes on the rubber. What truly struck me was the casual feeling in the stands. The people in this crowd hadn't paid sixty-five dollars for their seats. They lounged around with newspapers and suntan oil. They sipped beer and lemonade as they kept one eye on the game and chatted in the warm breeze. It was like going to a baseball game at the beach.

I caught sight of Ira making his way laterally across the stands. And I thought about Jimmy Zacharias and the showdown we were certainly building up to. Maybe Ira was right. Whatever was going to happen was going to happen, and there was nothing I could do to change it.

Chapter Twenty-nine

Felix had called as we'd made our way back down I-95 to Miami, so we made a stop at his command post at The Suites. He was prepared for us. He had stacks of information—printouts, copies of news clippings, and what looked like SEC filings. They were laid out across one of the double beds in what he called the "Cray Room." He asked us to sit. I took a seat on the other bed. Jack pulled out the desk chair and turned it around so he could sit in it with his arms across the seat back and rest his chin. He looked exhausted and I wondered if he'd had any sleep since the night in the hangar.

Felix handed us each a neat packet that was stapled in the upper left hand corner and fronted with a cover page. It had a table of contents, an executive summary, appendices, and bullet points all presented in PowerPoint landscape orientation. It was as polished and professional a presentation as any you might find in the densely carpeted, mahogany-paneled boardrooms of old economy corporate America—and it was chock-full, I was sure, of stolen and pirated information. Gen-X meets General Motors.

Felix paced back and forth. I halfway expected him to whip out a slide projector and pointer, but all he did was continue to pace, head down, lips moving, and no sound coming out. It took me a second to realize he was rehearsing.

"Felix."

"What?"

"Go."

"Oh, sure. Sorry. Okay. Uh . . . Miss Cray graduated from the London School of Economics, where she took a degree in Economic History. If you turn to Appendix I you'll see her transcript."

Appendix I was an official-looking list of all the courses young Vanessa had taken in undergraduate school. They were heavy on economic history in places like Latin America and Europe. There was one called The Internationalisation of Economic Growth, and one I found particularly interesting called Gender Theories in the Modern World. Equally interesting was the fact that Vanessa's class grades covered the full range from A- to A+. Wow.

"How did you get this?" Jack wanted to know.

"I called the school and told them I was from Data Processing and that I was, like, upgrading the system and I needed the password."

"And they gave it to you?"

"No. So I put out an APB to some hackers at the school. I told them what I needed and they told me how to get it."

Jack and I looked at each other. "It's a whole new world," he said, and I resolved right then and there never to put my credit card number out on the Web again for any reason.

"She spent the year after graduation traveling abroad. She attended a gourmet cooking school in Paris, and took flying lessons in Germany. She speaks, like, six different languages—English, Spanish, Portuguese, French, Italian, and Farsi."

"That's not like six," Jack said. "It is six."

"Oh, she also speaks some Russian. I forgot to put that in. Sorry."

"Seven," I said, stretching across the bed and sinking down on one elbow.

"She came back to the States to attend business school at Stanford, graduating with an M.B.A., concentration in Finance. That's, um, Appendix II." I flipped to the back. Another 4.0. Perfection can be so monotonous. "After graduation, she was recruited by, like, every Wall Street and consulting firm in the world."

No kidding. "How do you know that?"

"It was in one of the articles about her. She went with a Wall Street brokerage house called Thierry Eckard & Dunn."

"Never heard of them." That's where the litany ended. I turned the page. "What happened then?"

He went over to his stacks on the bed, picked up another handout, and handed one to each of us. My heart rate elevated instantly when I saw the title—INDICTMENT. Now we were getting somewhere. I sat up straight, glanced over the executive summary, which seemed to be a chronology, and went straight to the detail pages. There were copies of articles from the *Financial Times, The New York Times, Barron's,* and *The Wall Street Journal.* They all described a joint 1992 undercover operation that involved U.S. Customs, the FBI, and the IRS. They were looking to find brokers with Wall Street firms who "willfully invested drug profits or otherwise engaged in transactions to conceal the source and ownership of dirty money." Felix had helpfully highlighted that passage.

"They were looking for money launderers," Jack said. He was perking up as well.

"And they found some." I was reading ahead.

It was an ugly scandal. Five brokers, all working out of the Panama office of Thierry Eckard & Dunn, were indicted in 1993 by a federal grand jury in Tampa on charges of money laundering. The next few articles detailed the slow, agonizing death of the firm as the case lurched slowly through the justice system. Still later articles profiled the brokers who'd been busted. Right there in the middle of a lineup of photos was Vanessa Cray.

"Our little Vanessa," Jack mused. "A money laundress."

"I can't believe it." I was up and pacing now. I had to be careful not to run into Felix, who never sat down unless he absolutely had to. "How can she run a hedge fund if she was indicted for money laundering?"

"They all got off," Felix said. "Some kind of technicality."

"What?"

"The indictments were thrown out," Jack said. "It doesn't say, but it sounds like a problem with the case." He turned to Felix. "This is good work, son."

Felix beamed. He was so pleased to be praised by Jack.

"Anything yet on George Speath, Felix?"

"Not yet, but there's more on Miss Cray. Did you notice her personal history began with college?"

I hadn't noticed. I'd been distracted by the juicier aspects of her story. But when he mentioned it . . . "Where is she from?"

"I don't know. There's, like, nothing, you know? No personal information anywhere that I could access about where she comes from, who her parents are. Brothers and sisters. I tried everything. Inoculation records, social security number, birth certificate—"

"What about the schools?" Jack asked. "She had to have filled out applications that included information about her parents. They would have had to sign them if she wasn't eighteen."

"Blanked out. No data in those fields. Nothing. It was like she was born at the age of eighteen. Weird."

I looked over at Jack. "Witness protection?"

"I thought of that," Felix said brightly. "I tried to hack into the federal marshals' database, but there was no way."

Jack blinked at him. "I think I'm glad to hear that, son. But if she went into witness protection at that age, chances are it would have been for something her parents did. Or saw."

"Maybe this has something to do with why you remember her," I said. "Or almost remember her."

"I don't know." Jack went back to the first package and flipped through the pages again. He ended up studying a page near the end. I looked over his shoulder. He'd ventured back to Appendix III, which was two sparse pages. The first was a list of three different associations with telephone numbers and addresses: the American Orchid Society, the Australasia Native Orchid Society, and the Associació Catalana d'Amics de les Orchídies. The second page was a copy of a newspaper clipping from the *Miami Herald*. It was an article with accompanying picture of a woman in full climbing gear hanging from the side of a rock. According to the caption, it was Vanessa. She'd scrambled up a sheer cliff face to see an orchid with a name I couldn't pronounce. Something quite rare, apparently, that not many people get to see.

"She doesn't do anything in half measures," I said. "You know what we never got from Vanessa, Jack?"

"Respect?"

"An alibi."

Chapter Thirty

Vanessa Cray was already forty-five minutes late. The ice in my glass was long melted. The water sparkled no more, and the slice of lemon I'd requested floated at the top like a dead goldfish. I was seated on the deck of the restaurant she had chosen, where I had been since I'd arrived, wilting in the humidity and watching the quiet street in front for a limousine, a Mercedes, or at least a black Volvo. But, as I was learning, Vanessa Cray did not always do the expected. She arrived by boat.

It was a sleek cruiser with a tall cabin, a powerful motor, and a wide deck to play on. The name of the boat, *The Crayfish,* was painted in fancy script across the back. As it approached the dock, one of the waiters hurried out to grab a line.

It would have been hard not to recognize the man that emerged first. It was the oversized Bee Gee, the same large, distinctive individual Jack and I had seen in Vanessa's office the day we had visited. Today he wore a gold chain, a diamond stud earring, and a dark, tight, V-necked sweater over black slacks. He stepped onto the deck in his soft leather loafers—not exactly deck shoes—and discreetly slipped the waiter a tip. He scanned the surroundings, turned, and offered his hand to the boat.

Vanessa stepped out of the cabin, took his hand, and practically floated onto the dock. They both started toward me, but the escort dropped off and settled three tables away. Vanessa approached my table and gazed over my head.

"Where is Jack?" she asked.

"He's busy."

She continued to stand, bag under her arm, hands clasped in front of her. Today must have been business casual for her. Her long black skirt hung low on her hips and flowed around her legs like crude oil. The matching top, which looked like a shrunken black T-shirt, came down only far enough to reveal a thin strip of her smooth, tight belly when she moved. Her ice blonde hair was up, hidden under a black straw hat with a very wide brim. Sunglasses—Sophia Loren ovals—and perfectly painted lips topped off the look. Simple, yet exotic.

I thought she might have been thinking about leaving, since there was no one here but "Jack's assistant" as she had referred to me. Turned out she was only waiting for someone—in this case the waiter—to hustle over and whisk her chair out for her. While he was there he offered a menu. She ignored it.

"I'll have the Salad Niçoise with no eggs and a glass of lemonade. Not too much ice." As she ordered she took off her hat and set it on the table. It was like lifting a serving plate off of her head. She never looked at the waiter once.

"And for you, ma'am?"

"Another—"

Vanessa's leather bag twittered. The waiter and I both stared as she reached in, extracted her cell phone, and flipped it open. She angled her body away, making clear the distinction between us and what was really important.

"Another bottled water," I said, handing over my menu. "With more ice this time, please."

Vanessa conducted the call in rapid French. I didn't need a translation to know she was not pleased with whatever news she was getting. When the call ended, she put the phone on the table. She sat back and crossed one narrow leg over the other, letting the billowy black skirt fall loosely around her.

"More questions?" she asked. "You seem to be the one with all the questions."

"I hate loose ends."

"And he was, after all, your friend, wasn't he? This murder victim?" She said it as if the mere act of discussing John's murder soiled her.

"His name was John McTavish. He had a wife and three small children. And yes, he was my friend."

"You knew him from your work at the airlines?"

I quickly replayed the interview we'd had in her office. If there had been any mention of my background in that conversation, I couldn't remember it. "How did you know that?"

She smiled. "I am an investor, Alex. I make very large bets every day with people's money. I have an excellent research staff."

"Did you find what you needed?"

"It wasn't hard. It seems your time in Boston was short but rather"—she pursed her lips, but delicately—"newsworthy."

She watched for a reaction. My reaction was how interesting it was that we were off in our respective corners researching each other. She had her staff. I had Felix.

"Given your background, this effort you're involved in, this quest to find a murderer seems a bit out of your realm. What on earth has drawn you to such a risky activity?"

"I wasn't drawn to it. I'm repaying a debt."

"You certainly could do that without involving yourself personally. Jack, for example, could handle this for you. Quite capably, I'm sure."

I hated when she called him Jack. She probably sensed that, which was why she kept doing it. The waiter stepped between us to deliver our beverages—cold drinks in sweating glasses on a couple of damp cocktail napkins.

"One could say the same thing about your ventures," I told her. "Making large high-risk bets with other people's money. Or climbing sheer rock faces to observe a rare orchid. I'm doing this because I have to. I'm not doing it for the thrills."

"Are you sure?" A thin smile spread across her flawless face. Behind it was enough ice to chill my mineral water without the extra cubes. Perspiration beaded on my forehead. I shifted in my chair. She'd kept me waiting for a long time, and I was tired of sitting.

"Perhaps," I said, "we could get to my questions now."

"Of course."

"We found a credit card receipt in one of your Volvos—"

"One of the company's Volvos."

"It was the one that was seen in the parking lot on the night we're looking at. Someone named Arturo Polonia signed that receipt. There's no Arturo Polonia on the employee list for The Cray Fund."

"Arturo would not be on the list. He's in my private employ, and yes, I forgot to tell you about him. I hope you don't misinterpret that. It wasn't intentional. Tell me"—she leaned forward and removed her glasses, revealing intense green eyes, and I understood why she had been so successful. It was her ability to focus every ounce of her being on whatever it was she was trying to understand. Or control—"what was it like to kill that man?"

The world around us went still, as if we were the only ones moving in it, and I wasn't moving very much. I could not believe she had asked me that question. Even stranger was what I perceived as real curiosity, the first genuine human reaction I'd experienced from her. It burned in her eyes like the fever I was feeling, and I began to understand something about her. This woman was an insidious infection that got inside you in ways you didn't understand, and began to break you down before you knew what was going on. She was a virus. I knew it for sure because I wanted to answer her.

"Is there some reason," I asked, "you're so interested in me?"

"As you point out, I myself am drawn to dangerous activities. The bigger the risk, the personal risk, the more I like it. They say it's what makes me good at my job. I'm interested in others who are, as well. But it's all right if you don't want to talk about it." A comment that was, of course, a challenge in itself.

"What makes you think I would discuss something like that with you? I don't even know you."

"Don't you? I think we know each other quite well. Did it change you? Taking his life?"

"I didn't take his life. He was killed in an accident."

"While chasing you."

"Yes."

"Do you blame yourself? Do you think about him? Do you ask yourself every day if you could have done something differently to change the course of events? I understand he died rather brutally."

A quiet but insistent breeze brushed the white cotton tablecloth against my knee. It was stiff with starch. The same gentle gust billowed her skirt, which was far more fluid. It was a hot breeze, or it was a breeze that felt torrid against my burning skin, and I thought maybe my rising temperature was an attempt to fight her off.

"The receipt, Vanessa." I looked beyond her to her boat, but I could feel her holding me in that radioactive gaze, and I knew she knew she was very close. I took a drink of water because if I was drinking I couldn't be talking. Talking to her and playing a game she obviously played with a great amount of skill. "Arturo Polonia?"

"Very well . . . Alex." She slipped the sunglasses back on, making it safe to look at her again. "What would you like to know about Arturo?"

"What does he do?"

She looked over at her escort seated across the deck. "Is that him?"

"Yes. He's my driver."

"And he drives the company cars?"

"Arturo has carte blanche when it comes to all of my vehicles or the company's. He typically takes the Volvos to run errands."

"Are you aware—" I dropped my voice, realizing he could hear us. "Are you aware of his extensive criminal record?" I looked down at my notebook. "Assault, possession, possession with intent—"

"I told you I have a thorough research process. And I do background checks. I hired Arturo when he was on parole. It was a risk, but . . ." She let the thought run into a nonchalant shrug.

"You like taking risks."

"And as you can no doubt see, he has certain . . . attributes that compensate for any nastiness in his background. In fact, the nastiness in his background is precisely why he is so effective for what I need."

"He's your bodyguard."

"He is my security team."

The waiter arrived with her salad. He set it in front of her, and paused with the clear intent of asking if she needed anything else. She ignored him until he got the message and faded.

"Why do you need security?"

"I like to invest in emerging markets, which means I travel a great deal. My work takes me to Russia, Eastern Europe, Central and South America. It is not uncommon for someone with my net worth to seek protection in those countries. Domestically, Arturo is my driver. Globally, he is my security staff."

"A staff of one?"

"He's all I need."

"Has he been in any trouble since you hired him?"

"Absolutely not. It's a condition of his employment. And he is very well paid."

I looked over at Arturo. He was like a cat in a window watching everything that moved until he could no longer see it, and then picking up the next target. "May I speak with Arturo?"

"That would be difficult, unless you speak Spanish."

"I'm certain we can find an interpreter. Perhaps at the police station."

"You would like his alibi. Is that correct? For the night of the murder?"

"Yes, I would."

"I'll save you the time and me the trouble. We were both in the same place." She reached her hand out. Arturo pushed himself up, lumbered over, and handed her a business card. "Arturo was with me on the night of March fifth. We were on the island."

"The island?"

"A private island in the Caribbean. I have a small compound there." She offered me the card. "This is the telephone number of my caretaker. He can tell you what you need to know."

I took the card, but didn't feel good about it. The whole situation felt so handled. I felt handled by her. "How did you get to and from the island?"

"On my G-IV, of course."

Of course. Why wouldn't I have guessed she had her own Gulfstream to fly back and forth to her small compound on the private island? I handed back the business card. "Can I have the phone number of the pilot who flew you over there?"

She seemed to consider that question for a long time. Arturo had gone back to his table. Vanessa spoke to him, eventually, in Spanish with more than a little impatience. Whether her impatience was with me or with him, I wasn't sure, but one thing was clear. Whatever possibility there had been for a convivial mood between us, contrived or otherwise, was long gone. I could feel her defense shield almost as clearly as I could see her dark glasses.

Arturo pulled out a Palm Pilot and maneuvered around the small screen with his large fingers. He found what he was looking for and started to rise from his chair to rumble across the deck again. She cut him off and must have told him to simply read out the digits, which he did. I wrote them down.

"So you do understand Spanish," she said.

"I don't believe I said otherwise. When did you return from the island?"

"I was back in Miami for a meeting on Tuesday morning. And I'm afraid I'm late for a meeting right now." She started to reach for the big hat.

"I have a few more questions. Please, Vanessa. It won't take long."

She didn't respond, but she didn't leave. She picked up the glass of lemonade instead of the hat.

"Do you know a man named Jimmy Zacharias?"

"No."

"Bobby Avidor?"

"No."

"Ottavio Quevedo?"

"Of course. I know who he is and what he does. We're not personally acquainted, if that's what you're asking."

"Have you ever worked in Panama? For Thierry Eckard & Dunn?"

"Yes, I was assigned to that office. And if you know that, you must know that I was arrested, along with everyone else in the office, and indicted on a money laundering charge. Which means you also know the government dropped their case. Was that your question?"

She so enjoyed asking all my questions for me, and then answering them. "I'm wondering how far your tolerance for risk extends."

"That, perhaps, is a conversation for another day." This time when she reached for her hat, she didn't stop. She picked it up and settled it on her coif.

"Vanessa, have you changed your name?"

"I beg your pardon?"

"Is Cray your married name? Or perhaps you've had a legal name change?"

She looked surprised, then burst into a musical, ringing laugh. "No. I have never changed my name. I rather like my name. And as long as my fund continues to do well, it is a valuable asset, indeed."

The waiter appeared with the check when she stood. He was not sure who to give it to. Arturo handled it.

"This was fun," she said brightly as she turned to go. With the glasses on and the hat pulled low, I couldn't tell if she was joking. "Perhaps we can chat again after you've found your murderer."

She boarded *The Crayfish* and disappeared below. Arturo followed. The waiter cast off the line. I stood on the deck, watching them go and hoping the sick, feverish feeling would leave with Vanessa. It didn't.

Chapter Thirty-one

Jack's office was an afterthought of a space, a geometric impossibility that must have been what was left over after all the surrounding spaces had been designed. It would have been eight by ten if there had been four straight walls, but there were more corners than feet of wall space. A large window above the desk was the only saving grace. The property manager must have slapped in a door, thrown down some carpet, and put it on the market just to see if anyone would bite.

We'd stopped by to check the mail. From the size of the stack and from the stuffy feeling in the office, he hadn't been to his office in a while. He opened a window, which helped immediately, and sat down with the pile at his desk. It was arranged so that he could look out the window as he worked; which left me staring at the back of his head. Or looking out the window and across the alley into the offices of the people who worked in the high-rise next door. They were doing what normal people did at work on Wednesdays, and I realized how relieved I was not to be one of them.

The only other thing in the office to stare at was a picture hanging on the wall in a dime store frame of a younger, happier looking Jack with a boy who looked to be six or seven years old. The boy was blonder than Jack, but they shared the same deep brown eyes and long lashes. With their faces side by side, the resemblance was strong.

"Is this your son?"

"Yeah. Better days."

"Are you in touch with him?"

"As much as I can be. I call him five times and he calls me once. That sort of thing. I keep trying to work the ratio down." His chair squealed as he leaned back in it and turned to look at the picture. The high-backed, dark blue leather chair looked, like most of the furniture in his office, as if it too had seen better days. "I thought you wanted to learn about money laundering."

"I do."

"Then come over here and sit down. I can't concentrate with you roaming around behind me." Given the size of the space, "roaming" was a generous term. I pulled a chair up next to the desk so he could go through the mail and talk to me at the same time.

"A good laundering scheme," he said, "is designed to be so complicated it makes your head explode, which is the reason it works."

"Do you understand the basic principles?" I asked.

"As much as I need to."

"Then explain them to me. I want to understand. I want to know what Vanessa was doing."

"What she was *accused* of doing. Pull that trash can over here, would you, please?"

I found the standard gray wastepaper basket and pulled it around so it was between us. "Whatever."

"All right. You're a successful Colombian drug dealer. You've sold a hundred million dollars worth of drugs on the streets of the U.S. But you, señorita Shanahan, have a problem. The hundred million is in ten- and twenty-dollar bills in the suitcases of couriers all over the country. Your goal is to convert that money into a form that you can spend."

"I can spend cash."

"Only a little at a time." He handed me a stack of flyers, coupons, and credit card offers. "You're in charge of trash."

I dropped the stack. It fell into the bottom of the can with a soft thud.

"You don't want to be paying for your 360,000 dollar Rolls-Royce Corniche convertible with tens and twenties. And you can't take your boatload of cash down to the bank and open an account because there are banking laws designed to detect people like you doing things like that."

"This is the ten thousand dollar rule?"

He nodded. "Any cash deposit over ten thousand dollars is going to raise the red flag, and the banker is going to call me, law enforcement, who is going to start asking you a lot of pointed questions about where that money came from. Eventually, because I am a good agent, I'm going to track it back to the predicate act, which was the sale of illegal drugs, and then I'm going to bust you."

"Okay, so I have couriers sitting around with suitcases full of my dirty money. All dressed up and no place to go."

"But you do have a place to go. What you need is to disguise the true ownership of the proceeds and the source, and change the cash into travelers checks, money orders, CDs, or a bank account that you can draw checks on so you're not carting around bricks of cash. All the while, you have to maintain control over your money. The person who can do all that for you is the professional money launderer."

"Let's call her Vanessa," I said, receiving another pile of trash. "For lack of a better name."

"Okay. Vanessa the money laundress is going to take that money and legitimize it for you, and for her troubles, she's going to take anywhere from ten to twenty percent off the top."

"She's going to make ten to twenty *million* off this transaction?"

"She is, but you don't complain because this service is absolutely essential to your business. What good is the money if you can't spend it? Besides, you have plenty left."

"Okay, so she's rich, but I'm richer. I'm happy."

"You're especially happy if she's professional, never steals from you, accounts for every penny, and generally does a good job."

"How do I know how much money I'm starting with?"

"What do you mean?"

"Who counts the money in the suitcases before it gets laundered?"

He turned in his squeaking chair to smile at me. "Now you're starting to think like a crook. It gets counted and audited all the way up the ladder. Drug empires are like corporations. Their systems of checks and balances and controls would make IBM proud. However, the penalties for noncompliance are pretty severe."

"How do I get the money to Vanessa?"

"You have your couriers contact her. She gives them the name of a bank where they can take their suitcases and deposit the money, as much as they need to, no questions asked. Someplace she's already scoped out. Paraguay works. Also Mexico—"

"We'll say Panama," I said.

"Panama's a good one. Getting the money into a bank is a big step because there are no laws governing bank-to-bank transfers. You can move as much as you want in transactions as large as you want without being questioned. That's how she gets the money out of the country and as far away from its source as possible, most typically to Europe."

"Why Europe?"

"Credibility. Banks in Europe are more tightly controlled than those in the southern hemisphere. She would open up a bunch of accounts in different banks in different countries with balances as small as she could reasonably make them. The goal is to take these massive chunks of cash and spread them around."

"These banks would take these deposits, knowing they came from Panama?"

"If she's been in the business for a while, Vanessa knows the banking laws in Europe. She knows, for instance, that Switzerland and Luxembourg are good places for her kind of business. Like any good business-woman, she's established relationships, so she knows which banks will take the money without probing too much."

"She's got her own banking network."

"Something like that."

"What's the next step?"

"Colombian surnames—Hispanic surnames are a red flag all by themselves all around the world, so the safest thing to do would be to move the money again, this time to accounts with fake names, like Kornhauser, or Lautrec. Or she could deposit it into brokerage accounts. The point is to move the money all around to as many places as you can, to create so many layers of confusing transactions that it's impossible to trace it back to its origins, and yet still maintain control over the accounts, and the funds. That, of course, is key."

"All right. So now Vanessa has all of my hundred million dollars, less her cut, in far-flung places around the world. How do I get it back?"

"That's the last step. You set up corporations where Mr. Kornhauser and Ms. Lautrec can invest their money."

"Real companies?"

"Real ones or fronts. They provide a way to prove that the money was earned legally."

"Where are these businesses?"

"Colombia, Europe, the U.S. . . ."

"Miami?"

"Anywhere. By this point the money is washed so clean no one would ever know to look at it, and if they did, they wouldn't be able to trace it back to you. And that's how it works. Here you go."

He handed me the last of the junk mail, which left a thin stack of what looked like bills. The sun was starting to go down, so it wasn't quite so stuffy in the office. In the building across the street, people were packing up in their offices to go home.

"What kinds of businesses make for good laundering?"

"Any business that is cash intensive. You'll find a lot

of restaurants and bars down here in South Florida that won't take credit cards for that very reason. I hear the video rental business is catching on as a sink."

"Sink?"

"That's the place where you wash the money."

Naturally. "What about a hedge fund. Would that work?"

"I don't know. I don't know enough about that business to understand how it could."

"Vanessa Cray travels all over the world with a bodyguard. She speaks six or seven different languages. Doesn't that sound like the perfect profile for a launderer?"

"It sounds like a reasonable theory," he said. "But what if she is? What does that have to do with John's murder?"

"I don't know. But her car was in the hotel lot the night he died. And we know we have some kind of a drug connection going on here."

He stood up and stretched and let out an enthusiastic yawn. "Want to go to dinner?"

"Let me check my messages first and see if Felix has come up with anything."

I dialed the hotel first and found that no one had called except George Speath. When I dialed into my cell phone box, he had called there, too. Nothing from Felix, but there was something from Dan up in Boston.

The message came out in his rat-a-tat staccato rhythm. *"So I drove up to that bar you gave me and had a beer and I asked around and it turns out one of the waitresses is Avidor's mother only she had a different name because she got remarried and I ask her about Johnny's phone call to that bar and she admits she knows him. She says he and Bobby grew up together and I told her who I was and that Johnny used to work for me and that you're down there doing what you're doing and she starts crying, which I hate. I hate when women cry. But long story short, Shanahan, Avidor sent her the logbook and the ring. He wanted her to keep it for him. She gave it to Johnny because she didn't want it in her house. Something about evil spirits or some shit like that. Are you happy now? Don't ask for any more favors. And one more thing, Shanahan. That was a long fucking drive. You owe me."*

Jack saw me smiling. I replayed the message and let him listen. It made him smile, too.

"Forget dinner," he said, looking rejuvenated. "It's time to go and see Mr. Avidor."

Chapter Thirty-two

Mr. Avidor had not been home. He had not gone to work that day and, according to Bic, had been out sick for two days. I'd come back to the hotel to messages three and four from George, all inquiring in the most polite way after the results of my audit. When Bic woke me up early the next morning and suggested in the least polite way that I get Speath Aviation off his back, I decided I had to go and see George. The problem was, I didn't have anything to tell him.

The last I'd heard from Felix, he was still trying to scale the firewall George had erected. Scale it, bypass it, blow it up, go through it, under it, or around it. George's firewall had left Felix and his hacker friends alternately frustrated and in awe. It had left me with a problem. George claimed to have given me full access to his computer files. As far as he knew, I had no reason to suspect he hadn't. And we'd found nothing suspicious in the data he had made available. Nothing to even hint that he was buying or selling bogus parts. But why does someone build a data vault if he has nothing to put in it? I had to talk to Felix.

I tried him from my hotel room. I tried him from my cell phone on the way over to George's. I tried him as I sat in George's parking lot. I called him at home, at the office, and at his temporary headquarters in room 484 at The Suites. If I'd had his parent's number, I would have tried him there. I hung up, cursing the fact that he didn't have a cell phone. I was going to have to make something up. That was my plan, at least before I walked through the door at Speath Aviation and saw the welcome sign. This time the magnetic letters were arranged in a greeting to FELIX MELENDEZ, SOFTWARE SOLUTIONS.

Dammit, Felix. Apparently he had hit upon a new approach for getting around that wall.

Margie's desk was empty, as usual. A radio was playing somewhere. Salsa music. And I could hear the normal banging and whirring and grinding from the other side of the heavy door that led to the hangar. I went down the back hall to George's office. The door was open and the lights were on, but no one was home. I came back out and followed the sound of the music, checking rooms along the way. The break room was empty. The bathroom was silent. I found the source of the music when I went into the stockroom. It came from a cheap radio playing on a worktable. No George. No Margie. No Felix.

The stillness felt odd. Wrong. The musical accompaniment, small and tinny, made the walls feel close. The nervous beat of the Latin rhythm put my teeth on edge, so much so that I wanted to get out of that stuffy, windowless, inside space.

I turned to go, moving with some purpose, and crashed straight into a barrier, which turned out to be another warm body. Head-on collision. Full force. It knocked me back and was so sudden it took a few seconds for me to feel startled. When I did, a wave of adrenaline shivers erupted. He had come out of nowhere, this slight man with a goatee and thick, black eyebrows, approaching silently to stand behind me.

He was about my height. His hair, like his eyebrows, was wiry and dark and it stuck out from under a Speath Aviation cap, the same kind George had given me. I didn't know his name, but I'd seen him around the shop. He was one of the few employees who hadn't spoken to me—maybe the only one—which gave his wide-eyed, silent stare the weight of the unknown.

I asked him if he spoke English. He shook his head. Using my limited knowledge of Spanish, I asked him where George was. He pointed to the hangar, still completely silent. When I stepped toward the door, he moved aside, but his eyes moved with me. And I didn't turn my back on him. I got such a creepy feeling from him. From the room. From the whole situation. As I went down the hall, I heard the music go dead.

The door to the hangar opened from the other side before I reached it. My heart slipped out of my throat when I heard their voices—George and Felix—but it flew right back up when they walked through the door and into the narrow hallway and I saw them together. George was his normal, affable self, but next to him Felix looked small, vulnerable, and very young, and it hit me hard how much he didn't belong there, and how I was the one who had put him there.

For the first time since I'd met him, George felt dangerous. Not for any reason except that he was standing next to my kid friend, and I didn't know for sure that he wasn't.

"Alex . . . my word, what are you doing here? I didn't know you were coming. Did you get my messages?" He laughed at himself. "Of course you did. That's why you're here. Did you meet Felix? He's a software consultant. Boy, this is my week for visitors, isn't it? Usually we can go for months in this place and only see each other."

I smiled at Felix and we exchanged what felt like obviously artificial, overly pleasant greetings. I had expected to see him, but he hadn't expected to see me—no one had—and he showed admirable restraint when I had popped up in front of him. He stood with his hands clasped in front of him, gazing directly but blankly into my face.

"We're going to lunch," George said. "Felix is trying to sell me a complete systems review. He's one of the few software people I've ever met who knows what he's talking about."

"Does he?" I asked. Felix couldn't suppress a grin that was equal parts bashfulness and bravado. I had to get him out of there.

George had a different thought. "Say, I've got an idea.

Why don't you join us? We'll all go. Maybe you can share some of your insights with Felix about our capabilities and our needs. If we're going to do work for Majestic, we might want to upgrade our systems. What do you say?"

I checked my watch—two thirty eight. "It's a little late for lunch, isn't it, George? I was hoping to get some time with you."

"No, come with us, Miss Shanahan. That's a cool idea."

Felix's big eyes were on me, imploring me, giving me a preview of what it would be like spending an hour in front of George pretending I didn't know him.

"I'm sorry, George. I don't have time, and neither do you. We need to speak in private. Maybe Felix could come back another time."

If I hadn't known Felix, I might not have noticed how all the starch went out of him, how his head sank back into his shoulders. But I did know him and I did notice and it was all for his own good. He managed a smile anyway.

"Not a problem, Mr. Speath. I'll go back to my office and work with what I already have. I'll see if I can scope out a plan for you."

"All right. I'll show you out. Alex, I'll be right with you." George put his big hand on Felix's back to guide him down the hall, much as he had done with me when steering me out of the path of the bomber pigeons. His hand covered almost the entire span of Felix's shoulders.

I fell in behind and followed them out. I was determined to see Felix walk out the front door, and was actually feeling a hint of relief until I glanced into the supply room on my way past. Mr. Goatee was there. We locked eyes as he turned away from the door, and something in the way he looked gave me the feeling he'd been standing and listening to every word of our conversation. And that he understood. Maybe he did speak English after all.

Chapter Thirty-three

Back at the hotel, I opened up my laptop and sent an e-mail message to Felix. It was similar to all the voice messages I'd left:

"Call me immediately."

"Get in touch with me ASAP."

"Do not go back to Speath's again."

"What were you thinking?"

I tried to reach Jack to tell him how Felix had popped up at George's, but he was off somewhere looking for Avidor. All I could do was wait. By the time I heard the knock on the door, I'd been swinging between worried and annoyed for several hours. I flew to the peephole and checked. When I saw who it was, I edged all the way over to angry.

I swung the door open. Felix looked at my face, and said, "Uh-oh."

"Get in here." I pulled him inside and closed the door.

"You can't see any of the airport from here. Wouldn't you want to be on the side where you could watch the planes taking off?" He was already at the window peering through my blinds.

"Felix, what were you doing at George's?"

"We tried again all last night to get past the wall. I decided to try another thing we sometimes do which is go in and pretend to be a software consultant or salesman. Sometimes if you offer a free upgrade to their system, they'll give you anything. Anyway, I started with the lady, Margie. She wouldn't give me anything. But then I met with Mr. Speath and he was so cool. He showed me a bunch of stuff. I think I could have gotten in there if you . . . well, you know. If I'd had a little more time."

"Why would you do something like that? These are dangerous people we're dealing with. You have to appreciate that. We're—Jack Dolan is a professional. He does this for a living, and he has most of his life. You and I, we don't."

"I just did what you did, Miss Shanahan. You went in as someone else to get information. That's what I was trying to do. I was trying to help."

"I know you were. I'm not a professional, but I've got good reasons to be taking risks like that. Felix, you don't. You have no stake in this at all. You have no reason to risk anything for me or for Jack or for John McTavish. I want you to be safe."

He started to respond and stopped short.

It was a soft brushing against the door, a sound that felt like cold fingers across my skin. He had heard it, too.

It was quiet, and then the brushing sound again.

Signalling Felix to stay back, I crept forward as quietly as I could. I moved in front of the door and latched my right eye onto the peephole.

There was no one out there.

I angled to scan left and right. The emergency exit was across from my room and half a door-length down, so it wasn't easy to see it, but when it happened, I saw it. The door moved. I fixed on the dark crack where the door was slightly open and saw four fingers, the four fingers of the person who was standing on the other side, holding it ajar. An icy tingle crept up the back of my neck because there was no way past him. There was no way out.

I turned around and stood with my back to the door. I thought about Mesh Man. I thought about the kidney car. I thought about Vanessa and Arturo and Jimmy and George and Damon and God knows who else who might have a reason to want to do me harm. Reasons I didn't even know about. And then I thought about a scene from an old Burt Reynolds movie where a woman was cut almost in half by a shotgun blast—right through the closed door of her apartment. She'd been looking through the peephole.

Quickly, I fled inside toward the bed and the telephone.

"What's going on?" Even when he stood still Felix looked hyper. It was the way his face constantly changed expression based on whatever he was feeling at that moment.

"Someone is out there," I said. "Across the hall in the stairwell. I saw him."

"Really?" He headed for the door at warp speed.

"*Felix*, don't go over there." I was trying to punch the buttons on the phone and pay attention to him. "Stay inside here."

Too late. He was looking through the peephole. "Hey, there is. It's—"

I hung up, followed him over, and pulled him into the bathroom with me. The two of us cocked our heads and listened. *"Señorita, por favor."* The voice was barely audible.

"Miss Shanahan, it's just this little dude with a baseball cap and a goatee and—"

"He has a goatee? What else did you see?"

"He's got black hair and he's not that tall. That's about what I saw."

"Stay here, Felix. I mean it."

I crept back over to the door, and back to the peephole. The black cap filled the line of sight at first. But then he tipped his head up and I saw his face. It was the man from George's stockroom. Only this time he didn't look menacing. He seemed more fearful than furtive. Behind his heavy eyebrows and neatly trimmed whiskers, he was more frightened than I was.

"Who are you?" I called, trying to air out my throat.

"Julio Martín Fuentes."

"What do you want?"

He responded by ripping into an impassioned and seemingly profound explanation of himself and his presence in my hotel—in Spanish. I motioned Felix to join me. He listened as Julio rambled. Whatever Julio Martín

Fuentes was saying went well beyond my high school español vocabulary. I did, however, comprehend a number of references to señor George sprinkled throughout the hyperactive monologue.

"What did he say?"

"He works for George, and he wants to talk to you."

"Why?"

"He thinks you're an auditor and he wants to come in right now. He's scared to be standing out there in front of your door."

"What do you think?"

Felix asked a question and Julio responded. Then Felix nodded for me to open the door.

"What did you ask him?"

"I asked him if he was here to hurt us and he said no."

Great. I felt better.

"Ask him," I said, "to step back against the wall."

While Felix did that, I watched through the peephole. Julio had taken off his cap and was glancing and blinking in the direction of the elevator. He still looked as though he wanted to melt into the carpet. When he stepped back, I didn't see any firearms, at least not any obvious ones, so I turned the knob and opened the door.

Julio came as far as the doorway and stopped. That's when I saw the tattoo. He had sleeves on his shirt, but they were short, and I saw it poking out below the hem. It was a cross of some kind. Julio was Mesh Man. He stood working the black cap with nervous fingers until I realized he was waiting to be invited in.

"Come in, please, *señor*."

Felix ushered him into the room. The two of them sat in the chairs at my tiny table. I closed and locked the door and joined them, settling in on the bed with my feet up. They were already deep in conversation. Words were flowing swiftly and they talked over each other a lot. What I could tell from Julio's animated and emphatic gestures was that whatever they were talking about, it mattered a great deal to him. He ended the conversation with multiple repetitions of *"muchas gracias."*

"He works at Speath Aviation," Felix said. "He's a

bookkeeper there. He's seen you around with George and he knows you're an auditor."

"What's his story?"

"First of all, he wants you to know how much he respects his boss. He's in awe of him. Julio used to be a mechanic, but when Mr. Speath found out he was trying to become an accountant, he took him off the line and gave him a chance to go to school." Felix leaned in and lowered his voice. "I think it's sort of a father-son deal there."

Julio had clean fingernails—the hands of a number cruncher, not a mechanic.

"This is the best job Julio has ever had, and he doesn't want to get Mr. Speath in trouble. He's good to his people, and he tries hard to run a good business. Every Christmas he—"

"Felix, the more good things you say about George, the more worried I'm getting. Is George laundering dirty parts? Is that what he came to tell me?"

"No." Felix's voice became quiet enough that I could hear a thread of tension running through his usual irrepressible enthusiasm. "Mr. Speath is using his business to launder drug money."

I sat up and edged to the side of the bed. I didn't want to make any quick moves. Julio offered a polite smile, but his forehead gleamed with perspiration, and both knees bounced as if he were trying to run somewhere sitting down. I knew the feeling. I wanted to call Jack, but I didn't know where he was, and looking at Julio, he wasn't going to want to hang around after he'd told his story. I found my notebook and opened it up.

"Drug money, Felix? Is that exactly what he said?"

The two of them nodded in stereo. Julio obviously knew a little English. Probably about as much as I knew Spanish.

"Does he sound as if he knows what he's talking about?"

"For sure. And he's way depressed about it. At first, he wasn't certain since he's new at this, but he's been paying attention and keeping good notes. Now he's sure."

"How is George doing it?"

Felix turned to Julio and they were off and running again in another high-speed dialogue.

Julio seemed excited that we were so interested. Felix was beyond excited.

"Mr. Speath plays with the inventory accounts and makes it look as if he's bought more than he really has. They make up the difference with laundered cash, and because parts are so expensive, Julio says they can wash a lot of cash with only a few fake transactions."

He paused, and I thought he was going to check with Julio again, but the pause turned into a full stop. "Felix?"

"I was just thinking, no wonder we're locked out of his system. This is what Mr. Speath is protecting behind his firewalls. I wonder how I can get around them."

Julio's knees were still churning, and I thought soon he might start rattling the lamps with his nervous fidgeting. He could hardly keep himself in his seat.

"Felix, ask him why he's so scared."

Julio responded to Felix with another blast of accents and tildes, and somewhere in there, I heard the secret password, maybe the word that would unlock the whole case, answer all the questions, and bring all the loose ends into a tight bow.

"Get this, Miss Shanahan." Felix was on his feet now. "It's money that belongs to this dude Ottavio, who's a big drug lord down in Colombia, which is where Julio is from, which is why he's so scared because he has family there and he's afraid if the word gets out that he's informing, his relatives will be wiped out. This Ottavio is some vicious dude who has all kinds of corrupt officials looking out for him. Wow! This is . . . this is unbelievable."

"Ask him if he'd be willing to talk to the authorities."

I didn't need a translation to understand Julio's response. His face turned so pale I could see all the individual wiry whiskers of his goatee. He had gone as far as he would go—I could see that—and told Felix that if asked to repeat the accusations, he would deny them.

"Ask him why George would do such a thing."

He did.

"He says he doesn't know, but he thinks Mr. Speath is under financial pressure. He has a whole stack of unpaid bills and they've been having cash flow problems."

No wonder George was so anxious for the Majestic business. "Felix, did he tell you who George is working for? Who represents Ottavio here in Florida?"

Julio didn't know, but I thought I might. I'd only met one money launderer while in Florida on my great adventure.

"They did change outside accountants about six months ago," Felix said. "He thinks that's when it started. He gave me the name. In fact—" I could see Felix slipping into his hacker's trance. He stopped in front of Julio and asked him a few questions, to which Julio responded.

"I am so psyched, Miss Shanahan. He just told me enough that I might be able to get into Mr. Speath's vault. I can't wait. Can I go?"

"No, you can't go and if there's any chance they can find out you've been in there and trace it back to you, I don't want you screwing around with it. We're talking about drug traffickers here. In fact, ask Julio if they have a way of tracking back to you if you try something like that."

"I don't think he'd know if they did."

"Ask him anyway."

Julio responded with a shrug and a blank stare. "He doesn't know, but I think I can figure that out once I get in. Anything else?"

I looked up at the sprinkler head in the ceiling of my room. It was a good place to focus.

"Speath Aviation is a repair station that we now find out is being used to launder—but drug money, not parts. Right, Felix?"

"Right."

"Who's the drug launderer in this little scheme we've

got going here? It's not Jimmy. Jimmy is parts. It's
Vanessa. Ask Julio if he knows that name. Vanessa
Cray."

He didn't.

"Ask him if he's ever heard of Jimmy Zacharias."

Never.

"Does he know if George is also laundering dirty
parts?"

No again, which blew up the elegant theory I was con-
cocting in my head. Too bad; it made a lot of things
make sense that didn't seem to make sense. But then
Julio kept talking and something came out about the
"effay-bee-ee." The FBI.

"What did he say, Felix?"

"Hold on."

I strained to try to understand, but it was all too fast
for me. I had to be patient and wait. Finally, Felix turned
my way. He was shaking his head.

"What? What, Felix? What?"

"He said that a bunch of parts had come through recently that Mr. Speath had suspected were bad. Bad paperwork. No traceability. They looked used and were
supposed to be new."

"Yeah. What did he do?"

"He gave them to the FBI."

"The FBI? George is a money launderer and he called
in the FBI?"

"Julio said that Mr. Speath couldn't stand the idea of
someone trying to sell substandard parts." It made no
sense, but in a way, it did. I thought back on George's
face as he'd gazed up at that beautiful Electra out on
the tarmac. He was capable of money laundering, apparently, but drew the line at washing dirty parts. George
loved airplanes too much.

"Ask him . . . Felix, ask him if he knows who at the
FBI George has been working with."

Julio listened to the question, hesitated, then pulled
out his wallet, a red nylon fold-over with a Velcro closing, and dug deep to find a business card, which he held
in his palm, hidden like a playing card.

Felix translated. "He said he and Margie and Mr. Speath are the only ones who know about the bad parts, and that Mr. Speath had asked him not to say anything to anyone because he was afraid if you found out, you would give them a bad audit and they wouldn't get the business from Majestic."

Julio handed me the card. I read it, handed it back, and thanked him very much. I didn't need to keep it. I already had one from Agent Damon Hollander.

Chapter Thirty-four

Jack put his glasses on and sat down on the couch, deftly avoiding the empty pizza box that had been lying fallow for several hours. Felix and I had been through many meals in room 484 as we'd tried and finally succeeded in using Julio's information to crack George's data vault. Actually, Felix had done all the cracking. I'd done the analysis of what was in there.

"How am I supposed to read all those tiny numbers?" Jack held the page I'd handed him under the lamp.

He was right. Felix had reduced the large spreadsheets so much the numbers looked like black pepper sprinkled across a white tablecloth. He took off his glasses and held it at arm's length. "What would I be looking at if I could see?"

"I'll summarize for you," I said. "I told you about how Julio the Whistle-blower came to see me and told us that George has been using his business to launder money."

"Right."

"For Ottavio Quevedo, famous drug lord."

"I got that part, too."

"That's what was in the data vault. George keeps records in there of how much money he's laundered and through what accounts. We spent all night going through it and we think we understand how he's doing it. And Felix found a pretty handy link in there, too."

"What kind of link?"

"It was a way for me to get into the accountant's mainframe computer, Mr. D. I didn't think I could at first."

Felix was starting to rev up. "But then I found some code I could use and I—"

Jack smiled and gently cut him off. "George's accountant?"

"When George started laundering," I said, "he picked up a new outside accountant. It turns out this accountant has a bunch of other aviation repair stations as clients."

"Maybe that's his specialty. He has a particular expertise. It's not that unusual. Word of mouth . . . that sort of thing. These aviation people all talk to one another."

"That's not this accountant's particular expertise. Give me the list, Felix."

Felix dug around in the pile around his computer until he found the page I wanted and gave it to me. I passed it over to Jack. "This is the list of the stations, all using the same accountant, remember. Do any of them ring a bell?"

Jack put on his glasses and glanced over the names. "Dirty parts. These are Jimmy's places. Many of them anyway. They're all suspected of moving bogus parts."

I pointed to the list. "Every one of those stations has cash coming in on a regular basis in some form or another from Panamanian registered corporations that do their banking in the Cayman Islands."

He looked again at the list. "Money laundering? These rinky-dink places?"

"Yep. Jimmy's stations are multipurpose laundering facilities. You can get your dirty parts washed there, or your drug money. Take your pick." Felix started to giggle. We were both a little bit loopy.

"Hold on." Jack wasn't loopy. "Are you saying Jimmy is a money launderer? That can't be. Jimmy is a compulsive gambler. He'd be dead within a week if he had access to that kind of money."

"No. I don't think he's the launderer and maybe he doesn't have access to the money. But he might have access to the records. Incriminating records, such as the ones we found tonight in George's vault. It's good stuff. Any up and coming FBI agent would die to get his hands on what we found."

Jack set the page of names on the coffee table at his knees and stared at it. He let his head tip back and forth, as if to look at the idea from all sides. Then he looked up at me with that deep crevice over the bridge of his nose and started nodding, and I knew he was putting the information together the same way we had.

"What you two found," he said, "is what Damon has been after."

"Yes. This is Ottavio's drug money, Jack. The same repair stations Jimmy uses to wash parts are also used by Ottavio to launder his drug proceeds. It's the only scenario that makes everything work. And it explains all the connections."

"How?"

I looked around for my notepad. I'd been writing down bits and pieces all night. "Felix, where is my notebook?"

"I think I saw it in the bathroom."

It was there, next to the sink. I retrieved it, sat down on the couch next to Jack, and turned to the page labeled "Jimmy and Ottavio."

"You were wondering, Jack, about how Jimmy and Ottavio were linked in this Sentinel parts deal. I think Jimmy knew Ottavio to begin with, because he was letting Ottavio use his stations to launder money. It was a preexisting relationship. When the crash happened, Jimmy had someone to call down there."

"Someone with a lot of juice," he said. "Someone with access to a C130 transport."

"Exactly. Ottavio used his ties to whatever guerrilla or paramilitary group he's aligned with on the drug side of his business." I turned over to Vanessa's page. "As for Vanessa, being the only one with laundering experience on her résumé and a stint in Panama, I nominate her for Ottavio's launderer. Although we still don't know who she really is."

"That makes her Jimmy's partner."

"That's right," I said. "And she claimed she'd never heard of him."

Jack stood up and started moving around. It wasn't

easy. The suite was covered over almost completely in spreadsheets and hamburger bags and printouts, but he made a path. He went to the window and opened the curtains. Felix and I both cowered like a couple of bats. It was light out there in the central atrium. The sun was up. What time was it, anyway?

Jack stared through the window. "Jimmy loans his repair stations out to Ottavio," he said, "for money laundering, probably for a fee, knowing him. Damon finds out. The next time Jimmy gets hauled in and charged with something, Damon is there waiting to offer him a stay-out-of-jail pass. All he has to do is sneak Ottavio's laundering information out the back door. Documentation of a money laundering operation. Damon would definitely be interested in that." He turned to me, grinning. "One sink, two laundering operations. Very synergistic. Isn't that what you would say?"

I smiled back. I liked when he teased me. "Synergistic indeed. I'll bet that was Vanessa's idea, being the 4.0 Stanford Business School grad that she is. But synergy works the other way, too. Jimmy, Ottavio and Vanessa, even Damon—they're all connected through the stations so that if Jimmy goes down, say for the Ecuador parts deal, he takes the stations down with him. And if the stations go down, the money laundering operation folds, Vanessa is out of business or in jail, and—"

"Ottavio loses his laundering operation, and a large pile of his drug profits gets confiscated." Jack finished the thought for me and added his own. "And Damon Hollander loses his big bust."

"That" I said, "makes a lot of people interested in maintaining the status quo." I shoved the pizza box onto the floor so I could spread out more on the couch. It had been a long way and taken a long time, but we were finally at the bottom line. "Which is why John is dead. When he came down and threatened Bobby, he threatened to knock down the house of cards. Someone killed him for it."

Everyone was quiet for a few minutes. I lounged on

the couch with my head back and my eyes closed. They burned from hours of staring at the computer screen in the dark and a sea of tiny numbers. Jack was back at the window studying The Harmony House Suites atrium. Felix was busy disassembling a balky printer that had given us trouble all night. He was on the floor with the parts spread out around him in a sunburst pattern.

I heard Jack take a deep breath. I opened my eyes and he had turned back into the room. "Okay," he said. "Part two. Everyone in this twisted scheme has something to lose, which gives everyone a motive for murder. The only person we know who didn't commit the crime, at least not that crime, is Bobby Avidor because he has a solid alibi."

"You didn't find him?"

"He's nowhere."

I sat up and looked at my wrist. No watch. I'd taken it off at the same time we'd unplugged the electric clock radios in the suite. Looking at the time had proved a distraction we didn't need. "What time is it, anyway?"

"It's one-thirty in the afternoon."

"Felix, it's one-thirty in the afternoon. Have we been . . . we must have—"

"We were here all day yesterday," he said, "all night, and all of this morning. Yes, ma'am."

"Don't you have to go to work or something?"

"I took a comp day." He felt around on the carpet for a screwdriver. "I've got about three weeks worth in the bank."

Felix looked the same as he always did—ready to go out and run a sack race at the company picnic. I felt like crap. My legs ached. The throbbing in my ankle, which had almost gone away, was back with a vengeance and had dispatched companion aches to all my other limbs along with my neck, my back, and my shoulders. We had to get this over with before my brain shut down.

"I'm going to give Damon the benefit of the doubt," I said, "and assume he's not a murderer."

"That's a good assumption," Jack said. "Damon would

have plenty of options short of murder to move John out of the way if he had to. What about your friend Vanessa?"

That was a trickier and more complex thought process. I had to rub my head some more. "Vanessa might have had a motive, but only if she knew that John was in town and that he posed a risk to her operation. How would she find out? I doubt seriously that Bobby has any lines of communication open to Vanessa Cray."

"No," Jack said. "Avidor would have told Jimmy. If he's not already dead, he can verify that."

I filed that away, the idea that Bobby was dead, for later processing. Right now I was still on Vanessa. "I don't think Jimmy would have told her."

Felix piped up. "Why not?"

"Why bring her in? If he's got a good deal going, why tell her something that might encourage her to take her business elsewhere? If he is working with the Feds to build a case against Ottavio, then he needs her to be in business with him. What do you think, Jack? Do you see Jimmy bringing her in?"

"Jimmy doesn't take unnecessary risks. Vanessa also has an alibi. Didn't you check that, Alex?"

"I did. She and Arturo both, although I still think it's suspect. The people who provided the alibi work for her." I stared down at my notebook. I really wanted some orange juice. I found the phone and dialed room service. "Is any of this making any sense?"

"It makes a lot of sense," Jack said, "and it brings us to the last man standing."

"Jimmy." I was on hold. "He didn't want to lose his stay-out-of-jail card. Would that be motive enough, Jack?"

"Jimmy would kill himself before he went to jail. And he'd kill John McTavish before he killed himself."

The room service operator came on and I ordered a large, fresh-squeezed orange juice. I was, after all, in Florida.

"There's still a piece of this thing that doesn't really fit," I said, after I'd hung up, "and that's the Sentinel parts. Felix and I have been trying to figure that out and we can't."

"What about them?"

"If Jimmy was interested enough in the status quo to kill John, why would he risk everything by stealing that airplane?"

"Yeah," Felix said. "It's, like, a way bigger chance to take." He thought about that. "I mean, it sort of is. Killing someone is worse than stealing an airplane, but . . . I don't know how to say it—"

"It's the magnitude," I said. "Jimmy could have killed John all by himself, although it would have been quite a fight. But stealing a jet from the side of a mountain, schlepping it to Florida, and hiring a bunch of mechanics to break it down . . . how many people must have been involved in an operation like that? I would classify that as an unnecessary risk."

"Not for Jimmy. For him it's a calculated risk. Jimmy's a gambler. And he's an old soldier. He loved everything about the military. This would have been a chance for him to throw on his cammies and his war paint and go play Delta Force. For him, it would have been worth the risk just to see if he could pull it off. Killing a man is easy. Stealing an airplane, that's a risk worth going to jail for. That's the way he thinks."

"I'm guessing he didn't confer with his FBI handlers before he went down there."

Jack smiled. "Damon must have been pissed as hell."

I leaned back against the couch and rested my eyes again. "I think we've got it. The question is what do we do with it?"

"That's easy," he said. "We're going to take inventory and see how much leverage we have. Are you up for it, Felix?"

Felix sprang straight up off the floor. "What do you need, Mr. D.?"

"I want to find out everything we can about Vanessa Cray. If she's going down with Ottavio, then she has just as good a reason as we do to get Jimmy. I want to know who she really is."

Felix was already at work, booting up the computer and cracking his knuckles.

Jack looked at me. "As for you, I think it's time we had a talk with our prime suspect. Do you think you can stay awake long enough to take a ride out and see Jimmy?"

Chapter Thirty-five

I had been chased by his dog. I had heard his voice. At long last, I was about to lay eyes on the man himself.

From a distance, Jimmy Zacharias looked tall and lanky, but as we came down the drive to his house, I saw that he was the whittled-away kind of skinny, the kind that suggested there had been more to him at some point, and needed to be more now. His lips were so thin they seemed to have been drawn on his narrow face with a sharp pencil. His eyes were dark behind the squint, and his face desperately pockmarked. He wore his hair parted straight down the middle of his scalp. He looked like an Indian warrior who had been doing heroin, lounging in the doorway of his house, shirtless, forearm braced against the jamb above his head.

The sight of Jack induced in him a dark laugh that turned into a deep wet cough. "What do you want, asshole?" He managed to spit the words out between sticky, sucking eruptions. "I thought they kicked you out of the FBI."

"You were misinformed." Jack climbed the steps to the porch and stood alarmingly close to Jimmy, close enough to get coughed on. "I'm retired."

"Then what the fuck are you doing here?"

"I think you know."

Jimmy was only slightly taller than Jack, which meant when they stood nose to nose, they were staring directly into each other's eyes. They seemed comfortable doing it.

"Where's Bull?"

Jimmy smiled. *"Hey, Bull!"*

I heard him, snorting and growling. The adrenaline spread through my body like grasping tentacles, twisted around my heart and squeezed. I prepared for the sight of that big ball of muscle with teeth to come flying toward me, but he never showed up. The sound of his barking never got any closer.

Jimmy enjoyed my anxiety. "He's in the back. Should I get him for you?" He stepped into the shadows. The next thing I saw was the front door wheeling toward us, which must have been the very reason Jack had pushed in so close. He caught the door before it slammed. "Thanks for asking us in," he said.

The feeling inside the house was dim and cramped. Thin mustard-colored draperies that looked like big dish towels hung on the windows. Helped by the aluminum awnings that hung outside, they kept out the direct sunlight. But that didn't mean it was cool. The air was hot and stale and smelled of cigarettes, garlic, and something like Lysol. I was glad for the floor fan and the open door.

"Stay here," Jack said. "I'm going to see about that dog." He disappeared into what looked like the kitchen. Jimmy had disappeared, too, and I soon heard where he had gone. The bathroom must have been nearby.

Alone in Jimmy's lair, I took a look around. Besides an ugly brown couch shoved up against the wall, the major piece of furniture in the front room was a console stereo, the kind with the lid that opens to reveal the turntable. My parents used to have one. On top was a small trophy, the cheap kind that gets handed out every summer by the tens of thousands to little league and high school teams all over the country. The inscription read *Jimmy Zacharias—Winning Pitcher—1969 City Champs— Everglades City, FL.* Next to it was a picture of him in army fatigues, down on one knee and leaning on a rifle. His hair was dark and chopped short, but the shape of his face and the warrior squint were undeniably his. I looked at it and wondered what Jack had looked like back then. Next to the stereo on the floor were a bunch of magazines piled into a fire hazard. I reached down to flip through the stack. *Aviation Daily, Aviation Week & Space Technology,* a big fat pile of yellow newsprint called *Trade-A-Plane,* and something that looked like a military weapons digest. Mixed in were copies of *Hustler, Screw* magazine, and a local *TV Guide* from three months ago.

"Who are you? And what the fuck are you doing in my stuff?"

Jimmy had emerged from the bathroom under cover of the flushing toilet. I hadn't heard him until he was practically standing on top of me. He had donned a grayish T-shirt that probably used to be white. "Superbowl XXVIII" was emblazoned in blue letters across the front of a big faded Georgia peach that covered his entire chest.

"I was just . . . I'm sorry. I didn't mean to—I remember that game." I pointed to the shirt. "The Cowboys won. Their second in a row, I think. It was one of those big blowouts, the kind you could turn off in the first quarter if you didn't care about seeing the commercials." I couldn't seem to find the appropriate point to stop talking. This man made me very nervous, even without his dog. "Were you there?" I asked him. "In Atlanta?"

His face tightened into what could have been a smile. "Who *are* you?"

"She's with me." Jack had returned, and his hasty response only served to arouse more interest from Jimmy, which made me very uncomfortable.

Jimmy's eyes never left me. "You don't have a name?"

"I do have a name." I wasn't sure what the best response would be to a murder suspect. "But it doesn't seem to be relevant to what we're doing here."

"Come over here and sit down, Jimmy. Let's have a talk."

"A mystery woman. I like it." Jimmy actually did smile then, in a way that made me think he could read the dynamics in the room as well as anyone. That may have been the scariest thing about him. He walked the three steps over to the narrow brown sofa and eased down on the flat cushions. He leaned back and put his feet up on the coffee table. His toenails could have used a good clipping.

Jack remained standing, so I did, too, although he looked more comfortable doing it. "That was some job, brother, you pulled off in Ecuador. My compliments."

Jimmy held eye contact and allowed a ghost of a smile. "I don't know what the fuck you're talking about, Ace."

Ace? Everyone seemed to call Jack something different, but Jimmy's name for him did not strike me as a term of endearment. He had let it roll off his tongue with a measure of contempt that seemed to instantly elevate the tension in the room a few anxious notches.

"Air Sentinel up on the mountain. The Triple Seven. That would be right up your alley. Mobilizing in the dead of night. Swooping in on helicopters. A tight military operation, well timed and perfectly executed. Lots of dead bodies. It's just the kind of thing to get your heart pumping."

"You and me both, Ace. You and me both." Jimmy waited for a response. When Jack gave him nothing, he moved on. "Air Sentinel. Now that was a tragedy. But all I know is what I see on CNN. Just like you."

"Did you make it down in time, Jimmy? Did you get to see the blood? Smell the bodies?" Jack glanced at me. "Jimmy developed an appetite for blood in the jungle and now he's got to feed it. It's hard to do back in the world."

"Everybody finds their own way back to the world. I adjusted to the world as well as you did." Jimmy cocked his head back and stared up at Jack. "You want a beer, Ace? We could raise a toast to old times."

Jack's jaw tightened. Now it was Jimmy glancing in my direction. I tried not to look as nervous as I was. "How about your friend? Maybe she'd like one. How much does she know about you, anyway?"

The air in the house was starting to feel explosive, and I could almost hear the sound of the two men brushing against each other like two sheets of sandpaper, raw and ready to throw off an igniting spark. The second Jack took a step toward the couch, I spoke up.

"I think I will have a beer. Can I get you one, Jimmy?"

I made a point of stepping between them instead of walking around behind Jack to get to the kitchen. He had to take a step back to let me through. As I did, I gave him a little shove in the chest to move him back farther. The tension didn't dissipate, but it did seem to stabilize.

Jimmy's kitchen was only slightly larger than a galley on a wide-body aircraft, and at least as organized and efficient. Dishes were stacked neatly to drip-dry on the counter next to the sink. A matched set of pots and pans hung from a rack in the corner. Bottles of exotic looking oils in various shades lined a shelf over the stove. Jimmy Zacharias may have been a no-account scum in every other part of his life, but his kitchen would have done Martha Stewart proud. Go figure.

"Beer's in the refrigerator, Mystery Lady."

"Coming up." I found the Tecate and took a bottle out for Jimmy. I thought it best not to join him. My brain was already mush and I was so sleep deprived I was only retaining about every fifth word anyone said to me, which made it difficult to keep up under the best of circumstances, which these most certainly were not.

I was looking for the bottle opener when I saw Bull. Actually, he saw me first. When I heard him snarling, I looked out the back kitchen window. It reminded me of standing in Mae's kitchen back home what seemed like a hundred years ago. I had watched Mae's dog Turner chasing after squirrels in his goofy not-quite-a-puppy loping gait. This dog was chained to a stake in the ground, which in my opinion was not nearly substantial enough. His eyes were like two shiny black marbles as he pulled against his restraints and watched me through the window. Mostly I saw his teeth. Long, white, and sharp, and covered with the foam that came frothing out of his mouth every time he threw another canine invective my way.

I brought the bottle out to Jimmy and handed it to him. Jack was at the front window, peeking out through the yellow curtains. He spoke without turning.

"Did you ever see the logbook from the Air Sentinel crash, Jimmy?"

"Did they show it on CNN?"

Jack turned his attention back inside the house. "Here's the way I've got it figured. Bobby Avidor was working for you, helping you salvage the wreckage that you stole, when he came upon the logbook. That's got to be worth something, right? The logbook from a fatal crash. So he stashes it. Sends it home to his mother. That wouldn't be a big deal except his mother found the whole thing ghoulish. She gave the book to an old family friend whose name was John McTavish. John figured out what was going on and came down here, looking for Bobby and loaded for bear. Bobby called you and had to explain the whole problem and that he caused it because he took this logbook without telling you. Because he did, you could have heat coming down on you. So you killed McTavish. What do you think?"

"You always could spin a good tale, Ace, but nobody gets killed over airplane parts. You're talking about the death penalty. It's not worth it."

"You haven't heard the best part. The book wasn't all Bobby stole from you. Somewhere in all that mess, he found a finger or a jewelry box or something and with it a diamond ring, and that diamond ring was worth twenty-five grand."

One of Jimmy's eyebrows twitched.

"Bobby didn't share that with you, did he? Somewhere in his pea brain he thought that little detail would get lost and he would never have to answer to you."

"How would you know any of this?"

"That's what I'm leading up to. I had a discussion with Agent Damon Hollander of the Federal Bureau of Investigation. Your handler."

"What the fuck, handler? What are you talking about?"

"Shut up, Jimmy, and listen. Damon knew about the book, but not the ring. That tells me his information came from you, and your information had to come from Bobby. Why would you be talking to the Bureau unless you were working for them?"

"You're the one with all the answers." Broad sweat bands were growing on Jimmy's shirt under his arms. "You tell me."

Jack took a step forward and squared himself so he was facing Jimmy head on. "Damon's got you by the balls, and he's got your little Ecuador operation out there in the swamp shut down, and he's got agents keeping the hangar secure. The way I see it, you scavenged a crash site, stole the parts, committed a whole list of federal offenses, and got caught. And yet here you sit in your crummy little shack, free as a bird. It just gets curiouser and curiouser, Jimmy. How far would you go to stay out of jail?"

Jimmy sipped his beer.

"The only thing I couldn't figure was what information you had that would be worth anything to Damon. And now I have that piece, too. What do you think Ottavio would do to you if he knew you were selling him out to the U.S. government?"

"First of all, I am no fucking snitch and I never will be. Even you should know that. I would never be a snitch for anyone." Jimmy threw an arm up and let it rest along the back of the couch. "And second of all, we're pretty isolated out here. I don't know any of these people you're talking about."

"Do you have an alibi for last Monday night? Because Bobby does."

"I don't have to account for my time to you, Ace."

Jack squared to face Jimmy. "You would have been better off taking out Avidor than a civilian."

"That's right. You've got a thing for civilians." Jimmy kept his head low as he looked up at Jack. "Are you sure you don't want a taste of something? Tequila is your drink, if I'm remembering right. A shot of tequila with a Tecate chaser sounds good to me. I might even have some lime out there. And if you're lucky, maybe the Mystery Lady will serve you, too."

A hot breeze wafted through the screen on the front door, bringing with it the smell of stale brown water and moss covered trees. The only sound in the room was the spinning of the fan on the floor, and before anything at all had happened, I knew it was already too late.

I stepped forward. "Jack, maybe we should—"

Jimmy was up. All in one motion, he had put his feet on the floor, dropped the bottle of beer, and started for Jack. His other hand, the one that had been dangling behind the back of the couch, came forward. He was holding something. A gun. Jack was over the coffee table and driving into the Georgia peach on Jimmy's chest. They landed in a heap on the couch. The couch shoved into an end table. The lamp on the table crashed to the floor. The bulb exploded. As loud as a gunshot, the pop reverberated through the steaming house and out to the backyard, where Bull heard it and went crazy.

They rolled off the couch to the floor. The coffee table shot across the room as if it had been on wheels. I had to jump out of the way or take it in the shins. Jimmy was on top of Jack. They were grunting, scratching, yelling at each other. They were a pile of swinging elbows. Their legs whipped at each other. Jack was larger and more powerful. He gripped Jimmy's right wrist, just below the hand that held the gun. I knew there was something I could have been doing, but it was happening so fast . . . I had no instinct for it. I stayed where I was, next to the kitchen counter, and somewhere at the edge of my concentration, I heard Bull. His deep chested, big dog bark was getting louder. I saw him through the front door. He was dragging the iron spike behind him at the end of a long chain, and he was almost to the steps. I made a dive to close the door, tripped over someone's foot, and fell flat, rattling my teeth and knocking all the air from my lungs. All I saw was Bull's broad chest as he launched himself up the steps and against the screen door.

I put my hands over my head. He was going to land right on top of me. I heard the crash against the screen door, which inexplicably held fast. I raised my eyes to see him there, still on the other side, his big paws braced on the collapsing screen. He was close enough that I could feel his hot breath and see the black stains on his pink gums.

I crawled toward the door, reached for it with my finger-tips, and sent it sailing shut. It bounced hard against the dog's snout and came wheeling back. Now he was really pissed off. With one strong jump, his whole head and chest would be through the flimsy screen—and he'd be bringing his teeth. I stood up, swung the door as closed as it would go, and threw my weight against Bull's. He was powerful, and close enough to tear off my ear. I dug my feet in and gave it one more push. The door closed and latched tight.

When I turned around, the room was in complete disarray, with furniture and tables thrown around and knocked to the side. Jack was sitting on the floor, propped against the couch with Jimmy's raggedy body draped over his like a blanket. His arm went easily across the smaller man's chest to where he'd grabbed hold in the opposite armpit. With his other hand, he held a gun, his .22, to Jimmy's ear. Jimmy's gun was on the floor next to them. I went over and picked it up carefully and laid it on the console stereo.

"Do you remember how heads used to fly apart in 'Nam? Did you ever wonder what that felt like, Jimmy, when you did that to people?" Jack's voice was loud enough to be heard over the dog, and as harsh and cutting as it had been in the bar when he'd been mad at me, but it came from someplace deeper, some toxic pit that was filled with more rage and hate than he could ever have for me, that was perhaps reserved just for Jimmy. "A .22 is not an M-16, but it will have to do."

His tone was odd, dead. It was like a trickle of icy water running through that sweltering place. I moved over to the window. Bull was on the porch. He had destroyed the screen barrier. He was now trying to tunnel through, scraping frantically with his sharp nails, working hard at it. The thought of being out there with him was terrifying. But it scared me less than the scene playing out inside the house.

"You know what, Ace? I never think about that shit anymore." Jimmy's voice was a tight rasp. "You're talking about your own nightmares, not mine."

"Don't fucking call me Ace," Jack lifted his elbow and jammed the barrel of the gun against Jimmy's ear.

"Jack." The dog threw himself against the door again. "*Jack, damn* it, we have to get out of here."

"You need to taste some blood, Ace?" Jimmy was yelling, too, now. We were all yelling over the yowling animal. "All good soldiers like the taste of blood. And so did you. You're no different than me, and you never were." Jimmy's face was sunburn red against his silver hair. "The job was to kill—kill as many of them as we could as fast as we could. And it didn't matter if you blew them up or cut off their heads or shot them fifty times. Dead is dead. And you did all the same things I did."

I could see every muscle and every vein in the forearm Jack had lashed across Jimmy's heaving chest. His face was almost completely hidden except for his right eye, which stared out at nothing, maybe into that same place he was looking the other night at the laundromat.

"I know you, Dolan. I've always known guys like you. You tell yourself you didn't like the killing. You know what I think? I think you liked it a little more than you want to admit to yourself. I think—"

"Shut up, Jimmy." It took a second for me to realize the words had come out of my mouth.

"You liked it, Dolan, and you know it."

I had to make him stop talking. I grabbed the gun off the stereo. It was heavy. A revolver. I knew a revolver didn't have a safety. I raised it and pointed it toward the door.

"That's why you're a drunk. That's why—"

"Stop talking right now, Jimmy, or I'm going to shoot your dog."

With both hands holding the gun steady, I prayed Jimmy wouldn't open his mouth again, because I didn't know if I could pull the trigger. And if I did, what happened then? Five seconds went by. Bull was still agitating, the iron spike clanging against the front steps. Ten. If it was possible for me to hold even more still, I did, willing my internal organs—heart, lungs, stomach, kidneys, liver—to pause their orderly function while I waited. Twenty seconds and he still hadn't spoken.

I walked over and crouched next to Jack. "If you're going to kill him, tell me now because I don't want to watch. If you're not, we're leaving here."

The two men breathed in unison, as if they shared the same set of lungs. I had no idea if Jack was capable of shooting this man in cold blood. He shifted his weight and drove the barrel into Jimmy's ear. I shrank back, believing he was going to do it. Instead, he twisted the gun until a stream of bright red blood appeared. It trickled down, met up with a river of sweat, and spread down Jimmy's throat. Jack put his mouth close to Jimmy's other ear. "Yours is the only blood I want to see." Then he dumped Jimmy onto the floor and staggered to his feet.

Jimmy crawled to the edge of the couch and pulled himself up. Several strands of hair that had come loose from his ponytail stuck to the sweaty, bloody stream that covered the side of his face and throat. He touched his ear with his fingers, saw the blood, then pulled off his shirt, wiped his face with it, and balled it into a compress for his wound.

Jack shook himself out. His head and shirt were soaked. I thought I saw his hands tremble as he switched the gun from one to the other. Jimmy was bloody, but still sharp-eyed and alert. If there had been a tremor, he had seen it, too. We had to get out of that house.

As I moved toward the window to look out, I realized I still had the gun and didn't know what to do with it. I wasn't going to leave it for Jimmy to take a few shots as we pulled out.

"Keep it," Jack said, guessing what I was thinking, "until we get out of here."

"Tell Bull to sit down, Jimmy," I said, still watching out the window.

"Fuck you."

"He's either going to sit down," Jack said, "or I'm going to shoot him. One way or another we're walking past him."

Jimmy stood up on shaky legs, walked over to the door, and called through the door. "Back off, Bull."

"Don't tell him to go away," I said. "Tell him to sit there."

Bull seemed skeptical when he heard his orders, but he was also well trained. He went down to the bottom of the steps and sat, waiting eagerly for Jimmy to emerge.

"Jack, I think we should lock the dog in the house and take Jimmy with us as far as the car."

Jack grabbed Jimmy's ponytail, wrapped it twice around his hand, and pointed the gun to the back of his head. "I'm not with the Bureau anymore, asshole. I don't have to play by their rules. And when I get enough to prove you killed McTavish, I'm coming back for you."

"Here's a bulletin for you, Dolan. I didn't kill anyone. And I'm not a fucking snitch. Stop telling people that I am."

"Alex, get behind me." I did. "Open the door," he said to Jimmy, "wait until we're off the porch, then order the dog into the house. I've got no problem putting him down. It's up to you."

Jimmy let his hand rest on the knob. When he opened the door, he let in a blast of humidity that seemed to have been leaning against the door, eavesdropping. I stood behind Jack with my hand on his back as Jimmy moved out first, opening the screen door. All that was left was the frame.

Bull watched intently as the three of us moved in unison down the steps and past him. Jimmy talked to him all the way, trying to keep him calm. He looked like a torpedo in the tube as he trembled against every canine instinct in his body.

Once we were past, Jack told Jimmy to order him into the house. After he'd done it, I crept up the steps to close the door. Bull stared at me from inside with vicious intent. The most perilous moment was when I had to lean inside to reach the doorknob. Bull looked at me in the grim light of that house and I figured I had one chance. I took a deep breath, focused on the knob, thrust my arm forward and grabbed it. The instant the door was closed, he was there, scraping from the other side, and it wasn't clear to me he wouldn't try to come through one of the windows.

"Jack, let's go."

Jack had Jimmy lie flat on his stomach in the yard and put his hands behind his head. He took Jimmy's gun from me, opened the chamber with a quick flick of his wrist, and emptied the bullets out in his hand. He threw them down the long driveway, then heaved the gun in the opposite direction.

It was my turn to have shaky hands, and I could barely fit the key into the ignition. Jack climbed in the passenger side and shut the door, sealing us in with the sour odor of sweat and fear.

"Go. *Go!*" he yelled, twisting around to see what I was seeing in the rearview mirror. Jimmy was up and heading for the front door of his house, and I wished I'd thought to lock it.

I finally got the key in, turned the engine over. I felt Jack's reaction a split second before I heard the thud. As loud as a gunshot, it reverberated, filling the inside of the sweltering car and making me feel as though the big dog had leapt with full force and fury right into my arms. In fact, he had thrown himself against the passenger side door—Jack's door—and stood there now, his big paws braced on the glass, his chain and his spike rattling, his big teeth banging on the glass as he tried to chew through it.

Jack had pulled away from the window to my side of the car; his shoulder bumped my elbow as I put the car in gear. As I hit the gas and pulled away, I caught a glimpse of Jimmy, watching from the doorway, lounging casually, shirtless. He was laughing. We left him exactly where we'd found him.

"Pull over." Jack's tone left no room to question.

I checked my mirrors and started to pull to the shoulder. Before we rolled to a stop, his door was open. He leaned out as far as he could, straining against the seat belt, and threw up.

I stared at my hands on the steering wheel and listened to him gasping and choking and spilling his guts out all over the side of the road.

When he was done, he pulled inside the car and fell back against the headrest. He left the door open.

I looked at his face, damp and pale in the midday heat. He raised his arm to wipe it with the sleeve of his shirt. This time his hand was clearly trembling.

"What happened back there?"

He turned his eyes toward me and did not appear to have the energy to respond. But he did. "You were there. You saw the whole thing. I did what I went to do."

"Put us both in the most absurdly risky position you could think of?"

His head rolled back to center and he closed his eyes.

"Did you know going in that he might pull a gun on us?"

The mention of a gun reminded him that his was still stuck in the waistband of his pants. He pulled it out and leaned down to re-holster it at his ankle.

"I asked you a question, Jack. Did you plan that?"

"It was a calculated risk, but you were safe."

I wanted to lay into him like a pile driver, but my tongue was thick with the fear that had started in that shithole house and, now that we were safe, was turning more to rage with every word he stammered. There was only one thing I could get out. "Fuck you, Jack. Fuck you."

The smell of sweat and vomit, the humidity, the re-heated adrenaline—it was all beginning to get to me, and my own stomach felt ready to blow. I opened the window on my side and took in a few deep breaths. The air was tinged with smoke. "What's between the two of you?"

"I told you what's between us."

"There's more. There's something you're not telling me."

"You said you wanted to tag along. This is how it goes sometimes."

"No." I turned in my seat to face him. "He knows

things about you. He knows things I don't know, which puts me at a disadvantage if I choose to stand next to you, especially, Jack, if you might murder him one of these days when I'm with you."

He turned and looked at me with that same dead calm I'd seen in his eyes back at the house, only now it just looked dead.

"Take me back to the Beach. Or anywhere close. I'll find my way home."

I turned and faced forward, hands on the wheel. "Would you have killed him?"

"Every time I see him I want to put a bullet through his head. I haven't done it yet."

"He's not afraid of you, Jack."

"I need to get out of this car, Alex. If you don't want to drop me somewhere, I'll get out and walk."

I completely forgot that his door was still open. But that was all right because I pulled out so fast it slammed shut all by itself.

Chapter Thirty-six

I lay on the bed in my hotel room staring at my favorite sprinkler head in the ceiling. I'd been watching it for a few hours and it hadn't moved, so I could have broken off surveillance, if only I could have closed my eyes. The sun was going down. I could tell by the way the shadows played across the wall. I'd been trying to sleep ever since I'd dropped Jack off and driven, in a complete trance, back to the hotel. I was thinking of going up to the track on the roof for a short run. That would have been stupid. My ankle was basically healed, but I hadn't slept in thirty-six hours. It was early evening, not too hot, clouds had moved in and turned the sky gray, and it felt like months since I'd been out. I thought if I didn't get up and move around, I might just fall into a permanent stupor from which I'd never return. Yep, running was a dumb idea, and I was lacing up my shoes when the phone rang. I answered, hoping it was Jack.

"Do you know who this is?"

It would have been hard not to recognize that blend of youthful arrogance and smug vitality. "Yes, Damon, I know it's you."

"We need to talk. Tonight."

I walked the long line of batting cages at the Miami Tides recreation center, peering into each one as I passed. Special Agent Damon Hollander was taking his swings in the very last cage. He was decked out in gray cotton jersey shorts, clean white socks, and cleats. His shirt-sleeves were three-quarter length, the kind baseball players wear under their uniforms. He looked as professional and crisp as anyone I'd ever seen in sweat clothes.

As I approached, he adjusted the shiny batting helmet on his head, assumed his stance, and waited for the next ball to come out of the chute and hurtle toward him.

"I'm here," I said. "What do you want?"

He hit the ball foul. He didn't look at me, just pushed up his sleeves, as if it was the extra weight on his forearms that had thrown off his swing. He then proceeded to pound four straight against the back netting—every one on the nose—leaving the perfect aluminum ping vibrating in the air. He turned and looked past me, back the way I had come.

"Is Dolan with you?"

"You told me to come by myself. Why is that, Damon?"

He dropped in the last of the quarters he had sitting on the machine and swapped his aluminum bat for a wooden one.

"Because Jack Dolan is a drunk"—*Thwack*. A low liner in the direction of left field—"and I don't trust him."

Crack. A hard opposite field arc that would have surely cleared the wall at Jacob's Field, or at least the short porch at Yankee Stadium. I envied his swing—so graceful, fluid, and consistent.

"You trust me?"

"I trust you not to be stupid and emotional."

"You might be giving me too much credit, Damon."

He hit the rest of the pitches, fastballs every one, right on the nose, and I was willing to bet anything he couldn't hit a curve. I wanted to see him try, but I was also willing to bet that Damon never did anything unless it was a sure thing. He came out of the cage and we walked over to a wooden bench where he had his gear. A light sheen of moisture had appeared on his forehead, which made him seem to glisten. He pulled a towel from his gym bag and wiped his face.

"What do you want, Damon?"

"I asked you to come so I could deliver a message.

The message is for you. You can give it to him, too, if
you want. Or not. I don't care."

"What's the message?"

"Go home."

He dug around in the gear bag until he came up with
a water bottle. He tipped his head back and squeezed a
long, slow stream into his mouth.

"You delivered that message already."

"And you're still here."

I sat down next to him. I was tired. "I might consider
going home if I had some assurance the FBI was looking
into my friend's murder."

"I'll do that. I'll see that your friend's murder is properly and thoroughly investigated."

The sound of ball bashing was all around us—tight
pings as balls hit aluminum, the sharp cracks of wooden
bats on horsehide. I looked up into the sky, black behind
the high lights. I knew what was out there. Dark clouds
heavy with rain, ready to open up and pour down, and
not a moment too soon if you were a firefighter. I
couldn't figure Damon's angle. There were lots of options. Easier to just ask. "Why would you do that?"

"It's my job."

"And . . . ?"

"People are always telling me I'm young to be in the
position I'm in, to have achieved all that I've achieved."

"You must be very proud."

"My success comes from a simple approach. I anticipate all possibilities and eliminate the ones that don't get
me what I want."

"And I'm one of those rogue possibilities."

"If it takes making that commitment to you, that John
McTavish's death—"

"His murder."

"That his murder is investigated, if that's what it takes
to get you to leave Florida, then I'm willing to do it."

"And if the investigation leads to Jimmy Zacharias?"

He shrugged. "I can't predict the outcome. The investigation will lead where it leads. All I can tell you is we'll
do a thorough and professional job."

A few cages away, a dad was showing his son how to hold a bat. It was a big bat and a little boy, but they were having fun. It made me think of John's sons, Matthew and Sean. Sean would never know his father. "He must have wandered into something really big."

"McTavish? He did. And he paid a price. If you continue to pursue this matter, you could easily be killed, which would be a shame. I assume Dolan has at least tried to impress that on you. If he hasn't, shame on him. There's no question if you stay here, you will compromise my operation."

"And you're unwilling to tell me what that is."

"It's better for you if you don't know."

He tipped his head back again and took in a long stream of refreshment. He was making me realize how dry my mouth was. All the time. I'd been dehydrated ever since I'd set foot in Florida. The rain was going to feel good. "I won't leave because you tell me to go. You're going to have to give me something."

"What would you need to be convinced?"

"Give me information so I can understand. Is Jimmy your informant?"

"I won't tell you that."

I stood to leave.

"What I will say"—he waited, and I decided not to walk away—"is I work with a number of confidential informants. I have one that is highly placed and in a highly sensitive position right now, and you doing what you're doing can compromise that person's safety."

I sat back down on the bench. "This hypothetical informant, why would he be cooperating with you?"

"Informants cooperate for all different reasons. They don't want to go to jail, they want revenge, they're scared. Sometimes they want a competitor out of the way."

"Would this informant give you access to multiple targets?"

"Why would you ask that?"

"Because I have more information now. I know, for instance, that you've been over to see George Speath. I suspect it was to clean up after Jimmy and pick up the dirty parts he loosed upon the town. I give you credit for at least that much."

"I can't discuss the details of my investigation with you."

I pushed out farther on the bench and angled so that I could watch his eyes. "I know that George Speath is using his station to launder dirty money." If Damon had a reaction, he didn't show it to me. He seemed marvelously calm and unconcerned. "And I know that Ottavio uses a bunch of Jimmy's stations to launder his drug proceeds, which might give you what you need to nail the drug lord and get the big bust."

One nostril twitched negligibly, but he could have been sniffing for rain. And I could have been quoting Dr. Seuss to him for all the tension in his face. He retained a pleasant, unbothered expression. "Let's just say it's a big investigation and leave it at that."

"Does Vanessa know that Jimmy is a snitch?"

"Who's Vanessa?"

"That's what I thought. So she would be very interested if I told her about Jimmy. That if Jimmy brings down Ottavio, she goes down right beside him."

"Why would you even think of doing something like that?"

"I'm checking to see how much my chips are worth."

"Your chips aren't worth anything if you're dead. The stakes in this game are too high for you." He had such a patronizing way of speaking to me, I knew I was in danger of doing something stupid just because he'd told me not to.

"Let me ask you something else, Damon. How does a confidential informant, a guy working for the government, end up with the wreckage of a Triple Seven in his garage?"

"Again, I don't know what you're referring to, but as a rule, you can't control a CI all the time, and sometimes they do stupid things. They are criminals."

"Would Jimmy have been stupid enough to kill John? If John were going to screw up whatever deal you made with Jimmy and it looked as though he were going to jail, would he have killed John?"

"I don't know who killed him. That's why we investigate. To find out."

I sat on the wooden bench and listened to the subtle rumbling in the distance. The thunder sounded far away, but the air was starting to feel electric with the coming storm.

"There's one thing I don't know, Damon, and I don't know how to find out except to just ask you. If Jimmy did kill John, would you let him get away with it to bust Ottavio? Is it that important to you?"

Another rumble in the sky, this one louder and closer, drove the father and his son out of the cage and toward the exit. The little kid wanted to stay.

"I'll tell you this much," Damon said. "I would never risk blowing my informant's cover for stolen aircraft parts."

"That much is clear, and it's not what I asked you."

He pulled a windbreaker out of his bag and pulled it on. "This operation you're threatening to screw up, I've been working on it for almost two years. A number of people have been working on it for a long time, and we're *that* close. I believe as much as I believe anything that taking down my target is the most important thing I'll ever do. He's that bad. What he does reaches farther and does more damage than a single murder."

He tossed the plastic bottle into the bag and stood up. "And this is not a perfect world. But you know that."

He zipped his bag with a loud rip and slung it over his shoulder. The aluminum bat jangled against the wooden one as he propped one foot on the bench next to me. "If you go away now, Dolan disappears back into his stupor or the woodwork or wherever it is he lives. If you stay here and keep pressing, there will be consequences—for both of you. It's up to you. That's the real message. It's your call."

Chapter Thirty-seven

When I got out to the dirt parking lot the air was thick with the twin menaces of smoke and the impending thunderstorm. The wind had shifted and picked up, but it felt as if the night was getting hotter. I almost wondered if the fires were coming closer and raising the temperature.

Inside the car it was quiet enough to hear my own breathing, so when I got on the road, I tried the radio. The first station featured a Spanish-slinging DJ rattling off something in a deep baritone. It was the verbal equivalent of a bullet train. The next two stations had music playing, loud, peppy salsa tunes that were too boisterous for my dark mood. I stopped surfing when I found an English speaker. It was a talk show where people from all over the South called in to praise Jesus.

I turned it off when I realized with a creeping sense of alarm that I didn't recognize any of the scenery. Had I . . . ? Did I miss . . . ? I strained to find a landmark, something to convince myself that I wasn't totally lost. But when I looked out, it was into a darkness that seemed to extend from the edge of my high beams to forever. Somewhere along the way, I must have missed my turn back to the highway. Back to the *lighted* highway—that wide road with street lamps and big green direction signs. I didn't even know if I was going in the right direction. I decided to turn around and try going back the way I'd come. Maybe something would look familiar from the reverse angle.

I stiffened in my seat and clamped my hands to the steering wheel in the ten o'clock and two o'clock positions, just as they'd taught me in driver's ed, and pretty soon my face was damp and my chest was tightening because mile after mile went by without a place to turn around. No exits. No U-turns. Just a wide median of grass that sloped into a deep trough, probably to discourage people like me from creating their own turnarounds.

I was straining just to see through the darkness when I heard the first dull thud on the windshield. Then another. And another, and the rain was no longer coming. It was here, and it was coming down hard. It pummeled the windshield. I looked in all the obvious places for the wiper controls—God knows I hadn't had to use them so far—and when I finally hit the magic button, I discovered that even though my rental car was equipped with windshield wipers, sadly, they were not the kind that actually functioned.

My choice was to try to see around the wide, cloudy streaks they left with each creaky pass, or turn them off and try to see through the pounding rain unaided. Some wipers were better than no wipers, I decided, but then I had to scrunch down in my seat to see through the one clear line of sight they provided. I forgot about finding the way back. I had all I could handle keeping my vehicle on the road.

When I first saw the truck in the rearview, it was a couple of bright, runny specks in my lane, but far behind me. I stayed the course, puttering along at a stately fifty-five miles an hour. When I looked again, the truck was closing fast. He must have been pushing ninety, and he wasn't changing lanes. I tapped the brakes lightly to make sure he could see me. His headlights got bigger—*huge*. Over the sound of the rain, I could hear him rattling over the wet road—that and the sound of my own thick breathing. I looked to the right for a place to bail out. If he hit me from behind, I didn't want to be launched over whatever was out there that I couldn't see. I made a move to the left lane, the inside lane, thinking I'd rather be down in the median trough than down with the alligators. But no sooner had I committed than he did, too, and there was no way he was going to change course again at that speed. His horn blared into the night as I jerked the wheel hard and skidded back to the right. I went onto the shoulder and ricocheted back, barely holding it in my lane.

He threw a serious backwash over my windshield, so I couldn't see him, but I could feel him thundering by my driver's side door, his wheels inches away from my left shoulder. And I could hear him. They probably could have heard him back in Boston as he laid on the horn, letting it blast out angrily into the night until he was well past me, still going ninety, his red taillights blurring together in my cloudy windshield.

My insides untwisted, and then shuddered with a dose of adrenaline that I could taste in my mouth. I wanted to stop moving. I wanted to be still for a moment and ponder what had certainly been a near death experience, and savor the fact that I was still breathing, but the rain was still coming down and I was getting farther and farther away from where I wanted to be. Now there was another car behind me, and what the hell did he want because he was almost on top of me. Must have been behind the truck.

I tapped the brakes. He sped up. I moved to the other lane, making a slow, gradual transition. He stayed right on my tail. I tried to see who was driving. Saw nothing. His lights were up in my eyes. It was a pickup or an SUV, something bigger and more powerful than my Chevy. Probably four-wheel drive. The wipers kept slashing at the rain with a terrible scraping sound, reminding me that I was in a driving rainstorm with limited visibility. There was no way I was going to outrun them, and there was no way I was going to outdrive them. I let the car slow down gradually as I felt around blindly for my backpack. My phone. My phone was inside the pack. *There.* It's there. He was honking now and I was pulling out my phone and wrapping my hands around it and flipping it open. No signal. I felt like smashing it against the dashboard.

I rolled to a stop but left the engine running and kept the car in gear. The truck pulled in behind me. The driver killed the headlights, and I saw them—two silhouettes, dark shapes visible from the shoulders up. As they sat and talked, I listened to my engine running and to the sound of the rain, which was tapering off to a slow, steady patter. I was breathing, but just barely, in a rhythm that was shallow and quick.

The driver's door opened. There was no mistaking the tall, skinny build of the man who stepped out, and I almost did stop breathing. It was Jimmy.

I bit my lower lip to keep from going numb. I could see that he was about to slam his door shut, and the loud pop still made me jump. He was wearing jeans, a cowboy hat, and a tank top with armholes that reached to his waist. As he approached, I saw that his shirt was oddly bunched on one side, held there by the gun stuck in his belt. I lifted an unsteady foot. He put his hand on the door latch. I jammed the gas pedal to the floor. The car hesitated, lurched, and blasted off the shoulder. The wheels spun on the wet roadway for an agonizing interval. Then the four tires caught hold, slung the car forward like a rocket, and slammed me back against the seat.

In the rearview, I saw Jimmy scramble back to the truck. I hadn't planned anything beyond the swift takeoff. All I knew to do was to keep going until something else happened.

It did. They caught up.

Jimmy pulled up close and rammed my bumper. My head snapped back. They were next to me. Then they were in front of me, and I had nowhere to go. I had to stop when they did.

In the seconds it took Jimmy to cover the space between our cars, I searched my car's interior, the glove box, the floor, for anything to use as a weapon. Jack's .22 caliber automatic was sounding like a good idea to me right then. Jimmy rattled the handle on my door. When he started to go for the gun I unlocked it. The dome light came on. I felt a hand on the back of my head, then fingers twisting into my hair. I tried to pull away toward the passenger side, but he yanked my head straight back. The rest of my body followed and I spilled out of the car backwards and cracked my head on the pavement.

It took a few seconds for my vision to clear and my brain to regain focus. This time, both men were out of the car. The passenger stayed in the shadows. I couldn't see anything but his thick neck and bulky shape. Jimmy stood over me.

"It's the Mystery Lady." He reached down, grabbed me under my armpits, and leaned me up against the car. When I could stand by myself and didn't feel dizzy, I pushed his hands away. I heard a low rumble, which was not thunder. Jimmy's pickup truck was parked directly in front of my Lumina, and standing in the back was Bull. His fur was slick from the rain. His glassy eyes were on me. He was hot and panting and when he saw me staring, another vicious rattle worked its way up from his broad, muscled chest. I blinked the rain out of my eyes.

Jimmy leaned in so his face was close to mine. A stray hair from his ponytail brushed my cheek, and his powerful scent drifted into my sinuses and stayed. It was oily skin and tobacco and dirty clothes and wet dog, and I wondered if he meant to kill me.

I tried to turn away, but he clamped a viselike hand on my jaw and held it. "I want you to give Dolan a message for me, and I want you to tell it to him exactly as I say it."

When he took his hand from my face, my skin burned where he had touched me. He grabbed my wrist, pulled it chest high, and stuffed something into my palm. It felt like a plastic bag filled with warm milk. He wrapped his fingers over mine and squeezed. Something leaked down my forearm. Bull sniffed the air, twitched, and went into a yelping frenzy. Jimmy told his dog to shut the fuck up. The other man didn't seem to want to go near the beast.

"Tell Dolan I am no fucking snitch, and tell him if he

doesn't back off, I'm not going to kill him"—he gave my
hand a sharp twist and whatever was trickling went all
the way down my arm and dripped off my elbow—"I'm
going to kill you, Mystery Lady. Tell him to remember
what happens to civilians who get in the way. In my
way."

Even in the dark I could see how he looked at me, how
he wanted me to be scared of him. It was almost as if he
needed for me to be scared of him, and I was. But I also
had a dim, throbbing thought that if I had something
Jimmy needed, I sure as hell shouldn't give it up. My lungs
felt as useful as a couple of big rocks and I could barely
stand up, but I locked my jaw tight, forced myself to
breathe deeply through my nose, and wondered if that
was blood splattering out of my nostrils. I grabbed on to
every vicious, angry moment that had ever burned inside
me, wrapped them all into one laser stare, and channeled
it directly from my eyes into his. Then I snapped my
wrist and twisted my hand out of his bony grasp.

He didn't seem to know what to make of it.

"Keep your hands off of me."

A couple of cars went by on the other side of the
median. The second man, who until then hadn't said a
word, called to Jimmy in Spanish from the far side of
the truck. Jimmy didn't move.

"Why—" I had to clear the dryness from my throat.
"Why don't you deliver your own messages?"

"I like this way better."

"Maybe it's because you're afraid of Jack."

His smile was quick. "He's afraid of me. He's always
been afraid of me. You can tell him I said that, too."

The lookout called again and must have pointed, because Jimmy's head turned. I looked to see where he
was looking, at two headlights approaching on our side
of the road. As they came closer, the car decelerated as
if the driver might be interested in the show. Please,
God, please make him interested enough to stop.

Jimmy leaned down and pretended to be looking at
my tire. Bull stared from the truck. He'd caught a scent

and was sniffing the air, whining miserably. Jimmy
straightened and gave the passing car a friendly wave.
They moved on.

"Deliver the message," he said. "Tell Dolan to fuck
off, you go back to where you came from, and if you're
real lucky you'll never see me again."

He opened his door, slid behind the wheel, and roared
out even as his door was closing. Bull slipped against the
tailgate, then found his balance and stood in the back of
the truck, head raised to the rain, barking.

I stood for a long time feeling as if I were suspended
there in the dark, hanging by the slimmest of threads to
something above that held fast and kept me from total
collapse. I couldn't swallow. My muscles wouldn't respond. I forced myself to breathe. Oxygen began to flow.
I began to feel my body again.

Jimmy had torn out a handful of my hair, but my
whole scalp burned from it. Something was trying to
bang its way out of my skull, hammering from the inside,
mostly in the back where I'd hit the pavement. I closed
my eyes. It helped, but neither bending over nor arching
my back relieved the sharp pain that followed the path of
my spine. My shoulder throbbed. Something was wrenched
out of place. I rolled it up, back, and around, trying to
work out the soreness. I reached down to my elbow to
pull it into a stretch and felt the damp streaks on my
arm. Whatever Jimmy had folded into my hand was still
there, soft and mushy.

Like an idiot, or someone who'd been hit on the head
recently, I tried to see in the bag, to figure out what it
was in the near total darkness by the side of the road.
Eventually, it occurred to me to get in the car and use
the cabin light.

I opened the door. The incessant bonging began, a
reminder to either close the door or take the keys from
the ignition. My automatic response was to reach around
the steering column to get them. When I did I saw the
bright red streaks, like ribbons flowing across and around
the pale skin of my other arm. I opened my hand.

It was red, it was in a plastic bag, and it was misshapen

enough that at first I didn't recognize what I was holding. My stomach heaved. I tasted bile in my mouth. I was holding *a human ear*.

I dropped it as if it were a live scorpion. It fell on my leg. I twitched and convulsed in the car like a bird caught in a trap. I swatted it away so that no part of it would touch any part of me. It landed in one of the cup holders inches from my thigh. I had to get out, to get air, and I was on my feet, walking quickly away from the car, up the shoulder of the road, shaking out both my hands. The car was still bonging. My head, God my head ached. I turned and walked the other way, toward the car, passing it on the other side and continuing down the shoulder. My hair and the back of my shirt were damp from the rain and sweat and I was shivering. Either that or I was rock steady and the whole world was trembling around me. When I was far enough away, I stood staring at the Lumina from behind. I didn't see the car. I saw a detached human ear surrounded by a vehicle.

What in *hell* was I doing out here in the middle of *Florida* with a severed human *ear* in my car? This was so far away from my real life. I felt like crying. I almost laughed. *What* was I *doing*?

I paced the width of the car back and forth a few times. I decided that on my tenth round-trip I would continue walking to the open door. I stood outside looking at the smeary red Baggie. I reached across, opened the glove box, and found the free map that comes with all rental cars. I laid it out on the passenger seat. Then with two fingers, I lifted the dripping bag of horror by one corner, laid it on the paper, and folded it up. I put the whole package on the floorboard on the passenger side. Only then did I feel comfortable enough to get back in the car and close the door.

I started the car and drove directly across the road, down into the grassy trough of a median. The car rattled and bounced, the tires spun in the mud, and it was a struggle to get up the other side. But I made it, and I found my way and I drove all the way back into town with the dome light on.

Chapter Thirty-eight

Jack opened the door and all I could think was thank God he was home. He was there and I was safe and I didn't want to but I couldn't help it and I cried. He reached out for me and I walked into him and held on and wept into his shoulder. The darkness and the rain and being lost and the way Jimmy had touched me and the way he had smelled; the way my own fear smelled; the ear in my hand—that small flap of cartilage and tissue through a warm, slick Baggie membrane. And then the thought of being in the hangar in the swamp with the corpse of a dead airplane and all the ghosts inside; the dog and the rat and the petrifying panic and the tension and the smell of blood and bones and bodies. A ring . . . a diamond ring torn from a dead woman's finger and slipped onto mine. It all came up and out with so much force—it was like a catapult that had been loaded up and loaded up and loaded up and finally launched and, once loosed, could not be called back.

I cried and cried and it was very possible I would never have let go if Jack hadn't disengaged to close the door. When he turned around I grabbed him again and he held on to me until I stopped shaking. I was still damp down to my bone marrow and I was getting him wet, too. I don't know how long it was before he gently took my arms and pushed me out far enough that he could check me over.

"Are you hurt?"

"No."

He took my left wrist and turned my hand palm up. "You have blood all over you."

"It's not my blood."

"Whose is it?"

"I don't know."

He looked at me, waiting for an explanation that I didn't think I could blubber out in any comprehensible manner. Instead, I handed over my car keys. "Go look on the floorboard on the passenger side of the car."

He took the keys. "Is it a surprise?"

I wiped my eyes. "It was for me."

Jack came over to the kitchen table and handed me my tea. I wrapped both hands around the cup, lifted it up, and felt the steam condensing on my face, which was still hot and thick from my crying. But at least I wasn't damp and cold anymore. I had taken a long, long, long hot shower and Jack had given me a sweat suit to put on. I sat at his kitchen table with my feet pulled up under me and a blanket wrapped around my shoulders.

The ear was there. Sitting on his kitchen table in the middle of the map-wrapping, it looked like some exotic specialty that had come straight from the butcher. Every time I looked at it I cringed. Jack reached over and pulled the blanket tighter around me.

"Tell me again," he said, "exactly what Jimmy said."

"That civilians sometimes die when they get in the way, in . . . no, in *his* way. Especially when they get in his way. That you should remember what happens then." I wasn't being terribly articulate, but it was coming out the way it had lodged in my head. "He said he's no fucking snitch and if you don't stop saying so, he's not going to kill you, he's going to kill me. And he said you're afraid of him, that you've always been afraid of him."

He nodded, then leaned down and poked at the bag until the severed appendage was lying flat.

"He said to give you that ear."

"Yeah."

"Why? Do you know whose it is?"

"No, but that's not the point. It's part of the message. There were guys in Vietnam who liked to cut off ears to show how many people they'd killed. Jimmy liked to do that. We had a few discussions about it." He went back to the sink and twisted a couple of ice trays and dumped the frozen contents into an aluminum mixing bowl. I heard the cubes sliding around on the bottom. "He used to string them together and keep them in a little pouch."

"Why does he call you Ace?"

"The Ace of Spades is the death card," he said. "The Vietnamese thought it was bad luck. Grunts would wear them on their helmets. Sometimes they'd leave one sticking out of a corpse's mouth. They did it to scare the enemy, and sometimes as a warning."

I sneaked a glance at the ear. "Do you think this means Jimmy's killed someone else?"

"I don't know, Alex. Why did you go out there by yourself?"

"Damon said he wouldn't talk to me if you came. I tried to call you, Jack. Check with your service. I left a message."

"I went to meet Bobby," he said, "and I tried to call you. We must have missed each other. Bobby called and asked to meet. He said he was ready to talk."

I searched my memory for the last thing I remembered about Bobby Avidor. "He's not dead?"

"He wasn't earlier this afternoon," he said. "Although he might be lighter by one ear. He could be dead *and* missing an ear."

"You didn't see him?"

"He never showed. Didn't call. I went to his house. No sign of him." He slipped the bowl of ice onto the table and set the ear gently on top. Most of what blood there had been in the bag had already seeped out when Jimmy had squeezed it into my hand. But there was still enough to dribble down and stain the ice cubes pink. He put the whole thing in the refrigerator, leaned back against the counter, and crossed his arms.

"Jack, do you think Damon set me up?"

"That's what it feels like to me."

"He didn't even give me a chance."

"A chance for what?"

"To go home. To . . . he said . . ."

I realized I hadn't shared with Jack any of the pre-storm, pre-ear conversation I'd had with Damon. "I need to tell you what he said."

"Tomorrow. You don't look too good. I want you to sleep."

"Can I stay here?" The words flew out of my mouth. The important parts of me were functioning on some back-up power system, because the primary source, my brain, had shut down.

"I wouldn't give you any other choice."

My eyes started to burn again. I pulled the blanket around me, but no matter how tight I made it, it didn't feel like enough protection. If I was going to sleep, I needed the protection of his arms around me. "Jack, will you stay with me?"

He tilted his head and looked as if I was handing him a monumental responsibility that he took very seriously.

"Until I fall asleep. I feel safe with you." I was afraid he would say no. Instead he came over to me and reached for my hand. When I gave it to him, he pulled me up, put his hands on my shoulders, and steered me into his bedroom. He pulled back the covers and tucked me in, then he lay down and pulled sweatshirt, sheets, blankets, covers, and me all into a sheltering embrace. I closed my eyes and the world disappeared and I fell asleep.

The sun was trying to get in through the blinds when I opened my eyes again. Sounds from the unit next door floated in from somewhere, through the walls or the windows or the vents. Kids getting ready for school, so it must not have been too late.

I felt the weight of Jack's arm across my waist. I felt the solid comfort of his body curved around mine. He was still asleep, his breathing steady against my neck. I kept still and enjoyed the feeling. It had been a long time since I'd opened my eyes in a man's arms.

My mobility was limited if I didn't want to wake him up, so I let my eyes wander around his bedroom and saw what I could in the alternating light and shadows. It was neat, but not in a finicky way. More utilitarian. There wasn't much—a bed with a headboard, a tall four-drawer dresser, a closet with the door closed. But everything that was there had a place. All the books were on the bookshelves. The hardback titles, which were the only ones I could read, tended toward biographies and war books, many on Vietnam. *Hell in a Very Small Place*, *Vietnam: A History*, *The Things They Carried* by Tim O'Brien. There were several books by O'Brien. Books on World War II and some on law enforcement, and rows and rows of what looked like paperback mysteries. A compact and not very complicated stereo system fit on top of the dresser and I wondered where the CDs were. Sharing the space on the dresser with the stereo were three framed photos. I couldn't see what they were, but one looked like a graduation day, maybe his son graduating from high school. Along the floor leaning against the wall were a few citations from his days at the FBI and I wondered if they were going up or coming down.

I reached up as quietly as I could to the headboard, remembering that I had put my watch there the night before. My fingers brushed across a row of plastic jewel boxes. The CDs. I tried to crane my neck without moving too much to read the titles.

Classical, jazz guitar, rock—not much after 1975, a big blues collection with B. B. King, Keb Mo', and John Lee Hooker, what looked to be everything Leonard Cohen had ever recorded. At the far end was an entire section of artists I'd never heard of. I slipped one out but had to reach across Jack to do it and, in the process, woke him up. I could feel the shift in his breathing, followed by the slow turning and testing and stretching that signaled the return to consciousness.

He lifted the arm that had been wrapped around me, and left a cold swath where it had been. And when he

untangled from me and rolled over on his back, I felt
the chill of sudden and unwanted exposure.

I turned toward him but got twisted up in all the covers. His weight on top of the sheets and blankets held
them taut and pinned me to the mattress. I had to pull
some slack from the other side of the bed so I could roll
up on my elbows and see his face.

His eyes were only half open when he looked at me
from the cushy middle of one of his big pillows. "Feeling better?"

"Like a new person." I showed him the CD. "Jack,
gospel music?"

He lifted his head enough to see what I was looking
at. It was a small move that seemed like a big effort in
the lazy glow of a good night's sleep. "What about it?"

"Do you like gospel music?"

"I do."

Huh. I'd never actually met anyone who liked gospel
music. Or at least that I knew of. "What do you like
about it?"

He let his head sink back on the pillow, rubbed his
eyes, and yawned. "The singers are glorious. Their voices
are amazing, and it's the most uncynical music there is.
You don't have to figure anything out. Just listen. Simple.
I like that."

"Quite a contrast to Leonard Cohen."

"I like them both." He smiled with his eyes closed. "I
guess that makes me complex."

He drew in a deep breath and let it seep out slowly
through his nose. He did it a few more times and almost
seemed to be breathing in the energy he needed to get
up and start the day.

"Thank you for staying with me last night."

"You slept well," he said. "I woke up a few times and
you never moved."

I had to reach over him to slip the CD back in its
slot. Everything in its place. I felt him under me—solid,
substantial, real. When I pulled back, he was looking at
me, searching my face. "Your eyes are gray," he said.

"Ever since I was born."

"They're pretty." His hand was close enough that I could feel the warmth from it, and I knew he wanted to touch me and I was desperate for him to do it, but all he did was barely brush close enough to touch my hair.

"Jack . . ."

He took my left hand, the one that had held the severed ear, and pushed up the sleeve of my sweatshirt. He inspected the palm, the fingertips, the fingernails. Every part of my hand with his hands. He was in no hurry, and he was driving me crazy.

"Are you sure you're not hurt?"

"My head hurts."

He rolled up on his side and reached around and felt the tender place on the back of my skull. He ran his fingertip along the bare ridge where Jimmy had pulled out a handful of hair. "Here?"

"Yes." My face was very close to him now, to his chest. We were both wearing his sweatshirts, and I could smell the scent of his laundry, the sweet fragrance of the dryer sheets that had filled the Miramar Coin Op the night I'd sat on a pile of his laundry and put my arms around him. This time I decided to hold still and be quiet, go at his pace and hope he went where I wanted to go. "Jimmy pulled me out of the car," I said. "I hit my head on the cement."

"I'm sorry." He pulled me closer and kissed the top of my head. Then he lifted my chin and kissed my forehead. And then he rolled back and looked at me. "Why did you kiss me the other night?"

"Because . . . I was . . ." His hand had moved from my head to my shoulder, and his fingertips were exploring along the edge of the collar and underneath. "I kissed you because I was attracted to you. I am attracted to you."

His fingers kept moving back up to my head, then slowly down again, lower each time, finding their own path along the folds and crevices of the sweatshirt, like a stream following a dry creek bed. I was getting lost in his eyes, brown eyes that looked at me with the gentleness I had seen there from the beginning, and the desire he was letting show for the first time.

"Why didn't you kiss me back?" I whispered.

"I wanted to." He pulled me closer so he could reach all the way down my back. "It took all that I had not to."

"Why?"

"What I said. I'm not good with people." His hand had made its way under my shirt. The stream was more like a river now, pushing where it wanted to go, making its own way across my topography. "I get tired of disappointing people." He brushed his lips across mine.

"I'm not disappointed." I moved with the rhythm of his hand floating over my skin. I reached for his leg and pulled it across my body. I wanted to feel him, too, but layers of bedding and clothing separated us and he seemed content to work through it all in his own time.

"I don't know why you want to be with me." His voice was getting ragged, and I could feel him against me, responding to me even through all the layers. I moved in closer and began to explore on my own, feeling along the vertebrae that ran down the middle of his back, climbing the steps one by one along the graceful slope up to his shoulders, and all the way down to the back of his legs, where I found thick, sturdy muscles. He shivered against me as I followed their line down and around and back up until I found the drawstring to his sweatpants.

"I don't think I'm good for you," he said, but not with much conviction.

"You don't get to decide that for me."

"I'm too old, I'm a drunk, I'm—"

I shut him up with a deep lingering kiss as I pulled the drawstring on his sweatpants. He'd already found mine and loosened it, and it didn't take long after that for me to crawl out from under the covers and for him to crawl out of his sweats and for both of us to kick all of it—covers and blankets and clothes and everything else that separated us—off of the bed and onto the floor until there was just the two of us making love.

*   *   *

We had pulled the pillows off the floor and the sheets over us as we lay on the bed together. Jack had gotten up to open the window, so the sounds of the wakening neighborhood were coming through along with a slight, cooling breeze. A gospel singer was on the stereo, someone I'd never heard of, but someone he liked. I liked her, too.

"Jack."

"What?"

"You're not like Jimmy."

He shifted, so my head rolled a little to the side and I had to readjust to fit again into the crook of his right arm and against his chest. He didn't answer.

"Jack."

"I heard you."

"That's what scares you, isn't it? You're not scared of him. You're afraid you're like him. You're not."

"How do you know?"

I raised my head and crawled up to look into his eyes. I turned his face to make sure he was looking at me. "The only thing you have in common with Jimmy Zacharias is you were both from Florida, and you both served in Vietnam, which put the two of you in the same place at the same time with the same set of crappy options." I curled into him and put my head down again. "It's not in you to be like him."

I listened to the music and tried not to think about the moment, coming soon, when we would have to get up and take showers—or maybe one together—and put our clothes back on and go back to the world. He was quiet, stroking my hair.

"Where did you grow up?" he asked.

"All over."

"Where were you the longest? Where do you think of as home?"

"Seattle."

"What neighborhood?"

"Ballard."

"Try to picture a company of North Vietnamese soldiers coming out of the trees one night in Ballard. It's

foggy and it's hard to see. They look like ghosts carrying
machine guns and hand grenades and rocket launchers.
But they're not ghosts and they woke up in the morning
pissed off and they walk in pissed off. They walk up and
down the streets of the neighborhood rousting people
out of bed, out of their homes. They bust into bedrooms
and kitchens and living rooms and basements. They're
looking for the husbands and the sons because this is
supposed to be an enemy stronghold. They think they're
there. They've been told they're there, and they find
weapons, but mostly what they find are mothers and sisters and grandmothers and daughters." The slightest
tremble crept into his voice. "They find babies."

I felt him stiffening. When I tried to put my arm around
him, he turned so that it was hard to be close to him at
all. I moved away and wrapped myself in the sheets.

"Now they're really pissed off, these soldiers. So they
go up and down the streets of Ballard from house to
house, killing the family pets—shooting the dogs and
running the cats through with their bayonets, just for the
hell of it. Just because they can. Now they're not sure
what to do because if they leave all these people there
alive, one of them could steal off and alert the enemy
and they could end up in an ambush and all die."

"What do they do?"

"After a lot of arguing, they set all the houses on fire
and they leave. They're walking out. They're almost out
of there, when someone fires a shot. A shot is fired and
all hell breaks loose. The soldiers become convinced
they're under attack. They turn around and start shooting and they empty their weapons into this little neighborhood. They keep firing until there's nothing moving.
Nothing."

The song on the CD changed, and he seemed to be
listening. "It was so easy to kill people over there because after you'd been there for a while"—he made a
flourish in the air with his hand, a magician's wave intended to make something disappear—"they weren't
people anymore. You got so that you didn't even feel it.
There never seemed to be any consequences."

"Is that story about you? Was it some village in Vietnam?"

"We killed them all."

"How many?"

"Seventeen."

"Were you under attack?"

"That's what the report said."

"What do you think?"

"I think"—he pressed the heel of his hand into his forehead just over his eye—"unless you've seen it, you can't imagine what the percussive force of an M-16 does to the human body. Bones shatter, organs and limbs explode, bits of skin and blood spray everywhere." He stared straight up at the ceiling. "I think . . . it didn't matter to us at all if we were under attack."

"Jimmy was there?"

"It was a good day for Jimmy."

I found his hand among the covers and held it and listened to the gospel singer. Jack was right about her voice. It was glorious—strong with the fervor of what she believed, pure in the simplicity of her convictions, and irresistible in the strong current of hope that pulled you along to be saved with her.

"Do you ever talk to anyone about this? Have you ever gotten help?"

"I've talked to shrinks. Bureau shrinks. I go to A.A. meetings."

"Do you share this stuff at your meetings?"

"What they tell you at those meetings is to put your faith in the higher power. The higher power. What is that? That's taking the weight off your own shoulders and putting it somewhere else. We all have to carry our own weight. In the end there's no getting away from the things you did."

I put my hand on his cheek and felt the hard cheekbone beneath his rough skin. I felt his whiskers against my palm. I felt the edge of his hairline with the tips of my fingers—all things that made him a human being.

"You said it yourself in the laundromat, Jack. The rules are different in war. You were twenty years old. It

was dark. You were scared. You thought you were under
attack. Whatever you did, you did. What happened there
is part of you. It's part of what you've become just as it's
part of what Jimmy has become. But in a different way."

"Different how?"

"You think about the people who died. You think
about them as fathers and mothers and sons and daughters, people who could just as easily have been living in
Ballard, Washington as some province in Vietnam. You
grieve for them. You understand that part of you was
lost over there. Jimmy probably thinks . . . I can't say
what he thinks. Maybe that's what makes him so mean."

"What?"

"He sees you, and there is so much about you that is
good and honorable, and so much about him that is
twisted and dead. He knows what happened to him. He
knows what he is, and it really pisses him off."

He smiled. "You give him too much credit."

"Probably."

"You give me too much credit."

"You don't give yourself enough."

He pressed his cheek against my hand and closed his
eyes. I looked at him and couldn't stop thinking about
something I'd seen once on the Discovery Channel. It
was about a climber who had fallen eighty feet down an
icy cliff and was stranded where he lay for two days.
When the rescuers came to get him, you couldn't tell by
looking at him what his injuries were. He looked perfectly fine. But when they pulled off his boots, they were
filled with blood, and when they cut away his pants, his
injuries were almost too gruesome to look at. The misshapen forms below his knees were unrecognizable as
part of the human leg. The sharp points of broken bones
poked out through bloody gashes, and his toes were
black, frostbitten stumps. Over thirty years later, Jack
was still bleeding into his boots, getting up every day
and trying to stand on broken and bloody stumps. I put
my arm around him and pulled him close and wondered
what, if anything, would ever help him heal.

Chapter Thirty-nine

We were both hungry when we finally got upright, and didn't like the thought of cooking with an extra ear in the house, so Jack took me to breakfast at his favorite Cuban restaurant. Once again, the man behind the lunch counter knew Jack and greeted him warmly and offered to seat us at the best seat in the house, which was like all the other seats in the house—vinyl chairs at tables with laminated tops under baskets of fake ferns. After we ordered, the waiter brought some plain old tea for me and a strange brew for Jack—Cuban coffee.

"Too bad you don't drink coffee," he said. "This is great stuff."

It was a coffee cup full of milk with the blackest coffee I'd ever seen served on the side in a creamer.

"Alex."

"What?"

He checked around and leaned in so only I could hear him. "Do you always carry condoms in your bag?"

That made me laugh. I hadn't been with a man in so long I'd almost forgotten how to use them. "No. I bought them the other day. After the laundromat." I shrugged. "In case you changed your mind."

"Ah." He stared down into his cup and concentrated hard on his Cuban coffee ministrations. Either it was a highly complex procedure that took great concentration, or he was anxious for a change in the subject.

"I never told you what Damon said."

"Tell me now."

I did. I recounted the warnings and the veiled threats. I told him Damon had confirmed without ever saying so that Jimmy was his informant.

"I knew it," was his response. And then, "So?"

"So, what?"

"Are you going to take his advice, and Jimmy's, and go back to Boston?"

"I told you the other day I was staying."

"Things are different now. Jimmy threatened you."

"Yeah, it seems really dumb to stay here. The problem is, I don't feel driven by rational impulses. I don't feel the danger. Even when I think back on what happened last night, Jimmy scared me, but I still thought . . ." I stopped and searched for the words, trying to articulate something I didn't understand myself. "I don't know how to say it except I should have been more scared of him. I was more pissed that he would do that to me."

"Jimmy is dangerous. Killing is no problem for him. It would be dangerous for you to stay. That's not complicated."

"I know that. I know it would be stupid to stay. But the 'being stupid' argument is not persuasive. Apparently I'm willing to be stupid. So then I look at the other side of the equation. What are the right reasons to stay? That's even more problematic."

He was grinning at me. "This is great," he said. "You're such an analyst."

"You're making fun of me again."

"Yeah."

"This is the way I think."

"I know. It's fascinating. Keep going."

"I keep picturing myself checking out of the hotel, getting on a plane, and flying back to Boston. I envision the scene where I tell Mae I've given up. I'll say something like, 'I did everything I could, but now the authorities have to do the rest.' She'll thank me for all I've done. She thanks me every time I talk to her just for coming down."

I stared over Jack's shoulder at the warped wood paneling on the wall and the hand painted mural of Cuba in better days. "The truth is I couldn't care less about a job I signed up for in a city I've never been to. I can't see myself sitting at a desk anymore in my hose and my heels and my earrings, filling out head count reports and apologizing to some overwrought passenger because there are only fourteen seats in first class and he's number fifteen."

"Why is that a bad thing?"

"Because I feel as if I'm using him . . . using John's death as an excuse to keep me from doing what I should be doing. That's my dirty little secret. I'm not brave and honorable. I'm just less scared to stay here and face a homicidal killer than I am to go home and face my real life."

"That's bullshit."

"Excuse me?"

"First of all, what John did for you at Logan, I'm sure it was something you needed and no doubt he did stand up for you, and I know that's important to you, but no one's motives are ever as pure as you're trying to make his out to be. He got something out of it, too. Maybe he had to be the hero. Maybe that's why he's dead."

I thought about Mae standing in her kitchen, telling me what I already knew, that John always wanted to save the world, and how she had wanted him to stop trying to save the world.

"And second, it sounds to me as if your old life is not enough for you anymore. You've found a life you like better."

"What life?"

"The life of an investigator."

"What?"

"You're good at this. You're a good investigator. You're smart. You ask the right questions. You can read people. You're tough enough, especially if Jimmy doesn't scare you, although that might fit in the category of recklessness. Or lunacy. I think you were born to do this work."

"I don't have any training. I don't even know how

to shoot a gun. I wouldn't even know where to start. I need money."

"You can learn. And you can earn money as an investigator. I'm not a good example, but take my word for it."

"It would never work."

"Why not?"

"It's not a real job. I already told you I'm a single woman. I live alone."

"You're making this far too complicated. Here's the real dirty little secret. Doing this work excites you. It gives you a thrill like a nine-to-five job never could. It gives you a rush. It makes you feel alive. I know because I get the same juice. You've found something you really want to do, and you won't let yourself do it. You've got some kind of repressed self-punishment thing going on. Are you Catholic?"

"Sort of."

"That would do it."

"You're saying there are no Catholic investigators?"

"I'm saying you should do what you want, not what you think you should, and see what happens."

That was a wicked thought. Do what I want? I tried to think only about where I wanted to be right then and what I wanted to be doing, and I started to get a thrill, a power surge, just thinking about directing my life that way. "I want to stay here and see this to the end. Jimmy killed John, and I want to see that he's punished for it."

"Do you care how?"

"Are you asking if I want to kill him?"

"No. I'm not suggesting that. Maybe something that's not your traditional approach to law enforcement is all." He smiled. "If the cops can't help us, and the Feds won't, we have to find someone who will, and give them a reason to do it."

"I vote for Vanessa," I said. "I think she's the key."

A cell phone rang. We both reached, but it wasn't my ring. It was Jack's. He answered and did a lot of listening. I heard a lot of uh-huhs. He started looking around for something to write with. I pulled a pen from my back-pack and handed it over. He used it to write an address on his napkin.

"How about a phone number?" He paused to listen. "Are you going to show up this time?" Another pause, shorter. "Okay"—he checked his watch—"half an hour."

He hung up and smiled at me. "Guess who just resur-faced?"

Chapter Forty

The address Bobby Avidor had given us turned out to be in a warehouse district along one of the seedier sections of the Miami River. We took a downtown exit off the interstate, turned away from the gleaming chrome and glass towers, and drove down into an industrial enclave of dead end roads and concrete docks, where bars covered the windows and air conditioners dripped on asphalt sidewalks. There were no tourists here.

We parked underneath a drawbridge, and before we got within a hundred yards of the building, we ran right into a stench that was overwhelming. And overwhelmingly familiar. The place turned out to be a small fish-processing plant, and I had last inhaled that odor while standing over my bag on the floor of Bic's inbound bag room.

"Is Bobby taking up a second career?" I asked.

"He said it's his cousin's place."

Inside the building I flagged down a small old man wearing nothing but shorts and unlaced track shoes. His brown skin hung on his chest like soft suede as he struggled to roll a metal barrel on its edge across the crusty floor. He didn't speak English. Jack asked him in Spanish to find Bobby and tell him we were there.

We waited on the dock behind the warehouse where the smell of dead fish was cut by the industrial aroma of the river. Every once in a while a boat would motor by. They tended to be working boats—trawlers and tugboats—rather than the pleasure craft that jammed other venues.

We heard Bobby before we saw him. "What the fuck . . . do you think I'm coming out there to stand next to you in plain sight?"

We turned toward the voice. It was so bright outside that looking back into the warehouse was like staring into the mouth of a black cave. "Where would you feel comfortable?" Jack asked him.

"Nowhere, goddammit. But if you want to talk to me, you come inside."

And so we had to wade back into an odor so thick you could lean on it, and stand on a cement floor caked with dried fish guts. When my eyes adjusted again to the dim interior, I took one look at Bobby and turned to Jack. "Another mystery solved."

Bobby looked as if he were wearing a cockeyed turban when in fact it was a thick gauze bandage wrapped around his head, with special consideration for the place where his left ear had once been. He reached up reflexively to touch that side of his head.

"Too bad." Jack stuck his hands in his pockets. "If we'd known sooner, maybe they could have reattached it."

"What are you talking about, reattaching? How do you know what happened?"

"I was the lucky recipient of your detached ear," I said. "It came to me in a Baggie full of blood. But it took me a while to figure out what it was, and I certainly didn't know it belonged to you."

Bobby turned, and the light from outside fell across his face. The sight of dried brown blood and yellow pus caked along the edge of his bandage was bad enough, but the thought of what it must have looked like under the bandage made my stomach lurch.

"Why did Jimmy take your ear?" I asked.

"He thought I told you he was a snitch."

Jack turned to me. "Where would he get that idea?"

"Beats me."

Bobby's jittery eyes shifted from one of us to the other. He appeared to be struggling for just the right word. Instead, he put on a spiteful smirk and walked

over to a bucket a few yards away. It was filled with the
same vile stew that had defiled my allegedly lost bag.
"Too bad about that bag of yours." He looked as smug
as anyone with one ear can look.

"Bobby, I can get a new bag."

The smirk faded and his hand drifted up once again
to tug nervously at the bandage. "I need protection."

"Apparently." I marveled again at how flat the left
side of his head was.

"You said you could do that, right? Keep that crazy-
ass Jimmy away from me?"

Jack took a step closer to Bobby. "How do you expect
us to do that?"

"Get him the fuck in jail."

I took a step toward Bobby. "How do you expect us
to do that?"

"I'll give you what you need. You make sure it gets
where it needs to to lock his ass away."

"No deal," I said, "unless you tell us what happened
to John."

"I don't know what happened to him."

"Let's go, Jack."

"Honest to God," he whined. "I don't know who killed
him. But I know who he went to see the night he died."

That was good enough.

"Bobby," Jack said, draping his arm around his neck,
"let's go next door and have a chat. I'll protect you while
you have a beer."

Next door was the deck of a run-down bar, where the
rats had the decency not to strut about in the open. It
had a silver disco ball, a stuffed parrot, and a chain-link
fence that kept patrons from pitching over the side into
the river. It also served tuna fish on Ritz crackers. They
weren't appetizing, but they looked better than the other
free condiment—a bowl of pickles swimming in sour
juice. I reached for a cracker.

Bobby drank beer and held forth while I took notes
and Jack drank strong, black coffee, which seemed a
cruel and unusual refreshment on such a humid day.

"It happened," Bobby said, "the way I said. Johnny showed up here out of the blue. He called me that morning and told me to meet him for a cup of coffee when he got in."

Jack seemed content to sit back and let me ask most of the questions. "What did he say to you?"

"All the things I would expect him to say, being the self-righteous bastard that he is . . . was." He lifted his chin into a defensive pose. "He said he was ashamed he'd ever known me, and he was sorry to say it on account of me saving his brother the way I did. He gave me two choices—go to the cops myself, or sit and wait to be arrested. One way or the other, I was out of business."

"And your mother gave him the logbook and the ring?"

"Fucking bitch. '*I don't want the ring from a dead woman's finger in my house.*'" He'd pitched his voice into a high, unkind imitation of a woman and made the sign of the cross. "'*May God have mercy on her soul.*' Ignorant fishwife. That's all she is and all she ever was. I shouldn't have even told her what was in the package."

"Why did you?" Jack squinted at him. He wasn't wearing his sunglasses.

Bobby turned toward him. "Because I thought it was so frigging cool, and I couldn't tell anyone about it. I couldn't show it to anyone. My mistake believing she would ever think anything I did was as good as anything the great Johnny McTavish would do."

Jack chortled over on his side of the round table. "Bobby, I don't think you're cut out for a life of crime."

"What else happened with John?" I asked.

"He told me I had twenty-four hours to think about it, that he would be at The Harmony House Suites, and at the end of twenty-four hours, he was going to walk into the police station."

"When would that have been?"

"Three o'clock the next afternoon. And I knew if he said three p.m., that's when he'd be there."

I reviewed my notes. John had checked into The Suites around four o'clock on Monday afternoon, so that would have made sense. "What did you do next?"

"I tried all the stuff that usually worked on him before." He set the beer bottle on the table so he could press his hands together in a prayer pose. " 'I'm sorry,' I said. 'I fucked up. I know I did, but I can fix it.' " His wheedling voice matched the exaggerated gesture of contrition. " 'Johnny,' I says, 'I would never want you to be ashamed of me, and I want to do my best for you. Give me another chance . . .' I could always get to him before, but not this time. He said I'd gone too far. He said stealing tools is one thing, or even selling drugs, which on my mother's eyes I never did, by the way. He said at least people make a choice to take drugs. But no one makes a choice to be on an airplane with a bad part. Pretty screwed up logic, if you ask me."

John was not the one who'd been screwed up and Bobby knew it. He tipped back and finished off the rest of his beer. Then he looked for the waitress to bring him another.

"After he left for the hotel what did you do?"

"I was on the phone first thing to Jimmy. I said we got a problem here. This guy Johnny McTavish, I know him from back home and he will do what he says he will do which is to turn us in. Jimmy says, 'He don't even know me.' He's testing me, right? I say, 'If I get picked up, everyone's going to know everything I know. I just tell you that up front so there won't be a misunderstanding. I'll flip on you in a second if it will help me.' "

Jack thought that was pretty funny, too. "Were you on drugs, Bobby?" The tone suggested he must have been.

Bobby's shoulders stiffened. "I wanted him to see that my problem was his problem, is all that was."

"You're an idiot. Not only did you turn yourself into a huge liability for Jimmy, you also involved yourself in a conspiracy to commit murder."

"There was never any discussion about killing him."

Jack pushed forward and stretched his arms across the table. "What did you think Jimmy was going to do? You gave him no choice. He either had to kill John, or kill you. He'd have been better off killing you."

"Jimmy wanted to scare him is all."

"What are you saying?" I set down my notebook. "Jimmy was just trying to scare John with a knife and things got out of hand?"

"No. Nothing like that. Jimmy asked me for personal stuff I knew about Johnny's family. Like where his kids went to school. I didn't know that. I didn't even know about the baby, but I told him what I knew, about his neighborhood, his address, and what the house looked like. He needed it to make Johnny think they were watching his family." He caught sight of the two of us staring at him. "I figured it was better than him ending up dead."

Jack sat back and crossed his arms. "You're a pitiful bastard." That pretty much summed up how I felt, too.

"I didn't ask him to come down here. If he'd have just stayed home and minded his own business, he wouldn't have got killed and I would still have both my fucking ears."

I looked hard at Bobby. "Don't say it that way."

"Say what?"

" 'He *got* killed,' as if some nameless, faceless force beyond anyone's control reached down from the heavens and for reasons none of us will ever understand snatched his life away."

He stared at me. He didn't get it. The fact that he never would just served to get me more cranked up.

"People who get struck by lightning, Bobby, are killed. People who drown in rivers or have houses fall on them in tornadoes are killed. But that's not what happened here. John was murdered. Jimmy Zacharias took a knife that was nine inches long and stuck it into his throat. He just about cut his head off, and when he thought John was dead, he tossed him into a dumpster. But he wasn't dead. When they found him, his arm was hanging over one side. He'd tried to climb out, Bobby. He was fighting for his life right up to the end. He wanted to live." People a few tables over were beginning to take notice of our conversation. I lowered my voice. "Don't ever say again that John McTavish was killed. Don't even think it. When you think about John, think about the fact that you're the reason he was down here. You're the reason he's dead."

He stared down at his beer, and then he found something out on the brown river to stare at. Nothing I had said was going to change anything, but it made me feel better. It helped purge some of the emotional toxins that had been building up in my heart like plaque. I wanted to be finished with Bobby before I felt the need to purge again. I picked up my notebook and looked at the time-line. "What happened after Jimmy made his threats? Why did he kill him if John was going home?"

"I didn't say Jimmy threatened him."

"You just did."

"I said I gave Jimmy the information. It was his idea, but I never said he was the one who did it. He got that little FBI prick to do it."

Jack put down his coffee cup. "Who, Bobby? Give me a name."

"Damon Hollander."

Neither one of us had an immediate response. At least not a verbal one. Bobby looked at our faces. "You didn't know about him? Why do you think I'm talking to you, and not the Feds? Jimmy's got that little prick in his pocket."

Everything about Bobby seemed to come into sharper focus. It was as if I had adjusted my zoom lens and I could see the tiniest details—the little scar on his jaw where his beard stubble didn't grow, a few nose hairs poking out, the way the perspiration pooled in the cleft of his upper lip. I tried to see inside his head, to figure out if he was lying and if he was, if he was smart enough to have a good reason for it. I thought no on both counts.

"Jimmy sent Damon Hollander to meet with McTavish the night of the murder." I said it just to see how it sounded. "Is that what you're telling us?"

"That's the only way it would work. I knew it would never work to just threaten him flat out. Jimmy thought if Hollander looked him up at the hotel, flashed his badge, and suggested he go home for his own good, he would. So that's what he did. Hollander picked up Johnny

at the hotel and took him for a ride. He told him he had
me under surveillance and some shit about a wiretap and
how he'd heard me giving all this personal information
to some bad guys. Like maybe we were planning to get
to him through Mae and the kids. He told him all the
personal stuff and said he'd got it from the wiretap."

"What does Jimmy have on Damon?" Jack asked.

"What do you mean?"

"Jimmy is a criminal. Damon Hollander is a federal
agent." Jack was speaking slowly in short, simple sentences, presumably so Bobby could follow along. "Why
would Damon do something that Jimmy asked him to
do?"

"I don't know. I never knew. Jimmy just is always saying
how he can do whatever he wants, that he has protection.
No one is going to touch him. Then when you two came
around and said he was a rat for the government, I
thought that had to be it. This prick Hollander was protecting his source. I figured if a little of that protection
rubbed off on me, so be it. Good for me."

I looked at Jack. "Damon tries to warn John off. He
picks him up and takes him on the ride. But Jimmy has
second thoughts about the plan. He decides no risk is
better than low risk. So he swings by the hotel after
Damon has dropped him off. He grabs John, takes him
out and kills him."

"It could have happened that way," Bobby said, "but
I don't think it did."

"Why not?"

"Because Jimmy called me the next day and asked me
if Johnny had gone back to Boston."

I could never remember to crack the windows open when
I parked in the sun. When we got back to the car, it
must have been pushing one hundred and fifty degrees
inside. The seat belt tongue was so hot it singed my
fingers. But I couldn't wait to get away from the curb,
and out of the odor radius of the fish factory. I closed
the door and took off.

All my thoughts and ideas were beginning to fuse together into a hardened, impenetrable lump. I couldn't pull the threads out anymore and follow them.

"If Jimmy didn't do it," I said, "who did?"

"I'm not convinced he didn't. He could have been covering his ass with that phone call." Jack had dropped his head back and squeezed his eyes closed. I didn't, since I was driving. "But if he didn't kill him, I bet he knows who did."

I'd already made two passes trying to figure out on my own how to get back up to the interstate, but I had somehow gotten caught up in an endless loop of one-way streets. It felt the way this case was going. "A little help here, Jack?"

He sat up straight and checked our position. "I thought maybe driving around in circles was one of your concentration techniques. Turn left up there. We have to go out of our way a couple of blocks to get back on the other side."

I made the left as he'd instructed, and was immediately buoyed by the fact that we were no longer trapped in the shadows beneath the interstate.

Jack pulled out his phone. "Let's check in with Felix," he said. "That kid always cheers me up. We'll see if he's figured out yet who Vanessa is."

Chapter Forty-one

Felix must have been standing at the check-in desk watching for us because when we walked into the lobby at The Suites, he was there, wearing his wide-armed polyester suit and brown striped tie. Something about seeing him back on duty, back in his normal job, gave me comfort.

"Wait until you see what I found on Miss Cray," he said. "You are going to be so psyched."

Jack leaned against the front desk. "Did you figure out who she is?"

"No. Better. Well maybe not better because that would be good to know too but what I found is awesome. It is so cool. I think you're going to really like it."

As we walked to the elevator, he called to someone at the counter to say he was taking a short break. They could reach him in 484. All the way up in the elevator, he was bobbing up and down, rocking back on his heels and forward on his toes. He was like a little kid that had to go to the bathroom.

He had straightened up the room since our marathon session had ended, and I wondered when or if this kid ever laid his head down to sleep.

He went to the place he was most comfortable, to the seat on the couch in front of his laptop. "So, like, when you asked me, Mr. Dolan, to find out about Miss Cray, I thought and thought and I finally decided to try something totally off the wall and I did and it worked and I got in."

I sat down next to him. "What did you get into?"

"Miss Cray's private files."

"How did you do that, son?"

"It wasn't easy because there are no references or links or anything in the accountant's files. But then I remembered all those orchid societies she belongs to and I called them up and asked them how I could buy their membership lists, how that would work technically for me to get that data, file formats and all that, and they told me enough that I figured out how to bust in and grab all the enrollment data myself and what I got was all kinds of information about what orchids she likes and . . . and anyway, I got her e-mail address. I got Miss Cray's private e-mail address, and then I just sent her a message from one of the societies. It wasn't about anything, but that's how I got in. Through her e-mail. I did a Trojan horse and accessed her hard drive from there."

"You got in because she loves orchids?" I found a certain amount of satisfaction in that.

"It took me a long time and I got lots of help, but we found this little quirk in her system and I was able to slide through. All you need is to find a portal and I did. And I went in and looked around and found what I needed. What you need."

Jack pulled one of the desk chairs over, turned it around, and sat in it backwards. "What did you find?"

"First of all, she is definitely in the money laundering business. And she makes a lot of money doing it. I couldn't believe it. She's got seventeen different clients." He started tapping the keys and I heard his external CD drive start to whir on the table at my knee. A spreadsheet appeared with seventeen rows and a bunch of columns.

"See?"

I did see, but it didn't mean much. They were in some kind of code, identified only by a series of numbers, maybe account numbers. "Can you tell who they are?"

"No. But she has one that's really, really big, a lot bigger than the others, and it's the one that channels cash to Mr. Speath's place." He paged down and zoomed in on one of the accounts. As he moved across the screen, I could see it was bigger than the others by at least a factor of ten.

"That's Ottavio," Jack said. "He's the biggest fish in whatever sea he's in."

"Okay," Felix said. "Here's the good part. So I'm in there and I'm cruising around and looking at the entries and seeing how she does it and all and I find this second set of numbers for Ottavio's account."

I leaned in to see the screen. "Two sets of books?"

"Yeah." He went down and clicked on another tab that brought up a separate analysis. "It turns out," he said, "she's stealing from him."

"Vanessa is skimming?" I leaned in closer. "From Ottavio Quevedo?"

"She's either very smart," Jack said, "or very stupid. Either way, she's got nerves of steel."

I pointed to one of the totals. "What's this number? Is that . . ." I counted the zeroes. "Is that fifty million dollars?"

"That's what she stole from him. She's got it stashed away in offshore accounts. I couldn't believe it, but I added it up and that's what it is and I wondered how someone doesn't figure out they had fifty million dollars swiped from them but then I looked at how much money she moves around just for Ottavio and it's a drop in the bucket and she's been doing it for a couple of years and—"

"Felix." He was getting more and more wound up, and I thought if I didn't step in he might twist himself into the couch. I was beginning to see what sleep deprivation did to Felix. "This is important. You need to calm down and think about this. Are you sure Vanessa can't tell you've been in her files?"

He was almost insulted. "No way, Miss Shan—"

"Think about it," Jack said. "Just sit there with that question for a few minutes and think it through."

That was asking a lot from the kid. He might have exploded if Jack hadn't given him the nod. "What I'm saying, I'm saying she had two different burglar alarms on and I found them both and disarmed them. They were pretty good, too. I learned a few things from her."

The CD drive whirred again. "Where are you keeping this data, Felix?"

"I burned two CDs."

"Take this one out," I said, nodding to the one he was using, "and give them both to us."

He did. He had already selected the jewel boxes for transport, one that used to hold a CD by Rage Against the Machine, and another by Matchbox 20. He handed them over to me and I turned them over to Jack.

"I put them in there to disguise them. A CD, you know, can hold up to 650 megabytes of data and—"

"Did you leave anything on your hard drive?" I asked him.

"No."

"Okay." Jack returned the chair to the desk. "Do you live with someone?"

"I have a roommate but he's in school and he's never home."

"Stay here at the hotel, then. Stay around people. Don't go out. Order room service. I'm very serious about this. You stay holed up in here until I give you the high sign. Is that clear?"

Felix looked at him with a mixture of excitement and concern and nodded. I knew he understood what Jack was saying. I did, too, and it scared me.

"Let's go, Alex." Jack held up the CDs. "We just found our leverage."

Chapter Forty-two

It was hot in Jack's truck, which inexplicably had no air conditioner. It wasn't that the AC was broken. He had purchased a truck to drive around in Florida with no cooling device whatsoever beyond the open windows.

"That's the place," he said. We were on Collins Avenue in front of the Delano, one of the old Art Deco hotels in South Beach that had been gutted and redone. It had a big circle drive in front filled with exotic cars, but the entrance was mostly hidden by tall shrubs. We made two passes and I managed to get a glimpse behind the green barrier. It had a spacious, covered porch, which was a good plan because their patio furniture seemed to be covered with chintz and silk. Not your standard deck chairs.

"We have half an hour." Jack turned to make the block again. "You should go in and look around. I want to find a place, too, where I can keep an eye on you."

We'd decided I would meet Vanessa, since she and I seemed to have a rapport, of sorts. We also thought it best if she didn't have us both in her line of sight at the same time.

"Tell her what we want," he reminded me, not for the first time.

"I will."

"Give her one disc and tell her we have the other one."

"What if she says no?"

"We'll think about that when the time comes. But she's

smart. She'll do what she needs to do, but she probably won't say yes right away. She'll tell you she wants to think about it so she can come up with her own plan. Give her the deadline, and try to set up the next contact in advance. Two hours. That's it. That's what I told Jimmy."

"What else did you tell him?"

"I didn't give him too many details. I told him generally what we were up to. He said he didn't kill anyone and to go fuck myself."

"What did you say?"

"I told him he's killed too many people, but if he didn't kill John McTavish, he should lay low for a couple of days. He said to go fuck myself."

He'd pulled into a pay lot and parked, so now we didn't even have the breeze from the open windows to keep us cool. It was two o'clock in the afternoon and sticky. I was sticking to everything—the car seat, my clothes, my leather backpack. Jack was low on quarters, but between the two of us, we managed scrape up enough silver to buy two hours on the meter.

We found a spot in the shade and stood there long enough for him to go over everything again. He seemed to be getting more and more anxious, pushing his hands into the pockets of his chinos, pulling them out again. It was starting to make me jumpy, too.

"Jack, I've got it. It will be fine."

"Maybe this is not such a good idea," he said. "Maybe I should go. Maybe—"

I pulled him down and shut him up with a long, deep, soul-scraping kiss. "Are you ready?" I asked.

"I'm ready."

"Then let's go."

Judging from the lobby, when they'd gutted the Delano, they had dragged out a whole lot more than they had brought in. To call it sparsely furnished would have been generous.

I had entered through the front door into a vast open space with planetarium-height ceilings. Instead of walls, they had huge columns to separate the check-in desk, sushi bar, lounge, lobby, and pool table, and long, delicate white curtains that tended to drift back and forth with the breeze every time a door opened. It was a capsule of cool on a broiling strip of Florida oceanfront, and I was glad for Jack's suggestion to come early and check it out. Otherwise I would have been too distracted to pay attention when Vanessa arrived.

Of the furniture that was there, every single piece was different from the next. Leather and velvet and fur were a predominant theme. The floors were wide cherry or mahogany planks, covered here and there with pieces that looked like Mark Rothko paintings that had been dragged down off the wall and turned into area rugs. There were tall vases filled with even taller stems of exotic flowers, and lots of candles, including floor candelabras. They needed candlelight because the electric version was either so indirect or so high up in the ceiling as to have not been there at all.

My very favorite feature was the unusually narrow interior doorways along the perimeter walls, including those that led to the bathrooms. They reminded me of the templates we used at the airport to catch oversized carry-on bags. "If your bag doesn't fit in here, it's too big. You have to check it." Only the message here was "If you're not thin enough to fit through this narrow door, you don't belong here. Turn around and check out."

It felt forbidding, but that was the whole point. It was an Ian Schrager hotel, designed with the in-your-face, you-don't-belong-here-no-matter-who-you-are veneer that he had helped create at Studio 54. He had somehow managed to import the attitude intact to his hotels, and I was surprised there hadn't been a bouncer out front to usher in Bianca Jagger and Liza Minnelli, or at least their new millenium successors, and keep out riffraff, like me.

Vanessa was not riffraff. When she slipped through the front door, she fit right into the airy atmosphere. She had on bright green linen Capri pants, a black sleeveless top with a high collar, and little black sandals. Her

blonde hair was plaited and wrapped on top of her head.
She could have been wearing cutoffs and a bra top and
still have looked right at home in this place. It was all
in the attitude.

"I'm early," she said. "And you're even earlier. Isn't
that interesting?"

"Shall we find a place and sit?" I asked.

"Down to business. I like that."

I let her lead the way into the lobby/lounge, as if I had
any choice. She chose a corner with a leopard-skin loveseat
and a chair that looked like a big, high-heeled shoe. It was
metal and didn't seem to have been designed for sitting,
but she went straight for it. Maybe she liked pain.

"How is your investigation coming? Have you found
your murderer?"

"My investigation is going well," I said.

"Did you check my alibi?"

"Of course."

"And did it check out to your satisfaction?" Her tone
was slightly mocking.

"It checked out."

"But not to your satisfaction." Her skin seemed particularly translucent in the early afternoon light that came
in through the patio doors. She was so pale, like a soap-
stone statue.

"An independent sighting would have been more satisfying," I said. "The people who claim to have seen you
all work for you."

"And here I thought you invited me out to tell me I
was off the hook."

A slim man with long sideburns who had been wander-
ing about stopped by. Turned out he was a waiter. Vanessa
ordered a Metropolitan. I asked for my customary spar-
kling water and couldn't wait to see what kind of bottle
came out. I knew it wouldn't be Poland Spring.

We settled back into our quiet conversation. "I've
found out some new things about you, Vanessa. About
your clients."

She sat back in that horrible chair, crossed her legs,
rested her elbows on the armrests, and made a steeple

with her fingers. She pointed it straight up under her chin, and I could tell by the way she waggled her leg that she knew where I was going. And she was ready. "I have many clients. I manage their money. Where they get their money is of no concern to me."

"I'm talking about your other business. You launder drug money for a living, your biggest client is Ottavio Quevedo, you use Jimmy Zacharias's repair stations as sinks, and I believe you know who killed John Mc-Tavish."

Her sedate, satisfied smile made me think she was not surprised, but pleased, at last, to be given full credit for what she was and what she did.

She raised her eyebrows. "And . . . ?"

"And I'm here to ask for your help in catching the person who murdered John."

"You want to bring him to justice?"

"Call me an idealist."

"Very well. Let's take these items one at a time, shall we?" She glanced around the general vicinity. The closest patrons were two knife-thin boys shooting pool in the corner. One of them had a lizard tattooed on his shoulder blade.

"You are correct," she said. "I do provide a service to individuals with a specific kind of problem related to their cash flow, and Ottavio is a particularly active user of my services. I know of Jimmy Zacharias through Ottavio." She leaned forward. "And why on earth would I help you do anything?"

"You skipped a point, the one about how you know who killed John."

"Jimmy killed your friend."

I had expected her to say that, whether it was true or not, but not so quickly and not without encouragement. "What did you say?"

"I said Jimmy killed your friend. That's what you wanted to know, isn't it? But I find that point to be irrelevant, unless you can convince me that it's not."

The waiter slinked by and set down two drinks, including my bottle of water, which was a tall, frosted glass cylinder. I'd never seen one like it. I waited for him to clear out.

"How do you know Jimmy killed John?"

"Arturo saw him at the hotel that night."

"You said Arturo was with you on the island."

She blinked at me over the martini glass and I knew if she hadn't been sipping, she would have been smiling.

"Did Arturo see the murder?"

"No."

"What was he doing there?"

"That's a long and complicated story."

"I have a big bottle of water to drink," I said. "At least thirty-two ounces."

She sighed and I wondered if I was going to have to whip out the discs to encourage her. Somehow I thought not. "Will you stop bothering me if I tell you?"

"I'll stop bothering you when I get what I need from you."

She turned her head to watch the boys playing pool. Like all pool tables, this one was covered in green felt, but not billiard green. Olive green. She let her top leg bounce a few times and didn't seem anxious to leave. When she turned back, she looked as if she was ready to gossip. "Several weeks before that night, I was contacted by Ottavio and told to use his funds to make a loan to Jimmy. A rather substantial loan."

"A loan for what?"

"Something to do with parts. I don't know. I hate that business. It's filthy and the people in it are filthy scum, Jimmy chief among them. I pay him and I pay him well not to use those businesses that way and he does it anyway. It's not worth the risk."

"Was the money for the Sentinel parts?"

"Was that the unfortunate incident in Ecuador?"

"It was."

"Then the answer is yes. As I understood it, Jimmy was to use the money to get an organization in place to refurbish and sell a large quantity of parts. A highly speculative venture if you ask me, especially for someone who claims to be so risk averse. Ottavio never invests in my funds. But he didn't ask me."

"Why would a drug lord get in bed with Jimmy on a parts deal?"

"Jimmy talked him into it. He kept telling him what a great business these parts were. Ottavio was on the fence, but he was intrigued, and then an airplane dropped out of the sky practically on his head. He took it as a sign." She shrugged. "What would you expect from an ignorant drug dealer?"

"Was he thinking of making a career change?"

"He was thinking of diversifying." She had already downed over half of her Metropolitan. The elixir seemed to loosen her tongue, although it was also possible she'd been dying to share this story with someone. "And, as I understand it, Jimmy also promised him several hundred cases of AK-47s if he would provide the backing on this job. Jimmy has access to those sorts of things."

"Tell me about the murder."

"All I know is this. Jimmy's been paying the loan back to me in installments. The night your friend died happened to be a night Jimmy owed us a payment. I sent Arturo to pick it up. Jimmy wanted to meet him at The Harmony House Suites."

"Why there?"

"He said it was convenient for him because he had other business there that night."

I felt a tug in my stomach, picturing what the other business had been.

Vanessa continued. "That's why my Volvo was seen in the parking lot. It was Arturo meeting Jimmy to pick up that week's payment. Nothing more than that."

"We haven't been able to put Jimmy at The Suites that night."

"I know he was there because Arturo came home with the money."

She had answered all my questions so quickly and logically, I had to regroup and find more loose ends. "Did Arturo have any business that night with George Speath?"

"George Speath?"

"Speath Aviation," I said. "One of your sinks."

"No. We normally don't do business that way. Only with Jimmy."

"Why would Jimmy have used Ottavio's MO for the murder?"

"Because he's a very clever boy. Maybe too clever for his own good." She'd drained her glass and ordered another drink before I'd finished half a glass of water.

"We'll need a statement from Arturo," I said.

"You're joking."

"I'm not. According to you he can put Jimmy at the crime scene."

"Please, I would expect better than that from you. Arturo is too valuable to me. It's out of the question. And obviously his activities can be traced back to me. I can't help you beyond what I've already told you, and I've already told you too much."

"Wouldn't it be better for you if Jimmy goes to jail?"

"Why?"

"Because he's a confidential informant for the FBI."

Her eyes brightened. "On whom would he be informing? Those scummy brokers he works with, or those—what does he call them . . . 'parts-pickers?' The U.S. government must be desperate."

"We think he's working with the FBI on an operation to take down Ottavio, and not for stolen parts."

"That would be a profoundly unintelligent plan, and Jimmy knows it. He generally has a keener sense of survival than that."

"Maybe he doesn't have any choice. Maybe he got nailed and this is his best alternative."

"Crossing Ottavio is never the best alternative. There is nothing the FBI can do to Jimmy that would be worse than what Ottavio will do to him."

"Isn't it true that if Ottavio goes down, you go down with him? You are, after all, his launderer."

"Jimmy has no access to anything important. I am quite well insulated, which is a necessary precaution when doing business with Jimmy and people like him.

I'm afraid you'll have to find another way to get him. I can't help you."

Someone opened the patio door, causing the air pressure in the room to shift. All the white curtains billowed out like parachutes, and I knew this was the moment. "What would Ottavio do to you if he knew you were stealing from him?"

She managed to control every part of her reaction, except that her already pale face turned white. I had her.

"Of your seventeen different clients, Vanessa, Ottavio's are the only accounts that are light. So we know it's not because you can't count. You've been stealing from him, systematically siphoning off funds that go straight into your own secret accounts. Fifty million dollars at last count." I pulled the jewel box out of my bag. "We have copies of your files, the whole road map, in a convenient CD format."

She had regained her equilibrium and even managed to pump some blood back into her face. "It's a mistake to threaten me."

"I'm simply laying out alternatives and hoping you'll choose the one that benefits me. Personally, I'd rather not meet Ottavio. But then I can always FedEx these files. Or . . . does he have an e-mail address?"

"What do you want?"

"I told you what I want. I'm tired of chasing Jimmy around. I want to nail him, and the best way I can think of to do that is for you to help me."

"If I help you, you will give me that disc?"

"You can have this one." I passed it over to her. I'd chosen Rage Against the Machine for her copy. It seemed to suit her.

"How many are there?" she asked calmly.

"Only one more. Jack has it. We'll turn it over when you give me something I can use. I'm not interested in your operation. If Ottavio had nothing to do with killing John, I'm not interested in him either."

"How do I know you won't keep copies?"

"There is nothing else I want or need from you,

Vanessa. You hand me Jimmy, I hand you the disc, and our business is over."

She considered that. "I will not give up Arturo. If I help you, it will be some other way."

"What other way?"

"I have other ideas, but I will have to do research and get back to you."

"You have two hours before we start looking for a way to contact your biggest client. I'd much prefer to work with you on this than Ottavio, Vanessa. But one way or the other, I'm getting what I came down here for."

Her eyes were burning. Glimmering green emeralds in a geisha-white mask. And I knew what she was feeling. She wasn't used to being pushed around and she didn't like it. I wouldn't have wanted to be in her position, either.

Jack wasn't at the truck when I got back. I started toward the beach to see if I could spot him when he sauntered over from the street side.

"Where were you?"

"Keeping an eye on Arturo." He unlocked the truck and we got in.

"Where was he?"

"Outside on the patio sitting where he could see her. He just drove her out. She was on her cell phone the second you left her."

"She said Jimmy did it. She told a convincing story, too." I relayed what she'd said, including as many details as I could remember.

"Maybe he did do it," he said. "We'll wait and see what she comes up with."

"We've got two hours." I was relieved to have the meeting behind me, but still juiced by the experience. I reached over and traced the curve of his ear. "Want to wait together at your place?"

He smiled and started the engine.

We had all the phones lined up on Jack's headboard—my cell, his cell, and his cordless. Vanessa was supposed to call me, but she had all the numbers. At one hour and forty-five minutes after the Delano meeting, it was my phone that twittered out my distinctive tone. I reached up to answer, and it was Vanessa.

She didn't even offer a cordial greeting. "Go to Jimmy's house and look for a box with all his Vietnam souvenirs. It's there. Check the fingerprints and you'll have all the evidence you need."

"What am I looking for?"

"The murder weapon."

Chapter Forty-three

Even as we made the turn and started down the long driveway, we heard Bull crying—sending forth long, high-pitched, wailing laments from somewhere in the back of Jimmy's house, from somewhere in the depths of his canine soul.

Jack had already reached under the seat and pulled out the Glock. "You should stay out here," he said.

I turned again to study Jimmy's stucco cube. It looked exactly as it had the last time we'd come to visit, except all the curtains were closed. I didn't see any windows open, at least not from the front. It would have been sweltering inside.

"What are you going to do?"

"I'm going to go see what's wrong with that damn dog."

My heartbeat started to drag, not accelerate. Everything seemed to slow down, and I wanted to ask if we shouldn't call the police.

"I want to go with you," I said, though that's not exactly what I meant. What I meant was "I'd rather do almost anything else at this moment than go in that house, but if you insist, I believe I should go with you so you won't be by yourself and since I'm the one who basically got you into this in the first place."

His answer was to reach down for the second gun, the one he carried in his ankle holster. It was the .22, the one he'd tried to give me the night in the swamp. Seeing it reminded me of how much I didn't want to carry it, then or now. But I also remembered that I had promised to take it the next time it was offered.

"That's an automatic," I said. "You have to tell me how to use it."

"Here's the safety." He pointed to a small red switch. "It's off now, ready to fire. It's a double action, so if you do this"—he pulled back the piece on top—"it's ready to fire. All you have to do is point and pull the trigger. Aim lower than where you want to hit. You've got a full clip, which is eight rounds. When you're not pointing it, hold it up in the air like this, away from your body and your head. You don't want to shoot your ear off. Don't shoot first. Don't sweep across me."

"What do you mean?"

"You'll be behind me. If a target moves across the front of me, don't follow him and shoot me instead."

"Good point."

He turned the gun and offered it to me. When it was my turn to hold it, I had a sudden, desperate urge to embrace my old life, the one where I sat at a desk and reached for a calculator, not a gun, and the most dangerous thing I did was go running along the Charles River after dark. That all seemed very far away.

I took the gun.

It was a Smith & Wesson. It said so right there on the barrel. It had a crosshatch design etched into the grip that I could feel when I wrapped my hand around it. I touched the trigger. It felt tight. He was right about there not being much to a .22. It certainly wasn't going to weigh me down with its heft, but it had its own gravity that had nothing to do with its mass. It made me nervous, holding-a-bottle-of-plutonium nervous, but I also couldn't deny that behind the anxiousness, and not too far, was a surge of something—power, exhilaration. I didn't want to admit to feeling it, but it was there.

We climbed out of the car. I kept my eyes nailed to the front door as we moved toward the house. He hadn't yet fixed his screen door.

Short rapid bursts of barking and slow stretches of inconsolable whimpering embroidered Bull's long, mournful howls. He seemed inexhaustible, and I wondered how long he'd been at it.

When we got to the door, Jack motioned me to one side and stood on the other. He started to reach for the bell, then pulled out a handkerchief and used it to press the button. Bull reacted instantly, pushing his howls to the next level, an almost unimaginable hysterical keening that made my spleen hurt. Something was definitely keeping him in the back of the house.

"Jimmy. *Jimmy*," Jack called out as he tried the knob. Locked.

Sweat ran into my eyes and made them burn. I wiped them with the sleeve of my shirt.

"Let's go to the back." Jack moved in that direction. "We'll see what that damn dog is so excited about. Either that or I can shoot him. Stay behind me."

"Don't worry." I had no plans to blaze any new trails.

Bull heard us invading his sanctuary as we approached the back door. He tried to tunnel out, frantically scratching the wall or door—whatever was holding him in. It was apparently an old habit of his; the outside of the back door was a scarred landscape of deep furrows and rough gouges.

"It sounds like he's trapped in an inside room somewhere," Jack said. "You were in this kitchen the other day. Do you remember if there was a closet or pantry? Any kind of inside room?"

I closed my eyes and tried to picture the kitchen from the inside. "Yes . . . there is a laundry room or pantry. If we walk in through that door, it will be to our right."

"Good. Let's hope he can't get out."

Jack held his gun in his left hand. I held mine in my right and tried to do exactly what I saw him do. As he reached toward the tarnished doorknob with the handkerchief, I flattened against the wall and breathed, but the air seemed to go somewhere else besides my lungs. He twisted the knob. The lightweight door opened with a pop. It sounded like a starter's pistol, and my heart began the race.

"Take the safety off." His voice was quiet and close.

"Don't touch anything." He disappeared through the open doorway. Just like that. No deep breath. No moment of contemplation or anticipation.

My fingers felt too thick, but I reached around and managed to flick the safety off. It made the gun feel different. Hotter. I had to take a contemplative moment to test and make sure all my limbs were working. When I was convinced they would respond when called upon, I started into the kitchen. Then stopped. Confused.

Ringing. Cell phone ringing. Panic. *My* cell phone ringing. Clipped to my waistband. Hard to get it open with one gun and two anxious hands. Ringing again, goddammit. Bull out of his mind. Open it. Hit the power button and turn it off. Wait. Sweat. Listen.

Nothing. Not even Jack coming back to see. Saved by Bull's raucous din.

Stale and humid air wrapped around me the second I stepped into the kitchen. And I smelled . . . I thought I smelled . . . it had to be. Blood smells like nothing else on earth. Once you smell it you never forget. The rich odor came in though my nostrils, permeated my sinuses, then raced throughout my body, crackling along every nerve ending until I felt the odor more than I smelled it.

"Stay close to me." As soon as Jack saw I was with him, he moved forward, through the front room, and toward a hallway where welcome sunlight spilled through the first door we came to. The room was what I think is called a Florida room, complete with full plantation shutters that had been left open. It must have been Jimmy's junk room because that's what was in there. Jimmy's junk looked the same as everyone else's—cardboard boxes, an old floor lamp bent in the middle, a pile of wadded-up beach towels, and an old toaster.

The next door led to the bedroom. The only piece of furniture there was the bed. It was made. One room left. If Jimmy was in the house, he was in the bathroom.

I watched Jack move toward that door and I concentrated on simply reacting to whatever he did. He motioned for me to stay back, then raised the gun and pointed it straight up toward the ceiling, keeping it away from his head. He called out for Jimmy. The only response came from Bull.

This time he did pause to gather himself, taking a breath as I had done on the back porch, and I wondered what he was contemplating. The scene I was imagining made my insides want to rupture. A gunshot blast. Jack thrown back against the far wall. Down on the floor. Eyes open and unseeing. It was the worst possible image I could think of, conjured up from the fact that I cared about him and I didn't want to lose him.

I kept my eyes open, maybe couldn't have closed them if I'd tried. He swung into the doorway. His face turned pale. He rose from his firing stance and let the gun drop to his side. He leaned his shoulder against the jamb and all the energy drained out until he looked like a coat hanging on a hook.

I made myself step in beside him, and looked at what he was looking at.

"Jesus. Jesus Christ, Jack."

Jimmy had been taking a bath. His arms, head, and most of his torso hung over the side, but his long legs were still in the tub, mostly submerged. His two kneecaps stuck out like white ice floes in dull red water that was as flat as the mirror over the sink, and now certainly cold.

Much blood and brain matter had sprayed across the back wall of the tub. More was on the floor, having gushed across the tiles from a large hole in the back of his head. The pool of blood on the tiles was thick with his long, silver hair. Whoever had killed him had probably shot him through the forehead, blowing most of the back of his head off.

But that wasn't his only wound.

His hair was pulled to the side to show the knife, a long knife with a thick, black handle buried to the hilt in his throat. The murderer had plunged it in below his left ear. The bloody tip stuck out the other side, and had lodged against the tub in a way that kept Jimmy's head twisted at an unnatural angle that left his dead eyes glaring up at us.

I put my hand over my nose and breathed through my

mouth. Jack still hadn't moved. His hands were trembling, and when I looked into his eyes, I saw pain. I reached out and touched the sleeve of his shirt.

"He was a soldier." He pressed his lips together hard. "I hated him. I hated the things he did, but he was a soldier once." He blinked up at the ceiling, and maybe he was back there in the jungle seeing the sights and hearing the sounds only he could hear, and when he looked at Jimmy again, maybe he was thinking there was one less person in the world who had been there with him. No matter what he had done later, no matter what he had become, Jimmy was one of the men . . . the boys who had stood next to Jack in a place where no man should ever have to stand.

He turned and walked down the hall.

I wanted to be with him but he had walked away from me, so instead I counted nails. Jimmy's was an old house and all the nails in the floor in his hallway were not flush with the hardwood. Some of them were coming up, making little booby traps, the kind that snagged your hose when you walked around in the morning with no shoes, trying to get ready for work. Or provided something good to stare at when you didn't want to stare at a bloody corpse. I counted twenty-seven of them. I counted them again. And then I went out to find Jack.

He was in the front room with his gun in his holster and his hands in his pockets, staring at the trophy for the State Champs of Everglades City, Florida, 1969.

Bull seemed to finally be running out of steam. His cries were more intermittent now, more mournful and desperate than angry.

"Are you all right?"

"He didn't deserve that. I thought I knew what he deserved, but it wasn't that."

"We should call the cops, huh?" I pulled out my phone and turned it back on.

He nodded. "Call Patty. Tell her we found the McTavish murder weapon."

The screen on my phone was flashing, telling me I had a text message marked urgent. I hadn't even known I

could get those. It had to be from Felix. I had no other
friends who were that technologically capable. I futzed
around with the buttons until I figured out how to pull
it up and scroll through it.

"Oh, my God, Jack."

Chapter Forty-four

Jack had looked bad at Jimmy's house. He looked worse as he put my phone to his ear and listened again to the voice mail message Felix had left for me. I tried to concentrate on the road. On my hands on the steering wheel. On getting us to The Harmony House Suites as fast as the Lumina would take us. Anything but what had been in that message. And anything but the fact that Felix had been the one calling when I had turned off my phone.

He had wanted to tell me that Vanessa knew he had been in her system. He'd been "busted," as he put it, by a superior alarm that he had overlooked—a "hacker trap" that he had never seen coming. He was sure they knew who he was, and was calling to find out what to do.

Jack was dialing again, as fast as the little cell phone buttons would allow. I knew he was calling the room at The Suites again. He'd been doing that compulsively since we'd walked out of Jimmy's house. If he hadn't been doing it, I would have. He pressed the phone to his ear and we both waited. And waited.

"C'mon, son," he kept saying. "Be there, kid."

The waiting was excruciating. Finally, someone answered, and it wasn't Felix. It was the hotel operator wanting to know again if Jack wanted to leave a message for room 484. Apparently, no one was home.

We had no way to get into the suite when no one was there to answer our knock. Jack kept knocking anyway.

Banging, really, taking out on the intractable door all the same fears that were pinballing around inside me.

"Felix," he yelled. *"Felix. Son . . ."*

The curtains in the room next door moved—someone wondering about all the commotion, no doubt. But nothing from 484.

"I'm going down for a key," I said.

The see-through elevator showed that both cars were on the ground floor. I went for the stairs and flew down four floors. By the time I hit the lobby, I was sweating, every breath had a catch in it, and my mouth tasted as if I'd been swilling milk of magnesia.

There were three agents at the front desk working a queue. According to one of the bellmen, the smallish, youngish, roundish woman in the middle was in charge. She was the other assistant manager besides Felix.

"Excuse me," I said, stepping in front of her.

"Hey." A guy with a salesman's gut and a suit that didn't fit because of it was fuming behind me.

"I need your help," I said quietly to the woman. "It's an emergency."

She seemed stunned and stood blinking at me. "What?"

"We have an emergency upstairs. I need to get into one of your rooms immediately."

"Oh."

Still with the staring, and I understood completely why Felix had been named acting general manager of the place.

"Room 484," I said, more urgently. "Can you make a key and let me in?"

She responded by looking down at her keyboard and typing. "That's Felix's room."

"Yes. We need a key. We need to get in."

She turned to the agent working next to her. "Sherrie, I need to help this lady—"

"Now," I said.

She turned and looked at me with stern eyes and a locked jaw.

"I'm sorry. Please. This is important. Can you just make a key and give it to me?"

Of course not. After she had made the key, we stood at the elevator and waited because I thought it would be faster than encouraging her up four flights of stairs.

Jack was on his cell phone when we arrived. It felt as if I'd been gone for an hour. "I called Patty to let her know what was happening. She's sending some units over."

We both stood back and waited as the assistant manager gave the door a dainty rap. "Felix?"

"Open the damn door now." Jack must have startled her. She fumbled the key. Almost dropped it. Recovered. Had a tough time sliding it into the slot. It didn't work the first time. The second time the lock clicked. She pushed the handle down and the door opened.

"Stay back," Jack said to her. "Don't come in here." He pulled out his gun and I thought she would faint. He walked in first. I went behind him sans weapon because in my haste I'd left mine behind in the car.

It was dark. Cold. The air conditioner was pumping and the chilled air made me shiver. The sound was faint because the bedroom door was closed. Felix was not in the front room. Most of his stuff was still there.

"Jack." He angled slightly to see where I was pointing. "His laptop is gone."

"Shit." He approached the closed bedroom door, checking the bathroom quickly as we passed it. Empty. He pushed back against the wall, put his hand flat on the door, and paused to look down and take a quiet breath. He wrapped his hand around the knob and turned it. I heard the latch release, felt the pop in my chest. A wedge of light slipped through, fell across the durable carpet in the bedroom, and widened as Jack pushed the door slowly open. The sound of the air conditioner seemed deafening.

The darkness inside the room scared me, not because I thought someone was going to jump us. If Felix had been in there and able, he would have answered. He hadn't.

Jack reached in to turn on the light.

"There's no wall switch."

We both jerked at the sound of the little girl voice behind us. The assistant manager had crept within a few feet without either of us hearing her. The trepidation had gone from her eyes, and now they were burning with a weird light that was beyond innocent curiosity, but not all the way to lurid.

"Step back," I said. "Get out of the room."

"You have to turn on the lamp that's on the dresser."

"Thank you. Please go out and make sure no one comes in here."

While she trundled out, I looked for and found the switch for the light in the ceiling over our heads. When I flipped it on, it threw enough light that we could see the bed where Felix had laid out his notes on Vanessa. They were gone. Jack was inside the bedroom now, and I was just outside the door. He found the lamp. Turned it on. I quickly scanned the room. Nothing. Jack looked on the other side of the far bed. He shook his head.

One more place to look. He moved to the closet and signaled for me to stand behind him. He rubbed the palm of his right hand against his jeans, and I felt my own palms dripping. He swung the door open, stepped around it, and stood with his gun pointed inside. I couldn't see around the door. The muscles in his forearms twitched and his face went blank and I felt the temperature in the room drop a few degrees. I pulled the door all the way open.

The closet was empty.

Jack seemed to want to lean on something. He used the wall. He holstered his gun, leaned over with his hands on his knees, and took a few deep breaths. I put my hand on his back and leaned on him. His shirt was soaked through, and I could feel his heart working hard.

"They took him," he said. "Him, his laptop, and all his notes. They've got him. *Damn* it all to hell." He straightened up and covered his face with his hands, then let them slide down, as if he could wipe away the ache. I felt it, too.

"My God," he whispered. "What did we do?"

Chapter Forty-five

The woman in the next room over, the one who had been peeking through her curtains, told us Felix had left with two men and a tall blonde woman about half an hour before we showed up. It was now an hour and a half after that and still no one had called. No ransom demand. No contact of any kind. The working theory, the only one we could stomach, was that Vanessa had snatched Felix and would trade him for the account information. I kept reminding myself that getting rid of Felix while we still had it didn't make much sense. But it was hard to ignore the next conclusion in that logical sequence—that getting rid of all three of us after what she needed made a whole lot of sense.

Jack and I were in the Lumina, out in the city, trying to stay in motion. Our first stop had been at Jack's bungalow to pick up more weapons. He was now heavily armed. Next we'd gone to Vanessa's office. She wasn't there. We'd checked the garage. All Volvos were in.

The police had been to her house. Someone had gone to the airfield and checked her Gulfstream. *The Crayfish* had been found, boarded, and eliminated as a possible refuge. It was hard to eliminate all the possibilities—to even think of all the possibilities for a woman with so many resources.

In place of conversation, we had the radio. It wasn't much of a distraction. Constant emergency reports interrupted whatever program we chose to listen to. I couldn't scan fast enough to avoid them. The wind was due to shift, and the smoke from the largest of the fires nearby would turn by afternoon and blanket the more heavily populated areas to the south and east, which meant Miami and Miami Beach. Small children, asthmatics, and the elderly were warned to stay indoors.

"Where would she go?" I asked. Again. "Where would she take him?"

"She has to leave town," he said, finishing the routine we'd been working over and over. He had his cell phone to his ear, checking his service and my hotel again for messages.

"I think she has to leave the country," he said. "When Ottavio finds out Jimmy is an informant, he will have to assume she was in it with him, especially if he finds out she's been skimming. The smart move is to take the money and go hide. Although, if Ottavio believes she was working for the government, there is no place for her to hide."

"But why take Felix? I would have given her the disc."

"Insurance. We fucked up. We underestimated her."

I drove around for another ten minutes or so, retracing parts of the town I had come to know in the past two weeks. Eventually, I was headed back toward the airport.

"Where are we going?"

"To George Speath's place," I said. "We know he had a connection to Vanessa. He was working for her, in a sense." He didn't answer and I wasn't thrilled about the idea. But it was all I could think of besides the fact that we had to be running out of time.

They may as well have had a "Going Out of Business" sign posted in the window. Speath Aviation was locked up tight. The hangar door was shut and padlocked. My car was the only one in the dusty, crushed gravel parking lot.

I peered into the front window of the dark offices. The only movement was from a screen saver on one of the computer monitors. It was a little antique biplane that did acrobatic aerial stunts across the screen. It always pulled up just as it was about to crash.

"I don't think anyone's home, Jack." I looked around and realized I was talking to myself. From around the corner I heard the sound of glass shattering and plinking to the ground. Jack had found another door around the side—this one with a window—and he had his entire arm inside when I arrived.

"Doesn't seem like much security," I said, "for a place that has parts lying around." I had begun to grow much more security conscious as I'd learned about bogus parts.

"Didn't you tell me this is usually a twenty-four/seven operation?" The door opened. He slipped in and I went after him and closed the door behind us.

"You're right. They probably always have someone around." Which made it particularly strange that no one was there now. "What should we look for?"

"Let's start with the files." He stared at the twelve file cabinets that lined the wall.

"He's got files in his office," I said. "Anything that would be of interest to us is probably in there."

I led him back to George's office. The door was open. Jack went behind the desk. I started with the credenza where a picture of a smiling George and one of his airplanes was proudly displayed. "It's still hard for me to believe George is a money launderer. I can't believe I was so far off on him."

"Sometimes good people do bad things."

Something banged against the wall from the other side. I stopped and listened. The other side of the wall was the hangar. More sounds—clattering and scraping. Someone was in the hangar.

Jack listened, too, head cocked toward the sounds. "Did you hear voices?"

I hadn't. He pulled his gun, and then he was out the door, feeling his way in the gray light along the hall toward the front of the offices and the noise we'd heard. This time I'd remembered to bring the .22, so as he approached the first corner, I fell in behind him, back flat against the wall. It occurred to me that I knew the way and he didn't.

"There's a short hallway around that corner," I whispered. "There are two doors on the wall closest to us. One is to the stockroom. The other is to the break room. There's one door on the far wall and it goes to the bathroom. There's an extra-wide door at the end of the hallway. It goes out to the hangar, which is where the noise is coming from. They had a DC-8 in there."

He nodded. "The door to the hangar, which way does it swing?"

I closed my eyes and pictured George holding the door for me. "In. It opens into the hallway. Toward us."

We crossed over to the far wall. We'd move a couple of inches. Stop. Listen. Move. We were halfway when we heard keys jingling. He was in the hangar, he was close, and he was coming in. Staring down the long hallway reminded me of the distorted view through the peephole, but it was only the sweat in my eyes. I took the safety off.

The deadbolt slipped. The knob twisted. I raised my gun and squeezed it in both hands. Jack rushed the door just as it opened. A flash of yellow. A loud, hollow boom as the door slammed shut. A man's high-pitched cry as Jack grabbed him and shoved him face first into the wall. Keys dropped to the ground. The man cried out again, a long, plaintive wail. I saw his face. It was white, a frozen twist of terror that pinned the heavy eyebrows to his forehead. Heavy eyebrows and a neatly trimmed goatee. A goatee?

"Do you have him?" Jack shoved his knee in the small man's back. "*Alex,* do you *have* him?"

I leveled my gun at Julio Martín Fuentes. "Yes. And I know who he is."

I must have subconsciously expected to see George, because I was surprised when it turned out to be a small Hispanic man in a yellow T-shirt. Julio's hands were uncomfortably high over his head. His eyes were squeezed shut, and if I understood his *muy rápido español*, he was praying.

"Jack, that's Julio. He's okay." I started to shove the .22 into my jeans, remembered the safety. "He's the one who told me George was laundering. We're scaring him to death. He probably thinks Ottavio sent you to kill him."

Jack let his hand slip from Julio's back, but not before frisking him first.

"Julio." I touched his shoulder. "Julio Fuentes." I wouldn't call what he was doing shaking. It was more violent than shaking. "*Está bien, Julio. Lo siento, señor. We're sorry to have scared you."*

He opened his eyes. First into slits, then wider. I didn't know how to tell him in Spanish, so I signaled for him to turn around. "*Está bien, Julio.*" He stared at me until recognition replaced panic, then lowered his arms and turned to face us. His cheek where he'd been mashed to the wall was imprinted with the texture of the concrete blocks.

"*Señorita?*" His voice was weak and wavering.

Jack picked up the keys from the floor and handed them to him. I picked up his baseball cap, which had fallen to the ground, and gave it to him. He accepted each offering with a small bow and a "*muchas gracias.*"

Jack also apologized. He spoke more Spanish than I did. I caught about every other word. One that kept coming up was *policía.* Julio asked to go to the men's room, then darted across the hall and shut the door behind him. Jack and I went to the break room.

"He thinks I'm a cop," Jack said, pulling out a chair to sit. "I didn't disabuse him of that notion."

"That's probably how the cops behave where he's from."

"Where's that?"

"Colombia," I said. "Can you understand him?"

"If he speaks slowly," he said.

We waited for Julio to come back. I was still hyped up and dying to pace, but Jack thought Julio would relax more if we all sat with our hands on the lunch table. I asked Julio if he wanted something to drink before we settled in. He wanted a Coke from the refrigerator. I set the can on the table in front of his chair, but he didn't sit. He stood holding his black cap in both hands, working it with nervous fingers the way he'd done at my hotel, and I realized he was waiting for me to sit down. I did, and put both hands on the table. Only then did he pull out a chair and sit. Stiffly.

The three of us communicated as well as we could. Jack knew some words I didn't and I had some on him. Julio knew almost no English, so it was a slow, painstaking process. Julio's Coke can was empty by the time we had ascertained that George had shut down the business indefinitely, but he'd asked Julio to come in and do the payroll. He wanted to make sure his people were paid all the way through the end of the pay period. When Jack asked him why George had shut down, he ripped into another of his energetic monologues that went beyond what Jack and I could figure out together.

I tried to tell him that we were looking for Felix, the kid who had been at the hotel with us. I thought he might have gotten it, but couldn't understand his response. I kept asking about Vanessa Cray in every way I could think of in my stilted second language. I could not help but be reminded of how Vanessa spoke seven languages. She must have found it very easy to move through the world. I tried to ask if he knew her name. Didn't seem to. I asked if he had seen George with a blonde woman. Margie, he wondered. No, I said. Vanessa.

"Jack, I have an idea." I pulled up my backpack and dug out a file. "I have visual aids."

Inside the file were pictures I'd accumulated of our suspects—mug shots for Arturo and Jimmy, and the newspaper shot of Vanessa hunting orchids. I asked Julio if he had seen señor George with either Arturo or Vanessa. I threw Jimmy's picture out there just because I had it.

Julio looked at the pictures and shook his head.

It had been worth the thirty seconds to try. I started to collect the pictures, but Julio reached down and stopped me. He stared at each face, first Vanessa's, which was a copy of a copy of grainy newsprint. He picked up Arturo's picture, squinting first, then holding it out at arm's length until he seemed to have satisfied himself. Then he looked at Jimmy's. He put the pictures down, put both palms flat on the table, and said something in

Spanish that I thought I understood, but wasn't sure I believed.

Jack leaned forward and asked him to repeat his statement more slowly.

I listened again. I had understood exactly what he'd said, and it was still hard for me to grasp. I turned to Jack. "I gather from the look on your face that he just said what I thought he said."

"He says the woman in the picture, the woman we know as Vanessa Cray, is Valentina Quevedo. Ottavio is her father."

"And Arturo," I said, "is her brother."

Chapter Forty-six

When we stepped outside of George's offices the air had thickened considerably. The sun was going down, and when I pointed the car to the north and west, I saw the eerie orange glow that made the horizon look like a throbbing wound.

Three and a half hours since Felix had disappeared and still no contact.

We had one more idea we had gotten from Julio. He'd told us about an old abandoned airfield where it was rumored that Ottavio used to bring in his drug shipments. On a C130. It was the same old airfield where Jimmy had stashed the Sentinel parts.

"It makes sense," Jack had reasoned. "If Ottavio brought the parts in for Jimmy, he would have used a place he knew."

Vanessa's regular pilot had been accounted for and her plane confiscated, so she might have asked Daddy to send someone to bring her home. It was a ridiculously long shot, but we had no place else to go.

"I can't believe it," I said. "I can't believe she's his daughter." I'd been running everything I knew about Vanessa over in my mind, filtering it through the lens of Julio's bombshell. "No wonder she changed her name."

"She changed her name after she was kidnapped."

"Who was kidnapped?"

"Vanessa."

"Vanessa Cray was kidnapped? Recently?"

He shook his head. "This was maybe twelve or fourteen years ago when I was working up in New York. She was taken from her private boarding school in Pennsylvania. She must have been about seventeen years old. It got interesting when Ottavio refused to pay the ransom."

"Refused to pay?"

"Like I said before, he's one of the more vicious strains of the disease. I should have remembered her. You don't run across too many fathers who refuse to pay, especially if they have the means. Granted, he probably wasn't doing as well back then, but even so, all they were asking was a million."

"What did Vanessa's mother think about withholding the ransom?"

"She was dead by then. Died of cancer, I think. Natural causes, anyway. She was an American."

Which probably explained where Vanessa got the blonde hair and green eyes. "Who kidnapped her? Was it for money, or was it some enterprising competitor?"

"Definitely money. A couple of crack heads."

"You'd have to be to grab a Colombian kingpin's daughter. Did Ottavio want her back?"

"Put yourself in his shoes. If he submits to a ransom demand from a couple of punks, he would have told the world, at least his world, that to get to him all you had to do was snatch a member of his family."

"I can see how some of his lifestyle choices put him between a rock and a hard place. At least it put Vanessa there. How is it that she's alive today if he didn't pay?"

"She killed her kidnappers."

"Both of them?"

"Shot dead at close range. One twice in the head. The other four times in the chest. She got free and used one of their own guns."

Close range. She had asked me what it had felt like to kill a man. She herself had two kills from a range close enough to have their blood spatter on her. "I guess she didn't like being a victim."

"But she was. They raped her. This damn thing dragged on and on. The more unhinged these idiots got, the more they took it out on her. They kept her chained in a closet and only took her out to rape her and beat her."

"I'm guessing things were never the same between Vanessa and Daddy."

"Can you blame her?" I had been changing lanes as I could, trying to pick the one that was moving. Every once in a while I had to turn on the wipers. They weren't much help in the rain, but they were great for flicking ashes. We were close enough to one of the bigger fires that the traffic had slowed considerably. We passed some cars that were parked along the side of the road. Some people sat sealed inside with the windows rolled up. Some held handkerchiefs and towels to their noses and mouths. Some stood on the hoods gazing in the direction of the blaze, even though all anyone could see was smoke. All along the side of the highway, home owners patrolled their rooftops, moving like ghosts through the haze with garden hoses, the only protection they had available. Eventually, I was all the way over on the outside shoulder, moving faster than I should have past traffic that was mostly standing still. But just because I had an unobstructed lane didn't mean the view was clear.

"Jack, I can't see anything. I don't know how much farther we can go."

Just as I said it, a Florida highway patrolman materialized in front of the car with his hand up. I hit the brakes. Before the trooper had even raised a knuckle to knock on the glass, Jack's door was open and he had one foot out on the road. "Stay in the car," he said.

I lowered the window and smiled at the trooper. "I can't let you go any farther," he said. He had to raise his voice to be heard over the chop of rotor blades overhead. "The road up ahead is closed. And," he added with a weary sigh, "you shouldn't be driving on the shoulder like that, ma'am."

"Officer." Jack approached the trooper, wallet in hand. "I'm retired from the Miami office of the Bureau . . ." And that's all I heard as Jack skillfully moved the officer away from the car and out of earshot. I saw him open his wallet and hand it over. When the trooper took off his glasses to read whatever it was, presumably Jack's license, I could see even from a distance how the air had soiled his face and given him raccoon eyes.

I sat in the car and thought about Vanessa, about how she must have felt locked in a closet waiting for her father to come through for her. Finally realizing he never would. I thought about how much she must hate him, and what kind of profit motive there must be to get her to go to work for him. How powerful her lust for money must be.

And then I thought . . .

I thought back over the conversation I'd had with Damon, the one at the batting cages. I pictured myself there, in the hot, humid night under the lights, listening to the sky rumble and watching Damon's face. I tried to replay every word, and then I played it over again, looking at the whole conversation, the whole case from a different angle.

Jack opened his door and slipped back into the car.

"She's the source, Jack."

"What?"

"Vanessa is Damon's informant. It wasn't Jimmy. It was never Jimmy."

"I thought you said Damon told you it was."

"He never said Jimmy was his informant. I assumed he was. I had it in my mind that it was Jimmy from the start, and Damon gave me just enough facts to let me convince myself. Then Vanessa fed me the story that Jimmy murdered John. She was absolutely convincing. But you said it right from the start. Jimmy never had what Damon needed to put Ottavio away. All he knew about was parts. It's Vanessa. She's got the records. She's got his money. And she has the motive."

"Which is?"

"Revenge."

Jack had his head back against the headrest. He was staring straight ahead into the smoke, running the facts through his brain, looking for holes. He must not have found any, because he was smiling. "Work for him, steal from him, stab him in the back, and send him to jail for the rest of his life. Take his fifty million dollars and move to the South of France." He turned to me, still smiling. "Revenge is a beautiful thing."

"And powerful. It's a brilliant plan," I said. "So diabolical. So . . . Shakespearean. It's almost a shame to screw it up."

"I bet she thought so, too."

"Yeah." The pieces were almost pulling themselves together now. "She killed John, Jack. Or more likely had that thuggy brother of hers do it and make it look like one of Ottavio's drug hits."

A couple of helicopters flew overhead. They sounded low enough to scrape their skids across the top of my car. "What's going on up there? What's causing this?"

"A real mess. It's not the fire that's closed the road. There are five tractor trailers piled up on each other about three miles down. They have fatalities and injuries. Those are medevac flights overhead. Along with news choppers, and Broward Fire and Rescue and the Division of Forestry bringing in more firefighters. They're trying to keep the fire from jumping I-75 and moving south."

It sounded like a disaster area, someplace I shouldn't want to go, but I was completely in my head trying to work through the details. To make it all make sense.

"Here's what I think happened. John flew down here, met with Bobby and gave him the ultimatum."

"Turn yourself in," Jack said, "or I'll do it for you."

"John went over to the hotel to wait for Bobby to do the right thing. Bobby didn't want to kill John, but he wanted John to be gone. So he called Jimmy and put the problem on him. 'If I go down, you go down. And by the way, here's the hotel where John is staying.'"

"Jimmy's sitting in his house. What is he thinking?" Jack was getting into the spirit. "He's thinking 'I stole an airplane and got caught and the only reason I'm not sitting on my ass in jail right now is because of this Damon Hollander.'"

"Do you think he knew why? Do you think Damon told him why he was keeping him out on the street?"

He thought about that. "I think that's why Jimmy was out. Whether Damon told him or he figured it out for himself, I think he worked a deal. Something like 'I know what you're up to and I'll keep my mouth shut until you bust Ottavio. But you've got to . . .' Fill in the blank. Keep me out of jail. Get me a reduced sentence. Whatever. So when Bobby comes along with the news that John's going to turn them all in, Jimmy calls Damon and gives him the problem. "Now Damon's thinking 'God-dammit, who is this asshole who's come to town and is threatening to screw up my operation right at the last minute?' He goes over to the hotel, flips his badge out, and tells him to go home before the bad guys do something to his family."

"I don't know what happened next," I said. "Jimmy called Vanessa. Or Damon called Vanessa. Someone alerted Vanessa, maybe just to tell her to lay low until they figured out what to do."

"Or," Jack said, "Damon called and told her what was happening, knowing exactly what she'd do."

"Whichever it was, Vanessa was not into waiting and she was not trusting her fate to the Junior G-man. She took matters into her own hands, and John ended up dead in the Dumpster. And as a bonus, one last dig at Daddy, she made it look as if he did the murder. It was her," I said. "All the motives we attributed to Jimmy still work, but it's Vanessa who did it. She had the most to lose. Think about how long she must have been working on this scheme. How long it took her to set the trap. She wasn't going to let John screw it up. John had no idea what he was walking into. He never had a chance."

"She's tying up loose ends," Jack said. "Like Jimmy."

He didn't say it, but I knew he was thinking what I was. To Vanessa, Felix was one big loose end.

"Start the car," he said.

"What?" I looked up and the trooper was waving at me. I rolled down the window and he told me to drive over the service road, go half a mile to the shopping center, drive under the police tape and park there. "Jack, what are we doing?"

"I got us a ride." Just as he said it, I looked up and saw a sheriff's helicopter dropping down to land on said parking lot.

"How did you do that?"

"I still have a few well-placed friends around town. Let's go."

The pilot told us he would have to fly out over the Everglades and come back to the old airfield in order to go around the smoke. He flew low, skimming over the thousands of small islands of grass and mud that made up the vast network of waterways and inlets. It was amazingly intricate, as complex and impenetrable as the network of arteries and capillaries that carry blood to and from the human heart.

We approached the airfield in a swooping roller coaster arc that disrupted the workings of my inner ear and left my stomach in a free fall. With all the holes in the roof, the hangar looked from above as if it had been bombed. The lights were on. Parked in the front were two flatbed trucks, one with a crane attached. Next to them, a silver Mercedes with a dark blue drop top, and a dark red four-door sedan—kidney bean red.

"Jack." I pointed, but he had seen it, too.

The sheriff's deputy wanted to make sure we really wanted to land there. Jack assured him we did, then gave him his card after writing Pat Spain's phone number on the back. He asked the pilot to get in touch with her and tell her where he'd left us.

He put us down out in a perimeter field, as far away from the hangar as possible. After he left, it took a few minutes for me to adjust to being still, and to the quiet. Between the visual pandemonium of the smoke and ash and haze, the incessant thumping of the rotor blades, and the chaos going on inside my head, standing on the ground in the stark quiet of the abandoned airfield felt like an altered state of being.

Jack was all business. Besides his Glock and what I was coming to think of as my .22, he'd brought a bag of extra goodies. It was a good thing we hadn't had to clear a security checkpoint before we'd gone up. He pulled out a pump action shotgun, and boxes and boxes of extra rounds, which he stuffed into the pockets of his hunting vest, the same one he'd worn the last time we were here. He gave me an extra clip for my gun and showed me how to load it.

We watched the hangar as we worked. The air was not very clear and we were far away. There could have been movement and we wouldn't have seen it. "Do you think they heard us?"

"It would have been hard not to. But between the news people, the fire departments, and the forestry service, a lot of helicopters have been flying around here the past few days. If we're lucky, they heard us and didn't pay any attention. We're lucky Jimmy's not with them. He would have heard us."

"Do you think Felix is in there?"

"If he's alive."

"Why didn't they contact us?"

He didn't answer. I wasn't sure I wanted to hear the answer.

"Did you check your weapon?"

"Yeah."

"Are you scared?"

"Yeah."

He put his hand on my shoulder. His solid touch and level gaze made me feel steadier, made me want to be steadier. "Follow my lead. Follow the plan. You can do this. And remember, we got lucky. We found them before they got out of here. One way or another, we're going to find that kid. If they hurt him, I will personally blow their fucking heads off. Ready?"

My eyes started burning and watering the instant we began to move. The air felt as if it was filled with tiny, searing particles that embedded themselves in my corneas. I could feel the soot and ash building up on my skin.

Jack carried the shotgun in his right hand away from his body. My .22 kept working its way out of the waistband of my jeans, so I took it out and carried it in my hand.

It was faster and easier getting into the hangar this time because it was familiar and I knew what to expect, and because of the intermittent noise overhead that served as cover for our movements. After scrambling through the window, the two of us stood in the bathroom and peeked out into the lighted interior of the hangar. It was my second time seeing the dead aircraft splayed out in pieces large and small across the floor and the workbenches. But it wasn't any easier. We heard voices toward the front, which was the part of the building with which we were least familiar. I recognized Vanessa's voice. She might have been talking to Arturo, but the man's voice was hard to hear, and I couldn't remember if I'd ever even heard Arturo speak.

"What about those FBI guys?" I whispered. "Shouldn't they be patrolling around here somewhere?"

"This area has been evacuated. I don't even know how these two got in unless they've been out here for a while."

A helicopter flew over and we used the opportunity to push through the door and move out into the wreckage. The smells were all still there, strong and acrid, blended into an aroma I was sure I would never smell again. Jack had said Vietnam had its own smell. So did this place.

We moved up slowly, taking our time, slipping from a pile here to a massive assembly there. It was easier to move through the wreckage if I thought of the pieces as my protection rather than what they really were. At one point, I caught sight of the two of them.

Vanessa, who I would have expected to be the cool one, was pacing and jittery. She wore a bright red pantsuit that made her look like the only flame of color in an otherwise black-and-white landscape. Arturo stood a few feet off to the side, his big arms folded over his chest. He wore his traditional black garb and even had on dark sunglasses. No sign of Felix.

When we were close enough to hear both sides of the conversation, we stopped and listened. My body, as I rested against a larger piece of the aircraft, was so tense my muscles felt as if they'd been wrung out and twisted dry. Their voices were hollow in the large warehouse, and they spoke to each other in Spanish. I had to strain just to hear the words. All I could really get were the tones—Vanessa's, as usual, arch and superior as she prattled on at her brother in clipped and forceful sentences. She may have been anxious, but she hadn't lost her abusive spirit.

Jack looked as if he might be getting most of it.

"What's she saying?"

"She's talking about Jimmy. About what a horrible place this is. Something about how disgusting this whole affair has been and all for nothing. A pile of junk. Tons of crap. That sort of thing. She's really pissed off. She called this place a monument to Jimmy's stupidity."

"Can you hear Arturo?"

"He basically agrees with whatever she says."

"Anything about Felix?"

"No. I think they're waiting for someone or something to happen, but she hasn't said what."

"Do you think it's just the two of them?"

"So far." He poked his head up. "I can't see anyone else, and she hasn't spoken to anyone else. But if someone else is coming, we need to do something fast."

I looked out and spied Vanessa pacing and Arturo standing. They were in an open area next to an enclosed office. "They're not expecting us," Jack said. "We can take these two. You and me. Let's figure out how."

I looked around to see if I could find where Vanessa had left her bag, and hoped it wasn't in the car. I spotted it, sitting on one of the workbenches with her keys on top. It was the same flat, black clutch she'd carried every time I'd seen her. Must have been a favorite. It wasn't an ideal placement for what I had in mind, but it would have to do. I pulled out my cell phone and looked at Jack. "I have an idea."

A few minutes later, Jack was working his way around

to a particular spot in the wreckage he liked. It was close
to one of the engines where the pieces were piled into
something like a box canyon. A long piece of wing laid
on its edge ran almost the length of the hangar on the
side closest to Vanessa's bag. I found a place to squeeze
in behind it and moved along to the end, which actually
put me past them, closer to the front hangar doors than
they were. From the looks of it, it was as close as I was
going to get and stay hidden.

Vanessa and Arturo continued to talk to each other,
mostly Vanessa rattling on in what was beginning to
sound like compulsive dialogue. It was good that I
couldn't understand her. It made it easier to tune her out.

When Jack's signal came, it was loud. Louder than I
had expected. The hollow, warped sound of a flat piece
of sheet metal hitting the ground, followed by the crashing and banging of things, multiple heavy things falling
on top of it.

I pushed the speed dial on my phone. Vanessa spun
toward me and her chirping bag. Arturo pulled his gun,
snapped at her, and headed for Jack's position. He must
have told her to silence the phone. She was ten feet away
from me, her back turned, her long red nails on the bag
as she unsnapped it. I heard something over in Jack's
quadrant. A shout. Couldn't tell whose. Vanessa's hand
was in her bag. The phone was still twittering. Do it, I
thought. *Do* it. *Now*. I pushed forward and up, raising
the .22, and yelled at her.

She turned, twisted in my direction, and shot at me.

She *shot* at me. The gun must have been in her bag.
It was small, smaller than mine, but just the same it made
a hole in the wing inches from my shoulder. I ducked
behind one of the workbenches. It didn't work as cover
unless . . . It was solid and heavy and piled high with
heavy tools and crap. The bullets were dancing around
me, splintering wood, bouncing off metal, shattering plastic. I could feel them whizzing by in the air. How many
damn bullets did she have? I put my back against the
bench, found something to brace my feet and pushed
with both my legs. It tipped. It teetered. It went. It crashed

over into the next bench, and the two of them went over in her direction like dominoes, dumping all those heavy tools and stolen parts at her feet. The firing stopped. She tried to turn and run, twisted out of one of her high heels, tripped, and fell flat on her stomach. The little gun banged the cement and went scuttling across the floor. Before she had a chance to even turn over, I was on her. I grabbed the collar of her jacket, put my knee into her back, and jammed the gun against her head. I was so pumped up, it was hard to hold still, but that's what I did. I stayed on her until I started to breathe again.

She turned her head. Her pale face was a sharp contrast to the dark floor. "Kill me," she said. Her tone matched the contemptuous sneer that turned her beautiful features ugly. "Can you do it?"

She had emptied her gun at me. She might have killed Felix. She was probably responsible for John's murder. I didn't know if I could pull the trigger and put one of those small, stubby .22 caliber bullets through her blonde head. But if there was anyone I could have killed, it would have been her.

I heard the sound of a helicopter outside. This one seemed closer and louder than usual. It masked the sound of Arturo coming toward me. I caught the motion out of the corner of my eye. His hands were cuffed.

Jack was behind, pushing him along. He smiled as he came upon the two of us and waited for the sound of the chopper to pass. "Good job," he said. "Any sign of Felix?"

"We've just gotten started." I backed off and pulled Vanessa to her feet by the collar of her jacket. She stood up, kicked off her orphan shoe, and smoothed the wrinkles in her suit. "Put your hands behind your head . . . Valentina."

She ignored me and beamed at Jack as she assumed the pose. "It's nice to see you again," she said. "Although I would have preferred different circumstances. Did you recognize me the day you came to my office? I was certain you knew my secret."

Jack's response was to raise his gun and point it under Arturo's chin. "Where's the boy?"

Her forehead crinkled. "What boy?"

He nudged the gun high enough to tip Arturo's head back. "What did you do with Felix?"

She looked genuinely perplexed and she stared first at Jack, then me. Then she asked Arturo in Spanish, "Who is Felix?"

Chapter Forty-seven

Either they were very convincing liars, which was entirely possible, or Vanessa and Arturo had never heard of Felix Melendez Jr. After another few minutes of tense, frustrating, and fruitless Q&A, Jack decided to take Arturo out and check the cars. That left Vanessa and me alone in the hangar. We had found a length of rope among the ruins and used it to tie her hands behind her. I had her sit in an old kitchen chair that came from the office, and I dragged over a stool from one of the workbenches. I liked towering over her. And I liked having the gun.

"You never told me," she said.

"Told you what?"

"You never told me what it was like to kill that man."

"You already know. You killed two men. At least."

"I know what it was like for me." Her smile grew more intimate, sultry even. She blinked at me coolly, and settled back in her chair. "A rush like I'd never felt before or since. I can't get it from money. Not from my orchids. Not from climbing mountains. Sex doesn't even come close. Revenge. Only revenge. I love the word. I love the way it sounds. I love the way it feels in my mouth. It's the best drug. The only drug. It fills you. It fills you in places you didn't even know were empty."

"Like the revenge you've planned for your father?"

"He is not my father. A father does not leave his child to die with the wolves. Not even wolves. Scavengers. Curs. Mongrels who take their pleasure . . . A father does not leave his daughter to die alone in a closet. To be . . ." Her face seemed to grow harder and softer at the same time, as if her shell was stiffening, but also turning transparent so that I could see what was beneath the surface—see it but perhaps never touch it. Probably even she couldn't touch that part of herself. She looked at me with stone cold killer eyes. "They raped me. They took turns."

"Ottavio deserves everything he's got coming to him. But John had nothing to do with it. John didn't deserve what you did to him."

"Necessary losses." She tried to cross her legs. It was awkward with her hands behind her back and God knows she didn't like looking awkward. She gave up. "Losses are sometimes unavoidable."

The hangar door slid open. I looked up for Jack, hoping to see an extra silhouette, a slight one with spiky hair, against the darkness. Felix wasn't there. I slipped off the stool and circled around to put Vanessa in front of me. There were five silhouettes, five men coming toward me. Arturo was no longer handcuffed. Jack walked with his hands on top of his head. Behind them were three new guests at the party, two of whom carried automatic rifles.

The last man to enter the hangar was not armed. He had dark olive skin, almost black eyes, a dark mustache that rivaled Bic's for thickness and camouflage. His hair was on the bushy side, black with signs of graying at the temples. His looks were wholly unremarkable, but he carried himself like a general leading an invading army, even if in this case it was only an army of three. When Vanessa jerked up from her chair as if I wasn't even there holding a pistol at her head, I knew exactly who had just walked in. I just didn't know what to do about it.

"Poppy," she said, in almost a whisper. "Poppy, what are you doing here?"

"My dear Valentina. As beautiful as ever. Every time I see you, I am startled by how much you resemble your mother."

Ottavio's English was as flawless as his daughter's. He turned his attention to me. "Lower your weapon."

"Poppy—"

He raised a languid hand that shut Vanessa down instantly. "Put your weapon on the ground and put your hands over your head. If you do not do that, I will instruct my associates to shoot this man"—he nodded casually to Jack—"and then to shoot you."

In the time it took me to find Jack's face, to understand that there was only one choice here and he knew that, too, Ottavio had gone back to stand between Arturo and his thugs. "Do it now." I knew it was the last time he would say it. I put the gun down and raised my hands.

"Excellent. Arturo . . ." He gave him an order in Spanish, which must have been to free his sister's hands. Arturo whipped out a jackknife and cut through the thick rope around Vanessa's wrists with one deft stroke.

Vanessa stood in her elegant red silk suit with pant legs that pooled around her feet because she no longer stood on high heels. "Poppy," she said again, "why have you come?"

"You said you wanted to be rescued."

"I said . . . I asked that you send a plane for my use."

"And where were you planning to take my airplane?"

"To Colombia. Back home."

"You haven't been home in seventeen years, *hijita*." He walked over and touched her face as tenderly as any father would touch his daughter. She let him, but looked as though it was all she could do to endure it. "Who are you?" he asked, facing me. "What is you business here?"

If it's true that whatever does not kill you makes you stronger, this man looked very strong, indeed. It was in his eyes. He was a man who had not just survived but prospered in the world's most dangerous profession, by his wits and his willingness to do harm. I wasn't about to lie. I wasn't about to test the instincts of a drug lord.

"Can I lower my hands?"

"You may both lower your hands."

I let my arms swing to my side. My hands tingled and my fingertips hurt as the blood rushed back. I swallowed to loosen my throat and took a breath that was meant to give me momentum, but only made me shudder.

"My name is Alex Shanahan and this is Jack Dolan. I came down from Boston to find information regarding a friend of mine who was murdered. The cops think you did it because of the way he died."

"How did he die?"

"Someone shoved a serrated blade into his throat and left him in a Dumpster."

He considered that. "What was his name?"

"John McTavish."

He couldn't exactly dismiss the idea that this murder would have been related to his business. He must have been sifting through recent events to see if John's name rang a bell. Perhaps one of his captains had turned in an activity report to HQ to that effect. "I had no business with a John McTavish. I have no business in Boston. I did not kill him."

"He had no business with you either." I pointed to Vanessa. "She did it and blamed it on you."

Vanessa didn't even wait to be asked. "I killed no one, Poppy. Jimmy killed him. I warned you not to do business with him. It was a disagreement over parts. I have nothing to do with airplane parts, as you know. It is a filthy business."

Ottavio nodded to Arturo. The big man walked over and I thought my legs might give out right there because he placed the barrel of his large caliber automatic weapon against my right temple. The air that was in my lungs got stuck there. I couldn't get it out. I couldn't blink. I felt the cold barrel against my head and I couldn't move anything.

"Hold on," Jack said. "Wait."

"No one speaks unless I ask you." Ottavio moved in very close to me. My head began to pound and my eyes to throb in rhythm with the blood hammering in my ears. The closer he came, the harder everything throbbed. "Are you lying to me?"

Jack tried to take a step toward us. One of the thugs raised his weapon and the other yanked him back.

I made myself maintain eye contact, hoping to convince Ottavio with the power of the truth. "I'm not lying. John was killed because he threatened to expose Jimmy's parts operation. Vanessa couldn't have that, so she killed him. Or she had him killed."

"*Es verdad,* Valentina?"

"Losing the stations would have been inconvenient, Poppy, but of little consequence to me. I have many other options." I could hear the calculations running in Vanessa's voice as she went through her high-speed emergency damage control. "And she's lying about this man from Boston. He found out Jimmy was stealing from us, Poppy. That's why Jimmy killed him. Jimmy killed him, and brought unwelcome scrutiny as a result. It brought these two. And he *was* stealing from us. *He* was our problem, Poppy. And I solved it."

Ottavio had no problem maintaining eye contact. "There is your answer."

"My friend had nothing to do with bad parts or drugs or anything else. He was a man with a family who came down here to try to put something right. He threatened to upset her plan to take revenge on you. That's why she had to kill him."

"Poppy, she would say anything right now to save herself."

Ottavio kept his eyes on me. "Tell me about this plan."

"Please remove this gun. I can't . . . I can't talk . . . I can't even think with it pointed at my head."

He glanced at Arturo and I felt the gun pressing harder against my temple, closer to my brain. I squeezed my eyes shut. "Your daughter," I said, and stopped. No air. I couldn't make the words come out. I knew what to say and couldn't make them come out. "Your daughter . . . is a government informant. She's . . ." There was only one thought in my head now. No room for any others. A tear squeezed out of the corner of my eye and ran down my cheek. Every muscle contracted and at the moment when I thought I was going to die . . . I wondered who was going to call the movers.

The gun fell away. I opened my eyes to find that Arturo

had stepped back. A flood of delayed . . . something . . .
rolled through me. Delayed stress. The room started to
spin. I found Jack's eyes, looked at him looking at me,
and I saw something there to hold on to. I centered my
breathing and tried to get the world back in focus.

Ottavio's eyes had narrowed ever so slightly. His head
was canted toward Vanessa, but he was still looking at
me. "What did you say?"

"I said your daughter is an informant for the government."

"What agency?"

"The FBI. She's been helping them build a case against
you. She couldn't let John turn Jimmy in. If he went, the
stations went. If the stations went, so did she, and the
federal case against you would have blown up. She
couldn't let that happen. She wants to see you in jail."

"Vanessa's the one who has been stealing from you,"
Jack said. "We can prove it."

The disc. I'd forgotten about the *disc* and Jack was
reminding me and thank God for his presence of mind.
"We have documentation of all of your accounts," I said.
"How much was taken from where and where she's got
it all stashed. I came here today to trade it for Felix. I'll
give it to you. It will prove what we're saying."

"Who is Felix?"

"He's . . . he's just a kid who was trying to help us
out. She took him, too."

Ottavio walked over to his daughter and reached out
to her. She shrank from his touch, and it occurred to me
she had just failed a test. "Valentina, do you still hate
me so much?"

"Poppy, I will open up my accounts to you and let
you see that I have never taken a cent." She started
moving back, stumbling over one of the many items left
strewn about by the crashing workbenches. "I have done
a good job for you. I would never steal from you. I have
all the money I need." She kept moving until she was
blocked from behind by one of the heavier pieces of the
aircraft. She pressed back against it, thinking perhaps she
could move the obstacle through the sheer force of her

will. It was how she had moved every other obstacle in her life—all but the one standing in front of her.

"Tell him," she commanded, glaring in her brother's direction. Arturo was a sphinx. "I said *tell* him, Arturo."

Ottavio approached her slowly. "He did tell me. He told me everything." This time when he reached for her she had no place to go. He drew in a deep breath as he let his fingertips stroke her hair. His voice was quiet. "I sent him to watch over you, Valentina. And he has been watching."

She clenched both arms across her stomach and bent at the waist. "You were supposed to take care of *me*, Arturo. You were sent to protect *me*." When she straightened, Vanessa Cray was no longer svelte and elegant. She was skinny and drawn. Her clothes seemed to hang on her in a different way. It wasn't just her facial expression that had changed. Her facial *features* seemed different. The shape of her eyes when she looked at her father, the fullness of her lips, the way the muscles in her face moved—they transformed her, or perhaps returned her to what I could now see was her natural state. With her father, she was still the terrified, brutalized teenager he had abandoned to a horrible fate.

"Did you think I could forgive you, Poppy?" Mascara stained tears streamed down her face. "Did you think I could *ever* forgive you?"

Ottavio was unmoved. "I never asked your forgiveness. Only your loyalty and respect."

"Loyalty?" She heaved back against the fuselage, perhaps trying to move out of his reach. When it didn't move, she turned that force on her father. "You arrogant, selfish bastard. I was chained in a closet for *six days*. Where was your loyalty to me? Where was your respect *for me*?" She banged her chest so hard it must have hurt.

"I have explained all of this to you. If you could not accept my decision, then you should never have come to work for me. You made a choice."

"You *ruined* me, Poppy. You wrecked me. You destroyed my life. I died in that closet. I was seventeen years old and I was already dead and the only thing that gave me reason to live was the thought of hurting you. Of making you pay for all that you took from me." She was moving, stalking back and forth. If her nails could have grown a couple of inches, I was sure they would have, the better to tear into his flesh. "I thought about having you killed. I could have done it. I know the ways to get to you. But you wouldn't have suffered enough. I wanted you in prison. I wanted you to be raped, Poppy. To be held down by someone stronger than you and forced to submit to his will."

Dressed in that red suit, she seemed like one big force of pure hatred. She launched herself at her father. Ottavio's bodyguards, including Arturo, started to go to his aid, but he stopped them with a loud, barking command. He grabbed Vanessa's upper arms as she struggled against him. When she couldn't use her fists, she tried to kick him. She wrenched and pulled and twisted for a long time. He let her fight. When she was spent, she sank to her knees on the ground in front of him and cried like a child with her head bowed. "Why didn't you come for me?" She reached out for her father's hand, took it in the two of hers, and laid her cheek against it. "Poppy, why did you not want me back?"

He bent down and pulled her up to her feet and into his arms. "Everything is all right," he whispered. He took her face in both of his hands and kissed her fully on the lips. It was a long, lingering, tender, creepy kiss.

Ottavio took a step back. Vanessa straightened. She was a wreck. As she wiped her tears and brushed the damp hair from her face, Arturo raised his gun hand and placed the barrel against her head.

If her father gave a signal, I didn't see it. What I saw in her last moment of life was that she closed her eyes, and then opened them. She was looking at me. I thought she started to smile. The gun exploded. The shock of the blast snapped my head back. I saw the bullet erupt from the other side of her head, and with it a fountain of blood. Her body dropped as if her bones had turned to lead. She fell on her back with her eyes to the ceiling. They were open.

The warehouse was completely still. Ottavio, Arturo, Jack, the two goons, and I made six people, but I couldn't hear a sound. I smelled the gun, the cordite stench. I was aware that Ottavio was looking at us, maybe even talking to us. I was aware of the sound of a helicopter overhead again. But I was staring at Vanessa, at her startled eyes, her interrupted skull, and the growing circle of blood on the floor. It looked like an extension of her bright red suit, as if her body were melting into a pool of blood. Ashes to ashes. Dust to dust. Blood to blood.

The noise from the helicopter grew louder, the loudest one yet, and I didn't even hear the big garage doors rolling open behind us. All I saw was a phalanx of men surging through the door. They were dressed in black with helmets and masks and carrying big weapons, screaming.

"Down . . . *down* . . . *DOWN*—"

". . . weapons *down* . . ."

"On the ground . . . *now.*"

My hands flew straight over my head without any conscious direction from me. Someone came up from behind. I felt the rough force of the heel of his hand between my shoulder blades, shoving me to the ground.

"Spread your legs. Hands behind your head."

I did as I was told and lay there frozen with one cheek mashed into the concrete, looking over at Jack, who was in the same position. Whatever panic I had managed to subdue until that moment came rushing over me in wave after wave of violent shivers. I was convinced that the slightest unexpected move would cause a chain reaction, that I might have survived the Colombian drug lord only to be killed by the good guys. I assumed they were good guys.

The commandos swarmed around us, guns drawn, shouting to be heard over the oppressive racket of the still hovering helicopter. I caught sight of a second group coming through the door, six people dressed in blue jeans, wind-

breakers, and baseball caps. Some had holsters strapped
to their legs. This group seemed alert, but not on testos-
terone overload, and I started to feel that maybe I
wouldn't be accidentally annihilated for sneezing.

The sound of the helicopter began to dissipate as it
must have moved off from a position directly overhead.
I started to pick out individual voices again.

"She's all right." It was a woman's voice, and it was
familiar. "Let her up."

Someone reached down and helped me to my feet. I
had to take a few seconds to reorient to an upright view
of the world. The warehouse that had seemed so massive
before was now teeming.

"Alex."

It was that voice again. I turned around. A woman
approached. She wore the dark windbreaker and the
jeans and a long blonde ponytail that came out of the
back of her cap. I stared. She laughed. It was . . . it
was . . . *Margie?* George Speath's *secretary?*

"I'm Agent Laubert."

"You're who?"

"Susan Laubert. George is over there."

She pointed toward Vanessa's body. His back was to
me, but it was impossible not to recognize George's
bulky shape, and for the first time I noticed the big yellow letters stenciled across the back of the windbreakers.
DEA. George was DEA. George and Margie. DEA.

Jack was getting to his feet. He was bleeding from a
small cut over his right eye but otherwise seemed fine. I
walked over and put my arms around his waist and tried
to disappear in his arms. I wanted to cry, but my eyes
were too wide. They wouldn't close. I felt dried up.

George was cheery when he saw me. "Hi, Alex. You
seem to be in one piece."

"Felix," I said. I was unable to get any of the thoughts
out of my head in a coherent manner save that one. "We
have to find Felix."

"Felix is fine," George said. "We had to pick him up
earlier this afternoon. It was for his own good. We've
got him back at the office debriefing."

"*You* picked him up?" The woman in the room next door had seen Felix picked up by two men and a tall blonde. I looked across the hangar at Margie. Tall and blonde.

"Smart kid," George said. "And boy can he talk. We might have to hire him just to keep control of him."

"Who are you?"

"I'm Agent George Weir." He held out his big hand to me and smiled. "It's nice to finally meet you."

Chapter Forty-eight

George stood on the tarmac around the back of Speath Aviation. I stood next to him admiring the old Electra. "What about that whole story you told me about your father running the company?"

"This company was run by a man named Howard Speath. He got into some trouble with us, of the money laundering nature. As a way of staying out of prison, he offered the use of his business as a cover. We'd heard about the inroads Ottavio was making down here in his laundering activities, so we decided to set up the operation."

"You've been running his business for two years?"

He couldn't suppress a satisfied smile. "I made more money in that time than Howard did in the five years before that. I got them back in the black, strengthened their balance sheet."

"That shot of Ottavio's dirty cash must have helped a lot."

He shrugged. "I could have done it even without the dirty cash. I could have gotten a bank loan."

He probably could have, too. George had turned out to be quite an impressive guy. "And Marg—Susan was part of the whole thing?"

"She's my backup. We had to teach her to type."

"Did you set up the operation to get Vanessa?"

"Ottavio by way of Vanessa. We'd tried to get her before in New York, and she always managed to wriggle out. It was Damon Hollander tipping her off. After we shifted our investigation down here, this Damon kid popped up again and we figured out what was going on. We decided not to bring the FBI in. Actually, I insisted. I wasn't about to have my cover blown by some snot-nosed kid bucking for a promotion."

"What happened with Damon?"

"As near as we can tell, he was working on the task force in New York that was investigating a money laundering ring down in Panama. He started watching Vanessa. One thing led to another and she came up with this scheme to get Ottavio. He was more than happy to oblige. He worked it—it's more accurate to say that she worked it out so that she got off the hook on that deal. They all got off the hook. Damon set up a formal relationship where she was his informant and he was her handler. She refused to work with anyone but him. Not too many people knew about it, even within the Bureau."

"Did Damon know she had John killed?"

"No, I don't think so."

"What's going to happen to him?"

"The FBI's Office of Professional Responsibility is very interested in talking to him."

"I don't understand why they killed John if he was going home."

"He was a good guy, your friend. He thought it over. He talked to his brother, and he came back to Damon and told him he wanted to stay and help."

"He wasn't going home?"

"He knew these boys were dealing in dirty parts and wanted to stop them. He trusted his brother to watch over his family. He told Damon he would stay, wear a wire. Whatever they needed."

That sounded like John. All the strength—and the weakness—that had made him who he had been. Mae would understand what happened. She wouldn't like it or agree with his decision, but at least she would now understand. She could make sense of it. And Terry would be happy to know that John had trusted him with the most precious thing in his life. His family.

"Did Vanessa provide any confidential information to Damon, or did it all go the other way?"

"She provided a lot of information to Damon, always in favor of Ottavio and against his competitors. He made some big busts up in New York. Down here too, from what I understand."

"And then she turned on Ottavio?"

"I think that was her plan right from the start. She was a good girl long enough to build up her bank account and his trust. Once she was set, she got Damon to start working on a plan to reel him in. But things started spinning out of control pretty fast. First Jimmy went and stole the airplane. Damon had that more or less handled until John showed up. And then you. She never counted on all that."

"And she never counted on her brother being a spy, I bet."

"Arturo was her half-brother. She thought Ottavio had sent him up here after the kidnapping to watch over her. What he was really doing all these years was watching the money. Arturo figured out that Vanessa was skimming. He told Colombia, and Ottavio came up so he could kill her himself. This is what we're hearing, anyway. He figured if he made an example out of his own daughter, no one would ever try to steal from him again."

"Did you get Ottavio?"

"We got him. We got Arturo, too. Like I said, he's no dummy. He's talking up a storm. The thing about being the head guy, the top dog, is you've got no bargaining power. You've got no one above you. The buck stopped with the big O. He's going away for a long time."

"So in the end, she got what she wanted. Vanessa sent her father to prison." I remembered the look on Vanessa's face just before she died. I remembered her looking at me, and the beginnings of the smile that died with her.

"What about you, George? Are you out of the parts business now?"

"Yeah. I'm going to miss it a little. I meant what I told you. I love airplanes. I've got a pilot's license and I

do restorations when I have the time. This old bird"—
he nodded to the Electra—"is a real job we were doing.
I hate to let her go."

He turned and looked at me. "What about you? Can
I buy you lunch?"

"I'm leaving today. I just stopped by on my way to
the airport."

"Back to Boston?"

"For now. I'm not sure where I'm going to be living."
I looked up at the Electra. "The only place I know I
won't be is Detroit."

My flight had already been called when Jack finally showed
up. I spotted him working his way through what must
have been a cruise group moving slowly through the concourse. He was easy to spot. He was the tallest, the youn-
gest, and the only one in the bunch who didn't have
gray hair.

"I thought you were going to stand me up one last
time."

"I had to stop for these." He handed me a box, the
kind they use at Logan to ship fresh lobsters. "Something
to remember me by."

It could only be one thing. "Stone crabs?"

"The best crabs in the world."

"Is the shell already broken, or will I have to unpack
my ball-peen hammer?"

"If you want it bad enough, you'll figure out how to
get it."

I set the box down, reached into the pocket of my
backpack, and pulled out a few things. First the ring.

"This is the address of Belinda Culligan Fraley. She
lived in Coconut Grove. Would you make sure it gets
back to her family?"

"It would be my honor," he said.

Next, the check I'd written that morning after a long
chat with my bank. I offered it to him. "I'm pretty sure
this won't bounce, but you might want to wait a day or
two to cash it. When I get back to Boston, I'm cashing
in a retirement account and I can send you the rest."

He opened the check and looked at it. I couldn't tell from his face if it was more than he expected, or if he was disappointed. "I know it may not be enough, but—"

"Why don't you wait and pay me after you've started the job?"

"I'm not taking the job. I called this morning and we had an amicable parting."

He smiled. "Was that hard?"

"Really hard. But more because of the position I put them in. But they were nice about it. And I gave them someone else to look at."

"Who?"

"Phil Ryczbicki. I told Bic if he'd give Felix a job, I'd pass his name along. Felix starts at Majestic next month."

He folded the check and ran one finger along the crease. "Do you know what you're going to do?"

"I'm going to do what I want to do. I just have to figure out what that is."

"In that case"—he opened the check and tore it in half—"take this and invest it in yourself. I can't think of any better use for the money." He handed me the two pieces.

"Are you sure?"

"I don't have room for a washer and dryer in my place, anyway. Just promise to come back and see me." I felt like crying. Maybe it was because we knew without even saying it that we didn't fit into each other's futures. Maybe because, for the first time in my life, my future was so uncertain. And exciting. Instead, I opened my arms for a hug. He walked into it, wrapped his arms around me, and squeezed tight.

"Take care of yourself, Jack Dolan."

"Ladies and gentlemen, this is the cockpit. We're next in line for takeoff."

I finished my drink and put my seat-back all the way up.

"It's a beautiful day for flying. As of last night, it looks as though the wildfires you might have heard about down

here are mostly under control, so you should have a good clear view out your window as we leave Miami today. So sit back, relax, and enjoy your flight to Boston . . . or wherever your final destination may be."